Enjoy!

Captivated by an Adventurous Lady

(Thieves of the Ton series, book one)

by

Sandra Sookoo

Thank you so much for reviewing book #6. I appreciated that. I thought you might like to see how it all started. Thanks for your support!
XOXO
Sandra Sookoo

Published by New Independence Books

ISBN-13: 978-0692784372 (New Independence Books)

ISBN-10: 0692784373

Contact Information:
sandrasookoo@yahoo.com
newindependencebooks@gmail.com
Visit me at www.sandrasookoo.com

Edited by: Victoria Miller
V.millerartist@gmail.com

Book Cover Design by David Sookoo
Couple: SKU: REG3130HIGH Category: REGENCY Tags: Ashlee, bare back, brunette, Couple, dance, dancing, dark hair man, Duke, Earl, embrace, Gown, Jesse, open back, regency | Hot Damn Stock
Texture: The ancient Egyptian symbols on background by Lina Shafeeva | 123rf.com
Cat: Lion cub sitting, looking at the camera, 10 weeks old, isolated on white by Eric Isselee | 123rf.com
Background: Abu Simbel, Egypt by Emanuele Mazzoni | 123rf.com

Publishing History:
First Digital Edition, 2016
First Print Edition, 2016

Dear Readers,

There are times in a person's life when a challenge is needed for both growth and shake out the fuzz.

When I set out my goals at the New Year, I wanted to write something that scared me, do something I've not done before, write something different, so the Thieves of the *Ton* series was born in January.

The only way, at the moment, I can travel the world is to research and write about places I'd love to see in person. I thought it would be a fun adventure to take my love of travel and of antiquities and world treasures, and combine them both into the world of the Regency.

I didn't outline this story (which scared me) so this was all a freeform endeavor; I went where the characters and the story took me, which turned into quite the awesome book. It's also my longest story to date. I'd say it's the start of an epic journey.

Come along with me, Miles as well as Emmaline and enter the glittering, and oftentimes dangerous, world of the Regency's *ton,* Sookoo style. Along the way we'll dive headfirst into adventure and travel, engage in heart-pounding action, survive spine-tingling peril and somewhere along the line find romance with a thirst for more.

Enjoy!

Dedication

For Michele Worley. Disney brought us together but through magic, pixie dust and the love of a good book, we'll remain friends.

You keep me going with words of encouragement and blatant fangirling. For that, I'll ever be grateful.

Acknowledgement

Much of the time while writing a book is a solitary experience. The author spends hours, days, weeks, months and sometime years behind a computer screen, creating worlds and crafting characters.

And sometimes, it's fun to ask for input and to let readers and friends have a hand in that creation on my author page.

Special thanks to the following people for helping me create Jane's personality:

Ilene Renee Bieleski, Beverly Gordon. Cheryl A, Ki Pha, Jessica Grove, Cindy Drennan von Hentschel. Melody Brooke May, Brea Essex, Crystal Marie, Betty Johnson, Michele Worley, Megan Shelton, Christine Kolshorn Marciniak, Lora Phegley Rhode, Karyn Ford Monroe, Ameila Ellis Andrews, Pamela Daake

Also, many thanks to the following folks for their input in choosing Emmaline's ballgown:

Kyla McLinn, Emma Lai, Gail Delaney, Michele Miller, Elaine Mauney Carlson, Brea Essex, Kristin Gearns Bane, Ann Gonzalez, Nicole Stein, Crystal Marie, Stephanie Smith

Other Regency-era stories by Sandra Sookoo:

Scandal in Surrey series

Lady Parker's Grand Affair
The Bride's Gambit
Misfortune's Lady
Miss Bennett's Naughty Secret

Scandalous Shorts (tie-ins to the Scandal in Surrey series)

Library Tryst
Bedroom Assignation
Staircase Encounter
Garden Affair (coming soon)

Darrington family series

Marriage Minded Lord
To Bed or To Wed
The Bridal Contract

Regency-era pirate romances

Act of Pardon
Angel's Master
Storm Tossed Rogue
Once a Pirate
Scoundrel's Trespass

Blurb

The quest to break a mummy's curse turns dangerous when a peer ends up dead.

Miles Lawrence Hawkins, fifth Earl of Archewyne, is alone and the last of his line, save for a young daughter, and he's made peace with that...Yet unexpectedly finding an attractive female thief in his library gives him doubts. Drawn into the lady's insane plot to retrieve various stolen mummies from around London—including the British Museum—he accompanies her merely to see what will happen next. Being captivated by her quest and intrigued by her talent for skirting the law is a much needed distraction from the stress of his own life's misfortunes.

Lady Emmaline Darling, skilled thief and only child to the Earl of St. Ives, is under a mummy's curse. Believing herself damned due to her father's penchant for removing antiquities from Egypt, she's vowed to return a pair of mummies to their eternal resting place in order to save his life and her own. Being caught by Miles wasn't in her plan, and neither was falling for his charm, but she'll do anything to see he's free of the curse as well, for their histories are too intricately connected for his ills to just be bad luck.

When a peer with ties to them both ends up dead and Emmaline's jewelry is found at the scene, Miles is honor bound to offer for her and lend her his protection. Despite her refusal, desire pulls at them and scandal surrounds them, and when Miles is summoned to once more embark upon a secret mission for the Crown, he must shed everything that will become a liability, but keeping Emmaline out of trouble—and out of his mind—is easier said than done.

Chapter One

Late September 1820
London, England

"Oh, bloody hell."

Miles Lawrence Hawkins, Fifth Earl of Archewyne, cocked his head at the muffled exclamation made by an as yet unidentified female. He paused in the hallway, directly between his study and the library on the ground floor of his Mayfair townhouse. Frantic shuffling of objects being dropped or moved behind the library door met his ears next and he frowned. Why was anyone on this level of the house and at this time of evening, especially when all invited guests should be mingling and flirting in the drawing room or playing cards on the floor above. Even more especially since dinner would be served within the next quarter hour on that same level? He glanced back down the passageway toward the blue parlor and garden. Only one wall sconce had been lit, and even then its illumination didn't reach this section of the corridor. The anemic light didn't help in this situation, for no one was scheduled to be here at this time.

Common intruder or someone more vile? In his line of work, one could never tell.

He took a step toward the library door when another utterance halted his progress.

"No, no, no, no, no! Don't you fall. Don't you—" Something thudded with a dull crash and the owner of that dulcet voice cursed in … was that Arabic?

His eyebrows soared toward his hairline as a reluctant grin curved his mouth. He hadn't heard scraps of that lyrical language since his youth. What the devil occurred behind that closed door, and why did he feel the sudden need to meet the owner of that voice? He strode toward said portal and laid his gloved fingers on the brass handle then quickly pressed the metal and shoved the door open.

Though the large, bookshelf-lined room lay mostly in darkness, the soft glow from a single candle provided enough illumination for him to discern his unexpected visitor had been busy during her time there. Books were scattered over the floor, bric-a-brac and Egyptian antiquities had been taken from the shelves and now rested in rough piles in and out of the golden puddle of candlelight while a four-foot statue of Anubis, the Egyptian god of the dead had toppled from its perch on a marble pedestal in the corner near a cluster of potted palms. The tip of his onyx nose had broken off. Presumably the statue was what had fallen to the lady's dismay.

And frozen nearby, with an expression of surprise on her oval face, was a woman of indeterminate years. The dim light prohibited him from seeing her clearly, but there was no hiding the sheaf of age-yellowed paper rolled in her pale hand. Her midnight-black hair gleamed in the candle's glow while her eyes widened as she caught sight of him.

"Buggar it." Shoving the paper into the emerald green reticule attached to her slim wrist, she inched around the perimeter of the library. "Well, I should go now." A good several or so inches shorter than his five-foot eleven-inch self, she possessed flawless milky skin and eyes that flashed green in the fleeting moment she glanced directly at him.

The eyes were familiar…

Miles gawked at her for all the seconds he was afforded until she approached a low table, bent, then extinguished the candle with a soft exhalation. Darkness flooded the room, but the rustle of her satin skirts alerted him to her direction and he moved in the same. The hard rush of his pulse through his temples kept time to his footfalls. "Who are you?" There were so many other questions hovering on the tip of his tongue, but this one trumped them all for the moment.

"Oh, that's not important." Urgency rang in her voice. For what?

"I'll wager it is." He had no idea if she was an invited guest or even what her purpose was in invading his private rooms, but he'd damn well find out. The fact she'd broken the Anubis was beside the point. It was merely a copy and could easily be repaired. He'd been looking for a distraction from the mind-numbing events the rout afforded. This was as good as any. The scent of violets wafted to his nose, as did the slight intake of her breath. She was close. And the door was nearby—her only escape. If she intended to pass him—

Devil take it, she did! The brush of her skirts on the tip of his boot and the slight slide of her reticule against his sleeve had his pulse racing and his curiosity climbing. With his reflexes on alert and honed from years being one of the King's men, he snaked out a hand and wrapped his fingers around her delicate wrist as she attempted to pass. Her heartbeat raced beneath the thin kid of his glove. "Indulge me in an explanation or four, if you please."

"We don't have the time." When she attempted to wrench from his hold and he tightened his grip, she merely tugged him along the corridor as if it didn't matter.

"Of course it matters." She didn't know that he answered his own assumption and his mind reeled at how to deal with the problem. "What did you take from my library?"

"Nothing of consequence." The woman yanked on her wrist, but he didn't let go. "Obviously, you won't miss it since I found it buried in a box with a false bottom."

"What sort of box?" Miles didn't recollect any sort of a box like that in his library let alone the whole of his townhouse, but then, the place was still very much decorated in a haphazard style since his wife's death. All of the Egyptian antiquities had been his father's and more or less left scattered about without thought.

"Oh, you know the type. Cedarwood, decorated with carved ivory figures, brittle. Came from Egypt. Nearly four thousand years old." She shrugged and the ripple of movement transferred to him as she marched down the corridor toward the front door. "I truly do beg your pardon, but I don't have the time nor the inclination to talk at the moment. I really do need to move on."

"I don't think so." Was she a spy, another sort of operative thinking to unearth government documents, or just a petty thief? He opened his mouth to give her the dressing down she so richly deserved when they arrived in the entrance hall. She looked back toward the stairs. Muffled sounds of gaiety drifted down to him from the revelry in the drawing room. Then she glanced to the set of double wood and glass entrance doors. "There is nowhere to run, my little thief." As much as he wished to gloat in this moment, he couldn't. Something in her strained expression left his gut clenching in sympathy.

"Shh!" She tilted her head slightly to one side. Was she listening? Nothing except the distant laughter and drone of conversation from the party met his ears. Seconds later, heavy pounding rained on the door. "Runners."

What the devil? "Bow Street Runners?" At her slight nod, his jaw fell open. "Why would the Runners be here?" And how did she know who was at his door?

A wash of rosy color infused her pale cheeks. "I... uh." She moistened her lips and Miles flicked his gaze to her mouth. She had the most delectable plush lips, slightly full and with the most inviting dip at the top—the sort of lips for kissing. "I might have already visited another residence in Mayfair this evening."

"And helped yourself to someone else's property." He glanced back down the corridor. "I understand, but if you don't wish to be seen, we must move." Without a second thought, he tugged her out of the entrance hall and into the stairwell. As they stood there waiting, deep voices erupted onto the scene. Alfred, the butler, answered the knock. No doubt faced with insistent Bow Street Runners, that austere man would have a footman fetch their employer—him. "I'll be needed," he whispered, not wishing to give away their position. Which was odd, but he couldn't say why. Instinct drove him at the moment, the same instinct that had guided him during his time in the Navy, the same instinct that drove him in his new, secret mission for king and country.

"I'm sure." She attempted yet again to extricate herself, this time adding her free hand. He refused to let his grip slack. "You would be difficult."

"That largely depends on one's perspective."

"Arse." Her huff of annoyance stirred the baby fine tendrils of hair at her temple and forehead. "There's nothing for it." The mad woman climbed the square-shaped staircase to the first floor and he had no choice but to follow if he didn't wish to lose her.

If nothing else, as long as she remained in his home, he could keep an eye on her. Whether he turned her over to the Runners later remained to be seen. And if she was here in a more worrying capacity? Well, he'd deal with her himself.

Before he could ask what she planned to do, she dashed along the hall then plunged into the crowded drawing room. Determined to see this madcap adventure through to its end, merely to satisfy his curiosity, he followed close on her heels, never breaking his connection on her wrist.

"Drat. I hadn't counted on so many people," she grumbled as she kept to the perimeter of this room.

"I do apologize," he rejoined in a somewhat aggrieved voice. "I had no idea that my birthday celebration would throw a wrench into your urge for flight or evading the law." More than aware of the eyes of marriageable ladies and their mamas on him, he kept his focus trained on the woman currently leading him through the maze of mingling people. The gossip columns would have a right good go of it by the morrow. Just who was this mysterious woman, and why the hell did he even want to find himself embroiled in whatever trouble she'd borrowed?

Because I've been bored for far too long and lonelier for longer. The need for adventure was certainly there, and it hadn't been met in his current associations. "I have questions, you know."

"Do shut up. I cannot concentrate on an appropriate plan with you yammering in my ear." She didn't hesitate in her quest. "What is the easiest and fastest way out of this house that doesn't use the front door?"

The chime of a bell at the entrance of the room interrupted his response. Conversation around them died as Alfred announced that dinner would now be served. He then invited the guests to move toward the adjoining dining room.

Miles glanced over his shoulder. He caught his butler's eye, and the older man preceded to gesture with a gloved hand that his presence was immediately needed. Not knowing what else to do, the earl nodded and the butler removed himself from the doorway, presumably to tell the Runners he'd attend them shortly.

A sharp rap from an ivory inlaid fan of emu feathers jolted him from his thoughts. He glanced at his companion with a frown. She'd hit him on the shoulder with a damn fan. From where had she retrieved it? Narrowing his eyes, he purposefully stared as it dangled from the same wrist as her reticule. "If you wished for my attention, you need only ask. I am, after all, still holding onto you."

"I did," she hissed back, never slowing. "You didn't answer." Another rap, this one to the back of his hand holding her wrist. "How do we exit this house and quickly?" Again, urgency threaded through the question.

"Through the garden doors directly across from the parlor on the lower floor. There's a small terrace at the back of the garden and from there, a stone staircase leads either to the street or the rear of the property."

"What's on the other side of your property? I mean, you're at Upper Brook Street and Culross. On the far end of Mayfair." She turned about and led him through a stream of guests who were going in the opposite direction. "Not exactly convenient for becoming lost in the city."

"Yes, well, it's a Mayfair address all the same, and that's what matters." His frown deepened. Being on the outskirts of Mayfair meant he was well away from the general hubs of the fashionable folk, which allowed him more privacy than if he'd settled in a more highly sought after address. In fact, he owned the townhouses on either side of his to ensure that privacy—among other things. If he allowed them for rent, at least he could vet the applicants. In his position, he couldn't be too careful and quite frankly, he held suspect everyone he met. Trust didn't come easily. "Hyde Park is a block east. Why?"

"We'll need some sort of ground cover to help in our escape."

"*Our* escape?" Into Hyde Park nearing the midnight hour? He smiled and nodded at a lady of his acquaintance he'd seen a handful of times in passing at one event or another but had never wrangled an official introduction. She looked at him with wide eyes, took in the woman tugging at his hand then gave him the cut direct and kept walking with the other lady by her side. Damnation, but this was turning out to be a trying night.

"Well, I could go alone if you'd only release my wrist." Again she tried wrenching from his grasp. He hung on, now more determined than ever to figure out what her game was.

"That is not going to happen." When they reached the hall, he led the way to the staircase they'd recently climbed. Down they went, turning left once they gained the ground floor. "This way." He kept his voice low so as not to alert Alfred. "Quiet now. No doubt Alfred showed your Runners into the parlor." Just before that off-limit door, he jerked her to an etched glass door and pushed it open. "Come." The sudden burst of cool air over his overheated skin, brought on by too many bodies and a wealth of lit candles as well as the chase, came as a welcome relief. "Where do you plan on going after you quit my property?"

"Through the park. After that, I haven't decided yet. I must think about what I've learned tonight." Then she moved over the stone terrace.

"You'll have to elaborate."

She huffed again as she led the way through an opening in wrought iron railing and further into the crisp, chilly fall night. "There is a certain Egyptian mummy I'm keen to track down, and I think I've found out where it might be. I need time to pore over the clues."

He stifled a groan. Ever since he'd been in short pants, all he'd learned from his parents was the history of Egyptian royalty as well as been taught the proper classification of pieces unearthed from dust-covered tombs and pits. If he tried, he could still remember the grit of sand stuck perpetually in his socks or the feel of the unrelenting sun beating on his head. No young man should be forced to spend his winters in the desert, bored to tears while in a tent with a succession of equally bored or superstitious tutors. Fighting Boney's forces had been only a notch better than that. At least that adventure had led him to other things.

Realizing she waited for an answer, he quickly said, "I want absolutely nothing to do with anything remotely connected to Egypt." He'd had enough of that in his life, and even if he wasn't a believer in curses, myths or superstitions, there'd been enough strange and unfortunate occurrences in recent years that it came too close to home.

And he had too many responsibilities now to give in to that sort of foolish thinking. Bad luck was merely bad luck, not chalked up to otherworldly things.

"Whether you want to or not, I have a feeling you're more than connected to them." Her skirts whispered over the well-manicured back lawn as they fled along a flagstone path toward a grouping of evergreen trees. "And you have more than enough of their relics lying about to deny a familiarity."

"I don't wish to have you add to the theories." It had taken him two years, but he'd finally reached peace with the misfortune in his life. Nothing out of the ordinary had occurred in the past two years, and he wanted to keep it that way.

"Come on!" She tugged at her wrist. "We need to keep going. At least if we gain the park, I can slip away and find a quiet spot where I can think."

"There are more than enough rooms here for you to do that." A shiver stole up his spine. Give them another few hours and the temperature would drop even more as was autumn's wont. He glanced at his companion and her short sleeves and thin skirts. Her elbow-length gloves wouldn't help. Was she cold?

Finally, she slowed to a walk and glanced at him from over her shoulder. Too bad it was a moonless night, for he still couldn't see her features clearly. "Are you daft?"

Apparently, he was. He shrugged. "It's a large townhouse."

"Which contains at least two Runners."

"You don't know they're here for you."

She snorted. "Are you in the habit of inviting the criminal element into your home then?"

That all depended on the type of criminal. "Well, no." *You're the first*, though she wasn't invited. He couldn't place her, that much was certain.

"There you are." When she darted ahead again, but this time their connection broke. "Thank you for your assistance in gaining your gardens," she called over that slender, elegant shoulder, and he was rapidly tiring of talking to her back, gorgeous and shapely though it might be.

"Oh no." Miles wasn't about to let such a mysterious woman slip from his life before he could have at least a name—or a direction where she could be found for the Runners. After all, right was right, and ever since he'd taken up the title of earl, he followed rules and kept his nose clean, and gave up the chance at adventuring as well. "Our business together isn't finished." She didn't fit the description of the master criminal he'd been tasked to find, but then, anyone and everyone could do harm, and everyone was capable of betraying their country for the right price. He chased after her, and just as they entered the copse of trees, he caught her around the waist, tumbling them both to the ground. "I have never run from anything and do not intend to start now," he said in a breathless voice as he untangled his limbs from hers.

Except, that wasn't entirely true. As long as he kept people on the periphery of his life, he couldn't lose them to the grave. That was a sort of running which, in retrospect, he'd been doing his whole life, from his early years in Egypt, to his commission fighting Napoleon and on through his marriage…

"Unfortunately, you cannot run from a curse." Amusement underscored her words. The woman pushed herself into a sitting position. "I suppose this is as good a place as any for an introduction." She held out a hand and her black satin, elbow-length glove became an extension of the night. Diamonds and emeralds of her bracelet glinted in the dim moon's glow, stark against that dark glove. "I'm Lady Emmaline Darling."

Why did that name sound familiar? Definitely on the dossier he'd committed to memory not a month prior in urgent and secret audience with Lord Liverpool, the Prime

Minister, so then, who the deuce was she? He remained on the ground with her, propping one booted foot in the grass with a bent knee while he kept the other leg stretched out. His valet would surely have his head for the blatant disregard of the evening clothes. The longer he sent her name circulating around in his mind, the more the familiarity grew until, finally, he gaped at her. Again. "Good God, not the daughter of Earl St. Ives."

A frown turned down her lips. "You don't need to say it with such disgust, though I am accustomed to such a reaction." She dusted her hands together to rid the gloves of the worst of the dirt, which caused the fan and reticule to knock together on her wrist. "I'm well aware of what Society thinks of Father."

No doubt she did. Alastair Darling was completely mad from all accounts. In his seventies now, he'd quit England decades before, more or less fleeing the country ahead of creditors as well as dissatisfied patrons since he'd spent every farthing he'd ever made or received on chasing down legends or on funding archeological dig projects, mainly in Egypt to no avail if the rumors were true. The last he'd heard, his daughter remained his companion for fear he'd wander off and do something crazy.

And she was purportedly following in his footsteps.

How... disappointing. "When did you return to England?" He took her hand and brought her gloved fingers to his lips.

"Two months ago." Her eyes glittered in the dark, as bright and cold as her jewels, and she struggled to her feet, but not before he caught a tantalizing glimpse of her slim ankles encased in black, silken stockings. Jet beads winked on her emerald slippers. Expensive fabrics and baubles for the daughter of a man whose pockets were allegedly to let.

How had she procured them? Yet another layer to the mystery that was her.

"Why?" He rose as well and tensed in the event she ran again.

"To break a mummy's curse on my family."

Not this again. "There's no such thing."

She waved his comment off as if it were an annoying gnat. "You can have your opinions. I have mine, and quite frankly, I've grown tired of all the unexplained misfortunes or plain bad luck that's befallen my family." Lady Emmaline peered up at him and a shiver wracked her shoulders. "My father lies wasting away, courting death, even now in Cairo, and if I am unable to break the curse, I fear it will come for me next."

Despite his resistance to anything remotely stinking of Egypt and foolish curses and long-dead things, his chest tightened. Miles felt for her in that moment. Though he didn't know her story behind the cracked veneer of the rumors, no doubt it would mirror his own. Memories of chasing other English children about the grounds of various dignitaries came to mind from back in his school days. While his parents gadded about with others in their field, Lady Emmaline had been one of those children. He stole another glance at her person and his gaze accidentally landed on her rounded bosom. The last he'd seen her, she was sixteen and still very much a lithe schoolgirl without a woman's curves. At least they had Egypt in common and could possibly lead to a better connection later. "Good to meet you, Lady Emmaline. Though I'm certain we knew each other before. In any case, I'm Miles Lawrence Hawkins, Fifth Earl of Archewyne, but please, call me Miles."

"Very well. Miles. I used to know a pair of Hawkins boys in my childhood." A slight grin lifted one side of her lips and jogged another memory, this time of an awkward, thin girl with sun-streaked dark hair who had that same smirk. A frisson of remembrance twined up his spine. He recalled being enchanted by that unique quirk of those lips. "You may drop my title as well. It makes for a rather messy business when one is trying to keep a low profile."

"I can well imagine." More than she'd ever know, actually. How had she become this woman before him from such uninspiring beginnings? The need to know burned strong in his chest, but he remained quiet on the subject. That was for another time.

She narrowed her eyes. "Your title is familiar. Perhaps I knew your father in passing."

"Perhaps, but I believe we knew each other as children. Comb the depths of your memories, my lady." Now was not the time to reminisce either. He held out a hand. "Will you at least consent to let me help you through the park?" If something happened to her while she traversed Hyde Park at this hour, he'd never forgive himself. He owed safe passage to her for the woman she was and the girl she'd been. His gut clenched. There had been a time in his reckless youth when he hadn't escorted her when he should have and she'd met with a fair amount of trouble.

Doing the nicety now wouldn't excuse his behavior then, but it would be a start.

"Knew each other as children, did we?" Seconds went by before she slipped her fingers into his. "I'd like that. Fortune hunting and curse breaking are often a lonely business."

"I'll take your word for it." But the first part of her statement rankled. Was this some sort of scheme on her part to have someone discover them together in an attempt to get at his family's coin since her own was depleted? The grand necklace that matched her bracelet negated that thought, however. Very curious indeed. He led her farther into the trees and followed a brick wall for a bit until they reached a tall wooden gate. "However, if your plan is to trap me into marriage, I will bid you adieu right now and point Bow Street in your direction with my compliments."

She wrenched her hand from his. "You overstep, sir." Disappointment filled her voice and that captivated him even more. "Why the deuce would I want another marriage when my first two ended with the deaths of both husbands?" She tossed her head. "And I do remember you, Miles. Some of those memories are not pleasant." With her chin thrust out and head held high, she sailed through the gap he made when he opened the gate.

If her previous actions hadn't secured his interest, her words now did. "May God forgive me, but I'm going to need a deeper explanation," he muttered as he followed her into the vast forests of Hyde Park.

Chapter Two

Lady Emmaline Darling's attempt to ignore her accidental companion failed miserably. What kind of a man, especially a member of the aristocracy at that, followed a woman he no doubt suspected was a thief even after she'd all but given him orders to leave?

She missed the warmth of his gloved hand upon her wrist, since they had been together thusly for the last fifteen minutes. And bloody hell, he had to bring up a previous connection, tenuous though it was at best. Yes, their parents had been in Egypt at the same time, when he and she were but children, still finding their way in the world around them. She'd thought him a dashing young man and, with a schoolgirl's crush, she'd gone adventuring, following him around hoping he'd take notice of her.

Now, she wished he'd forgotten the memories. They were of no use in the present and made her feel foolish besides. With a frown she kept to the trees and set off through the perimeter of Hyde Park. Damn and blast but she needed a place to think and a light to better read the scrap of paper she'd filched from Miles' library. That was what she had to focus on. Not sun-drenched remembrances of a dark-haired boy who'd seemed to hold the secrets of life in his titled palm. Of course, that would require some sort of illumination, which would be easily seen in the darkness shrouding the park.

Drat! Perhaps I should have planned this scheme a bit better.

"Do you plan to ignore my inquiry, then?" The deep tenor rumbled through the night and sent heated shivers of awareness skating over her skin. At least it chased the chill away. "I believe I asked for enlightenment."

"If that is what you're after, might I point you in the direction of any man of religion? No doubt you can find them all over the city, merely choose your faith and ask accordingly." She crushed her skirts in her fists as she traversed a particularly rough patch of ground.

"Emmaline, stop." Authority rang in the command. It wasn't softened with the use of her given name. Once more he encircled her wrist with his fingers and his touch stayed her flight. "Before we go any further, I do need more information. It's only fair."

No, fair would be the curse leaving her and her family alone. Too much death was… well, too much, and she spent enough time around the dead as a vocational choice. It didn't need to follow her into her personal life as well.

With a sigh, she faced him and gasped in surprise. He was entirely too close. And tall. A good several inches taller than her average height. His raven hair blended with the night and his eyes were just as inky. As a young man, he'd spent so much time in the sun that his skin was as dark as the natives, which had only added to his appeal. Of course he'd have to be all the more enigmatic now. She shook her head. It didn't matter, not when more important things occupied her time, and that time was slipping by at an alarming rate. Memories were only memories after all. The longer she tarried in the area, the more likely the Runners would close in. How they'd tracked her here, she'd never know. Over the years, she'd become quite skilled at being a thief, something she'd acquired from her days in Egypt, where such things abounded. "What would you like to know?"

"You won't run if I release you?" He held up her wrist, and she had the errant thought that if they weren't wearing gloves their skin would touch.

Would his hands be work-roughened or soft like all the titled gentlemen who didn't know a day's hard labor? She glanced at his fingers, strong in their kid casing and moistened her lips. "I promise I won't." *At least, not in this moment.* Obviously, she couldn't promise the future. When he let her go, she sighed again. "Well?"

"Where to start?" Instead of loitering, he clasped his hands behind his back and led the way toward one of the walking paths that crisscrossed the land. A few dried leaves crunched beneath his boots. She hurried to catch him up, never pausing to properly appreciate his broad shoulders that strained the confines of his black evening coat. "I've been presented with so many arresting topics since meeting you—or renewing your acquaintance—that I confess I'm a bit at sixes and sevens of which one interests me more."

For the first time since she'd been caught pilfering his library, a genuine grin tugged at her mouth. It had been a long time indeed she'd conversed with a gentleman. Though there was a large English population abroad, it wasn't the same as finding oneself alone with a nobleman in the dark. This aberration to her daily routine was most welcome. She hadn't lied when she'd said adventuring was a lonely endeavor. That brought a frown. *I am not looking for a romantic entanglement.* Thank heavens for the freedoms afforded a widow, else they'd be in the drink for certain if events of this night came to light.

"What is the most pressing?" She cringed when her step fell on a large pebble and the rough edge pushed sharply against the sole of her slipper.

"I don't recall your name on my guest list."

Out of everything, *that's* what he'd choose to ask her? "I'm not normally invited to the homes I plan to—"

"Steal from?" he interrupted. When heat hit her cheeks and she nodded, he continued. "What did you purloin from my library?"

Emmaline remained silent. How much to share with this man she didn't know past vague memories, one especially annoying of him pulling her braid when she'd been not much older than eight or of him chasing her with a monkey on his shoulder? Even that slight connection wouldn't help what she'd become now.

"You're already in over your head, my lady," he murmured in a quiet voice as he held out a hand to help her over a series of branches that had fallen across the road. "Telling me more isn't going to help or harm your case anymore than what's already there."

What could it hurt, truly? After tonight, she'd never see him again and even this meeting would be consigned to memories. "I took a map of what should be the complete layout of tombs in the Valley of the Kings."

"And you believe I had such a thing why?" He didn't release her hand, and she didn't pull away. For whatever reason, keeping such a bond felt natural, companionable even.

"Your father was the last known person to own the priest's mummy."

A sharp inhalation was his only answer. For many moments they walked in silence before he finally broke it. "Yes, my father had a mummy in his possession, but I donated it to the British Museum two years ago after…

well, that doesn't matter now. They assured me they were happy to have it but doubted it would go on display as they are currently overrun with mummies." A slight snort gave away his humor. "Sounds like a deuced bad problem to have."

"I don't doubt that." Her lips twitched but she didn't give in to the mirth. "It's quite a fashionable thing to leave a tour of Egypt with a mummy, regardless of how irresponsible it is." Bitterness rang in her voice.

"Yes, well, that being said, I didn't want it in the house, so off it went."

"Then that is to be my next stop." A tug on her hand halted her forward movement. "What?"

"The museum is closed."

Silly man. She found his gaze in the darkness and answered with a scoff. "Do you really think such a thing as operating hours will stop me from continuing my quest?"

"At this point, I'm not certain what you're capable of, but I have a healthy respect for it." He looked around. "This is as good a spot as any."

"For what?"

"Telling me what you stole from the other house in Mayfair as well as how you came to decide this mummy curse needs to be ferreted out now." He drew her over to a thick fallen tree. "It's not exactly a parlor, but it's the best I can offer."

She perched on the smooth birch trunk and stifled a shiver. "If I tell you, do you promise to keep the knowledge to yourself?"

"Of the stolen goods or the mummy history?" He crossed his arms in front of his chest, and with his legs planted apart, she could easily envision him on the deck of a naval ship. Had he done a stint in His Majesty's service during the war?

"Um, both." She played with the strings of her reticule, which she'd laid in her lap. "As you can imagine, trust is a rare commodity and what I value most from the people I take into my confidence."

"I understand that more than you could know. However, there are times when the suspension of disbelief is greater than the need for trust." He stared at her, but she couldn't read his eyes or expression in the dark. "Start talking, my lady. I'm not of a mind to stand here all night."

"Ah, then you and I are of an accord, for there is precious little time to waste." Emmaline yanked open her reticule then withdrew the item she'd taken from the residence before his. She let the necklace dangle from its delicate golden chain. "This is the Amulet of Mutemwiya, who was the mother of Amenhotep III." The oval-shaped pendant with four, thin, white quartz wings sprouting from the body twisted on the chain. "It's made of malachite, and though you can't see it now, it's dark green with marbling of lighter green woven throughout. A beautiful piece, really." It resembled a bug of some sort but didn't have a head.

"I agree that it does have a visual appeal. What's its significance with your mummy?"

I only wish it was my mummy, then at least I'd known where the blasted thing was! She shook her head. "Malachite was used to promote inner visions and the headdresses of pharaohs were lined with it in the belief that it would guide them and encourage them to rule wisely. Because Mutemwiya was the mother of a powerful pharaoh, she often aligned herself with priests like the one I'm hunting.

It only goes to follow his wife was in the faith as well, no doubt a priestess in her own right."

"Ah, so they embarked on a bit of black magic to protect the king and his rule?"

"Yes, basically." She fingered the amulet one last time before she put it carefully back into her bag. "There's a short inscription on the back, like a tag on a gift, from Mutemwiya to the priestess. It took me an hour of searching through Lord Leventhorpe's study, but I finally found it, and it proves that he did have the mummy in his possession at one time."

"Or it proves he had the necklace of said mummy and that was all. He could have bought the bauble on the black market, which means a rather dead end for you."

Dead. There was that word again. "Perhaps, but I hope that's not the case." Another shiver wracked her shoulders, and this time she couldn't stifle it.

"Damnation, woman, you'll catch your death." Miles removed his dress coat after a heroic struggle then he handed her the garment. "Put this on."

"Thank you." She didn't protest or play coy like so many women of her acquaintance. The bald fact was she had indeed felt the chill. This would help. Quickly she shoved her arms into the sleeves and pulled the jacket tight about her. His warmth still clung to the superfine and his sage and citrus scent wafted to her nose. It comforted her in a moment when she didn't know she was discomfited.

"Was Lord Leventhorpe in residence when you were there?" Slight censure rang in the question.

She frowned. "He was not. It wasn't until I reached the drive that his carriage pulled up. I was forced to flee through the shrubbery and gardens. I ran through the streets before ducking through more gardens until I could ascertain I wasn't being followed any longer by his footman. Leventhorpe's servants are rather more in the ogre category, if you ask me."

"Ah. But that doesn't explain why Bow Street was called in. Yes, Leventhorpe saw you and could identify you by sight, for I assume you and he are not on socially speaking terms, but unless the theft was of some significance and more than the necklace, the Runners wouldn't care. Leventhorpe certainly wouldn't press for charges, not with all the alleged crimes the man himself has committed."

"Well, I don't know how much of my identity he ascertained. We've never met and don't move in the same circles, as you said." She might be part of the aristocracy, but she didn't aspire to breathe the same air as the black-hearted marquess. "I make it a habit to stay on the outskirts of Society, and when I don't, my father's name secures that urge." None of that bothered her. The importance that members of the peerage placed on rank and worth and connection aggravated her more than it impressed. A person should work hard for what they wanted instead of letting their name or coin secure it on a whim.

"Even still, I don't like the sound of it. I suppose the Runners—if that's indeed who was at my door—aren't here for you, but it is coincidental. How long after you quit his townhouse did you enter mine?"

Emmaline shrugged. "Perhaps forty minutes to an hour. I needed the time to double back through the streets then study your home before finding out the best way of entry."

"Which was?"

"The front door, of course. Since you'd opted to throw a party and I was already dressed for such a thing due to wishing to blend into Leventhorpe's own soiree in the event I was discovered at his home." She frowned. "That doesn't explain why he'd arrived late for his own affair at his own home."

A dark look crossed Miles' face. "He is an enigma."

"Quite. In any event, I simply told your butler my name, pretended I belonged there all along and the man granted me access." She giggled. "Truly, you should retrain your staff, Miles. There are unsavory people out there who will take advantage of you."

"I am well aware of that fact." When she remained silent, he sat beside her on the tree trunk. "You're in a spot of trouble. Leventhorpe's not exactly the kindest peer."

"I know that." Rumors abounded about the cruelty of that lord, but when one gleaned their news from the weight of rumors, it made one rather an idiot. However, there were facts behind each rumor.

"He will make your life miserable." Part of that lord's dark persona was the existence of a ledger or notebook of some sort wherein he recorded every favor he'd ever done to any member of the *ton,* and he'd demand repayment on a whim. "I've had a couple of incidents with him since becoming earl, so I can vouch for the degree of tarnish on his soul."

Which only added to Miles' air of mystery and intrigue. "I don't plan to tarry in England long enough to find myself apprehended or to come into contact with Leventhorpe." Her belly twinged, and once more, the urgent need to run raced through her veins, especially now that she began to realize just what exactly the notebook in her reticule was. "Even if I did, what else can he do to me that the curse has not?" Already, her father's townhouse was understaffed and hopelessly out of date, not to mention the blunt he owed to keep the place running would not be forthcoming any time soon. She'd be lucky if she wasn't run out by creditors during her hopefully brief stay. Selling off pieces of jewelry she'd managed to hide away from her father over the years would only last so long.

"What if your mummy is still in England?"

"Then obviously I'll have to make other arrangements." He didn't need to know at this point that she was fully prepared to smuggle a mummy out of the country by whatever extreme means necessary. Over the years, she'd tucked away enough funds so she could finance the trip, and if she needed more, she had jewelry and antiquities to sell in an emergency.

"I see." He brushed something from his leg. "Why me? Why steal from me?"

"Your home was the next logical step on my quest because your father had owned the mummy at one time, perhaps he'd taken it from Leventhorpe or the marquess acquired it from the museum after you donated it. I need the map so I know exactly where to return my mummy once I locate it." She shrugged. "It's a fairly detailed map. Done by members of Napoleon's expedition, dated 1799."

"This is significant?"

"I should say so." She snorted. Honestly, how could the man not know? Then she tempered her reaction. Not all people she met were as interested or as well-versed in Egyptian folklore as she. "Whatever happened to your history lessons as a boy in Egypt?"

"I don't think about those days if I can help it." A note of finality rested in his response.

"Understandable." Thank goodness her father had been adamant she learn alongside him instead of the boring subjects the governesses insisted upon. "This map also contains detailed drawings of the Western Valley. It's where Egyptologists Prosper Jollois and Édouard de Villiers du Terrage located the tomb of Amenhotep III—"

"Who was the employer of your priest and where his tomb was—"

"—is—"

"—is no doubt housed."

"Exactly." She gave a tremulous smile. "So you see why I had to have it." Perhaps now he'd understand why she needed to be on her way. "I don't know how you came to own such a thing. It was only luck on my part that you did have it, but I'm not complaining. It's not a collector's item, and you don't seem all that interested in ancient Egypt." Not anymore. He'd lost his enthusiasm for adventure he'd had during his youth. That was more than disappointing, yet there was a certain edge about him, like a cloak he drew about him that proclaimed otherwise.

He cleared his throat. "I may have come into possession some of Napoleon's papers during my stint working for the Crown. Those deemed unimportant to the war were handed back to me. I kept them for posterity, as a remnant to that part of my life, I suppose, in the event I'd forget..." His eyes flashed before shadows clouded them again.

Ah ha, so then he did have a military background. "That's an interesting tidbit I do wish I'll have time to explore later."

"Indeed, that is a story for another day, as they say, but then, you're impatient to quit the country. Your curiosity will be destined to go unchecked." Was that a snicker he stifled? "Did it occur to you that you could have asked for the map?"

"Would you have given it to me once I told you my name or my purpose?" She looked askance at him but doubted he saw the expression in the darkness.

"I might have considered it."

"Don't patronize me. We both know you would have treated me with kid gloves and escorted me from the property." Though she loved her father, she did regret how he'd conducted his life that made their name the subject of joking through the *ton*. Why couldn't luck shine upon her just once and let her make an important discovery? Well, she knew why. The curse wouldn't stop until she was as dead as her mummies. Perhaps then Society would find respect for her and her father once they were parted from the earth.

"We should agree to disagree." He held up a hand. "What difference will that map make if the priest's wife has gone missing as well?"

A shiver moved through her that didn't have anything to do with the autumn chill. She put a hand inside her reticule again, her fingers brushing over the soft, worn leather of a small notebook she'd also purloined from a false bottom in Leventhorpe's desk, and this time pulled out a few scraps of dirty bandages attached to a dried up and shriveled hand.

"Good God!" Horror infused the exclamation.

She ignored his reaction. "In addition to the necklace, I have this. I have reason to believe Lord Leventhorpe is hiding the female mummy somewhere on his property. Clearly, it belonged to a female. God only knows why he might have had it. Unless…"

"Unless?"

"What if he thought the curse had touched his life due to his brief possession of the priest's mummy and he wished to reunite them both, the same as I?" Interesting theory and one she'd not considered before. She didn't know that much about Leventhorpe's history outside of his penchant for blackmail. "Regardless, I found this with the amulet, both thrown into an ivory-inlaid trinket box and shoved into a drawer." She waved the hand about.

Miles sprang up from the tree as if a snake had bitten him. "Why? Why are you gadding about town with a … a…" He gestured at her offering. "A human hand stuffed in your bag?"

She bit her lip to keep from laughing at him as a trace of memory trickled in. Another time and another place he'd reacted similarly to a gathering of bones they'd found on an adventure. It would seem he'd never conquered the fear. It only added to his appeal. "Calm down, my lord. It's merely a piece of a long-dead mummy." But in order to keep the peace, Emmaline replaced the antiquities. "I took them as proof. He might not have the mummy. I realize this, but why have a hand and an amulet that belonged to that same?"

"Theft. Crime of opportunity. He could have ripped the hand as well as the necklace from the mummy somewhere else." Miles fell into pacing before her. "None of this will solve the question of the curse. You have mummy pieces; not a full mummy or mummies as it were."

"I am aware of the failure, my lord." She rose to her feet. In the distance, the howl of a dog cut through the silence and drew her focus back to the urgency of her mission. "That won't dim my determination to locate at least one of them." Unbidden, her mind went to her father, who even now lay suffering from a mysterious lung ailment the doctors said would ultimately steal his life unless a miracle occurred. She wasn't so naïve that she thought bringing the mummies back to Egypt would cure her parent, though the fond thought was certainly there, but she was hopeful the curse would break before it set its sights on her.

"I didn't think it would." He closed the distance between them and lifted her chin with his finger beneath it. "Also, this is not a failure. It's merely a stumbling block or a time to reevaluate your options."

"Thank you." A tremble moved up her spine that had nothing to do with the chill in the air or the subject matter. Ever impulsive and a firm believer that everything good came with a risk, Emmaline lifted onto her toes and pressed her lips to his. She lingered perhaps a second, not long enough for him to react or for her to think about it before she pulled away and retreated a step, breaking their connection. Not nearly long enough for her to become accustomed to the masculine firmness of his lips or the warmth exchanged in that fleeting instant.

Even in the midnight gloom, his frown was evident. "What was that for?" Amusement hung in the question, which chased away the sudden tension in her shoulders.

"A parting gift let's say. I appreciate the fact you've treated me like any other person instead of thinking I'm mad due to my family name."

"Of course. Actions and accomplishments and dedication to one's causes show a person's mettle more than rumors and gossip." His eyes glittered in the gloom. "Despite what I personally think of you chasing after mummies, you believe wholeheartedly in it. That's enough for me to believe in you."

"I appreciate that." She nodded. "Well, it's been lovely spending part of my evening with you, Miles." In some reluctance, she removed the jacket and held it out to him. "Thank you for your kindness. In a world where that is sorely lacking, small gestures like this leave a big impression." Lord knew she wasn't afforded kindness from the *ton*. Merely another reason to quit England as soon as she could. Society in Cairo lacked certain things, but at least they were understanding.

"Where are you going?" He took the jacket from her fingers, but made no effort to don it.

"I already told you. To the British Museum."

"How do you plan to travel there? Besides, it's still closed for the summer holidays."

She peered into his face. "My mission cannot wait." His dark eyes glinted and didn't give up their secrets. "I thought I'd hire a hackney. I'm sure there a few drivers prowling around the more popular locations of the park."

"Absolutely not. Woman, you are inviting trouble doing something like that alone. Nothing good happens in London after midnight."

"Neither does good happen after midnight in Cairo either, but you didn't care about that years ago, did you?" Why she'd choose this moment to rehash that memory, she had no idea. Perhaps she wanted to put him off his line of questioning. The remembrance sent chills down her spine.

One winter, when their parents had been in Cairo for a Society event of some sort, Miles had been tasked with escorting her then twelve-year-old self to a home of one of her father's contemporaries. When the adults had departed, he'd cried off, citing he had other amusements to attend to. He'd left her in a questionable section of the city, where she'd been eventually pounced upon by a band of boys not much older than he'd been. They'd cornered her, pulled at her clothes until she was left clad only in a petticoat, her skirts shoved up about her waist as she writhed on the ground, held there by multiple pairs of hands. Her savior that night had come in the form of her father's man of all trades, Samir, who'd followed her discreetly on what he'd called a nudge from his god.

"I apologized for my lapse and my father took a rod to my backside after the incident as well, but again, I was lax in my duties and honor to you." He softly cleared his throat. "My younger self had much maturing to do." His sigh had enough force that it might have come from his toes as he stared at her. He offered the jacket, holding it out and open to her. "Put this on." The order was no less commanding than it had been a half hour ago.

"Why?" She couldn't shake the feeling that every male she'd ever known had left her vulnerable to life's wolves more times than they hadn't.

"I'm coming with you." He shook the jacket, obviously expecting her to comply.

"Absolutely not," she said, repeating his exclamation. Emmaline popped her hands onto her hips. "This doesn't concern you."

"Like hell it doesn't. I didn't escort you back then. I won't make that same mistake now. My honor is a good deal more developed." When she didn't put the jacket on, he came closer. "If you don't wear the jacket, my lady, I will be forced to take drastic measures." His low voice rumbled in her ear and sent delicious tickles throughout her body.

"How does a missing mummy and my father's declining health have anything to do with you?" She ignored the fact her question sounded breathless while she also ignored the fact that she slid her arms back into his jacket.

"If you want to discover how our lives might be connected, you'll have to let me accompany you to the museum." A healthy dose of smug victory laced the reply. "At least I can offer you the ride."

She smiled. "Fine. It will save me the cab fare and I'll have someone to converse with." She set out down the path. "Most of the men I talk to or talk about are older by a few thousand years and have the decided disadvantage of being dead."

Perhaps there was something to be said about being among the living after all.

Chapter Three

I must be as mad as her father is reputed to be.

Accompanying her anywhere at this time of night was the very definition of insanity and went against every rule he'd put to himself regarding the opposite sex. But then, no one of the opposite sex had voluntarily kissed him, not even his wife. She'd always waited for him to initiate contact, even when he knew she'd wanted that sort of attention. His dear Constance had always been a shy one, and that had never changed with marriage. It had been one of the things he'd loved about her. *May God keep your soul at rest.* Yet… He touched the tip of his tongue to his bottom lip and could swear he still felt Emmaline's brief kiss. How did he reconcile with the fact he liked her way of doing things too?

Yes, definitely as mad as a man can be in such a situation. He didn't know her from Adam—childhood adventures notwithstanding—but she sparked an interest, if only it was to see what she'd do next before he'd made it a point to remain alone.

A nice diversion from the high stress world he usually dwelled in now.

Near Rotten Row, they found a growler for hire. While Miles didn't like the looks of the scruffy individual driving the unmatched set of brown horses, it was better than either loitering around Hyde Park after midnight and being easy pickings for footpads or worse. Beyond that, Emmaline had an air of determination about her that meant she'd take off for the museum on foot, which was just as dangerous as staying in the park. Whatever else she was, he couldn't, in all good conscience, let her go by herself even if she did appear highly capable.

Once he handed her into the hack, he focused on the driver. "British Museum if you please."

The man gaped. "You sure about that? Ain't open for another week or so." His raspy voice could conjure demons from the thick night around them. "It's summer holidays and near midnight besides," he added, no doubt in the event Miles was a nodcock.

"I'm well aware of that, but if you'll stop at the address, I'll pay you handsomely for the effort." As soon as he gained agreement, Miles swung inside the closed carriage, shut the door then the conveyance sprang into motion. "Because going to the damn British Museum in the middle of the night during holidays isn't suspicious," he muttered as he wrinkled his nose against the odors of stale smoke, faded perfume and unwashed bodies.

"Think of it as an adventure," his companion offered. She arranged her skirts over her legs. "Something you can talk about to your grandchildren."

"Not likely." His jaw clenched and he had to tell himself to relax, that she had no idea such a jesting comment would rankle or that he had years ahead of him yet before Jane would be old enough to worry about that.

"Ah, the overprotective father type, for of course you'd have children." Her chuckle filled the interior of the carriage and left pricks of awareness over his skin. "You have that attitude. Your daughters will have quite the time of it during their Seasons."

What the devil did that mean? "No. I don't and I am not." He curved the hand that rested on his thigh into a fist. He was always sensitive where it came to Jane.

Children and wives made a man all the more vulnerable and targets to those with a score to settle.

"Ah, no daughters. All to the better, then, with your title that you'd have male children."

"Well, I do have…" He huffed then hurried to add, "My wife and I lost our son on the day of his birth a little over two years ago." The words were pulled from a tight throat.

"Please accept my condolences." Emmaline turned to him and her leg jostled against his. Heat sprang from the point of contact. "I do hope you and your wife will be blessed with many more children."

The agony that always pierced his heart when speaking about his deceased family came, but it was somehow lessened albeit slightly. There would be time to ponder that later. "We will not. She followed my son into death, I'm afraid. Died of blood loss after the birth." He turned his face to the window, and when he pulled he ratty curtain open, he stared out into the empty London streets. "Grandchildren are the farthest thing from my mind seeing as how securing the line is the more pressing problem at present." Not even the thought of his little Jane could lift those gloomy musings. She wouldn't inherit, of course, and unless he had a son to take up the title… He cleared his throat. "Not that I'm interested in trying to align myself with anyone at the moment, for…" He let the explanation die off. Reasons she did not need to know at this time. Reasons that didn't matter anyway.

Greater things were at stake that would affect more than just his future if he failed in his mission. He huffed. How the hell did she manage to tug such private information out of him when he rarely told anyone of his acquaintance of that time in his life? As a general rule, if someone didn't know his history, he didn't offer it.

"Oh, Miles." Remarkably, there was no pity in the utterance. Only understanding. Then her hand was on his cheek and she forced his face back around until he looked at her. Their gazes met, and the illumination from the gas lights on the street allowed him to definitively identify her eye color—vivid emerald green, like her gown. "You have no idea how much of a parallel our lives are and of how much I fear for your future because of it."

He thought often of his future, but not because of an alleged curse. The warmth from her gloved palm seeped into his skin, and he hated the fabric that kept her separated from him. "Did you lose a child as well?" After all, she'd mentioned two prior marriages. Surely children had come of those unions.

"I have not." For the first time her gaze faltered. Now, she stared at the reticule resting in her lap. It was so unlike the forthright woman from his library and the park that his chest tightened and his mind spun to find ways to make that woman return. She removed her hand from his person and he mourned the loss of her touch. "This is just one way the curse has affected me. I have never been able to become with child." The last word broke on a strangled sob, and then she took a deep breath and regained her composure.

"Ah." Shock filtered through his mind as he searched for words. "Did you, ah, have it confirmed?" Deuced awkward stuff.

"I did." She remained silent for long moments before resuming her narration. "After my first husband's death, I saw a midwife who told me there was nothing physically wrong with me." She sighed. "But then, one doesn't actually *see* a curse, does one? It's not a shroud."

"Yes, but—"

"It's probably for the best my husbands died, for it became unbearable after a while to live month after month without..." She forced a cough. "Well, I'm sure you can guess."

"I can." He peered out the window once more. The conversation was highly inappropriate and indubitably uncomfortable. Yet her speaking on such a topic made her more approachable somehow, more human, more vulnerable than the sophisticated thief. Almost, in that vulnerability, he could easily see her as she was back in those childhood days in Egypt when they'd dined out on dreams and everything seemed possible.

Before the ugliness of humanity exploded all around them.

"Yes. Such is life." The quiet words rasped across his consciousness.

Again, he hung on to his theory that bad luck was simply bad luck. Yet... "We're nearly there." How could a simple carriage ride go so quickly? A frown tugged at his mouth, and he berated himself for enjoying something he shouldn't. It was accompanying a woman to a destination. Nothing more. When she remained quiet, he looked her way once more. "I'm sorry for your loss of what might have been." Feeling compelled to touch her, he covered her hand with his and squeezed before pulling away. He'd become wildly out of practice being close with anyone. It wasn't for his welfare he didn't—couldn't—do it, it was for theirs. Everyone in his life had died and everyone had borne a connection to him. No one else needed that sort of luck. Especially now that he had close connections to the Crown. "That, I think is a more profound disappointment than death could ever be." He sympathized with that loss, and it speared his heart in the dark of night when he was alone in his chambers at times.

"It is." She drew the curtain on her side open. Her soft sigh echoed in the carriage. "In some ways it's a powerful reminder of failure."

He looked across as the carriage passed one of the city's orphanages then he flicked his gaze to her face. Even in profile, longing and desperate sadness lined her expression, gone with the next blink of her eyes. In close scrutiny, the fine lines at the corners of those remarkable eyes bore silent testimony to the trials she must have lived through. "I won't offer you the empty platitudes. I'm certain you've heard them all anyway." He had after he'd laid his wife and child to rest. Those types of words never helped. "However, I will say this: live for the days you have left and enjoy whatever they bring you. Life sometimes doesn't happen the way we hope it might. That doesn't mean it's not a good life nonetheless."

"You're right." She let the curtain fall back into place. "I do enjoy my life as it is now, and I hope that you follow the same advice for I rather think you do not."

When a hot protest sprang to his lips, he tamped it, for she would be correct. It was something else she didn't need to know. There were times he couldn't bear to look at Jane; she resembled Constance so much. How could he when each time he remembered and it near broke his heart? But he'd never tell his daughter that. As such, he'd love her with everything he was, because of Constance.

Emmaline glanced at him with a smile that didn't reach her eyes. "At the moment, I need to break the curse so I may live out my natural life and discover all I'm capable of."

"From what I've seen, I don't doubt you'll set the world on its ear, my lady." He looked away, unable to process the wealth of confusion this talk and her presence had brought into his life in such a short time. His was a world of order and quiet days, not the adventure and chaos she represented. Well… He gave in to a slight smile. He did adventure when the Crown required it. But Emmaline didn't need to know that either.

The opportunity for further conversation ceased as the carriage rocked to a halt before Montagu House on Russell Street. The gardens lay sprawled in the darkness, the shadowy silhouettes of the trees much like an eerie skeleton leading up to the building. Miles exited the vehicle and spoke to the driver as he pulled a sovereign from his pocket. "This should make the trip and your silence more than worthwhile." He flipped the coin to the driver who deftly caught it. The coin disappeared up his sleeve.

"Mum's the word," the driver growled.

Before Miles could go around to the other side and help Emmaline down, she followed him out of the conveyance. "Are you available to wait for us?"

"Us?" He gawked at her in some surprise, for he'd only vowed to escort her to the museum.

"Of course." She shrugged. "I assumed you were coming inside with me." A determined glint twinkled in her eyes, a glint that winked with gold flecks.

Damnation. No way could he leave her to her own devices now. Who knew what trouble she'd find inside. "Quite right. I'm accompanying you."

The driver cleared his throat. "It'll cost you. I'm losing out on fares cooling my heels here."

Miles rolled his eyes. How many clients did the man expect to find in the middle of the night? Well, respectable customers that was. No doubt the seedier side of the city churned with life. "You'll be paid accordingly."

"Yes." His companion unclasped the emerald and diamond bracelet at her wrist and held it out to the scraggly man. "I'm giving this to you as a down payment and guarantee you'll wait for us. Drive around the streets if you must, but remain in the vicinity. We shouldn't be longer than an hour." She fingered the matching necklace at her throat. "This will be yours when we're done. However, if you breathe a word to anyone of us or where you stopped this night, you won't get any more of this, and I'll see that the authorities take a hard look into your personal history."

The man's eyes widened and he quickly grabbed the bracelet from her gloved palm. "Deal. I'll be here looking for you."

"Very good." Emmaline turned to Miles. "Shall we go?"

Not having anything else to do and not wishing to leave her to it alone, he nodded. "Lead on, my lady." She swept by him in a rustle of skirts. He followed her through the gardens, the grass muffling their approach as they ran. "Why are we not walking up to the building like the proper people we are?"

A trill of laughter rang out behind her. She glanced over her shoulder. "Why would you want proper when you can be spontaneous?"

Why indeed? But there was a certain comfort in being proper and it was an image he needed to maintain for a while. He knew exactly how to do that, how to conduct his life as an earl, how to make decisions that hinged on the title and the obligations therein. He understood all too well what he owed his king as well as the prime minister, but he did not know how to be spontaneous. Not even slightly.

Until tonight.

"Oh, and don't worry," she added as they gained one of the wings. "You're doing an excellent job."

"I'll take your word for it." He paused beside her and the window they waited near was shrouded in shadows. "What now?"

"We follow this wall around to the back. There's a particular door that leads into an abandoned room used only as a makeshift holding area. Not much more than a glorified supply closet really. I stumbled upon it on one of my last visits and had it confirmed while talking persuasively to one of the curators."

Did he even want to know what that persuasion entailed? His chest tightened. "And you plan to break into that room, thereby gaining access to the museum." He resisted the urge to forbid that activity. She'd only do it anyway.

"Of course." Emmaline kept close to the building but her steps were quick and light. Soon she ducked around the corner.

With a curse, Miles dashed after her, somewhat noisier in his approach. She'd disappeared around another corner since the edge of the wing was only six feet in width. "Emmaline, at least have the sense to wait for me," he groused.

"Ah, then you have knowledge on how to pick a lock?" She'd stopped in front of a door somewhat hidden by shrubbery.

"I do not." He frowned as he stood behind her, no doubt more a hindrance than a help.

"Mmm, in light of that, you must plan to provide defense in the event we encounter a guard or other impediment."

When she glanced at him with a question in her eyes, he sighed. "Again, no. I'm afraid I declined to arm myself before attending the ball this evening." A stab of disappointment moved through him. Had his dismal showing affected her as well? Not wishing to perpetuate the problem, he added, "I can use my fists. I've tallied quite a few victories at Gentleman Jackson's salon these last two years."

"I'm glad to hear it." She slid her skirts up her right leg, higher, ever higher revealing not only her black stocking-clad limb and beribboned garter but also the creamy pale skin of her thigh. He gaped.

What the devil? His gaze stuck on a worn leather sheath that hugged the delectable limb. "What are you doing?" He glanced around, fully prepared to shield her from prying eyes. No man had a right to see such a glorious leg without her permission.

"In case you stumble with those fists of yours, I have other ways of rendering men quiet who are too curious for their own good." She yanked a dagger from that sheath and held it up for his inspection. "This was given to me on my sixteenth birthday by the Egyptian ambassador to England. At the time, my father was somewhat less … fanatical than he'd become in later years, but he's still highly respected. At least out of England." Emeralds, rubies and diamonds on the hilt glittered in the dim light. The blade itself was of brass and the tip looked as sharp as any deadly weapon. "In case you're wondering, yes, I have defended myself with this a time or two."

"It's beautiful." Beautiful and deadly, as he was beginning to suspect she was. And quite surprising.

"Thank you." She pressed her lips to the blade before resheathing it. "Shall we proceed to the actual breaking and entering portion of our evening?"

Miles gestured at her to hurry. "Of course." At this point, his curiosity to see how she'd perform such a feat had grown exponentially. When he thought she couldn't surprise him anymore, she proved him wrong.

"You're lucky," she said in a conversational tone. "I don't let merely anyone see this." She took up her fan, and instead of snapping it open, she held the closed accessory in both her hands, twisted then guided the top part off. Inside the thin tube, for it was indeed not just a fan as he'd thought, she removed a slim metal instrument. No wonder it had stung when she'd rapped him with it. "Watch and learn."

"Uh, if you could speed the process, my lady, that would be best. We're in a bit of a vulnerable position." How the devil would he explain away their reasons for being here at this time of night? But he followed her movements with avid interest. She inserted the slim piece of metal between the door and its frame. When she jiggled it a few times and still nothing happened, she cursed and frowned. "Not working?"

"I don't understand. Must be this rubbish door." She continued to move the strip of metal this way and that with no success.

"Have you done such a thing before?" Of course she must have. She had the tools for it.

"Yes. A few. I never had one fight me." Annoyance echoed in the words.

"Step aside."

"But, I can—"

"Emmaline, move." He infused every bit of authority into his voice that had made him the earl of some import over the past five years. She took a few steps backward with her mouth slightly agape. Miles braced himself then delivered a sound and solid kick to the door with the flat of his boot. Wood splintered at the frame around the mechanism, and he easily pushed the useless portal open. "After you." Fantastic. He'd vandalized a door at the

British Museum. Who was he becoming and how the devil would he explain that to Lord Liverpool?

"You know, it's not very noble of you to show off your prowess like that." She lifted her chin a notch as she sailed past him with her lock picking tools still clutched in her hand.

How adorable that she assumed he had a skill for bashing in doors. "Well, if we had to wait for you to do the deed, we'd be here all night. I was simply hurrying things along, since you *are* on a mission," he responded while following close behind her, careful not to let her see him favoring his foot.

"Do shut up, Miles." She halted suddenly and because it was pitch black in the room, he smacked into her.

"I apologize," he murmured. He told himself he wrapped his arms around her merely to steady her until she found her footing. Something fragile crashed to the floor and he cringed. "Damnation there's junk everywhere in here."

"I should have retracted my offer to take you with me." She grabbed his hand once she'd disentangled herself from him. "The second you become a hindrance to my investigation, I will lock you in a gallery or tie you to one of Elgin's pieces."

He didn't stifle his snicker in time and she elbowed him in the ribs. "I'll endeavor to be the perfect burgling companion." He threaded their fingers together. "But I must insist on some sort of light. I don't want to be responsible for permanently damaging something priceless." Well, anything further.

"Not until we reach the gallery. It's on the third floor of the main building." A squeeze on his fingers reassured him. "Not to worry, my lord. I've been here many times before. I won't steer you wrong."

That he wasn't sure of. Since their first meeting had been when he'd caught her stealing from his library and now they were breaking into the British Museum, how much worse could it get? Surely once she found the mummy, she'd make arrangements to have it transferred or relocated or reserved for transport, and then she'd go on to her adventure.

Where does that leave me?

Chapter Four

Emmaline tugged her companion through the silent, stifling halls of the British Museum. The smell of old things and dust tickled her nose as did the scent of stale air. Being closed up for nearly two months had done nothing for the indoor climate, and if she was beginning to sweat, she could only imagine what such unmoving air was doing to the priceless antiques housed within the building.

"The way this place smells reminds me of much of my time as a youth," Miles mentioned while they walked. "My father's library often had the look of unorganized chaos. Books abounded in stacks and piles as he continued his studies." Fondness flowed through the words. "I suppose one of the best things a title can afford a man is the ability to do what he pleases and to travel. Before my father died, he certainly lived that motto."

Ah, so in addition to the loss of his wife and child, he'd suffered through the death of a parent. Interesting. "I can understand that. My father is much the same. Well, he was until he grew too sick to visit the great libraries of the world or dig up the earth to see if his theories were correct." A tiny smile curved her lips. "Though I will say he has books and papers around his bed now. Learning, it would seem, never ceases even when one's body is failing." She cried out when she stubbed a toe on the first marble step. "At least we've found the staircase." The throbbing pain distracted her from thinking overly much about the state of her father's health and what that would eventually mean for her.

"Ah, then I somewhat have my bearings now." He readjusted his grip on her hand. "I've visited the reading rooms many times, but going through the actual exhibits hasn't been a top priority for me in recent years."

"Due to your wife's sudden departure from this world?" She spoke in reverent tones that echoed off the walls and seemed magnified in the darkness.

"Among other things." His tone didn't invite further inquiry.

"You and I will need to chat about those things soon. I sense there is more to your story than you've revealed." Yes, losing a wife and child was tragic enough, but what wasn't he telling her? And in that omission, how much of that could squarely be laid at the curse's doorstep? Perhaps his secrets went beyond that.

"Perhaps we will if we're afforded time."

That didn't sound promising. Which brought her to another thought. Once they were done here, would she see him again? She frowned as they ascended the steps. A right turn at the first landing presented them with another set of stairs. Of course she wouldn't. Why should she? No doubt he'd only accompanied her tonight due to a misplaced sense of honor or nobility, or even guilt from that incident in their pasts. Her path would take her away from England while his would remained firmly fixed in this country.

Again.

"I can practically hear you thinking," Miles said into the gloom as they reached the second landing.

"Why is that a surprise? You should have figured by now I am a woman of some intelligence. Therefore, it's not a shock I should do more thinking than the average cotton-brained female that society values." Her frown returned at her acerbic tone. It wasn't fair to unleash a foul attitude upon him. Her worries were her own and didn't need to include him. "Too many men in these modern times, too many lords for that matter, condemn women to the shadows and prohibit higher learning on the grounds our minds cannot handle anything beyond child rearing and household management. Not to mention the alleged values the *ton* has regarding wealth, position or titles."

"Codswallop." The word echoed through the empty stairway.

"Pardon me?" She dragged him along with her as they completed the last set of stairs.

Miles halted and put an end to her forward momentum. He didn't release her hand. Instead, he pulled her toward him and didn't stop until they stood a mere hand's span apart. "I call codswallop." His breath skated across her cheek.

"Because?" What he found objectionable was beginning to grate.

"Assuming that I think you couldn't be a woman of greater than average intelligence." He brushed his thumb over her knuckles. Curious flutters raced down her spine, which she promptly dismissed to the thrilling and dangerous atmosphere of the museum. "I've been in your company for little more than an hour, and in that time period, I've been impressed by how your mind works and the reasons behind those thoughts, so please, don't believe that all of us—men and peers—categorize women as the weaker of the species."

Emmaline's jaw dropped open. He'd done something not many men could—left her completely flabbergasted and without words. As the seconds ticked by, she shook her head. "Well then. Let's carry on, shall we? There should be a collection of candlesticks close by." This earl would be trouble, certainly. Perhaps it was a good thing she'd quit his company soon. Having a man in her life who questioned her motives and set her at sixes and sevens at every turn would undoubtedly become a hindrance after a while.

Even more troubling and terrifying was a man who understood her. Those types she had no idea how to interact with, and she didn't relish giving the upper hand to anyone. Best to keep this one at arm's length. Purely for self-preservation, of course. Until the curse was broken, it wasn't a good idea to maintain friends for fear they'd be somehow tainted.

"I gather you're not often tongue-tied?" His soft-pitched question and sudden release of her hand had her fumbling in the dark for a familiar side table where the candles and tinderbox with spills always rested.

"Not generally." Finally, her fingers encountered a brass candleholder. "Forgive me, but I'm just not certain how to respond." She rooted around for the tinderbox and the lid knocked against the candles with a dull thud. "Drat."

His laughter rumbled in the air between them he batted her fingers away. "Let me." In short order, he had a spark lit and a spill ignited. Seconds later, flames danced merrily on two tall beeswax candles then he extinguished the spill, leaving it on the table in an empty brass bowl. The silver holders gleamed and sparkled in the weak illumination. "Ah, a beautiful woman by candlelight is rendered all the more gorgeous."

She strove to ignore the sudden heat in her cheeks. "Save your flattery, my lord. I have not the time for it nor the inclination to indulge in banter." And drat her hand for shaking. The shadows on the wall jumped and tilted in crazy patterns until she calmed herself. "The Egyptian gallery is this way." Their footsteps rang on the marble and the farther they moved into the exhibition gallery, the more stifling the air became.

"Interesting that you're a woman of high intelligence, possess a no-nonsense approach to life, have more than enough skill in the criminal realm and you dislike men paying you compliments." Amusement threaded through his words. "I wonder why that is."

"Why does it have to be anything?" She glared into the gloom lurking past the small circle of golden light from her candle. Flattery led to flirting and flirting led to engaging her heart into something she had no business indulging in.

"It doesn't. I'm merely making conversation."

Yet the questions he left unspoken banged around her head like gongs. "I told you I was married twice before."

"You did." He didn't prod for more information, which she appreciated, yet why did she feel compelled to offer more pieces of herself to him? "That in and of itself is a mystery, for you still go by your maiden name, Lady Emmaline Darling."

"Why shouldn't I?" She avoided glancing at him as he kept pace beside her. "I know who I am under this name more than my married names, and since those men didn't stay with me long enough, why should their names live on?"

"Interesting way of looking at it." Several seconds of silence passed before he spoke again. "How did they die, if you don't mind me asking?"

A sigh escaped her before she could recall it and the flame on her candle flickered wildly. "I don't mind, for it is merely history after all." So much of her life was lost to memories. Would she end up the same way soon? She kept her focus on an arrangement of jewelry, all decorated with scarab beetles in different jewel tones. "James expired five years ago. We were walking along the Nile in an effort to move closer to some ruins near Luxor. A crocodile launched from the reeds and attacked. They move quite quickly when properly motivated. We scattered but James faltered. The croc got hold of his leg. Nothing he or the other men with us did would loosen those powerful jaws." She forced down a swallow. "The croc pulled him into the water and it was all over in less than thirty seconds." Her voice caught on the last part, and she gave into a shiver. Sometimes in her dreams she'd still hear his screams and see the bubbles in the water as his life extinguished. "So quick. So bloody. We'd only been married eleven months. We'd met at a diplomatic dinner party. He'd been the secretary to one of the British ambassadors."

"Good God." Horror and sympathy rang in his voice.

"Indeed."

"And your father agreed to you marrying beneath your station?"

She snorted. "I'm very much my own woman, Miles. And love doesn't separate by class."

He blew out a breath. "True, but that is a horrible story and not even to your first anniversary."

"You asked. Egypt, for all its beauty, is fierce and dangerous." A faint smile tugged at her lips. "Then, three years ago I married Benjamin. He specialized in shipping. We met at the docks of Alexandria of all places." An unexpected laugh escaped her. "A British tourist had carried off part of a fresco from a tomb. I protested. Benjamin took a blow to the face aimed at me."

"A true hero." An answering grin pulled at Miles' sensuous mouth.

"Yes. He was and another man my father had to accept as my choice despite his grumblings. He always tells me I need a man who was strong, crafty and honorable." She trailed the fingers of her free hand over a collection of broken and cracked statuary assembled on a velvet-lined tray. "A whirlwind courtship ensued and we were married on a dahabiya at sunset while heading to Thebes." Such a romantic time that had been. "I adore the waterways of Egypt at sunset. For all the danger that lurks beneath, they are unbeaten for sightseeing."

"Dare I ask how long this union lasted?" Nothing except solicitous concern sounded in his voice.

"Not long." She frowned at the antiquities. "In fact, he died on that honeymoon trip. We'd made a stop along the way to picnic. Apparently, the dates he'd bought from a villager were tainted and he fell victim to poisoning. The particular vendor had assumed that packet of dates would go to another and didn't recognize his error until we'd gone back through each stall." Emmaline closed her eyes against the images of her second husband writhing in agony as white foam flecked his lips. "It was quick but violent. There was nothing I could do. Intrigue and vengeance is alive and well in Egypt, and woe to anyone to stumbles across those paths by accident."

I've always known death. Even with both marriages, they hadn't lasted long enough for the romance and charm to fully bloom. Now she was alone and it was better that way, for if she was truly as cursed as she believed, she couldn't pass along that horror to anyone else. Except… Now there was the earl, back in her life with seeming serendipity. While she welcomed a renewed friendship, she had no choice but to keep him at arm's length.

For his own good.

"Damnation." Miles shook his head as she glanced at him. "I'm sorry you had to witness such things. No woman should."

"I agree, but in the world of travel and adventure, this is the reality, my lord. Things sometimes do not go as we would like and we must accept that." Her candle flame danced in the air currents stirred by their breath. "I've grown tired of making funeral arrangements for loved ones. I'm hoping to never do it again soon, which is the reason for my current mission." Except, her father did indeed lay near death.

"Practical yet harsh. Just another layer that shrouds you." He clicked his tongue. "I can't help but think what will happen when you stop drawing those layers about you for either protection or comfort and let the woman you are shine through, tears and all."

Was her outlook as extreme as he thought? Perhaps. Did she assume the layers as he said as some sort of protection? Most definitely. When one was unlucky enough to have a curse follow one about, one learned these things. There was only so much a person's heart could take before it would stop repairing itself. She'd managed to keep men at bay and from her heart for over two years. That wasn't likely to change any time soon. "I didn't survive this long by being vulnerable or weak."

"I'm sure, but sometimes letting down that guard allows someone to help, to come at your problems with their own understanding, to help carry that burden for a while."

"I don't need that." Until the curse was broken, she refused to let another person in. To throw him off, she said, "I wonder what would happen when you cease to do the same." For if she was as mysterious as he claimed, so was he. The man hadn't volunteered much in the way of personal information, but why should he? They weren't exactly on a bosom pal level. "I suspect you've become an expert in keeping yourself apart from life's thorns."

"Touché." They entered the gallery and were forced to go through single-file. "Perhaps we're more alike than we're not, and self-preservation is what we both excel at."

"That's terrifying to contemplate, for I know why I wish to avoid life. I hope and pray it's not the same reason that you do." Dear heavens, had his existence been as plagued as hers? Mayhap their time in Egypt as children had carried forth more than memories.

"Perhaps we'll never know, as we're on a mission of some import and not afforded a drawing room or tea to converse over."

"Indeed." Emmaline frowned as she drew to a halt before a giant bust of Ramesses II. Finally, she peered at her companion and for the first time had a good look at him. Black hair, slightly longer than what was proper, curled at his collar. A hint of dark stubble clung to his jaw and gave him a rakish air that quickened her heartbeat. In his shirtsleeves, the bold breadth of his shoulders and the strength of his upper body was on display through the fine linen. Her husbands had both been slight of frame and gentle in spirit. Miles wasn't like either of them, and that worried her. Quickly, she forced moisture into her suddenly dry throat. "Behold the Younger Memnon." Her voice emerged on a squeak in her rush to distract herself. She lifted her candle and he did the same.

"Ah, yes. Another piece of history yanked from its rightful place and shipped here so the people of England can come and gawk at it." Bitterness wove through the statement as he gazed at the much-abused statue.

Surprise stabbed at her chest. "I thought I was one of the only ones who felt that way."

"You're not, my lady." He rested his gaze on her, and the passion shining in those dark brown depths stole her breath. "My father was one of those men who thought nothing of stealing antiquities whenever he wished, while my brother and I fought him each step. Eventually, we won, or rather convinced him, but not before he had accumulated quite a collection. It's taken me years, and in some cases, considerable expense, to send most of the pieces to museums or back to their countries of origin. What remains in my townhouse are particular favorites of mine or things that are forgeries and copies because I couldn't bear to keep the original."

For the second time since they'd breached the museum, her jaw dropped. "Ah." He'd mentioned a brother, but hadn't talked about him in the present. Had that sibling succumbed to death as well? Not able to withstand the heated fervor in his eyes, she switched her attention to the statue once more. "I detest it when explorers, travelers or tourists carry away pieces of the past and destroy the proper cataloguing of the same simply because they feel they can."

It was one of two colossal granite heads from the Ancient Egyptian mortuary temple—the Ramesseum at Thebes—which depicted the pharaoh Ramesses II wearing the Nemes headdress, complete with a cobra diadem on top. The matching statue was still at the temple—at least she hoped.

"Indeed." Miles lowered his candle and long shadows crept along the bust. "Thanks to that idiot Henry Salt who hired the self-proclaimed adventurer-turned-tomb robber, Giovanni Belzoni, many treasures of Egypt, and from that whole region, have been absconded with. Raping tombs and depriving the people of their history is abhorrent and an action those of us who know better should be actively opposing. And why do they do it? So arrogant collectors can show them off in parlors and studies? Then when they grow tired of them, throw the artifacts in boxes to molder in storage? Or worse, toss them out like so much rubbish?"

"Exactly, but without the authority and funds on the part of the preservationist, it's a battle being sorely lost." She wandered up and down the tight rows and shelves of artifacts, funerary accessories, jewelry and scraps of pottery. Elongated shadows bounced and moved before her, eerie in the silence. "Some of this collection isn't categorized correctly, and some of it shouldn't be open to the air. Simply stuffing the museum to its gills isn't helping."

"Just because the tide is against you doesn't mean you should give up." He joined her as she paused in front of a row of mummies, all three encased in glass. "Are any of these the fortunate man you're in search of?"

Emmaline looked at the identification plaques and shook her head. She pointed to each. "Too old, too young and not even a male."

"So, what now?"

She glanced toward the back of the gallery where the darkness lay heaviest. "There has to be some sort of store room close by. From everything I've been told, there is more inventory at the museum than its halls and galleries can display. If they have superfluous mummies, that's where they'll be. Of course, there are vast storage chambers in the basement too." Searching would take days and they didn't have that long. "I'm rather hoping to avoid that just yet."

"Then let's start looking. The longer we're here, the more likely something could happen to put us in a bad position. I would have thought there'd be a guard or a custodian at the very least making rounds."

"Oh, there is a caretaker."

Miles narrowed his eyes. "Now you share this?" When she merely nodded, he sighed. "I take it you know when he'll come 'round?"

"Once at the top of the hour." What did it matter when they wouldn't linger long enough for that?

"I see." He pulled out his pocket watch, flipped it open and checked the time. "Twenty to the hour." Once he'd replaced the instrument, he led the way toward the rear of the gallery. "While we're searching, perhaps you could explain more about why you think there's a curse attached to these mummies."

"I don't think it." The response came out with rather more prickles than she'd intended. She trotted to catch him up, using her free hand to shield the candle. "I know it. How else do you account for so much death connected to my family name?"

"Sometimes misfortune is merely misfortune. No curse needed." His long-legged stride ate up the floor space.

"Yes, but that misfortune didn't occur until my father unearthed that damn mummy twenty years ago. Even his removing it from his life didn't keep the curse's finger from touching him." She gasped. Her family had been dealing with ramifications of that day since she'd been a girl of three and ten. "My mother left this earth directly following, maybe a few days after he'd taken the mummy from its tomb."

"Something about poison perhaps?" He didn't stop in his trek. "I beg your pardon. I should know that, but I was a young man back then with other interests to occupy my mind."

"She was bitten by an asp that had hidden in a broken pot they'd collected from that tomb." Her throat grew crowded with tears. Though it had been a long time ago, losing her mother at such a tender age had shaped her into the woman she was today. "I'd been sent back to England for school at my mother's direction. At thirteen, I thought I'd left my beloved Egypt forever."

"Obviously, you did not, though I do remember your father leaving the country that winter abruptly. When he spoke of his loss at his last dinner with all of us, that haunted look in his eyes…" He shook his head. "It will forever remain with me."

Unshed tears crowded her throat. "They were very much in love. Oftentimes I'd wished to have a relationship as theirs was." Briefly she bit her bottom lip. "Regardless, Father traveled home with the news—and the mummy. After that, my schooling was conducted while he was on digs. I…" She cleared her throat. "I simply couldn't bear to have him out of my sight. Though the winter of my sixteenth year was my last in Egypt for some time."

"Understandable. I believe that winter was my last spent in Egypt." His voice had taken on a faraway quality. Did he recall when he'd said goodbye to her in the cool darkness of that tomb?

"It was. Subsequent years without you and the others who were older brought a different sort of melancholy to existence. As was being in London that was as far from the tombs of Egypt as I was comfortable with." He'd kissed her in the privacy of that tomb—her first kiss. Though it had been fleeting and sloppy, she'd reveled in it and kept that memory close to her heart. To him it had probably been one of many he'd bestowed on young ladies that year. "But sadness of one kind or another seems to be my fate or part of the curse. It's a terrible thing to hear such news in the parlor of a school with a headmistress staring on. Not to mention it had occurred some weeks earlier."

"I can only imagine." He slowed to a halt then faced her. Sympathy lined his expression. "Death is rather a poor companion."

"Yes." She moistened her lips. "Mother had been laid to rest by the time I arrived at our estate outside of Cairo. I've made a memorial of sorts for her on the property there." When he held out his free arm, she frowned. "What?"

"I'm offering a hug in the event you simply require the touch of a caring human." A grin lifted on side of his mouth. "Unless the only comfort you gain is from long dead men?"

"Don't be an arse, my lord." But she closed the distance between them.

As he slid his arm around her shoulders and hugged her close to his side, he said, "It's Miles. No more my lording."

"Then no more my ladying." As surreptitiously as she could, she breathed in his sage and orange scent. Dear Lord, the man smelled good and gave her a slight reprieve from the stagnant air. She stirred and parted from him. "Let's go find that mummy. I'm hungry." And his pleasing scent wasn't helping any.

"What, no breaking into a bakery at some point this evening?"

She rolled her eyes at his quip. "Don't give me ideas."

Chapter Five

"That is a bloody lot of junk." Miles stared with mounting trepidation at seemingly endless glass and wooden shelves filled to the ceiling with boxes, bottles, baskets and bags of, for lack of a better term, ancient things. He set his candleholder on the top of a nearby packing crate.

"Most of it will never be on display for public consumption," Emmaline rejoined and her tone suggested how idiotic that was. "Good thing we're only searching for a mummy. It looks like the big stuff is off to that side." She hooked a thumb toward the right side of the storage room where row upon row of coffin-shaped boxes lay haphazardly stacked and piled.

"Great." Poking through dusty relics was not how he'd thought he'd spend this evening. "Happy birthday, Miles. Hope you enjoy your next year," he muttered under his breath.

"I beg your pardon?" She rested her candleholder on a crate that stood upright, nearly as tall as she. "Is it true today is your birthday?"

"Yes." He rested his hands on his hips as he surveyed the room.

"And you've reached what fanciful age?"

He huffed. What difference did it make? When she continued to look at him, he said, "I'm seven and thirty today. Which was the reason for the party at my house tonight."

"Was it your idea to host it?" She raked her gaze up and down his person with such precision his skin prickled as if she'd touched him. "Somehow I don't quite see you as a lord who enjoys mingling with the glittering, empty side of the *ton*."

"I am not, this is true." He rubbed at the dust on an urn but couldn't read the hieroglyphics. "It was thrown for me by the Marchioness of Wellesley. No relation to the Duke of Wellington, however."

"Why? Is she someone special to you?" Emmaline blew out a breath and it ruffled a dark strand of hair that had come loose from her coif.

"Not more than anyone else." He shrugged. The woman had connections and ones he wished to cultivate. "She's recently come into my circle in the last year and told me it was time I looked into marriage again." No matter how much he'd told her she didn't need to constantly check in on him, the woman wouldn't take a hint. Too much more of her brand of smothering and he'd be forced to lay it out bluntly. Already, he hid in his townhouse when she came visiting and had instructed Alfred to inform the marchioness he was out.

"Sounds like a fair weather friend." Emmaline frowned. "Where had she been before?"

"In mourning for her husband I assume, though I heard she'd been traveling the Continent. Had become interested in paintings by the Masters so had gone touring museums." Which was another facet that could become useful. "In fact, you might remember her from our old childhood days in Egypt. She was known then as Lady Georgiana Hartsford."

"Vaguely." Her frown deepened and she let his jacket slide from her arms. "I remember a stunningly beautiful blonde girl who complained about the sand, grit and 'dirty' local people while ordering everyone about and reminding us all she had a title, as if we didn't. I don't think I ever gave her much thought beyond wishing to throw river mud on her pristine dresses."

"That's exactly who she is!" Amusement trickled up his spine from her turn of phrasing. "She was rather managing back then."

She snorted. "I'd wager she's still the same now. Back then, she kept hanging around me and you boys, whining about everything when she wanted us to do her bidding or hang attendance on her. Well, mostly she wanted male attention. She couldn't give two jots for me."

Miles snickered. "She's much the same indeed, and her attempts at matching me tonight proved ineffective."

"Do you wish to be matched?"

"I do not." For many reasons, none of which she needed to know right now. "I took to walking my halls just to be away from the crush and noise. I can't very well tell her off." Though he was mighty tempted. "There are proprieties, after all."

"Proprieties can hang. If we paid them any mind, you and I wouldn't be here."

"True enough." He glanced her way as slight disappointment cooled his chest. Emmaline had the ideal life. She didn't need to dance attendance with her peers to keep up appearances, and she was afforded the freedom to travel on her whim. Issues of national security didn't dictate her days. "What are you doing?"

"Unless you'd like for me to perish away on this floor from the heat, I simply must remove some of these layers." As she yanked off her elbow-length gloves, she continued the discussion. "How often do you see this marchioness? I don't understand why you'd want to continue a friendship with such a woman if she annoys you so."

His eyes widened at her penchant for plain speaking. Ah, but then she'd never understand the need to keep connections with various members of the *ton*, moving them about like pieces on a chess table.

Had there ever been such a woman of his acquaintance that he didn't feel the need to hand out a dressing down? No, there had not. "I don't see her often and generally not unless I attend a *ton* event." Too often, the women he had cause to associate with were either young society misses too shy to have an opinion or older peer's wives who excelled at spreading gossip with forked tongues. Then there were still others constantly on the prowl for nothing more than a man's title and worth or furthering her connection. Still others prowled around him for entirely different—and more dangerous—reasons, which meant keeping even enemies close, all in an elaborate dance.

Gah! How jaded he'd grown since his wife's death, since the day the prime minister had recalled him into service.

"Which, knowing you, is perhaps once every six months, when your closest friends cajole you into it because they fear you're hiding yourself too much away."

"Again, this is true. However, Lady Georgiana does pay calls—"

"That you avoid as much as you can." There was enough cheek in that statement to elevate his eyebrows.

"Uncanny how well you know me." And more than a little disturbing.

"Well, we did more or less grow up together while in Egypt. We have more than enough memories between us to form a life-long bond."

A bond that had been forged in childhood. He'd never talked of those days with his wife, for they had no bearing on his future. He'd thought. From the depths of his memories, a scrap of conversation came forth. It had been the last winter season she would be in Egypt before her parents sent her to England for schooling and refinement. Both he and she tarried in a dark tomb at the end of the evening while the adults and workers packed away finds and tools for the day.

"I suppose you'll leave soon?" he'd asked as he leaned on his arm next to her. The coolness of the stone had seeped into his bare palm.

She'd stood, her smile amusing in the light of a last flickering candle, her hands tucked behind her.

"Yes. In two days. Father said it was what Mother wanted even though I pleaded with him to remain here with him." Her breath, lightly scented from the peppermints she adored sucking on, skated over his cheek.

"I will be lonely without you, Emmy," he'd said, using the nickname only he called her by.

"You won't." She'd snorted and tossed her head, her green eyes sparkling in the dim light. "You have your fellows and there is always Georgiana. She makes calf's eyes at you, you know."

"She's grasping and won't be happy unless she marries well. The man she lands will be miserable enough." Even back then, he had no use for women of that sort. *"Will you leave broken hearts behind?" He'd cupped her cheek with his free hand.*

"If I will, I certainly don't know as no one has paid the slightest attention to me in that way. I'm too much a hoyden I suppose. Not even a dance partner, I'm afraid."

"Never change, Emmy. You're a delightful handful. Never let the ton *dictate who you should be."*

He'd taken advantage, he knew that now. But he'd been a young man full of courage and lust, and she'd made an impression on him. He'd kissed her then as the candle had guttered out. A chaste kiss though it was, those fleeting seconds had remained pressed into his memory as one of the turning points of his life.

Indeed, he'd missed her and noted her absence even as he continued to chase adventure. Why had he never inquired into what had happened to her between then and now? He frowned. Because life had gotten in the way and he hadn't been afforded freedom of a second son as he'd been meant to be.

"Woolgathering?" She snapped her fingers and grinned, recalling him to the moment. "Holding a title yourself and struggling to do your duty to said title must constantly be at odds with wanting privacy."

How eerie it was that she seemed to think of things the same time as he. "It is." Again, he felt the consistent urge to reveal everything of his life to her. How did a woman he'd only just met do that? But then, they hadn't just met. They did have a previous connection, albeit if only in memories. He battled the whim and removed his gloves as well. "We should start our search. The caretaker will be by soon." Once he'd rid himself of the gloves and his palms could breathe, he undid the cufflinks at his wrists, dropped the jewelry into his waistcoat pocket then rolled up his shirtsleeves. "Might as well be comfortable for this, unless you're squeamish about seeing a man in such a state of undress?" He darted his gaze to her with mild inquiry.

"Hardly. I've seen men garbed in less, and even then they weren't as well turned out physically as you." Her gaze jogged first to his bared forearms then to his shoulders. Was that a touch of rose infusing her cheeks?

He couldn't be certain due to the low lighting, but her regard made him want to preen. He didn't, of course, but that didn't negate the urge.

"I appreciate the compliment." Further conversation ceased as the echo of footsteps came to their location, steady, evenly paced as if the owner was even now climbing the marble stairs. "Extinguish the candles and hide them behind something. Quickly!" He came around a stone sarcophagus that had a shiny black veneer in the places it wasn't chipped and scratched. An idea tumbled into his mind. The heavy lid covered only half the container and had been shoved against one wall. The surrounding detritus of boxes, crates and parcels would make poking around difficult. *It's as good a place as any.*

"We'll have to go back for the flint. I haven't located the mummy yet!" Low-grade panic ran through her voice.

"One task at a time." Even now, they'd tarried at least thirty minutes, and he didn't wish to push it past a full hour. Not only would their driver not wait longer, but their position could easily be compromised. Inky darkness descended once more. He dropped his voice. The open doorway loomed shadowy in the distance, but it might as well have been fifty miles away. "He's too close and would hear the door if I were to shut it, so we'll be left exposed."

"Now what?"

"Into the sarcophagus." Miles felt along the lip then before he could convince himself to change his mind, he threw a leg over then slipped into the cold stone coffin. *I'm ready for Bedlam, that's what.* There was no other reasoning behind this insanity. The man who'd formerly spent his days thinking up ways to make his estates run better and more efficiently, who tried to keep his contact with others limited was now skulking about a closed museum, hiding in funeral equipment to evade notice by a caretaker.

With a woman who was much a stranger and a thief besides.

"You're mad, do you know that?" Emmaline whispered, neatly echoing his thoughts as she dropped in on top of him. When he stifled an oath because her knee found purchase in the sensitive flesh between his thighs, she smothered a giggle. She stretched out flat, lying the whole length of his body with her cheek pressed to his. "This is highly unusual."

"So has been the bulk of this night. Now hush." Not knowing what else to do with his hands, he wrapped his arms around her in an effort to settle her more comfortably on his person. Her violet scent seeped into his nostrils and he couldn't help but drink it in. The memory of that scent conjured up childhood where her hair had always smelled thusly, and in a country full of exotic aromas, it was a welcome reminder of the gardens from home. He swallowed hard, but the satin glide of her cheek against his put him in mind of other places her skin might also be silky soft and what he could do with his tongue and lips on such skin.

Stop thinking, Miles. She's not for you and her life is too chaotic. Attachments slow a man down and make him vulnerable. Once you leave this museum, you'll never see her again. There is other work to be done.

And Emmaline as she was now would become yet another memory.

He took in air through is mouth in the attempt not to luxuriate in her scent. The footsteps drew ever closer and he feared the sounds of his breathing would ring out for the man to hear. When the caretaker paused at their doorway and the golden pool of his lantern light crept into their sanctuary, his heart faltered. *This is it. This is how my life will crumble about me. I'll be skewered in the papers, not only caught in a compromising position with a thief and the daughter of a mad earl, but given over to the Runners for my part in this farce of an evening. Not to mention needing to face Lord Liverpool.* Yet he held onto Emmaline, pressing her closer in case her back or her gown were visible over the top. Her exhalations warmed his ear and awakened his member. After his wife died, he hadn't thought he'd have such urges for anyone and neither did he want to. Now…

Stop bloody thinking, man!

Every beat of her heart, he heard. Every rapid flutter of her pulse, he felt beneath his fingertips. He concentrated on regulating his breathing. Why didn't the caretaker move off? Had he seen something that gave away their presence? His heart seized. Damn and blast, no doubt their gloves were on the floor as was his jacket. He slid a hand to the small of her back as a distraction. She gasped, the sound so soft he nearly missed it, but it was there all the same, and rang through his head with all the clatter of a church bell. She shifted slightly, putting undue pressure on his growing length.

A moan escaped the back of his throat despite the attempt to tamp it. Another gasp burst upon the room, this time from the caretaker. Miles' heartbeat raced and he feared that organ would gallop out of his chest from discovery. The caretaker moved deeper into the room, the lantern light bobbing crazily around the walls and ceiling. Then Emmaline's lips were on his skin. She nibbled a path beneath his jawline. When she reached a particularly sensitive spot near his ear, he moaned again.

"Ghosts! The mummy curses are real!" A yelp came from the direction of the doorway followed by quickly retreating footsteps that echoed throughout the gallery. The golden pool of light diminished as quickly as it had come.

Miles tilted his head while he listened for evidence the caretaker had indeed fled the area. "I don't believe he'll return, but in the event I'm wrong, we should remain where we are for a few minutes." He damned his breathless voice and hoped she'd assume the reaction was from their circumstances and not her kiss.

"I understand."

"Why, uh, why'd you do that?" Though he wanted to know what had prompted such an amorous activity, part of him shied away from her answer.

"You were about to panic, so I did something guaranteed to drive any man wild." He felt rather than saw her shrug. "When you moaned, I couldn't have asked for a better response. Fancy the museum finding anyone to caretake the property now that it's reportedly haunted, and by one or more of their mummies to boot."

"Good thinking." His chest tightened. It was a blow to the ego to find out she'd only done that for a certain reaction and not because of personal feelings. As if there would be. They'd shared a similar childhood and that was all. *Don't be a nodcock, Miles.*

"Thank you." Her words steamed his cheek and didn't provide quite the reprieve he'd hoped. "What shall we do in the meantime?" She moved a hand and curled it behind his neck. After all, quarters were rather cramped.

Oh, God. He needed a distraction. That kiss under his jaw might have been staged, but she didn't have to keep touching him as intimately as she did. "Tell me of the mummy's curse."

"Very well." She squirmed, presumably to find a comfortable position, except her soft curves fit against his harder angles too well and too closely. Would she feel his reaction and take offense? When she didn't comment, he relaxed by increments and contented himself with listening to her whispered voice. "My father discovered the priest's mummy twenty years ago as I've told you."

"And the curse came from a spell the pharaoh's mother put upon it?"

"No. Don't be silly."

Of course he wasn't trying to be, but he had taken in much information this night, and at the present, his mind was scrambled. "Pray continue."

"From what I could understand, the priest's last request was the curse. One of his high ranking followers must have spoken the words once he was laid to rest with his wife."

"I take it the poor woman was already dead once that occurred? I thought I'd read somewhere that a few of these fellows were quite fanatical and they wanted their households to go with them into the Underworld, dead or alive." A shiver raced up his spine at the thought. He couldn't imagine either being locked in a tomb to wait for starvation or worse, being murdered just because your spouse had died.

"That did happen, yes. Servants, family members, pets." She paused and brushed her fingers along the side of his neck in the silence. "Those were different times."

"Thank goodness." He slid his hands to her hips. The thin satin of her gown was warm from her body heat. "Can you imagine the outcry today?"

A huff of annoyance escaped her. "Do you want to know the tale or don't you?"

"I do. Go ahead."

"Then stop interrupting me." The last word ended on a slight squeak, for he'd slid a hand to the curve of her rear, merely for something to do, not because he wanted to know how she'd feel beneath his palm.

"I beg your pardon," he whispered, for interrupting or the touch, he couldn't say.

"From what I can gather from reading the hieroglyphs is he was well respected and held an inordinate amount of power."

"The church usually does." He skimmed his palm up her back. When he encountered the lace edge of the garment, he followed it with a fingertip. "No doubt he had an agenda too. Probably had many ways of nudging the pharaoh into doing his bidding."

"Perhaps." She huffed again, but it sounded more like a sigh. "Not only was he a spiritual advisor, he apparently could weld a certain amount of magic. There were stories on some of the tombs nearby touting things he'd done that could only be accomplished by the occult."

Miles rolled his eyes. Curses and magic didn't exist. A man's life was a series of actions and reactions. What he did had consequences and no amount of other-worldly nonsense had a hand in those choices. "Now you're having me on."

"Buggar it, Miles." Emmaline shoved at his chest. "You're mocking me. Our association is over." She attempted to struggle into a sitting position, and in the process straddled his waist.

Such a posture would reveal too much, so he tugged her back down over his body. "I promise to behave." Though it would tax every amount of his willpower. Which was odd in and of itself. He wasn't one to jump into scandal. "Tell me the rest. I'll try to mind my manners." He grinned into the darkness, knowing she couldn't see. The longer he lingered in her presence, the more he remembered of her as a young girl. Though she'd always been self-possessed and fearless, she'd flown into a temper when he or the other boys would tease her. Nothing had changed in that regard and he appreciated that.

"Hmm, I don't believe you, but what can I do?" As she spoke, her lips brushed his jawline again and sent charged tendrils of need through him. "Well, because of this power, the priest was more feared than the pharaoh in many circles. He had a much revered wife, a close advisor to the pharaoh's mother, and Father had removed him from her. The inscriptions found in the sarcophagus after the fact provide dire warnings for any who separate the two from the eternal sleep of true love. Of course, I paraphrase since I'm not able to remember the exact wording of the original script."

"Ah, even in ancient Egypt there were fools who believed in such fairy tale endings." He pulled a face and was again glad for the shroud of darkness. "True love might exist, surely, but that power—if there is any—wouldn't extend beyond the grave. Hell, it rarely is respected in today's day and age."

"How sad that statement is." She drew abstract designs on his shoulder with a fingertip. "Did you not love your wife?"

His gut clenched and he stilled his hands on her back. "I did, of course, but I refuse to believe that our romance was so pure and true and exclusive she'd wish for me to pine for her until I, too, joined her in the grave." Did that sound too harsh or uncaring? For the bald fact was he'd adored his wife and had selfishly thought he'd have her to himself for more years than the mere five they'd had together.

"You poor man." Emmaline stroked her fingers down the side of his face leaving heat and chills in her wake. "Though, as weird as it sounds, I do understand why you said what you did." Her sigh sent her breath skating along his cheek. "I loved my husbands, but I foolishly thought my love would keep them from the grave. Perhaps I didn't love hard enough. Grand passion is just that, but unless it's founded in deep feeling, it's fleeting."

"That's a lie and you know it." The fierceness of his reply startled him. After all, he didn't know anything about her, yet in a way, he did. They were much the same—trying to survive a world after people who'd pledged to be at their sides suddenly weren't.

"Thank you." She wrapped her arm around his neck and held on tightly as if he were the only thing keeping her anchored to the here and now. When she laid her head on his shoulder, he froze. It shouldn't feel as right as it did, and he didn't know how to process that. His life and his fate weren't going in the same direction as hers. "Forgive my lapse. In my chosen field and in my life, loneliness becomes a constant companion that you don't realize is trying to strangle you."

"Yes, and then there are those of us who prefer being alone for fear of dooming others to the same life we've been given." It was as close to admitting that he might have been touched with the curse as he would come. "Or, for other circumstances altogether." The less personal connections he made kept people safe. "Please, continue your story."

For long moments, she hesitated before finally speaking once more. "Despite our realities, over the centuries, everyone has believed in the power of true love. Why shouldn't the story of the priest's curse be true?"

He shrugged. "I'll agree to listen with an open mind." Mostly because he enjoyed the melodious pitch of her voice. Sometimes during their winters in Egypt, she'd read stories to the local children and had even then managed to infuse a thrill into her voice.

"Well, when I decided to chase down the mummy and return it to his wife's side to break the curse, imagine my surprise when, upon visiting the still unnamed tomb shortly before coming to England, I discovered it had been vandalized a few months before. The wife is also missing."

His chest tightened. "And of course your lead is Lord Leventhorpe." His mind rested on that mummy hand she'd tucked away into her reticule. "But you said you didn't find the mummy at his residence."

"I was rather in a hurry when I was there, and yes, unless he has the mummy hidden away, I didn't find evidence of it with the exception of the amulet and hand. However, one of my contacts in Egypt told me that a man of his description had been seen in that tomb during that time frame."

"And this troubles you why?"

"The legends scrolled on some of the grave trappings confirm what the tomb writings say: if the mummies are not laid to a forever rest side by side then a curse will be unleashed that won't stop until every person who had contact with the mummy, as well as their family members for four generations, will find themselves in the grave, thereby depriving everyone of a long and natural life. Any and all lines and lineages will die out." Her voice had risen during the telling and when she came to a stop, the words echoed around the storeroom.

"Well." He cleared his throat as cold dread crept over his skin. It was silly to believe anything of the sort held such power. Yet, how else could he explain what had happened in his own life if it was plain bad luck? Would that lead to further misfortune in his current endeavor? "Those Egyptians certainly enjoyed being dramatic."

This time when Emmaline sat up, he didn't restrict her. "You'll think dramatic when you breathe your last prematurely, as will my father." Apparently gripped in a right proper temper, she climbed off him then out of the sarcophagus. She grunted when she hit the floor. "You can believe me or not, my lord, but I *will* find that mummy and I *will* break this curse if only to see that my life will continue on as it should."

Damnation. We've moved back into the 'my lord' business, have we? He sat up too fast and smacked his temple on the lid's edge. A few white starbursts erupted behind his vision and he let out a string of vulgarity. How did he tell her he wanted the curse broken as well and for the same reason for his life after he'd cast water on her theory? Hell's bells, this interacting with people was tricky. "Your cause is noble, truly." And if the curse was indeed uttered with magic and ancient help from the beyond, how did she think she'd manage to break it? "I wish you well on your quest."

Her sharp inhalation was the only indicator she still stood in the room. After a few minutes steeped in tense silence, she said, "But you will not accompany me on the remainder after this night." It wasn't a question, and the chilly disappointment in her tone pierced him deeper than if he'd seen that emotion in her eyes.

"I have my duties here. My work and my daughter…" His throat constricted, for he hadn't told her about his firstborn child who'd just turned four last month.

"You have a child?" Emotion graveled her voice, but he couldn't determine what. "You'd mentioned losing a son but didn't mention other issue."

"Yes." The admission seemed pulled from him. "It would be the height of irresponsibility to drop everything merely to gad about the world playing at adventuring." Especially when his duties to the Crown required him to remain on England's shores for the moment. "We are no longer children given the relative freedom we enjoyed back in those days." Curse or no curse. The words were designed to wound, but he hadn't counted on being collateral damage in the exchange. What was the more irresponsible decision—not breaking a curse he didn't know if he believed in and letting it consume his child or leaving his estate and his duties and obligations to someone else on his staff merely to chase what? Memories?

"Very well." The response was so soft he strained to hear. "I suppose it was foolish of me to think a titled peer would be anything except what he's always been meant to be."

His throat constricted. "I'm the second son. I was never meant to be anything." *Until it was forced upon me.*

"As if that matters now, Miles Lawrence Hawkins, Fifth Earl of Archewyne." Was that a sniff? Never say she was crying. "I'll just find the flint, retrieve the mummy, and then you and I can go our separate ways and pretend our paths never crossed. And God save your daughter's soul if I'm proved to be correct. Children are too precious to be left to chance. May you never live long enough to see that to fruition."

And if the curse was truly real, he wouldn't.

Before he could respond, the rapid tap of her heels against the marble floor signaled her flight from the room.

Chapter Six

Miles combed through the mummy cases with barely a clue as to what he was looking for since his companion hadn't bothered to tell him what dynasty or other identifying information he hunted for. Emmaline did the same not five feet from him with a carefully averted gaze. Though her face was in profile, he spied the damning trails her tears had made through the dust and dirt on her cheeks. They hadn't spoken since she'd returned with the flint for the candles and even now, tension simmered in the air between them.

He had no idea what to say that would end this terrible silence and restore the easy comradery they'd formerly enjoyed, for it was as she'd said, once she found her mummy they'd go their separate ways. It's exactly what he'd told himself since this adventure began, yet faced with that eventuality now? He didn't know if he could let her go without knowing what would happen to her. Emmaline's story was every bit as fraught with misfortune as his own, and he desperately wanted to know the ending. Would she find happiness? Would she survive into old age? Would he and his daughter?

If I have breath left in my body, we will – all of us.

But right now, he couldn't stand the silence, so he'd fix that then consider the future. He might not be as spontaneous as she'd hoped, and he might not see things as she did, but he could be every bit as commanding when the right circumstances occurred. He wasn't an earl or a spy for nothing. He cleared his throat. "Do you remember the time when I, and some of my fellows, thought it would be a good idea to race Egyptian-made boats down the Nile?" It had actually been his brother's idea, for Nigel had been easily bored with the tedious work of unearthing artifacts and cataloguing them. Never a day went by when Nigel didn't wager someone something.

Which had proved a problem once he'd gained the title.

Several seconds ticked by. Just when he thought she'd ignore him, she said, "I remember. I had my own team of rowers, only mine were children of workers in the tombs and we had more experience and knew the nuances of the river." A soft chuckle followed her words. "You made a rather poor showing of it, and if I recall correctly, most of you ended up in the drink when the older boy in your party left your boat in a huff."

"That was my brother. His arrogance at that age was already out of control. He was every bit my father's heir. I'm not ashamed to say my friends and I wasted no time in calling him out for the prick he was, pardon the language." All couldn't be lost if she'd laughed.

"I've heard worse, my lord." His hopes died as she used the formal address in a chilly tone. Not long after, she squealed and this time there was no disguising her glee. "I've found him." Excitement wove through those words. "This one is the Priest Akanamakhet." She pointed to the box three rows in. "I'm sure of it."

"How can you tell?" To him, one mummy of shrunken, dried out bones looked the same as any other.

Her eyes sparkled in the candlelight. "The priest I need had a unique condition handed down through the men in his family." She waved him over then pointed at the mummy's left hand where it lay in folded repose over his right. "His pinkie finger never formed past a stump. Same with his pinkie toe on the same side."

Miles peered into the makeshift coffin at the brittle bones in questions. The deformity was indeed on the digits specified. He moved his gaze to the head, with its mouth agape in a silent scream, the empty eye sockets staring and the shock of surprisingly still-red hair. "What now?"

She glanced at him as if the answer were obvious. "We're taking him with us." Her tone brooked no argument.

"How? Surely you don't propose to carry him out in the box."

"Of course not." He'd barely relaxed when her next words had him jerking straighter. "You're going to put him in your arms as if he's a person."

He fought off the shivers of revulsions. "I can't carry a mummy out of the museum. Those bones will simply fall apart." Or fall off the skeleton. *And they'll touch me.*

"You can and you will." Emmaline began drawing up her skirt once more.

"What are you doing?" He eyed the thin white linen of her petticoat then glanced away.

"Removing my gown so that I might take off my petticoat. After that, I'll put the dress back on and we'll wrap the mummy in the petticoat in an effort to have it remain intact." She stared at him with wide eyes. "Well?"

"Well what?" He shrugged. "Did you want me to tell you it's a bad idea?" *Because it is. It's a deuced bad idea.*

"No." Her eyes narrowed. "Turn around so I may do this."

"But I…" When it became apparent she had no intentions of stopping, he sighed then pivoted around with his back toward her. "Do you require assistance?"

"Not at the moment. Since my life is somewhat unconventional, I've had my gowns made so that I can manipulate them myself in the advent there is no maid." The sound of rustling fabric muffled her response. "It's difficult to secure reliable help in Egypt and even more so if they know of my father's reputation."

When she cursed and the rustling grew more frantic, he glanced over his shoulder and his breath caught. While Emmaline's attention remained fixed on struggling with the gown and trying to pull all the folds of fabric down over her head, he looked his fill. Pale, creamy limbs were set off by the ivory of the fine linen shift, covered with her white, lace-edged stays that only accentuated her already thin waist and the flare of her hips. Without her gown, her stockings were fully on display, as was the sheathed dagger strapped to her slender thigh. The hem of the shift barely covered it. Her petticoat lay in at her feet in an ivory puddle.

"Damnation," he whispered and followed it with a hard swallow. Ever so slowly he raised his gaze up the length of her body, barely lingering on the soft swell of her breasts nestled within that dainty lace edging. Coupled with the flash of the emeralds around her throat, she appeared every inch an ancient goddess they no doubt shared the room with. "Dear God in heaven." Need shuddered down his length and awareness hardened it. *Stop looking, Miles!* She was magnificent. How could any man not admire her?

"Has the caretaker returned?" Mild panic infused her question and her struggles intensified.

Just as the top of her head appeared through the fabric, Miles faced the other way once more with his heart racing. "Uh, no. I thought I saw something in the, ah, shadows. A rat perhaps." He cleared his throat, hoping to calm his pulse as well as his body's response. It wouldn't do for her to see the bulge pressing against the front of his breeches. "Are you about finished? We should go."

"Almost ready." Seconds slipped by. "You may turn around." When he followed instructions, she snagged her petticoat from the floor. "Thank you for not peeking."

His crime chewed through his stomach. "I'll let you in on a secret." As she raised her gaze to his, he gave her a tiny, though forced, grin. "A hero always peeks."

In the golden candlelight, rosy color infused her cheeks. One of her finely shaped eyebrows arched. "Did you?"

"Yes." Disappointment speared him as she shredded him with her eyes.

"You're not different after all." Emmaline threw the petticoat at him. "Hold this. When I lift the mummy's back, slide it beneath him."

Suddenly, he desperately wished to be that different man after all. Perhaps if fate had taken a different direction… He shook his head. It didn't matter. "Hurry," he urged as she took her time maneuvering the bones. "It'll be a miracle if our driver is actually waiting for us, and another miracle still if no one sees us leaving this Godforsaken place with a body." *I left my birthday celebration to assist in bundling bones in a woman's petticoat after vandalizing a highly valued British institution. Yes, indeed, I'm a fit candidate for Bedlam.*

"Have some faith, Lord Archewyne. They are bones, not a body." Her whisper tugged him back into the moment. Gently she guided the mummy's upper half upward. "Now slide the fabric under with care." As he did so, she urged him into the exact positioning. "The good thing about absconding with a mummy is that the resins used in the mummification process will keep the bulk intact. We might lose a few digit bones, but I cannot see how that would render breaking the curse null and void."

"If I have any say about it, every piece of this priest will make it home." Since she believed it needed to go back to its final resting place, he'd damn well see it intact as it did so. Miles spread the skirt of the petticoat beneath the mummy's lower half then pulled the edges over the thin bones, which were stark brown against the ivory. As best she could, she knotted the fabric in intervals, making an envelope of sorts that contained the appendages. "We're ready."

"Carefully lift the mummy into your arms. I'll guide you through the museum."

He tamped the urge to shiver. "Fine, but gather up any trace that we were here. I'd rather have the staff believe this museum is haunted than give them confirmation humans broke in." Once Emmaline did as asked, he gingerly lifted the mummy into his arms. The rasp of dry bones and the remnants of grave wrappings sounded in his ears, magnified in the cloying silence. When its head lolled onto his shoulder and the face with its frozen scream turned toward him, sour bile hit the back of his throat. "I cannot do this." It had taken years after he'd quit Egypt before not to dream of things he'd seen then.

"You can and you will." She extinguished one of the candles, slipped her arms into his jacket and stuffed their gloves into her reticule that was near bursting at its seams. "Breaking the curse is more important than your discomfort." She met his gaze and hers blazed with determination. "I'm going to put out the last candle, but I'll take your hand and guide you. Agreed?"

"Fine." He didn't have to like the insane plan, but at least they'd be headed out of the building. Danger from that quarter would be averted.

Seconds later, the room was plunged into total darkness and the sharp scent of smoke filled his nostrils. He shifted the burden in his arms so that he held it with his right arm, and thank heavens for the petticoat. It kept everything but the head and neck contained, but none of that stopped him from nearly jumping out of his skin when she grabbed his left hand.

"Woman, next time warn me," he bit out as she tugged him into forward motion. "This place is already spooky enough without our theatrics."

"As I said before, my lord, consider this an adventure and let it happen."

He uttered an oath when he ran into a door jamb. The throbbing in his knee assured him he wouldn't soon forget that accident. "Emmaline." There was enough of a warning in that growl she should be warned.

"Apologies. It won't happen again. Just consider that retribution for peeking." She pulled him into the exhibition hall, and he tried not to think about how close the mummy's face was to his. What was that breathing on his neck? "We're approaching the stairs. Be advised that going down won't be as easy in the dark as coming up."

"Noted." Rather proud he only missed one stair on that set, he shifted his bundle at the landing. "Slow down else I'll lose our cargo."

"You won't." Emmaline didn't slow her pace. By the time they reached the ground floor, Miles' breathing was slightly labored. Absconding with a mummy in the dark was significantly different than boxing with Gentleman Jackson. "This way," she directed in a whisper with the tug of her hand. "We're almost free."

Free was a relative term. "Thank goodness." Would his mind know peace when they parted? He rather doubted it. Once he returned home, he'd call immediately for a bath then scrub every inch of his skin in the hopes of forgetting the touch of the mummy. Soon enough they waded through the supply room and stepped through the outside door. He gulped in deep lungfuls of clean fresh air. "That was interminable."

"Please try and locate your backbone, my lord. Our evening isn't over yet." She gestured toward the street where their growler waited. "Once we're away and you've been dropped off at Hyde Park, you can collapse into a quivering ball. Not before. It seems as though you traded your childhood sense of adventure for adulthood sense of duty. I'm not certain that's a fine quality."

She had no idea the sacrifices he made on a daily basis for duty or honor, and she'd never know because he wasn't at liberty to tell anyone. "No need to be rude." Or unfair. Just because a man disliked cooling his heels in a dusty museum then becoming intimately acquainted with a mummy didn't mean he was a coward. He wrenched his hand from hers then strode over the grounds toward the hack.

Damn managing female. He didn't need another one of those in his life, so once they parted ways this evening, good riddance. Fate knew what it was doing after all. Memories would be enough.

"Do hurry, Miles. I'd rather the caretaker not catch sight of us from a window, if he's still in the building," she urged as she hitched up her skirts and ran toward the hack.

At least she'd slipped back into using his given name. "If you want our friend to remain more or less intact, you'll be content with my pace." But he did quicken his steps. By the time he reached the road, Emmaline had already engaged the driver in conversation.

"...and you'll receive the necklace when we've both been conveyed to our respective destinations."

"I'll hold you to that, ma'am," the driver ground out. "About time you came back."

"We were unaccountably delayed." Her voice rang with annoyance as she climbed into the cab. "Not that I owe you an explanation."

Miles ignored her clipped tones and said to the driver, "Thank you for waiting."

He lightly touched his cap. "Where to?"

"The same place in Hyde Park where you picked us up." He handed his bundle to Emmaline before jumping into the seat beside her.

"Will do."

Miles swung the door closed and the carriage sprang into motion. He leaned his head back against the worn squabs and closed his eyes. "This has been quite an evening." And not exactly how he thought he'd spend his birthday celebration.

"I've passed worse."

He didn't care to know any more of her history. Truly. Silence descended between them. She dropped her reticule and fan on the seat between them while she shifted into a different position. "Where in London will you go?"

Not that he wanted to know overly much.

"My father still maintains a townhouse in Mayfair, such as it is. The estate pays for its staff the best it can with the remaining funds in our family coffers. Who can say what will happen once Father succumbs to his illness, but I'll stay there until arrangement can be made for me to travel to Cairo. I'm not sure what will happen to the title after that."

"With our crunchy companion."

"Yes."

"I see." He opened his eyes and looked in her direction. "What about the missing female mummy? Wouldn't it make better sense to stay in the city until you locate that one then take them both back to Egypt together?"

"Though I would love nothing more than to do that, I cannot fathom how I could break into Lord Leventhorpe's home again in order to search for that mummy, though I will devise a plan." She sighed, in frustration or exhaustion he couldn't say. "At least this way I can be assured the priest will rest in peace, and then I can decide what I'll do about his wife."

"Which will amount to months of delay and no guarantee the priest's mummy won't be stolen again all in the pursuit of eternal true love." He shook his head. "It's not a great plan." She needed at the very least, a keeper and at worst, a protector.

Was he volunteering for the position? How could he with his current obligations?

"It's the only one I have at the current time. I did tell you adventuring was a lonely but necessary business." Her voice sounded a tad waspish.

They lapsed into silence once more, and all too soon the carriage rocked to a halt. He pulled back the curtain and assessed the area. The Serpentine glimmered in the distance with the gaslights reflecting off its surface.

"This is where I leave you," he murmured as he opened the door.

"Oh, wait!" Her cry halted his movements. His heart hammered with a hope he dare not put much faith into.

"What of your jacket? If you'll wait one minute and hold the mummy, I'll return the garment to you."

"Keep it." He closed his fingers around the bead-encrusted satin of her reticule. "Perhaps we'll meet again someday. You can return it to me at that time."

"All right." Was that a touch of disappointment in her voice? "Well, thank you for your help this evening. Though I could have accomplished this mission myself in half the time, I appreciated having someone to talk to."

By sheer willpower, Miles stopped himself from rolling his eyes. "Most of the evening was enjoyable for me as well." He scooted to the edge of the bench. "I wish you well in your future endeavors, Emmy. I hope you break the curse." Would she notice his use of the childhood nickname?

"Thank you." She turned her face to the window and wouldn't look at him as he climbed down from the carriage. Not being able to see her expression meant he was destined for disappointment.

Miles dug out a few coins and threw them up to the driver. "Make certain the lady reaches her destination unharmed."

"You can count on me," the other man responded as he tucked the money away.

He took his leave of the carriage and strode into the park without a backward glance, though a large grin spread over his face, for clutched in his fist was her reticule and all of its contents. It would guarantee that he'd see her again and soon. He wasn't a spy deft in sleight of hand and manipulation for nothing.

Perhaps Fate needed a kick in the arse, and he'd decide what happened to him without it.

By the time he'd tramped through the park, over his lawn then onto his terrace, his good humor was restored.

He whistled as he passed into the corridor. As he crossed the hardwood toward the staircase, his footsteps echoed.

The sound of a masculine throat being cleared pulled his attention to the stairs, where Alfred approached from the basement level housing the servants' quarters. "As relieved as I am to see you've returned to the house, my lord, I'm afraid there is pressing business still awaiting your attention."

"What would that be?"

"There are two Bow Street Runners waiting in the Blue Parlor, my lord. They've been here for over an hour and refuse to leave. Even after I served them tea. We've had no recourse except to end the party early and send your guests home." He drew himself up to his full height. "What shall I tell them?"

Of course he couldn't escape his obligations. A shard of envy speared his breast when he thought about Emmaline and her freedom. "No need to tell them anything. I'll attend to them straightaway." He glanced at the reticule in his hands. The emerald green satin glittered with jet beading—the perfect match to the lady's gown. "While I do, please put this in my rooms, or better yet, give it into Peterson's safe keeping. I have a feeling this will play a pivotal role in the next few days." Of all the missions he and Peterson had run together, tackling Emmaline would be, by far, the most enjoyable—well, it would be to him. He wouldn't let his valet be that close to the lady.

"Very good, sir." Alfred took the reticule, dangling it from a string on his finger as if it would contaminate him if he gave it further purchase. "Though may I suggest you give some thought to your appearance? Whatever has kept you away, you look rather worse for the adventure."

"Duly noted." He waited until his butler departed the room before he strolled into the cozy morning room next door to the parlor. At a mirror on the wall, hanging in an ornate golden frame, he sighed. "Adventuring, indeed. She has no idea of what I do." How would she react if she knew about the covert missions for the Crown he accomplished? One peek at his reflection brought out a rueful grin. Smudges of dust and grime dotted his face while his drooping cravat betrayed his exertions from the evening. Without a bath and the chance to change into a whole new set of clothes, there wasn't much he could do in the way of making himself tidy. Yet, he loosened the length of once-snowy white fabric and slid the cravat from his neck, using one end to scrub at the more damning splotches of dirt on his cheeks. The rest would have to wait. "On to the next." He tossed the soiled garment onto a nearby chair.

Miles clasped his hands behind his back and continued into the hallway. Clearly, his night wasn't yet over and that suited him just fine.

I'm growing rather accustomed to this spontaneous way of living.

Chapter Seven

"Gentlemen," Miles greeted as he entered the parlor not four steps away. "Pardon my tardiness, but I was delayed with some prejudice." Unbidden, Emmaline's chosen way of distracting him from his nerves came to mind and a wave of warmth slipped over him. Much prejudice indeed. She wasn't all that innocent; it was but one facet to her that made her intriguing and most definitely captivating. Without much thought to the thin man or the fat one, he crossed the room to a carved wooden cart in one corner that held a few bottles of assorted spirits. At times, when he wasn't in his study, he hankered after a drink and didn't wish to bother Alfred with fetching one, so he'd had the cart installed. "Would either of you care for a drink? It's late, or early if you think of it as the morning, but I'd say a glass or two wouldn't be amiss."

Both of the men declined.

"We have already had tea." The thin man cleared his throat and glanced at the detritus of a tea tray still laying on a low table before a settee. "Lord Archewyne, if you don't mind, my associate and I have tarried here for rather a long time and—"

"Well, that all depends on one's perspective, doesn't it?" Miles interrupted as he poured a cut crystal glass of deep ruby port. In the flickering candlelight the liquid resembled the most expensive jewel. What would garnets look like nestled in the hollow of Emmaline's collarbones?

That exact color in a gown would set off her hair and eyes to perfection.

"I beg your pardon?" Confusion ran riot through the man's expression and added additional lines to his middle aged face.

A smile twitched Miles' lips, whether from thoughts of his companion of the evening or the man's befuddlement he didn't know. He joined his guests and took a seat in the worn but comfortable chair he wouldn't let his butler consign to the attic with all the other old and broken furniture. Much to Alfred's chagrin. According to his erstwhile servant, furniture should never be allowed to show its age. However, Miles had protested for reasons that were his own.

"Perspective," he said into the silence. "To me, the last hour or so has gone by at an alarmingly quick rate. I'm rather surprised by that, actually." As he sipped his drink and the satisfying wine slid down his parched throat, he uttered a sigh. A man didn't realize quite how straining having an adventure could be. "It's most peculiar, really."

"What is, my lord?" The fatter man asked the question with a frown to his companion.

Miles flicked his gaze to the speaker. Dark circles rested beneath his deep-set eyes. "Time passing for me doesn't usually happen with such haste. I plod along behind my desk, working on my accounts or what have you, doing my duty in Parliament, sometimes wishing I were elsewhere." Or the long hours in the field he sometimes was required to spend. He'd never met anyone quite like Lady Emmaline Darling and honestly, he couldn't wait until their paths crossed once more. She'd brought life with her, and with life the remembrance of his boyhood and spending time in Egypt, the country he'd formerly held no love for. But in the memories and her, perhaps he hadn't been focusing on the important parts. In the small window of time he'd spent with her this night, he'd felt more alive than he had since his wife had died. Even now he was near breathless with anticipation of her next move.

Watch it, Miles. Remember, you are not looking for romance. It won't fit with your lifestyle at the moment.

"Yes. Peculiar. This night has been rife with such things." The thin man tugged at his collar and cravat. "Speaking of which, we're here about something in that vein." He rose to his feet. A shower of crumbs, no doubt from various cakes and cookies he'd had during tea, fell from the folds of his clothes and rained down upon the Aubusson carpet. "By the by, I'm John Ratterly and this is my partner, Yardley Flummert."

"A pleasure, I'm sure." Miles flicked his gaze first over the tall, thin fellow who wore his lifeless hair to a part on one side. The pomade in the dark tresses shone in the candlelight. "Did you know you have a spot of jam on your chin?" While Mr. Ratterly dove for a discarded linen napkin, Miles regarded the portly man still seated on the settee. He was as round and short as his partner was lean and tall, and his thick shock of blond hair was as lustrous and abundant as an adolescent's. It quite distracted from his piggish brown eyes. No doubt if the Runners stood side by side, they would resemble the number ten.

The thought made him snicker and he allowed the fledgling grin to spread while he continued to sip his port. Never would he have thought of something like that until Emmaline. Remarkable. Her explosion into his life had more or less resurrected his sense of humor from where it had been buried due to the rigors of life and grief. His stomach growled and the men exchanged glances. Damn, but he wished the tea tray wasn't empty save a few crumbs. When had he eaten last? He couldn't remember and gallivanting with Emmaline had assured that he'd missed the buffet supper his guests had no doubt partaken in during his absence.

When he became aware that both men stared at him, he sighed. "I'm glad to meet both of you, but pardon my ignorance. Why are you here? I wasn't aware Bow Street would have a presence on my guest list this evening. It's my birthday, by the by."

"Felicitations of the day, my lord, but how did you know we were from Bow Street?" The round one rocked his body to the edge of his seat. A scuff marred the shine on his left boot and a dollop of whatever the fellow had to eat days ago decorated the bridge of the right.

"Uh..." Miles' mind raced. Obviously he couldn't give up the information that he'd gleaned from Emmaline. He darted a glance toward the doorway and spotted Alfred as he traversed the hall. A sigh of relief escaped him. "My butler informed me of the fact. No doubt one of you told him when you first arrived."

"Right." Was that disappointment in his voice? "In the event you didn't know, we *are* from Bow Street as previously indicated, and we've been dispatched here while following the trail of a brazen thief." His tone suggested a thief was the pinnacle of criminal activity a person could aspire to.

"I see." Miles took another sip of his drink and let the liquid linger in his mouth a few seconds before swallowing. "So you harkened to my residence because?" Better to let them explain than for him to jump into the fray and give over information they might not have.

Mr. Ratterly cleared his throat once again. The raspy sound was beginning to grate on Miles' nerves. "We have reason to believe the thief came here, perhaps with the stolen items, and we'd like to know if you could tell us of her whereabouts."

"Her?" As much as he could feign surprise, Miles raised his eyebrows.

"Yes. Our witness stated the thief was a female."

"Do you have a name?" There was every possibility Leventhorpe couldn't identify her by sight.

The thin agent nodded. "We believe it was Lady Darling, daughter of Earl St. Ives."

Apparently, the peer did indeed know her. "Is that so? I had no idea she'd even returned to England."

Mr. Ratterly's face grew pinched. "How did you know she'd been out of pocket? Is there a prior relationship?"

"There is not." Which was true. Being in her company for the hour or so didn't mean any sort of relationship. "However, it is common knowledge that St. Ives and his daughter are more than a bit eccentric. As children, we knew of each other since our parents often spent the winters in Egypt. They often funded and worked on archeological digs." This farce needed to be moved along. The longer these men lingered in his house, the more he might slip and give himself or Emmaline away. With all the authority he'd learned over the years since taking the title, he added, "I am not in the habit of harboring criminals, gentlemen, or aiding and abetting them." Lord but he hoped his face didn't convey that lie. "So if you wish to accuse me of something, I suggest coming directly to the point."

"You have us wrong, my lord," Mr. Flummert interrupted as his face reddened. "We aren't accusing you of the crime, only that we witnessed the thief enter your residence, but your man Alfred refused to let us search the house or grounds until we gained your permission."

"Which now it's too late since you were apparently missing. No doubt she's gone," the thin man followed up with a frown. "Since we had to wait for you to return." He pinned Miles with a direct look. No emotion reflected in those dark eyes.

"Don't think to intimidate me, Mr. Ratterly," Miles warned. He set his glass on a small table at his elbow then stood. "Do you assume this thief of yours is hiding somewhere in my house?" Of course it was untrue since he'd just left that same woman not ten minutes earlier.

"I have no idea, but seeing as how you weren't available to immediately accommodate us, you can understand how there'd be some suspicion raised."

"Yes, my lord," the fat Runner interrupted as he rocked ponderously to his feet.

Miles narrowed his eyes. "I'm certain you'll understand if I refuse to rouse my staff or anyone else from their beds merely so the pair of you can tramp through the house in a ridiculous search." He would absolutely not allow them to wake Jane.

Ratterly paled. "No, we wouldn't dream of that."

"Yet you resolved to wait for me even though I was out without a return time. Why, I wonder?"

"I, we, that is to say, we are under orders to question you and to not return to our offices until those inquiries are answered." A sheen of sweat appeared on his brow.

"I see." Why, when they could have better used their time interviewing others in the Mayfair area?

His associate wasn't as cowed, but his face flushed. "Where have you been for the last hour, if you don't mind me asking, my lord? From what we managed to gather from your butler, the soiree held tonight was to celebrate your birthday, yet you weren't in attendance. Even you have to admit that's highly suspicious."

Hot anger snaked through Miles' insides. He wouldn't have been put into this position if it wasn't for Emmaline and her deuced wish to break a mummy's curse. There was already enough stress weighing on his shoulders. "I do mind, in fact, but in an effort to help with your investigation, I'll answer you." Except, what could he say since it obviously shouldn't be the truth? He might not agree with her penchant for sneaking about or stealing items that didn't belong to her, but he certainly didn't intend to throw her to the wolves of Bow Street. Unless she continued her criminal career then perhaps. "I felt stifled from the crush in the ballroom so went outside to take in the clear air."

Most of that wasn't a lie. Exactly. He had quit the ballroom for the reasons stated, but he'd gone on a walk through his halls, where he'd come across Emmaline in his study.

Mr. Ratterly eyed him with a fair amount of doubt. All the while, Miles' gut clenched and he resisted the urge to wipe his suddenly sweaty palms on his breeches. "And you lingered out there for over an hour?"

"I did." God, even a nodcock could see the holes in that story. He rushed to continue and vowed to use this experience to help in his missions for the prime minister. "It's such a nice night, I decided to walk the property and that led to a stroll through the streets of Mayfair. I've lived here most of my life and would you believe, I've never really taken in my surroundings before?" He would have said Hyde Park, but then that might send these two to look for clues near the Serpentine and put them into the vicinity of a certain growler driver who may or may not remember the promise he'd made.

"I suppose you misplaced your evening coat somewhere on that walk?" Mr. Flummert stared pointedly at Miles' shirtsleeves which bore streaks of dust and dirt as well as wrinkles from being rolled to his elbows during the search of the museum.

"I..." What could he say to that? He glanced at his sleeves then back at the Runners. Thank goodness he'd had the presence of mind to hand off the reticule. "Actually, since I'd felt rather heated, after I quit the ballroom, I did remove my jacket. At the present time, I'm not exactly certain where I left it while I walked." In his mind's eye, an image flashed of Emmaline wearing that much talked about coat and how well it looked about her slender shoulders. "But I cannot see how that matters. Once the sun comes up, I'll send a groom out to look for it." And good luck with that.

"I see, yet that doesn't explain the general mess of your clothing. Did you find yourself in a spot of trouble? Perhaps engaged in fisticuffs with someone while you walked?" Mr. Flummert eyed the dust streaks on the front of Miles' shirt as well as his gaping waistcoat. "I'm certain you didn't present yourself to your guests looking a fright like that, which tells me you never intended to either get yourself into trouble or return to your guests at all." He shifted his gaze upward. "Is that a spider web in your hair, my lord?"

"I'm sure I have no idea to what you refer." Sweat trickled down his spine and his body temperature rose. How to explain his appearance or his absence? He shoved a hand through his hair and when his fingers came away with gossamer strands of a web, he rubbed his palm on his breeches. By sheer willpower, he forced the reaction away. He was better than this and had been in worse situations. "You know how the out of doors can be. A messy business at best."

"Yes." He managed to draw out the word, but Miles didn't fail to notice the skepticism in the answer. "I'm told you're not a lord who prefers the hunt scene or other activities requiring one to be out of doors for long periods."

"Who told you this?" He crossed his arms over his chest.

"We had the honor of speaking with the Marchioness of Wellesley before your guests were told to leave. It would seem the lady is intimately acquainted with you. She was worried when your absence was discovered."

"What gammon." What else did the blasted woman go on about and why would she be so loose-lipped? Obviously, she wasn't well-versed in discretion. "We are merely acquaintances. Nothing more."

"Interesting. We'll follow up on that."

"I'm sure you will." Miles traced a small tear on the shoulder of his shirt.

Mr. Ratterly focused on his face. "That's a rather large lump on your left temple, my lord. Mind telling us how you received that while you were out on your walk?"

Damnation. He'd forgotten about that. "This?" He slid a fingertip over the small knot on his left temple where he'd banged his head on the lid of the sarcophagus. "Easy enough to explain." He swallowed to force moisture into his dry throat. "Upon my return to my property, I tripped over an exposed tree root near the terrace stairs. I ended up glancing my head on the balustrade." No doubt he'd have to pay for each one of the lies he'd told this night, but if he could protect Emmaline, he would. Newgate wasn't a place for a lady.

"That's quite a tale, my lord." Mr. Ratterly lifted an anemic eyebrow. "I'd caution you not to leave your home from now on if you're that prone to injury."

"Yes, perhaps taking in nature isn't the pastime for you," Mr. Flummert rejoined. "I suggest in the future you stay indoors." The agents glanced at each other then laughed and the round agent resumed his seat. "Let's forget about state of your garden for the moment, shall we?"

Miles breathed a relieved sigh. He retrieved his glass and gulped the remainder of the ruby liquid inside. "Indeed. If you know the identity of the thief, surely you know she still maintains a residence in Mayfair." That wasn't a betrayal since it was common knowledge. "Why do you tarry here when you could pay Lady Emmaline a visit?" Would that he could be present during that exchange. He had a hunch Emmaline would lead these two a merry chase indeed and they'd be the ones thanking her as they left, with no doubt considerable less information than they'd come with.

Perhaps the prime minister could use an agent of her ilk in their fold.

"We intend to call on her tomorrow morning," Mr. Ratterly replied with considerable annoyance riding on his reply.

"This is an unsavory task? If you're after her, why not go there straightaway?"

Again, the Runners exchanged a glance. Finally, Mr. Ratterly said, "Lady Emmaline is a bit odd, and there is talk that whole family is cursed." He cleared his throat and Miles cringed. "I'd rather not have to spend time over there unless it's vitally necessary."

"And is not thievery from a peer not vital?" Miles frowned. "I should think any delay on your parts would be a waste. Considering you're the ones who are here at my home with her name on your lips, I'd venture a guess it's necessary to bother her instead of me. Do bear in mind that odd doesn't necessarily mean bad, and that a curse could spread." Was his family suffering from the same? It bore more pondering.

Ratterly paled. "She has a lion, my lord."

"And you are not fond of cats? I'm afraid this interview is over." He stood to his full height and hoped to hell it intimidated the two of them. If they only knew his covert actions kept their measly futures secure and their country safe... "Was there anything else? It's been a rather busy evening and I find myself fatigued."

The thin man cleared his throat as he tugged on his cravat. "The reason we've come is more grave than simply tracking a petty thief."

Ah, then they didn't think she taken anything of value. Interesting. "No doubt graver than hinting I'm harboring a criminal or inferring that I've had something to do with an alleged crime?" Of which he had. How soon would they become aware of the bashed in door at the museum? Regardless, he didn't want to hear anything else of what Lady Emmaline might have done this night. The memories he did have of her, he wanted to keep untainted, wished to remember the silky feel of her lips on his skin without these two staring at him. Miles slipped over to the cart and poured himself a second glass, this time of brandy. "I wouldn't think there's been time for anything else to go awry, but then, the two of you have been cooling your heels here instead of investigating the rest of Mayfair."

"Be that as it may," Mr. Flummert rose once more to his feet. He took a wheezing breath then let it out and swiped a hand over his brow. "There is a complication in the matter of the alleged theft, and if Lady Emmaline is involved, there will be hell to pay."

"Out with it, man." Miles detested delay. He sipped his drink and grimaced as it burned on the swallow. "You'll either speak it or you won't, but as for me, this interview is concluded. You can show yourselves out."

Mr. Ratterly took up the tale as he gained his feet. Worry formed deep grooves in the man's forehead. When he cleared his throat yet again, Miles was hard put to restrain himself from flying across the room and throttling him if only to stop him from uttering that sound. "It would seem that Lord Leventhorpe is dead."

The glass slipped from Miles' suddenly lax hand. It crashed upon the hardwood and broke into glittering shards and pieces. The puddle of amber spirits spread between his boots. "Dead, you say? Are you certain?" His blood ran cold. Had Emmaline put an end to Leventhorpe's life before she involved him in the convoluted events of the night?

"Quite certain, my lord. We found him in his study, as dead as a post not ten minutes after we completed a look about his townhouse for the thief's possible hiding place. Dead, with us in the house. Exceedingly odd, that." Mr. Ratterly's eyes narrowed into slits. "Shall we sit down and have a more in-depth conversation?"

"Regarding?" His pulse thundered in his temples and throbbed in his fingertips. His only thoughts were for Emmaline. As reckless as she was in her pursuit of breaking the curse, he doubted she'd be a killer, her jeweled dagger notwithstanding.

"Exactly how well do you know Lady Emmaline and where do you think she went once she left this residence?" The Runner gestured toward the chair Miles had vacated earlier. "If you please, my lord?"

Well, he did not please. For the moment, he had little choice. Since he'd spent the bulk of the interview prevaricating on his whim, he supposed he could continue doing it for a few minutes more. "Very well, but this will be our last meeting, gentleman. I cannot be expected to do your job for you."

Please let me be the arrogant and unhelpful lord Emmaline thinks I am.

Chapter Eight

Emmaline yawned. She rolled onto her back and squinted as the late morning sunlight streamed through the fine lace curtains. Once white, they were now ivory with age and no doubt needed a good washing, but that wouldn't happen without a full staff and quite frankly, she didn't have the time to spend on the townhouse's upkeep herself even if she wanted.

A loud bout of feline purring from the foot of her bed brought her into a sitting position. "I suppose it's time to start the day, Sanura," she said to the ten-week-old lion cub who currently reposed in a rumpled heap amidst the emerald satin gown Emmaline had removed last night. She hated to think of what the exuberant kitten had done to that fabric with its claws and teeth.

The lion, upon hearing its name, glanced at her and the amber eyes widened, the pink tip of its tongue stuck out, the dark brown tipped ears pricked. She uttered a faint mew then went back to licking a front paw. Morning sunlight glinted off the dark sapphires in the lion's collar. She especially liked the blue flash of the stones and the silver buckle of the collar's leather against the tawny fur. Against the butler's wishes, she didn't keep the cat chained. A lion shouldn't be fettered. The speckled brown spots along the spine and into its tail gave the cat a personality but would vanish as she grew.

"So that's how it is, eh?" Not to be deterred by the dismissive feline greeting, Emmaline swung her legs over the side of the bed and groaned. Her muscles ached and her mind immediately revisited the events of the previous night. "We'll need to be creative with excuses over the next few days. No doubt the Runners will come calling."

The lion cub offered only a snuffle, and she couldn't determine if that was even in agreement.

Often Emmaline indulged in talking to herself or the cat. Being alone was satisfying on one level, but when she craved companionship and the only living creature she had to talk with was the lion, she did what she could. After all, one could always pretend the cat would reply. Unbidden, her mind went to Lord Archewyne and the fact he'd been so easy to talk to and with. Perhaps their prior childhood relationship had helped. It certainly didn't hurt. Neither did his masculine perfection or his delicious scent that even now she swore she still smelled.

His biggest fault, besides having a healthy fear of mummies, was telling her things were a bad idea or that her fears were groundless.

Men!

Once she'd cleaned most of the muck and grime from her skin, brushed and caught her hair in a low knot at her nape then changed into a day gown of deep plum, she glanced at the lion. Recuing the cub from its former cruel master had been the best thing she'd done before departing Cairo that last time. The kitten had only been a babe, perhaps a few weeks old then, but it had been yanked from its mother and deserved a chance at a good life. So, she'd challenged the dirty, ragged street vendor for the cat. If kissing the man with garlic-scented breath was the price, she'd gladly pay it twelve times over to prevent abuse. Yes, owning a domesticated lion in England wasn't exactly the most proper of things, but neither had the whole of her life been the modicum of what was expected of a member of the *ton*.

Truly, it didn't matter now, and besides, she'd be back in Egypt soon enough. Then she could regale her father about her adventures here and hopefully make him laugh. Her chest tightened. *Just hang on long enough, Father. My return is imminent.*

She shooed the lion from her gown then rooted beneath it for her reticule. At least she had proof that Leventhorpe had the female mummy in his possession. All she needed now was to sneak back into his home and do a proper search. Once she found the mummy, perhaps she could persuade Miles to help her remove—

Where is my bag?

Emmaline whipped the garment from the bed then shook it out. Where the devil did it get off to? Emmaline fell to her knees and dug beneath her bed for the mummy. After she'd slid it out, she rummaged about the bandaged limbs from where it still lay swaddled in her petticoat. No reticule there either. "Drat." The mummy was shoved back into hiding and she shot to her feet. She looked at the lion who stared back at her with anticipation in its eyes. "Bloody hell."

The deuced earl stole her reticule and with it Leventhorpe's highly reviled notebook. Or, she hoped he had; otherwise, she'd left it in the hackney and Lord only knew where it would be now. Yes, the more likely fact was Miles had it. Did he plan to blackmail her or use it against her in an effort to make her do … what? Heat swept into her cheeks. Had he read too much into her overture in the sarcophagus? Besides, as far as she knew, her name wasn't listed in that book of accounts and favors, but her father's might be. Best to steal the book back and destroy it.

"I cannot believe I was so stupid." She threw the dress down. Sanura jumped to the floor, all twenty-two pounds of exuberant lion, and pounced upon one of the ties. The jacket he'd given her lay in a rumpled heap and she went through that garment next, even going so far as to check the sleeves. The missing accessory simply was not there. "For a man who doesn't believe in the mummy's curse, he certainly waited no time in taking the proof." But for what purpose? Surely he couldn't want the mummy for himself.

A slight scratching on the door pulled her from her musings. With one last glance at the cat, Emmaline crossed the floor and wrenched the panel open. The one maid she could afford to employ stood in the hallway beyond. "Sarah, is there something amiss?"

"Not that I'm aware of, my lady." The young woman, probably not more than five and twenty, offered a tremulous smile. Rosy color bloomed on her pale face. "It's time for Sanura's warm milk."

Ever since Emmaline had returned to England with the lion in tow, Sarah had taken to the animal with alacrity. Once she'd learned of the cat's dubious start to life, the maid insisted she and Emmaline nurture it, and she practically demanded the morning feeding responsibilities.

Not that Emmaline minded. Taking care of the lion was a full-time job which required help. Something else she hadn't thought through when she'd appropriated the animal. Wouldn't Miles read her a lecture on the impulsiveness of that?

No doubt she should have had the maid accompany her to the British Museum instead of Miles. The girl would take to adventure like breathing. Of course, she wouldn't be nearly as interesting in the manly ways the earl was, due to her not being, well, a man. While pressed so intimately against him, she'd felt the evidence of his desire and had lost countless seconds wondering what sort of lover he would be.

She yanked herself from her thoughts before they could take a naughty turn. With a few rapid blinks, she gazed at the maid with a fair amount of speculation. The younger woman was pretty enough and could turn heads if she wanted, and that might be advantageous during certain escapades. *I'll keep her in mind.* It was always good to have accomplices. "Right, but after that, I need to pay a call to a gentleman who lives at the end of Mayfair. He, ah, has something of mine I wish to have returned."

"Oh?" Sarah arched a blonde eyebrow. "Should I tell Thompson you need a carriage?"

"No." That would mean they'd have to hire a hack, since she didn't own a carriage anymore. Emmaline shook her head. She refused to fall victim to the bold curiosity sparkling in the other woman's blue eyes. "No need to burden Thompson with such a task." The man had served the household since her father had come into the title, and as such, he was too old and doddering to handle much of anything, but she hadn't the heart to tell him he should retire. Any time she'd hinted at it, he'd responded in a frosty voice that his place was with her because her father would have wanted it. Keeping him employed meant he had a safe place to stay, meals to eat and a salary if the funds were there. "We shall walk over. It's good to take in the morning air."

"We?" Those blue eyes rounded.

"Well, I'll need to maintain some sort of propriety, won't I? Traipsing through Mayfair is one thing, but calling on someone here means I have to try to be respectable even though these rules annoy me more than they should." England had too many rules and restrictions where women's freedoms were concerned. When Sarah grinned, Emmaline sighed. "Plus, I want to take the lion out. She's been restless."

"Very good. Once I feed her, I'll set up the pram." With a click of her tongue, Sarah called Sanura to her. The lion trotted at her heels, nipping at the hem of her black skirt as they retreated down the corridor.

Thirty minutes later, Emmaline pushed the rattan and brass pram down the street. Beneath the Brussels lace blanket she'd thrown casually over the basket, her lion cub rested, and from the squirming beneath said blanket, she wasn't thrilled at being confined, but Sanura could still see through the lace.

"In another month, I won't be able to take her out like this. She'll jump out and she already loves to run." Though Emmaline adjusted her grip on the rattan-wrapped handle, her knuckles felt tight. What if the earl wasn't in residence? What if he refused to see her? Why appropriate her belongings?

"Well, Sanura is a lion, my lady," Sarah replied from a few steps behind as if the problem was obvious. "She cannot continue to fit into a mold never meant for her."

"This is true. I quite feel her pain." A frown pulled at the corners of Emmaline's mouth. Perhaps it had been wrong of her to take the lion, but it wasn't as if the cat had been in a natural habitat even then. "Yet I'm firmly of the opinion I have at least given her a chance a life. Once I return to Egypt, I shall endeavor to set her free." Her stomach clenched. How would that increase the lion's likelihood to live out her life if she didn't have the skills to hunt? She glanced at the lion through the lace. "I hope you appreciate all I've gone through for you, you furry menace," she said to the cat. The lion pawed the lace and four lethal-looking claws put four tiny holes in the fabric. "Buggar it."

A snicker from her maid was the only response.

They arrived at the townhouse all too soon. In the light of day, the stucco gleamed and the gray shutters gave the unrelieved white a cheerful feel even if it wasn't a gay color.

Emmaline pointedly ignored the stares from passersby. Oh, she knew they gawked; she felt the prick and burn of their gazes as if they were invisible darts. She told herself she didn't care what anyone thought of her, that the opinions of others weren't her issue but theirs. Still, heat swept over her skin, of embarrassment or shame she had no idea. Perhaps it didn't matter. No doubt her family name carried a great dollop of both within the *ton*. As did the fact she pushed a pram down the fashionable streets of Mayfair when everyone knew she'd not borne children from either marriage. Nothing she did or didn't do was likely to ever change the wagging tongues or stares, so there was no use worrying about it. None of that logic stopped her from *knowing* it though. "Help me lift the buggy up the steps, please."

Once the pram rested on the wide stoop with them, she raised her right hand then rapped sharply on the gray-painted door. Such a proper, boring door for a proper, rule-following lord. There were a few glorious moments last night when she thought Miles wasn't the boring, staid peer she'd expected, but he'd disappointed her in the end. He'd lost that certain spark he'd held as a youth. Perhaps that was all to the good. Now she wouldn't be tempted by him any longer. Kissing him had been a mistake, surely, for even now her lips tingled and awareness danced along her spine.

How could the man from the sarcophagus be simply confined to memories?

No sooner did the echo of her knock fade than the portal yawned open and an old and stately fellow stood in the frame, promptly scattering her thoughts. She recognized him as the butler she'd glimpsed the evening before and the same man she'd been obliged to hide from at least twice on her way to the earl's study.

He lifted his bushy gray eyebrows then raked his assessing, judgmental gaze up and down her person. A trace of surprise lit his dark, intelligent eyes. Did he recognize her? "Yes?" He stood as straight as his spine would allow. No trace of wrinkles marred the crispness of his gray livery. "May I help you?"

Why, he's as gray and boring as this house!

Of course he'd treat her like a second-class citizen. She tipped her chin up a notch and straightened *her* spine. "It's imperative that I speak to Lord Archewyne straightaway." The thieving bastard.

The butler flicked a glance to the baby pram then to Sarah beyond her shoulder then met her gaze once more. Disapproval lined his face. "The earl is not receiving visitors."

Poppycock! She'd wager the rest of the jewels she'd hidden away that the earl was enjoying coffee and his paper over the breakfast table. Her stomach growled at the thought of food. *When will I learn to eat before tearing out of the house?* She hadn't eaten since perhaps luncheon yesterday, and the edges of her temper were frayed. She was never more waspish than when she was hungry. "Be that as it may, I do need to talk with him immediately, so if you'll be so kind as to show me into a parlor?" With that, she took firm hold of the carriage and shoved her way past the frowning butler. The tap of Sarah's heels on the marble foyer echoed as she followed.

The man's huff of disapproval carried to her ears as he closed the door. "Miss—"

"Lady Emmaline, if you please." She looked over her shoulder. "And the parlor is where?" When she caught Sarah's eye, she grinned at the shock on her face. There were times that being ladylike and polite didn't get one anywhere within the *ton*. Thank goodness she excelled at being managing.

"This way," the butler muttered in a highly aggrieved tone. He led them down a hallway lined with watercolor paintings in gilt frames. The Italian marble beneath her feet glittered every so often in the sunlight streaming in from the windows at the front of the house. Finally, the man paused at a door at the rear of the hall. "Please wait while I inform Lord Archewyne of your arrival."

As soon as he left them alone and his heavy footsteps dimmed, Emmaline turned to her maid. "What are the chances I'll actually have the opportunity to see the earl?"

"I couldn't begin to say, my lady," Sarah answered in a whisper. She darted her gaze to the open doorway then retreated to a chair in the farthest corner of the blue-and-gold appointed room. "I hope it's soon. This is a real fancy place."

"As opposed to the wreck of my townhouse?" The slight clearing of a masculine throat had Emmaline facing the door just as Miles came into the room. She took a step backward at the thundercloud expression on his face. "I suppose you're surprised to find me here," she began and hated every word uttered in that tentative voice. Why did he discomfit her so?

"I am not." He looked at Sarah, the pram and then focused fully on her once more. "I know why you're here." His deep tenor rumbled through the air and sent goose flesh sailing over her arms.

"I'm quite certain you do." If he could be chilly then so could she. After all, it had been him who'd dismissed her and ended their temporary partnership. "You stole my reticule."

"I did not, but even if I had, it could be said that I was perhaps attempting to take back that which you'd stolen from me." He gestured to the baby pram. "I wasn't aware you had children." The frost in his voice thawed ever so slightly.

"I do not. As I'd already shared with you." He reached for the blanket. She put out a hand to stop him from pulling away the blanket. "Buggar. I wish you hadn't done that."

"Then what's this little one?" Miles recoiled with shock etched on his face. "A lion cub?" He dropped the blanket and retreated another few steps. "You brought a bloody lion into my house?" He gaped at the animal in the pram. "You walked through Mayfair with a wild animal, who is not tethered then were going to allow me to pet it?"

"She needed the air and I didn't think it was fair to make Thompson watch her yet again. He, uh, cannot run as fast as needs be..." Not that the man deserved an explanation. "Also, if she had bitten you, it would have been your own fault for sticking your hand near a lion's head. Now, if you'll return my property, I'll be on my way."

Sanura uttered a mock-growl. She swiped a paw in Miles' direction and gave him the tilt of the head that always signaled trouble.

"What the devil?" He moved away just time to avoid having his watch chain clawed. She did so adore shiny objects. When the cat leaped from the pram, the earl apparently lost pieces of his mind, for he darted toward the door. "Recall the animal, Emmaline!"

"Oh, bother. I really wish you wouldn't run." She glanced at Sarah, who gawked with wide eyes and expression of fear mixed with amusement. "Why do they always run?" When she faced Miles again, he'd dashed into the corridor with the lion cub in pursuit. "It's one of Sanura's favorite games. She does so enjoy the chase." Obviously, instinct couldn't be undone.

A few minutes later there was a resounding thump in the hall followed by an, "Argh!"

She sighed. "I suppose I'd better rescue the great and powerful lord from the kitten." As Sarah giggled, Emmaline quit the room only to find Miles stretched out on his back, lying on the marble with Sanura sitting proudly upon his chest, staring down into his face. "What a good girl you are, Sanura. You've brought your prey down nicely. And in record time, too. I shall see you are awarded with a nice hunk of meat when we return home."

The cat uttered a throaty meow then went back to staring at Miles.

When he tried to touch the cat, the feline nipped at his fingers and he snatched back his hand with a curse. "Lady Emmaline, please remove your pet from my person this instant."

"But you're missing out on a chance to bond with her." She crossed her arms beneath her breasts and smiled down at him. Served him right, and she rather enjoyed seeing him helpless. "She's a sweet cat once you come to know her. After all, how often is a person afforded the chance to interact with one of nature's most majestic creatures?"

"I don't wish to further an acquaintance with a lion." He reached again for Sanura's neck, but the cat rolled over onto her back and batted at his hand with both front paws. "I'm not that good with animals."

"You're doing a fine job, my lord." Gripped by her wicked mood, she grinned as the cat writhed in apparent amusement on Miles' chest. A tremor tingled at the base of her spine. How idyllic it was, him unlaced and vulnerable, trying to ignore and giving in to the furry paws by turns. *Perhaps he isn't as unyielding as I'd first thought.*

The steady *tap-tap* of tiny feet bore down on them from the front of the townhouse. Emmaline peered over and her stomach tightened. A little girl, probably not much older than four, ran toward them. Blonde ringlets ran riot over her head and her dress of the palest green was bedecked with lace frills and ribbons. "What a beautiful child," she breathed before her logical mind could recall the words. This must be his firstborn.

"Oh, bloody hell," Miles whispered seconds before the girl gained their location. "Jane, go back to your nurse." He tipped back his head and the moment his gaze fell on the small person, his eyes softened to a chocolate brown. The affection lighting his gaze sent flutters through her belly. "Please, poppet?" The entreaty went straight to Emmaline's heart.

"Papa, is this my kitten?" Wonder and excitement wove through the question.

"No. It belongs to Lady Emmaline. Leave it be."

"It's pretty." She ponderously stepped over Miles' arm and reached his side with a delicate, pale hand outstretched. The tip of her tiny slipper tapped to a beat only she could hear. "Wion goes rawr." The girl made a fair imitation of a weak lion's roar.

In typical Sanura fashion, the cat uttered a soft meow of inquiry. She did so love to meet new people, though she'd never been into contact with a child. A warning niggled at the base of Emmaline's spine. How would the cat react to a tiny human?

"Don't touch it," he warned. "It bites and I won't have you hurt due to someone else's negligence."

Even as Emmaline opened her mouth to give the same warning *sans* the last part, for Sanura was temperamental at best and naughty at worst, but it was too late. The child had laid a hand directly on the fuzzy belly of the cub and the world seemed to freeze. *This is how the rest of my reputation will die. I'll be in the* Times *because my adopted lion cub shredded the face of an earl's daughter.* Yet she couldn't look away. Rarely did the cat let her rub its belly and such an action usually resulted in scratches or bites. But this little girl with her dimpled hands and rosy cheeks and delight sparkling in her big blue eyes soothed the savage beast. Sanura lay patiently still with all four paws up in the air, her tawny eyes locked on the small human, speculation glimmering in those topaz depths. Emmaline blew out a relieved breath. "It will be fine."

"My kitty." The small girl patted the lion upon its head then she scrambled over her fallen father as if he was of no more consequence than a tumbled play thing in the nursery. "Come." She glanced at Sanura, who regarded Jane with a tilt of her head. Then, with an answering mew, the cub flipped over on Miles' chest, bounced to the floor and trotted after the girl. Her tail wagged in the air. As they disappeared into the parlor, part of Jane's continued conversation floated to her ears. "This is my house. We can pway everywhere. Do you wike dows?"

Dows? How very heartwarming the girl couldn't yet pronounce words with "Ls" in them.

"Never take in a lion cub, my lord," Emmaline confided as she held out a hand even as her pulse pounded hard in relief. One never knew what such animals would do. "They become quite the traitor when presented with a better looking female. I suppose I've lost my status as the alpha with the cat."

"Don't try to charm me, my lady." He ignored her offer of help and struggled shakily to his feet. He brushed at tan fur still clinging to his once-immaculate bottle-green superfine coat. The ivory waistcoat embroidered with gold swirls also contained cat hair. "My daughter is now in there with a blasted ferocious beast. And it's all your fault." His eyes roiled with accusation. "You brought the bloody thing here."

He apparently indulged in vulgarity when in a mood. "Honestly, it's not as bad as you think." She shook her head and had no recourse except to follow after the aggravated lord. *I hope.* "As long as she doesn't turn tail and run like her father, Sanura won't pounce."

"Good God!" Miles took the last steps at a trot. Both he and Emmaline arrived to the sound of girlish giggles and the lion chasing her tail.

Chapter Nine

Miles surreptitiously studied the woman on the settee opposite him.

Despite her bringing a damned lion cub into his house and putting his daughter into danger, he had to admit, Lady Emmaline looked as gorgeous today as she had last night, perhaps even more so now. The deep plum velvet suited her skin tone though he would have preferred the short sleeves of her gown from the previous evening. But the most startling thing was her hair. Caught at her nape with a plum-colored ribbon, no doubt it started life bound in a chignon, but with the contretemps of the morning, it now wound down her back in a riot of midnight curls.

How much would he give to tangle his fingers in those tresses while settling her lips firmly beneath his?

He shook his head in an attempt to dislodge the highly inappropriate thoughts. Time to address the matter at hand, especially while her maid sat quietly in a chair near the window. "When did you notice your reticule went missing?" he asked in a low voice so as not to startle both his daughter or the lion, both of whom were sitting calmly on the Aubusson rug not far from his chair. For whatever reason, the cat seemed completely fascinated by the way his daughter moved a set of tin toy soldiers around on the rug's design. Every once in a while, the cat would put out a paw and knock over the closest soldier, much to Jane's annoyance.

Emmaline didn't slow in her consumption of the last tiny teacake on her saucer. She chewed then thoroughly swallowed before washing the confection down with a sip of tea. There was apparently nothing wrong with her appetite. Oddly enough, he appreciated the truth in that. Where most ladies of the *ton* only pecked at their food for fear of what others would say or the possibility of mussing a gown, Emmaline ate with great gusto. Already she'd ingested four seed cakes and two scones with jam and cream. At last she said, "As soon as I began dressing for the day." Her eyes narrowed to slits that spat green fire. "I'd never think you'd stoop so low as to stealing, my lord, after you chastised me for doing the same."

"Perhaps you've had a detrimental effect on me," he rejoined in a low voice.

His daughter jerked up her head and focused her gaze on Emmaline. "Papa's name is Miwes. My name is Jane."

He held his breath. How would Emmaline respond, and when she did, would she treat his daughter as a person and not an object to be shoved aside? Already, he routed convention by even letting the girl spend time with him when she should be with her nursemaid.

"Jane is a lovely name," the lady said with a gentle smile that pierced his heart. He expelled a relieved breath. "And your father's name is very nice as well."

Jane nodded and paused in moving her soldiers about, wherein the lion cub made use of that opportunity to take one of the figures into its mouth and carry it off to the far end of the room near Emmaline's maid. "What's your name?"

"Emmaline." Her eyes twinkled as she continued to regard his daughter.

She attempted to form the word with her lips and with her inability to pronounce l-words properly, she'd no doubt stumble. Miles inserted, "*Lady* Emmaline, actually, poppet." The girl needed to know the title, at least. When she still struggled, a wicked streak ran through him and he said, merely to see Emmaline's reaction, "If that's too hard, you may call her Emmy, if the lady agrees."

Jane stood. She approached Emmaline with cautious steps, her blue eyes focused on the lady's face. "Is Emmy your name too?"

The color leached from Emmaline's cheeks for a few seconds before she nodded. "It is."

Her eyes rounded to small moons. "You have two names?"

Emmaline nodded. "Your father used to call me that a long time ago when we were children." She did not look his way but rosy color infused her cheeks.

His daughter's forehead wrinkled as it did when she thought hard about something. Constance used to have the same gesture. "You can be Emmy to me too." One of her tiny eyebrows arched. She'd fit into the role of earl's daughter without incident, it seemed. "Yes?"

"Yes." The word came out on a whisper. Emmaline's hand shook and she swiftly returned her teacup to the low table in front of her. "That would be lovely."

"Good." With a sunny smile, the girl skipped back to her toy soldiers, noticed one was missing then glared at the lion cub. "That's not nice." The lion's response was to put the toy back in its mouth, and then it darted across the floor and left the room. Jane pelted in pursuit with the cry of, "Mine!"

Seconds later, a muffled scream drifted to their location and Miles sighed. No doubt one of the maids spied the lion cub. "I suppose I'll not have order in my home as long as you're here." The quiet he'd become accustomed to was shattered as the sound of running footsteps and Jane's high-pitched squeals of delight rent the air.

"Stiff upper lip, my lord. Change makes a person grow," Emmaline said as she added another scone to her plate. All traces of emotion from earlier had vanished. "Now, suppose we discuss the return of my reticule and the reasons why you took it in the first place?"

"At the moment, it's in the possession of my valet, Peterson." Miles cocked his head as another shriek met his ears, followed by a shout from Alfred and a crash of crockery. "Devil take it. The lion is terrorizing my household." Why had he wanted to ensure a visit from this woman who'd turned his life upside down?

Emmaline heaved a sigh. She slid a glance at her maid. "Sarah, do be a duck and retrieve Sanura for me. I don't expect to linger much longer here."

"Yes, my lady." The young woman left the room at a decorous trot.

The steady ticking of a carriage clock on the mantel filled the sudden quiet of the room. Emmaline calmly slathered clotted cream onto her scone as if nothing untoward had occurred. How did she spend her days in chaos? Or did chaos merely flow around her and she was the eye of the storm? He cleared his throat. "What does Sanura mean?"

A slight smile curved the lady's lips. She rested her intense green gaze on him. "It's Egyptian for kitten. I thought it fitting but realize it might not last as she grows."

"And you, ah, have a lion cub in your possession why?" Another suspicious crash sounded from deeper within the townhouse and set Miles' teeth on edge.

"Why not?"

Why not indeed. He cast a longing glance to the cart that contained his collection of spirits then discarded the idea. It was just past ten-thirty in the morning. Bad form to imbibe and in front of a lady no less. "Knowing you, the cub was rescued from a fate worse than death." It was like her, championing the plight of the powerless.

She paused with her teacup halfway to her lips. "I cannot abide the ill-treatment of people or animals, so yes, I plucked Sanura from the clutches of her previous owner and took her home with me to England."

"You always did have a soft spot for philanthropy," he said in a low, almost reflective voice. "How many times did you bring food to poor children in Cairo or interfere when you thought tomb workers were being beaten?" Even as a girl of three and ten, she'd had more of a social conscience than a half dozen peers he knew.

"How could I walk by those obviously in need?" she asked in an equally quiet voice. "People who have the means and ability to help should do so. Ignoring a need doesn't make those problems go away and it won't give rest to the observer in the dark of night." She took a delicate bite of her scone. A dot of clotted cream clung to the corner of her mouth and that became the only thing in existence Miles could concentrate on.

What would she do if he came across the table, sat down beside her and licked away that tiny bit of fluff? When she eyed him with a slight frown, he flicked his gaze to the teapot. "You're quite different from the other ladies of the *ton*, Emmaline. It's a refreshing change."

She uttered an unladylike snort then wiped her lips with a linen napkin, taking away the tempting dollop of cream. "Which is why I'm always on the outskirts of it." With a dust of her fingers, she settled the full weight of her attention on him. "Would that you were different as well, but we both know that's not possible."

"What do you mean?" Hadn't he gone far outside his comfort zone for her the previous evening?

"Don't play coy, my lord. Your world is one of order with everything just so. You rely on tradition to fill in the gaps and you glean great satisfaction if your holdings turn a profit." She drained the remainder of her tea then set the cup on an equally empty saucer. "The adventuring young man from childhood I used to know exists only in memories now. Perhaps that boy was chased out by responsibility; perhaps it was the horror of life that sent him into hiding." Her shrug lifted her shoulders and brought his attention to the slender line of her graceful neck. "Only you can know the truth."

What would she say if he told her of his secret missions for the Crown? Then she wouldn't accuse him of never adventuring. Yet, he remained silent. There were orders, after all.

"And here we are with you holding my property for an unknown ransom. Tell me how it is that you've come so far from what you used to be?"

Throughout her speech Miles' ire rose. Who was she to call him out and chastise him for being forced to grow up and take on the responsibilities thrust upon him? "It's Miles." A muscle twitched in his cheek and he relaxed his clenched jaw.

"I beg your pardon?" Surprise lit her expressive eyes.

"My name is Miles, not my lord. I would appreciate it if you would call me that from now on." He brought his gaze to hers and held it until she wavered and looked away. "As for your assumption on my character and the reasons I am who I am, suffice it to say a life filled with bad luck will sometimes take its toll."

"It's not bad luck, my…" When he glared, she corrected, "…Miles. It is very much the curse of the mummies."

He rolled his eyes. "Spare me the melodrama. I do not believe in that any more than you do." As her eyebrows rose, he plunged onward. "You are merely searching for something to blame for all the misfortune plaguing your life. Sometimes bad things happen and there's nothing we can do about it."

"What gammon." She surged from the settee and paced with agitated strides between his chair and the window. "However, if you can look me in the eye and tell me in full truth the string of deaths in your own family can only be attributed to bad luck, then fine. I'll consider what you say, but I think, deep down, you know it's because of the curse and you're searching for bad luck to be the cause because there is more hope and comfort in that explanation." When she pinned him with her glare, her eyes flashed green lightning. "The curse is real. I know it is, which is why I will return those mummies whether you wish me to or not."

"You may go or not. My opinion has no bearing on your life," he bit out, feeling as full of restless energy as she. Yet he remained in his chair and studied the scars and scratches crisscrossing the wooden arms. Telling her to do anything was like demanding the wind not blow.

Frustrating female.

"It does not," she agreed then drifted over to the window and gazed outside. Did she see the streets of Mayfair below or did she peer inward into her musings? "Quite frankly your objections grate and I grow tired of being told by everyone—men and women alike—that how I see the world and what I wish to accomplish in it aren't important or that they will never happen." She clenched her hands into fists at her sides, then relaxed them and wiped her black lace-covered palms on her skirts. "I will do this, and if my father dies or something happens to me," her voice cracked, "then and only then will I consider that it might not be the curse's fault."

His gut contracted as if he'd been punched. He hated being thrown into the same pile as every other person who'd thought her odd, who'd relegated her to the outskirts of Society, who dismissed her as if she didn't matter. In the grand scheme, he wasn't his father; he wasn't the obvious sort of peer one would expect regardless of the carefully crafted veneer he'd shown to the world.

Was he? God, he didn't wish to be seen that way by her. For whatever reason, knowing she'd lumped him into the same collection of callous peers bent only on their pleasure or furthering their coffers rankled. The urge to be a better man took hold. He stood and slowly made his way to the window, stopping at her shoulder slightly behind her. "I apologize for making you feel small, Emmy. That was never my intention." Where did these words come from? As an earl with some power in the peerage, he never made it a habit to apologize or even deviate from a decision once he'd made it. That had been one of the qualities that had gained him the attention of Lord Liverpool. "I am, however, concerned for your safety. That's all."

"Why should that bother you?" She turned and crossed her arms beneath her breasts, pushing those creamy mounds further into the lace edging the bodice of her dress. "If you hadn't intercepted me last night, we would not be standing here right now and you'd be unaware of me and my life. I'd happily continue on my path and you on yours."

Unless the Runners caught up to her. Or she fled the country, never to be seen again. "Well…" He couldn't deny what she'd said and truth be told, he didn't wish to. "While that is true, I've only become aware of your existence again and don't wish to lose touch with you this time." His chest tightened at the admission. Just last evening, as he stood in the corridor outside his library, he hadn't wished to align himself with a woman who might want marriage. Why now was he nearly tripping over his words in an effort to show himself in a good light? Would she throw those words back in his face?

"Why?" Her instance on asking the same question put him in mind of his daughter's propensity for the same. "You certainly didn't give me a thought in the intervening years."

This was also true. "Forgive me for that lapse. There were duties and obligations…" None of them made the situation better now, and it wasn't as if he didn't have more added to those. "I'd like to make it right, and…" And what? He couldn't very well blurt out that she'd captivated him last evening and he wished to see what else she was capable of. Even she, who believed in mummy curses and true love's power past the grave, would eye him askance. "…and I rather enjoyed myself in your company. I'd like to help you on your quest if I can."

Damn and blast! Where did that come from? Didn't he have responsibilities and a life here? A child? Duty to the Crown where he could be called upon to leave at a moment's notice? An entanglement of any sort with this woman would prove a deuced bad complication he didn't need.

Emmaline's eyes widened with surprise. Her lips parted slightly with an ever-widening grin. "You will?"

For a glimpse of that smile that set the pools of her eyes to dancing with golden flecks and made a dear little dimple in her right cheek flash, he'd do almost anything. God help him. He had to resist the urge to tumble into those fathomless green depths. His chest tightened as did his groin. "I will. My connections are at your disposal," most of them, "only if you promise no more breaking and entering." Neither of them needed that. "Unless…" Gah, what was his propensity suddenly for not finishing a sentence?

"Unless?" Trepidation hung on that one word.

"Unless you want to teach me how to utilize your lock picking instruments," he said in a low voice even though they were still very much alone.

Yes, no doubt about it, I'm destined for Bedlam. Besides, that skill would help him in his current work.

"I knew you weren't as stodgy and proper as you let everyone believe!" In typical Emmaline fashion, she threw her arms around his neck and hugged him. "Thank you, Miles. Your support means the world to me. You have no idea how lonely this journey has been."

"Yes, well." He slid his hands to the enticing flare of her hips and cleared his throat as heat from her body seeped into his. Her violet scent overwhelmed his olfactory senses and he set her away. *I can bloody well guess at the loneliness.* "After all, what's the point of having a healthy coffer if one cannot help those in need, eh?" God, his father would be turning over in his grave. "Jane should know how decent folk act."

"You're a good man." Her genuine smile had the power to turn his knees to jelly. *Dash it all, infuse iron into your spine, man!* "Perhaps with your keen eye for practicality we can locate the second mummy post haste. Even you must admit our last adventure was great fun."

"Perhaps." Another muffled scream rang in the bowels of his house and recalled his attention to more urgent matters. "Let me ring for Patterson and I'll return your reticule to you." He strode across the room to the blue tasseled bell pull. "Also, I feel compelled to tell you that when I spoke to the Runners last evening, they informed me that Lord Leventhorpe is dead."

Her eyes rounded and her pupils expanded. "What—"

"I beg your pardon, my lord," his butler Alfred interrupted from the open doorway. When Miles glanced at him, the older man continued. "The Marchioness of Wellesley to see you, sir." He stood aside and seconds later, she swept into the room with the rustle of satin skirts.

He tamped down a groan. Of all the bloody times for Georgiana to call. His attention should have been firmly on Emmaline as he told her how the other lord had died, and that he'd expired shortly after she'd left. That expression of distress and shock wasn't manufactured—she'd had no idea. Though relief trickled through him, he'd need to hear her confession or admission from her own lips. To analyze her body language. Some people were masters in prevarication. Instead, he took the marchioness' offered hand and brought her fingers to his lips. "What a pleasant surprise, my lady. I certainly didn't expect to see you again so soon."

The woman was no less striking than she'd been last night. Of the same height as Emmaline, Georgiana possessed masses of strawberry blonde hair, elaborately dressed in ringlets and curls beneath a smart beribboned hat. Her russet gown, more revealing than a morning social call would deem wise, molded to her Aphrodite figure and proclaimed her every inch on the prowl. She was the light to Emmaline's dark, but her eyes didn't pull him in like Emmy's.

"Don't be silly, Miles." She released his hand only to give him a playful smack on the shoulder. Her blue gaze sparkled. "Your party ended on a rather awkward note last night, and you were nowhere to be found when the cake was wheeled out, so of course I wanted to come over here this morning and find out if you were quite all right." She leaned closer and her breasts brushed his arm. "I couldn't even find you to give you my personal felicitations," she said with a pout. "Oh." She shifted her gaze past his shoulder to Emmaline. "I wasn't aware you had a guest." Her voice had lost the purr she'd started with.

Miles glanced between the two women. His business wasn't concluded with Emmaline and he'd be damned if he'd let Georgiana run her off. There was too much left to discuss. "Lady Emmaline Darling, I'm sure you'll remember Lady Georgiana Montross. She also wintered in Egypt during our childhood days."

A flash of recognition entered Georgiana's eyes, gone as quickly. "How lovely to see you again," she said into the shocked silence, but she didn't move to greet Emmaline in any other way. Though a smile graced her flawless face, it gave no warmth. "I had no idea you were in Town or that you'd rekindled an acquaintance with Miles."

"I'm in London on a time-sensitive matter," Emmaline responded, her voice guarded, her expression bland. "In fact, I really should be going—"

"That's not necessary," Miles said quickly as he held up a hand. "I'm certain that once I convince Georgiana I am, in fact, as right as rain, she'll continue on about her day. No doubt she has many other visitations to keep."

Please God let her not linger. Before he could say anything else, Emmaline's maid returned with the lion cub held securely in her arms. Jane trailed after her, the tin soldier clutched tight in her tiny fist. Peterson and Alfred brought up the ragtag procession, each carrying various bits of broken crockery or shredded fabric.

He blew out a frustrated breath. How much worse could the day be?

Chapter Ten

Emmaline's heart pounded out a quick rhythm as the parlor exploded with sound. She had no time to puzzle out the reason why Miles had pledged his assistance or even wonder over the news regarding Lord Leventhorpe, for chaos reigned. Her maid kept hold of Sanura's collar, much to the annoyance of the lion cub who kept swatting at Sarah's hand and nipping her fingers. The butler held up a broken platter for her inspection while telling her in a condescending tone that her animal had crashed through the breakfast room, jumping onto the table and eating all the hamsteak and kippers before knocking the platter to the floor.

Emmaline held up her hands, palms outward in a soothing gesture as she addressed the older man. "I apologize for Sanura's behavior. If you'd like, I can replace the platter—"

Before he could answer, the other man—tall, thin and with a mop of curly red-gold hair—stepped forward with a man's jacket, the navy superfine shredded on one sleeve. "Your animal snatched this right from my hand as I carried it to the earl's wardrobe. True, Lady Jane," he threw a reproachful glance at the little girl, "knows better than to play in her father's rooms, but she brought the lion there and this is what happened."

And, off to the side, the marchioness asked, "Miles, why are all of these ... people invading your parlor?" As if the aforementioned people where somewhat less than that. "I rather thought you held greater control over your household."

"Papa." Jane tugged at the hem of his jacket. "Pick me up." She raised her arms.

"Of course, poppet," he murmured and followed instructions.

Georgiana eyed the child as if she'd turn into a dragon in two seconds. "Does she not have a nursemaid?"

"She does, and I'll return her to that woman once this mess is sorted," Miles replied in a low, even voice that rumbled with warning.

"I see." The marchioness rested her bright blue gaze on Emmaline, apparently ignoring the rest. "I had hoped for a more private meeting."

Oh, good God. Emmaline couldn't stand the accusation in every pair of eyes, plus Miles' apparent oblivion when it came to Georgiana's bald hints turned her stomach, and that brought out a frown. Why should she care who the earl spent his deuced time with? She cast a frantic glance at Miles, who appeared to be as overwhelmed as she felt. *Bloody hell. I'll take care of it like I always do.* "Attention, please!" She raised her voice just enough that it cut through the din. Looking at the butler, she said, "Mister...?"

"Alfred, my lady," he intoned.

"...Alfred, then." Emmaline laid a hand on his forearm. "I would like nothing better than to replace your platter. It seems a particular favorite of yours, correct?"

His dark eyes softened. "It is, ma'am. It belonged to Lord Archewyne's mother, and she left it to me when she passed."

She nodded. Dear Lord, his mother was gone too. And the man still denied a curse at work in his life? "I thought so, and I would love to hear stories of that esteemed lady when we have a more appropriate moment."

"I'll see that we'll have tea at the ready when that moment comes, my lady." The butler went out of the room with a smile. From the side of the room, Miles gaped at her while the marchioness narrowed her eyes. Jane laid her head on her father's shoulder.

Her wild heartbeat began to slow as she turned to the tall man. Anything could be accomplished with a firm directive. "I do apologize, but I never heard your name."

"It's Peterson, my lady. I'm Lord Archewyne's valet, among other things," he said with a sniff of his long nose. He held up the ruined jacket. "About the garment—"

"I must say it is a terrible tragedy to see such fine workmanship destroyed by my wayward lion," she said with a frown she hoped would defrost the valet. "If it's all the same to you, I'd be delighted to purchase the ruined jacket. Perhaps my seamstress can remove the sleeves and take in the shoulders as well as eliminate several inches from the back. I think it would become a lovely vest to wear with a walking skirt and a shirt with flowing sleeves, don't you?" She refused to give in to a blush. What was the world coming to when she so blatantly, and in front of the marchioness, stated she wished to repurpose the earl's jacket?

Nothing says pockets to let like saving ruined clothing others would throw out.

"I couldn't let you do that, my lady," Peterson said in dubious tones. "Not with you being one of the Quality."

She fought the urge to roll her eyes. *I'm no more accepted in the* ton *than you would be, my good man.* "I'm certain you can." Gently, she took the jacket from his lax fingers. "On my way out, I shall make the necessary arrangements for your funds." She handed the jacket over to Sarah while priding herself on her willpower. At least she hadn't brought the garment to her nose in order to see if it still smelled of *him*.

The valet dipped his head. "Very well." As he headed for the door, Miles waylaid him with a soft order.

"Peterson, the item I gave to you last night? Please bring it here if you would."

"I will, sir." The man quit the room.

Emmaline breathed a tiny sigh of relief. The occupants were down to more manageable levels. The best way to divert suspicion or interest off oneself was to throw it back onto someone else. "Well, this has been a rather busy quarter of an hour, hasn't it?" She moved toward the settee where she'd been shown earlier. "Why don't we all sit down and have a civilized conversation, for old time's sake, hmm? How interesting that we've all come back into each other's' lives, even for a season as it is in my case." As if it were her parlor, she arranged her skirts as she settled on the cushion. "Miles, shall I order a fresh pot of tea?" Her hands shook so badly at her presumptions that she hid them beneath the folds of her skirt.

"Uh..." Of course he'd wear a shocked expression. Who wouldn't when someone he barely knew practically took over the running of his household? Then he physically shook himself, glanced at Georgiana and back to her. "That won't be necessary. I'm here at the bell pull." So saying, he gave the tasseled rope a tug with his free hand. "Georgiana, please come and have a seat. You can tell me why it is you've come."

Jane roused slightly. "Papa, Wady Emmy's kitty did a naughty in the haw."

"Oh? How so?"

The young girl giggled. "Her piddwed on the rug."

"She did?" The corners of his lips twitched. "No wonder Alfred was in a black study."

"Miles." Considerable annoyance hung in Georgiana's voice as she fought to regain his attention. "I already told you why I came. To check on you after last evening's events."

"Capital, then." He waved her over to the seating area. "We'll talk about the weather and the state of Parliament as per society's ridiculous rules then conclude the morning's visitations." He'd barely collapsed into the chair he'd occupied before and had Jane settled in his lap when Alfred arrived in the doorway.

"Was there something you needed, my lord?"

" A fresh pot of tea and refreshments for my guests."

Alfred nodded. "I shall have them brought immediately."

Emmaline's attention wavered from the bizarre setting when Sanura jumped onto the settee next to her with a soft, inquisitive meow. "Poor thing. It's nap time, isn't it?" Sarah snickered then resumed the spot across the room. Usually by this time of the morning, after the cat had caused enough trouble, she spent an hour sleeping in whatever sunny patch on the floor she could find. As she stroked the cub's thick fur, the lion dropped beside her, half on her lap, half off. Feeling the other two staring, she shifted her attention to Miles. "I do beg your pardon, my lord. Something had to be done, so I took it upon myself to do it." Even if it wasn't remotely what she wanted to do. Neither was sitting here preparing to discuss banalities with a woman she barely recalled from childhood who apparently had her sights set on him.

He waved a hand. "No apology needed. The situation found me at sixes and sevens momentarily." His eyes softened as he looked down at the cuddling bundle in his lap. "But now, everything is as it should be." He pressed a kiss into the top of Jane's head.

Dear God. Emmaline's heart spasmed. Did he know how domestic he appeared and how natural it was? There they both were, seated tranquilly in his parlor, she with her furry charge on her lap and he with his child on his. What must life be like living out such halcyon days, perhaps with a book in hand or discussing favorite music or where Parliament could stand to be reformed? *Remove him and that scene out of your mind, girl. He isn't for you. You're not looking for romance, remember?* Since someone—anyone—needed to break the pregnant silence that had fallen over the room, she blurted, "Georgiana, have you been back to Egypt since we all left?"

Her laugh tinkled and was every bit as bright and beautiful as the woman herself. "My parents might have loved that country and its people, but it never called to my heart." She brushed at her satin skirts and resettled herself on the settee opposite Emmaline's. "When I kicked the dust from my heels at sixteen, I never looked back."

How terribly sad for her. "Do you do much traveling?"

The other woman's eyes lit. "When my husband was alive, we toured the Continent, did a tour of India and even visited America. Wherever England had holdings, we went. Dear Harold was quite the navy man and nearly an admiral besides a marquess when he passed. His rank allowed us into many places others were not." A hint of smugness threaded through the words and her satisfied smile rubbed against Emmaline's sense of decorum.

Tamping the urge to say something unladylike, she replied, "How nice for you. Did you have a favorite place?"

"I cannot decide." She leaned forward as a maid entered bearing a tea tray. As the young woman exchanged the fresh service for the old, Georgiana continued. "I don't mind telling you that I adore bringing back tokens from everywhere I've visited."

"Tokens?" Though Emmaline knew she shouldn't perpetuate the conversation, she couldn't help it.

"Yes, you know, things that one finds in the old and moldy places." The marchioness waved a hand about, undoubtedly to signify *everything*. "Old paintings, trinkets, baubles. Sometimes, if I admired something in a museum around the world, it didn't take much to see that item in my possession." She rested her gaze on Emmaline and smiled as if it was second nature to rob the world's citizens of their culture. "I recently acquired a mummy, which I thought would be more exciting than it was." A bored expression lined her face. "The person who I took it from wasn't using it, but what does one *do* with a mummy? I grow bored having all that chipped and tarnished junk lying about. I've had all of that relegated to one of the bedrooms upstairs." She shrugged. "Do pour out, Emmaline. I'm quite parched. I don't wish to discuss anything remotely linked to Egypt now."

Sanura uttered a half-hearted protest when Emmaline moved her so she could manipulate the teapot. As soon as her hand landed on the handle, she was dismissed from the conversation and Georgiana's attention. Which was fine; she'd learn more by listening than by talking.

The marchioness turned to Miles. "Obviously, you're otherwise engaged at the moment," she began, and though her voice sounded pleasant, her expression didn't show it. "However, I did come on a mission of sorts."

"I thought you had," he answered with a hint of a grin. "Please tell me it had nothing to do with your continuing efforts to find me a match. It's simply not an ideal time in my life at the moment. I have too much occupying my attention."

"Pish posh." Georgiana accepted a teacup from Emmaline. "You're the type of man who needs a woman to look after him."

Actually, he is not. She handed Miles a full teacup as well. *He might find himself lonely at times, but he's quite independent.* When their fingers briefly brushed, tingles moved up her arm to her elbow. *And potent. A woman should only enhance his life, not run it.*

"I don't know about that," he hedged and smiled his thanks as he accepted the small plate with a lemon scone upon it. Jane had slipped into a doze and now lay haphazardly across his lap with the solider still clutched in one hand.

"If I may be so bold," Georgiana continued as if he hadn't spoken, "your virility is wasting away while you play at domesticity." She quirked an eyebrow as she took a sip of tea. "But that's easily enough rectified. I've brought you an invitation to my rout in two days' time. It's quite last minute, which necessitates the personal delivery."

Emmaline bit down hard on the inside of her cheek. *Well, aren't you just a managing baggage?*

"I see." Miles set his saucer on the small table at his elbow. "You assume I want to attend any sort of *ton* function. I've told you I'd rather spend my time here."

"Don't shut yourself away, Miles." The marchioness' perfect lips formed a moue of displeasure. "Besides, I'll be there as hostess, and you wouldn't want to disappoint me, would you?" She set her teacup on the table in front of her and as Emmaline looked on, the other woman fished a small envelope of ivory vellum from her reticule then handed it to him. "Please come. I do so want you to meet a couple of ladies who are looking for a match. I've heard rumors you're interested in Viscount Chamberly's daughter."

A snort escaped Emmaline, which she turned into a cough. *That's a tale straight from Drury Lane, isn't it, Lady Georgiana? You want him for yourself.*

He took a large gulp of tea. "I asked after her well-being once. That doesn't mean I'm anxious to become leg-shackled to her. In fact, I believe I told you I'm not anxious to invite romance into my life a second time."

"You cannot mourn forever."

"Perhaps." He put his cup next to his saucer then finger-combed Jane's hair as he shot a quizzical glance to Emmaline. The invitation he tucked into an interior pocket of his jacket. "I also assume you will be inviting Lady Emmaline, since it is bad form to proffer mine without one for her, and in front of her no less." One of his black eyebrows lifted in challenge.

Heat slapped Emmaline's cheeks. "Please, do not think you need to invite me—"

The marchioness huffed, interrupting her. "Since I didn't know you had returned to England, I hadn't planned on you attending my rout, and I'm afraid the numbers are already even." Her smile was genuine—like a wolf's. "You understand, I'm sure."

"Absolutely," she assured. She slid a glance to Miles and her belly clenched. He peered down at his sleeping child with a vague smile curving his lips. Regardless of the independence he craved, if a woman was lucky enough to win his heart, he'd be happy enough indeed. "I'm certain your event will go off with grand results."

So why did the thought of him with any woman make her want to scream with denial?

"Oh, I plan for it." Georgiana finished her tea. "Have you seen the scandal sheets yet today, Miles?" And just like that, Emmaline had once again been effectively cut from the conversation.

She gritted her teeth. *The scandal sheets are for people who have more space than brains between their ears. Why not go to the source for the truth?*

"I don't read that rubbish," Miles responded. Exhaustion rang in his voice. "Why anyone does is beyond me."

"Whether you do or not, at least part of it is based in truth." The marchioness simpered. "Lord Leventhorpe made an appearance in today's edition," she continued. "It's said his death was caused by poison, they say likely in the brandy bottle found near his body."

Emmaline choked on a nibble of her scone. "Brandy?" Oh, dear. On her way out of his home, she'd offhandedly told the footman in pursuit she hoped Lord Leventhorpe enjoyed his brandy, that it would no doubt calm his nerves after the night's events. It was supposed to be a sarcastic barb, for everyone in the peerage indulged in those spirits, but now? They'd claim it damning information. "How do they know that?" She hadn't had time to discuss the news with Miles, yet here was this woman, offering up further information.

"Why, it's filtering through the *ton* even as we speak." She flashed a small smile. One of her eyebrows rose. "So is the rumor that a woman matching your description was seen fleeing his home late last night, not a half hour before he allegedly died." The marchioness pinned Emmaline with an icy blue gaze. "What have you been doing in London since your return, my lady?"

Emmaline's voice and heartbeat quickened at the same time. "What, exactly, are you implying?" When she'd left Leventhorpe's home, he'd been very much alive. No less than two servants could verify that, if they hadn't already been paid to turn a blind eye.

"Why, nothing." Georgiana blinked in surprise. Slowly, she stood and cast a glance to Miles. A tiny frown pulled her lips downward. "Obviously, this is a bad time. I'll return at another when you aren't entertaining." She swept to the door in a flurry of rustling skirts and cloying honeysuckle scent. "Perhaps you'll call on me soon? We do need to catch up, and you still haven't explained to me what took you away from your own party last night or how you came to renew an acquaintance with Lady Emmaline." Her tone of voice suggested that was a severe waste of his time.

Emmaline once more bit down on her lower lip. Words had long ago ceased to sting, but she did so detest when they were uttered to sway another's opinion.

"I look forward to it," he responded. He struggled to his feet, gently displacing Jane, who mumbled in her sleep. "Let me escort you out."

Once he left the room, Sarah softly cleared her throat. "We should go, my lady. The earl has other interests, and we should probably keep moving."

"Right. The Runners. No doubt they'll pay me a visit today," she said in a low voice. As soon as she roused, Sanura dug the claws of one paw into her leg, piercing the fabric of her skirts and Miles returned with an apologetic grin. "Buggar," she said to the cat.

"Indeed," Miles replied, incorrectly interpreting the reason for her vulgarity. He took a seat on the settee the marchioness had vacated. In his hand, he held her reticule from last night. "I intercepted Peterson in the hall."

"So I can see." Anxiety rode her spine. Sanura stretched, and again the claws came out. Another set of tiny holes appeared in her velvet skirting. "My lord, I'm afraid I should be going. I am on a mission of some import, as you know."

"I do know, and as *you* know, I have pledged my support and assistance in that very mission," he reminded her in a low voice with a hooded glance at her maid. "We should discuss Leventhorpe's death," he said in an even lower voice that sent goose flesh crawling up her arms.

Emmaline's heartbeat kicked up a notch. Did he think her responsible? He'd talked with the Runners last night. Would he turn her in without letting her explain? Never had she been more glad of the freedoms afforded a widow. "Sarah?" Her voice broke on that one word. "Please take Sanura home. I have a private matter to discuss here but shouldn't remain longer than half past the hour."

"Yes, ma'am." The young maid came forward. As she gathered the cat into her arms, Sanura woke with a sharp meow.

"Do put the lead on her this time. She's had entirely too much stimulation," Emmaline instructed.

"I will." Sarah walked to the buggy where she procured a lead of braided rope dyed sapphire, which she tied to the cat's jeweled collar. "Let's go home." She put the lion into the buggy then wheeled the contraption out of the parlor without a backward glance.

Emmaline relaxed only slightly. "I had nothing to do with Lord Leventhorpe's death, my lord," she began but quelled beneath his annoyed gaze. "I hope you'll believe—"

"Miles. This will be the last time I ask you to call me by my name. Otherwise, I'll be forced to do something that will leave an indelible impression so you will remember." His eyes glittered with wicked intent.

"Right." She nodded and forced a swallow into her tight throat. What would be his chosen means of persuasion? "Miles."

"Perhaps you should tell me your tale. All of it and no shortcuts." He rested an ankle on a knee. "As much as I did pledge to assist you, I'd rather not keep company with a murderess if it can be avoided."

Chapter Eleven

Miles hated that he'd had to infuse such authority into his voice, but he needed to hear the truth and from her own lips. Though, he'd only renewed her acquaintance last evening and would have no idea how to tell if she lied to him, he liked to hope that he could read her well enough to know. Hadn't he been trained in less?

"There is nothing to say that I haven't already told you in Hyde Park," Emmaline said in the same dulcet voice he remembered from meeting her the previous night. "When I left Lord Leventhorpe's residence, he'd just stepped out of his carriage. Upon seeing me leave his home from the front door, he ordered a footman to give chase."

"Were you at any time in his study?" The Runners had informed him that Leventhorpe was found sprawled on his study floor with a broken brandy glass nearby and that amber liquid in a puddle. Apparently, it hadn't been his first glass. "Did you perhaps tamper with his sideboard or his brandy?" He laid her beaded reticule on the cushion beside him.

A trace of rosy color jumped into her cheeks. "I did look through his study during my search, but I swear I didn't touch anything having to do with his brandy. And why would I?" The spirited woman he'd first come into contact with returned after having been apparently eclipsed by Georgiana's arrival. "His tastes might run to fine wines and imported liquors but that's not what I was after." Her color deepened. "And I tossed off an ill-thought comment about him enjoying his brandy to a footman as I ran."

Good God. They could put her away with that circumstantial evidence at the very least. "Have you previously had cause to visit Leventhorpe's home? Has he perhaps treated you with less than respect and you thought you might gain revenge on him?" Every word that fell from his mouth had the power to wound her. What was the lesser of the two evils: hurting her or investigating the case and discovering she did indeed kill a peer? If she had not, perhaps his queries would keep her at arm's length. "The Runners told me there were no fingerprints left at the scene, and weren't you wearing gloves last night?"

"No!" So great was her agitation that she sprang from the settee. Jane mumbled in her sleep from his chair but didn't wake. "Well, I was wearing gloves, of course. I've not had dealings with him before in my life other than seeing him in passing at the few events we've attended together." She shook her head. "The fact you'd imply otherwise shows me the caliber of your character, and for that I'm disappointed."

As am I. "Please understand my position. You've come into my house. You've met my daughter." *Plus, wormed her way under my skin.* He lowered his voice. "If you are, in fact, a murderess, I cannot in good conscience let you further your acquaintance with her." Not to mention, she'd managed to charm the leading members of his staff. How the deuce she'd managed to soften his curmudgeon of a butler, he'd never know. And Peterson? The man needed a reminder of where his loyalties lay.

"I do understand, and I apologize." Emmaline drifted toward the window though she stood with tensed muscles, poised and ready for flight. She cast a glance to his sleeping daughter and the fight left her eyes. Longing shadowed the depths. "I'll limit my interactions with Jane if our relationship goes any further. Hurting you or anyone in your family didn't enter my mind."

And that convinced him of her innocence more than anything else she could say. She might be clever and cunning in other aspects of life, but she wasn't a killer. His original instinct still rang true, as did his hope that they wouldn't lose the connection they'd recently established. "Jane is my only family. She's what's left since…" Again he let the statement die. Did he even wish to tell Emmaline about the wretched luck that had been his these last several years?

"The curse."

"No." Though, why wasn't he as certain as he'd been in his denial before? "As you refuse to believe there is no power in a curse, I refuse to believe my life's misfortunes are due to the same." Though, it would be so easy to have a scapegoat.

She faced him and their eyes met across the room. Her expression remained clouded. "Perhaps common ground is needed if I'm to convince you." He didn't initiate more of the conversation. After all, what would he say? As she moved her mass of hair to the other shoulder, she sighed. "Typical tight-lipped British man. Unwilling to share anything of his life."

"Now that's not fair. I didn't have the chance. A man—British or not—must have time to compose his words." He gave into the grin that threatened. Of course she knew that. Her sparkling eyes gave her away. Not to mention parts of his life simply weren't up for sharing. The secrets he kept for king and country must remain just that.

"Regardless, it's time to give me the information regarding your life that I've been curious about since the museum." Emmaline crossed the floor, her steps light, and paused as she came to his worn out chair. "How extremely odd this piece of furniture is." She frowned while she traced a fingertip along the threadbare velvet of the wing-backed chair that had long ago lost its sheen.

"Why would you say that?" Would she side with Alfred or with him on the fate of the chair?

"In a room full of delicate French furniture, this doesn't fit with the theme." She smiled down at Jane then returned her focus to him. "Which leads me to believe either your butler is slipping in his duties by allowing such a shabby addition or else this chair serves more than merely a functional piece of furniture."

The woman was intelligent, and though he appreciated that, he also cursed it too. No one else suspected the reasons he retained the chair. What else would she divine about him? "Your summations are correct." Unable to remain inactive any longer, he stood in favor of pacing. "I'm reluctant to let Alfred consign the chair to the obscurity of the attics."

"That's obvious, but I want to know why because the key to your character lies in that story." She folded her arms along the back of the chair. "Why does a man so bent on proper and following rules keep such a chair. Are you caught up in sentimentality?"

"I don't know how much of that is true, but to me, this chair does harbor deep memories that I perhaps don't wish to forget." He clenched his jaw and when a muscle twitched in his cheek, he blew out a breath to relax. "Yet, there are times I don't want to remember," he said in a low-pitched voice.

How wise would it be to tell Emmaline the reasons while his daughter slept nearby?

"Another thing you and I have in common, Miles," his guest replied in an equally soft voice. "In the recollection, one must relive the pain."

"Yes." He moved across the floor toward the cart containing his favorite spirits, but he didn't retrieve a glass. Not yet.

Emmaline followed. At least now as they conversed, Jane might not overhear should she wake. "One could say pain is a signal that we still live, and where there is life, there is hope." A tiny note of wistfulness crept into her response.

"Perhaps, or perhaps one doesn't wish to have hope for fear of what will happen based on previous knowledge." He fingered the crystal stopper on a decanter containing brandy.

"One must never let go of hope even if one is terrified at what allowing oneself to think of future might entail." She wandered to the window then faced him with an expectant expression. "Tell me why your hope has dimmed. Explain to me why you don't think you're worthy of being close to someone again."

He fought to keep his expression calm while, inside, he reeled from her insight. How could she know any of that when he never shared those fears with anyone? His pulse rushed through his ears and throbbed into his fingertips. The longer she looked at him, more he wanted to talk about everything still locked in his soul. Perhaps, after all, the burden of keeping his history to himself was too much to bear. "That chair has marked milestones in my life." In this he would share. Everything else would remain a secret based on the oath he'd taken.

"So I assume." She tucked her hands behind her and leaned her backside against the window ledge. "And?"

He offered a small smile. In her, assertiveness didn't rankle like it did with Georgiana's penchant for being managing. "It's not a happy tale."

"Strong people don't usually have idyllic origins."

"Indeed." Her story certainly wasn't. "Five years ago, my parents were touring Greece. This was a couple of years after my marriage to Constance. They'd gone to attend a wedding of a mutual friend. At one point, a group of them decided to go for a picnic lunch to some of the Santorini cliffs only accessible by winding roads." He dropped his gaze to the beverage cart and this time he poured himself a tumbler of brandy with a slightly shaking hand. "On the way, a portion of the road crumbled beneath the carriage wheel. In the space of a heartbeat, their vehicle tumbled from the road and plunged twenty feet. No one survived."

"What a horrible tale." Shock warred with sympathy in her eyes. "Did the Grecian trip come after your father had taken possession of the mummy?"

"I believe so." Miles raised the glass to his lips and paused. "If I remember correctly, Father bought the mummy at a private sale ten years ago. Somewhere in Surrey, I think but cannot recall clearly as I was rather busy fighting Boney's forces at the time. Well, not hand-to-hand combat, but through the navy, and even that wasn't strenuous for my skills were honed as a spy. Once my commission expired, I went on to perfect my career as a rogue." His continued work for the Home Office as a spy didn't have any bearing on the tale. He took a hearty sip of the brandy and welcomed the burn of the alcohol as it slid down his throat. "Second son, you know. Nothing much was expected of me." And neither did he push himself to find a suitable challenge, for where his family and friends assumed he was charming women into his bed all over the world, in reality he'd been chasing down enemies of the Crown.

Twin spots of color jumped into her cheeks. "That was my father's country home. At the time, he'd been gripped by some gammon I needed a Season at the ripe old age of three and twenty." She snorted and shook her head. "That's a rather long in the tooth for any lady, title be damned. In any event, he held the private sale for many of his prized antiquities, furnishings and paintings to raise the required blunt. Eventually, the estate was sold as well." She frowned. "I haven't been back to Surrey in a long time."

What a fascinating tidbit, and quite scandalous as well. Imagine a member of the peerage selling off possessions for something so pedestrian as funds. "How did the Season go?" At that age, had she been more like he'd known her at sixteen—wild and carefree—or was she more like the woman before him now—independent but with caution and sadness in her eyes?

She sent him a look brimming with annoyance. "After spending agonizingly boring months attending *ton* functions where I was ignored or mocked or inspected as if I were horseflesh instead of a woman with her own mind, I escaped at the winter holidays still unwanted by any man." Her shrug drew his attention to the delicate slope of her shoulders and the dip between her collarbones. "Of course, I remember that time fondly as it was where I learned to hone my lock picking skills."

"From who?" Surely she didn't hang about in dark alleys while mixing with an unsavory element of society.

Her smirk held a decidedly wicked edge. "Lord Lothbrine's youngest son. He was twelve then and way too smart for his own good."

Given that that particular duke left his four children very much to their own devices with a parade of governesses in and out of their lives, the news didn't surprise Miles in the slightest. "Isn't the lad shut away in Newgate at the moment?"

"He is." Emmaline's laugh lifted some of the melancholy that had settled over the room. "You see, the best of thieves don't manage to get caught. But then, only a nodcock would try to steal from Prinny himself. He was still the Regent then."

"You did."

"What?" Her eyes rounded. "I've never approached Prinny or any of his court. I have no use for his sort of lifestyle."

"No, I mean you were caught." He hid his smile by taking another drink. "Only last night. Does that mean you aren't a very good thief?"

"Don't be an arse." She tempered the words with a grin. "It means your interference in my task was a poor coincidence, nothing more. Had you not come upon me, you'd never know I was here."

"True." He drained his tumbler. "Needless to say, once Father passed, Nigel had the title thrust upon him. He was nine and twenty and already as arrogant as if he'd been an earl his whole life. He embraced the role with relish." Memories of his brother flashed into his mind. In Egypt, in school, in London, his sibling had practiced for his eventual role, and when his time came, he'd slid easily and naturally into their father's footsteps. He'd never given Miles much thought after he'd become earl.

Not that Nigel had noticed anyway. Father had trained him all along, which meant Miles was left with unaccustomed freedom and more jealousy than he'd any right to.

"Nigel had been busy with the holdings and gambling while my attention had been occupied with the arrival of Jane." Once that little miracle had come into his life, everything else had paled, even his career as a spy for a time. He hadn't much concerned himself with his brother's problems.

Though, in retrospect, he should have since he hadn't a blessed clue when it became his turn.

"Dare I ask what happened to your brother?" She hadn't moved from her position, but the intimate tone of her voice, the way her words sounded made him feel as if she stood right next to him. Strange indeed but not unsettling. More of a comfort than not.

"Where you are involved, I suspect you'd dare anything," he replied, more to himself than her. Needing something to do with his hands, he poured out another two fingers of brandy. "Nigel held the title of earl for a couple of years before fate visited."

Emmaline shook her head. "Fate let him have the title. The curse took it away."

"Be that as it may, three years ago my brother came down with what we thought was a summer head cold." Miles clutched the tumbler tighter in his fingers. "Over the following weeks, he'd recover then decline by turns until the ailment went into pneumonia." He took a large sip of brandy and swallowed it. "His lungs couldn't recover, and already weakened from that condition, he contracted a fever. Within days, he was gone."

"And thus you came into a title you should never have been responsible for and didn't ever want," she whispered, and this time she came toward him a few steps. "I'm so sorry."

He waved his free hand. "Thank you, but sometimes life doesn't work out the way we would have wished."

"So you've said before, yet we're left behind to muddle through the remnants." She eyed the drink cart, and when he thought she might have asked for a glass, she said, "I assume your wife saved you from your circumstances?"

"In a way." He stared at the amber liquid still in the crystal tumbler. "Constance was the one constant in the muck my life had become." A snort escaped him. "I hadn't thought much about her name meaning so very much until this moment." Miles carried his drink over to the window, where he peered out at the garden area. "I was soul-weary from burying the whole of my immediate family. I suppose I took solace in her, for soon after she gave me the happy tidings of a second pregnancy."

"It's a romantic story to be certain." Anyone else would have missed that slight, telling catch in her voice that was the only betrayal to her feelings on babies. "And as it should be."

"Perhaps." He drained the liquid from his glass. "Though that year was a difficult one. The title and its responsibilities took much of my attention and time." As had his presence being recalled to active duty for the prime minister and reporting directly to either him or the Duke of Rathesborne. He'd answered the call, but not without a heavy dose of guilt for being pulled away from his growing family. "The pregnancy drained her and she was sick, eventually confined to bed." He shook his head as cold regret gripped him. "I should have made the effort to spend more time with her, but she'd always wave me off, saying once the child was born we'd have all the time in the world, that my work was of more importance." She'd been one of the few to whom he'd confided what exactly he did for the Crown.

Perhaps that had been a mistake.

"You don't have to continue if it pains you." Emmaline's voice sounded from behind him.

"It's all right. The worse of it has faded though I'll never forget." He glanced slightly over his shoulder at her. She'd raised a hand. Did she intend to touch him in comfort? In the end, it didn't matter as she lowered it to her side, yet disappointment stabbed him. Her gesture would have been welcomed. "I've already told you that Constance did indeed die with our son. He was stillborn." He clenched the glass harder. "I often wonder what the boy would have been like. He had my dark hair." But the rest of the infant's features had resembled his wife. His heart squeezed, but that ever-present ache had somehow lessened.

"It's a natural thought. I think we all wonder about the what-would-have-beens." The violet scent she wore drifted to his nose, much different than the rose Constance had favored. "However, you are still strong, my lord. You have survived the curse, and from all accounts have escaped it for the last two years." She sighed. "I must say I'm envious of that."

Why the devil wouldn't she consistently call him by his name? Miles faced her, pleasantly surprised that only two feet of space separated them. "Have you not survived as well?" He closed the distance, his tumbler still clutched in his hand, and didn't stop his advance until their bodies nearly touched and she leaned backward to maintain eye contact.

"There are times when I don't believe I have, that I'm almost a shell of myself until my sense of self-worth returns and brings confidence with it. When that happens, I can successfully shove my failures to the back of my mind and look only forward." Her eyes rounded and she slid the tip of her tongue along her lush bottom lip, leaving it glossy and oh so tempting. "What are you doing?" Her breath warmed his chin as he leaned into her.

"I told you I'd need to do something drastic to help you remember to call me by my Christian name." Gripped by the urge to touch her, he slipped his free hand around her waist and held her to him with pressure at the small of her back. "I'll wager you won't soon forget now." He dipped his head until his lips merely hovered above hers. "Say my name, Emmy. I want to—need to—hear it. Right now." His heartbeat slammed through his veins. When had he ever given a woman such a mad request?

The muscles in her delicate throat moved with a hard swallow. She clutched his shoulders to keep from bending backward. "You're really becoming overbearing ... Miles. I'm not sure how I feel about that."

If she moved even slightly, their lips would touch as she spoke. Every nerve in his body hummed with anticipation. A jolt of desire sped through him. "Sometimes, it's best to keep people at sixes and sevens." His lips glanced across hers. That fleeting pass didn't begin to satisfy his curiosity. He remembered all too well the feel of her body pressed against his while in the sarcophagus or when she'd flung herself into his arms in spontaneous thanks this morning. "Wouldn't you agree?"

"Yes." Her gaze fell to his mouth and the dark of her eyelashes formed black arcs against her pale cheeks. "Miles, I—"

"And that is the story of what my life has been like these last five years," he said as if the small interlude or the indefinable connection had never occurred. Just as she currently fascinated him, he wished for her to feel the same about him. He straightened and put much needed space between them before his body could react any more to her presence and even that taxed his self-control, for he couldn't think of anything as interesting as feeling her lips beneath his. Would she be as enthusiastic in kissing as she was in everything else? "Do you still honestly believe I've been the victim of a curse?"

Emmaline stumbled and blinked before staring at him with a dazed expression. "I do." She softly cleared her throat. "Every person who has contact with either of those mummies, however brief, is affected." She shook her head. Had she felt that charge between them too? "Bad luck would only be your parents dying. A curse is taking the rest."

"I'll consider it." He crossed the room to the cart then set his tumbler upon it. However, if he did acknowledge such a thing existed and was even now creating havoc in his life, then he'd be forced to realize his own life was every bit as suspect, as was hers.

I refuse to let a bit of magic or the occult determine the end of my days.

Or Emmaline's. What a tragedy indeed it would be to deprive the world of her presence.

"There is one thing I'm still uncertain about," she said in tones more like her usual efficient self.

"By all means, please ask any questions you have." Within reason.

"What does any part of your story have to do with your chair?"

He glanced at the piece of furniture in question. Jane slept on, with one hand flung over the cushion while the other still clutched the soldier. "I cannot let the chair be forgotten."

"Why?" She didn't make any effort to come near to him again.

"It means more to me than merely a piece of furniture or an object." Miles heaved a sigh. He shoved a hand through his hair. "More than memories, really." He looked at the worn fabric stretching over the chair's frame then back at her. "I was sitting in this chair reading when I received word of my brother's last breath and realized my life had forever changed." He rubbed his hand over his face. Honestly, he'd thought the admission would go to his grave with him. "In this chair, my wife crawled into my lap and told me of the babe that would make us parents." His throat tightened. "I held Jane for the first time in that chair and…" God, why was it both difficult and freeing at the same time to finally tell someone the reasons? "… I was sitting in that chair when the doctor gave me the news that not only was my son stillborn but that Constance had died during the process."

Tears sparkled in Emmaline's eyes. "It's a living scrapbook."

"Yes." His voice broke.

"I agree with you. The chair should stay, but I would suggest putting it in your private rooms. It needs a place of honor and not to invite commentary from people who would never understand."

Out of everything she could have said, he appreciated what she did impart. "You're right. I'll ask Peterson to help me move it as soon as our meeting is concluded." When he rested his gaze on her once more, the pressure in his chest lifted. Perhaps it had been cathartic to impart that secret to her. "Speaking of Peterson…" He crossed the room with efficient movements, his bootheels ringing on the hardwood. Once he reached the settee he'd occupied earlier, he snatched up her reticule. "I believe this belongs to you."

"Thank you." She came toward him with a hand outstretched. "I suppose I'll be on my way then." A decided frown pulled her lips downward.

Taking a liberty he didn't have, Miles delved into the bag and procured the folded map as well as a small leather notebook. "This is collateral that you'll make use of my offer of assistance." And thus ensure he'd have another adventure to look forward to—along with his fascinating companion.

"Fair enough, but do you, uh, know what that notebook is?"

He glanced at the unassuming black book then on a whim slipped off the tie and flipped through some of the pages. Familiar names of peers met his gaze. "Surely this isn't Leventhorpe's famed notebook of accounts and favors and revenges?" Good God, how had she come upon it?

"It is. I'd found it in hidden in his study."

"You said you never went into his study."

Rosy color suffused her cheeks. "I liked, but it was a quick pass and truly I had nothing to do with his brandy." Her throat worked with a hard swallow. "Something so painstakingly hidden must be important, and it wasn't until you'd mentioned Leventhorpe's book that I realized…"

"Ah. I see." He tucked both the book and the map into an interior pocket of his jacket. "I'll put it into safe keeping and thereby relieve you of the responsibility." And tear out the damned page that recorded his family name.

"Thank you." When she took the reticule from him, her lace-covered fingers brushed his. Heat shot up his arm. "I don't know when we shall see each other again."

Perhaps she wasn't the only one who could be impetuous. Miles pulled Georgiana's invite from that same jacket pocket. He held it aloft. "Why not be my guest at the marchioness' rout in two days? I'll even give you full permission to wander about her house in the hunt of a mummy." He waggled his eyebrows. "Who knows? I might join you."

A wide smile full of delight crept across her face, and that was more reward than he could have hoped for. "I cannot think of anything else I'd rather do."

For the moment, neither could he, but none of it answered the question of who had killed Leventhorpe and why.

Chapter Twelve

Two days later, Emmaline fidgeted inside Mile's closed carriage as the equipage rumbled slowly through the Mayfair streets toward Georgiana's Grosvenor Square residence.

"Is there a reason you are unable to sit still this evening?" he asked in a low voice with just the hint of a grin.

"It's nerves. Nothing more." She smoothed a gloved hand down the front of her gown and took comfort in the richness of the deep sapphire color of the satin bodice. "Knowing I wasn't officially invited has given anxiety the opportunity to take root." She arranged her skirts over her legs once more and the flash of the silver beading and embroidery on the ivory satin overlay caught her eye.

Of all the gowns she owned, this one was a favorite. The silver handiwork extended to the bodice and crisscrossed the fabric in bold swirls and dainty scrolls. Paired with long ivory gloves, heirloom sapphire jewelry and matching satin slippers, it was a striking ensemble guaranteed to draw eyes and turn heads.

After all, if she had to make an unannounced entrance, she wanted the assembled company impressed.

"You are coming as my invited guest," he said—again—and the confidence in his voice reassured her.

"Except your invitation didn't say to bring anyone," she reminded him and turned her face to the window. When she pulled back the black velvet panel, drops of rain streaked the window glass and she sighed. "Arriving with you gives quite the wrong impression. Of course it would have to rain."

"Look on the bright side. The gloom of the clouds will better provide you shadows as you skulk about the house." He leaned forward and patted her hand that lay on her knee. "Perhaps you'll be fortunate and find the mummy who is missing its hand."

Despite their gloves and her skirts, the heat from his skin seeped into hers. "We can only hope," she managed to squeeze out from a suddenly tight throat. Her mind revisited that morning in his parlor two days ago when he'd nearly kissed her. Even now, her lips tingled from where they'd brushed his.

What sort of man didn't follow through on a kiss?

"Also, I don't pay any mind to what impression people might take seeing you with me. Our history goes back to childhood. Why shouldn't I wish to seek you out in such a public capacity, especially since you plan to leave at the first opportunity?"

Why indeed? "There might be hurt feelings from ladies who wish to further a connection with you and become your next countess." What type of woman did he favor?

"I am not seeking a countess," he replied in a quiet, authoritative voice that didn't invite more speculation. "Not at the present time. Life is—"

"—rife with uncertainty, and you don't want to subject anyone else to the alleged cloud of misfortune hanging over your head?"

"Yes, something like that." Miles leaned back against the squabs as his grin widened. "Uncanny how you can read me."

"Not at all. Our thoughts travel much the same lines." She brushed again at her skirts. The design and cut of the gown mimicked an Indian style and that carried her mind to her father. Had he improved or did his condition worsen? *I really should return soon.* "Gah. It takes forever to travel anywhere in London."

"I realize I haven't known you for longer than a handful of days, but I can't help but think this anxious side of you isn't normal."

"It's not." She let the curtain fall into place and glanced at him. The man was positively splendid in black evening clothes. She especially adored the military-style cut of his jacket. It gave him a certain edge and would set him apart from every other gentleman. "However, I'll let you in on a secret not many people know about me."

"Oh ho! Another confidence you'll share with me." His chuckle filled the carriage interior. "I'm honored."

Emmaline nudged his leg with the tip of her slipper. "Suffice it to say I dislike appearing vulnerable in front of anyone. It takes away some of my control. Makes me seem less than I am." She huffed and her breath stirred the artfully arranged tendrils of curls on her brow. "Regardless, when it comes to people, especially those in equal or higher rank, I'm intimidated. I always having a sneaking suspicion they're judging me, judging my father, and finding me severely lacking." She gave into a shrug. "As if I don't matter and will never, regardless of what I accomplish in my life."

"The *ton* will always talk and follow gossip or rumors. They feed off it. Have a sick interest with it. Makes them feel superior to cut down others beneath their forked tongues." As the carriage passed a gaslight outside, his dark brown eyes glittered. "Do not let them pull you down to their level, Emmy. At times the *ton* is nothing better than gutter trash." The words echoed a speech he'd given her in Egypt long ago.

They'd sneaked about an ambassador's residence and listened beneath the open windows during a dinner, hosted by the ambassador for all the adult members of the *ton* who had wintered in Egypt that year. The old adage about listening at keyholes came to pass when they'd overheard a couple of the men ripping apart her father's academic reputation and his intelligence. She'd been devastated, as that was the first time she'd become aware of how her father was received in Society. Miles had consoled her, and then they spent the rest of the evening in the courtyard of her father's modest estate in Cairo inventing outrageous scandals for every one of those peers while eating an indecent amount of dates and figs dipped in honey.

"No happiness can be found in that direction." A nudge from his foot to hers brought her back to the moment. "Show them the gild of your heart and know you have a mission to complete."

Those words perfectly mirrored what he'd said all those years ago as well and brought her the same amount of comfort.

As the carriage rocked to a halt, Emmaline bit her bottom lip to stave off stupid, silly words that would show her in a bad light or worse, embarrass her when she had no right to utter such things. She couldn't afford to form an attachment to any man while the curse was still active. "Thank you. I appreciate the reminder."

"Never think you're anything less. No one can make you feel that way unless you let them." Miles swung open the carriage door before a footman arrived. He hopped out then waited as the steps were lowered. Turning toward her, he held out a hand into the carriage. "You are every bit as important as any of those people in there, and you're infinitely more interesting."

When she slipped her gloved fingers into his, her hand shook, and she hated that show of emotion. "I'll bear that in mind." She let him help her down, and a stab of disappointment moved through her when he released her hand immediately. "Though I'm hopeful I won't need to spend that much time with our peers."

"Lucky you." He waited as she shook out her skirts then fell into step beside her. "While I'm suffering through boring dinner conversation, you'll no doubt gallivant through Georgiana's home searching out treasure and finding adventure." He grunted as the front door was swung open and a middle-aged butler showed them inside. "Such freedom you have."

"The same could be yours if you'd just accept that's where your soul is pointing," she responded in a soft voice shortly before they were ushered into a lavishly appointed drawing room and sent down the receiving line, which cut all opportunities for more conversation.

Unfortunately, Emmaline's plan to immediately investigate the marchioness' home didn't take root. She was greeted with unaccustomed enthusiasm by Georgiana, who said she would gladly accept the last minute addition since she'd had a cancellation and her numbers were off.

Now, as she swirled her spoon through a bowl of creamed leek soup, Emmaline deeply regretted that she hadn't a chance to escape before being thrust into the mix of the dinner party. On her left was Lord Gastonberry, a pompous, round and balding fellow of undetermined years who talked incessantly of nothing but hunting and the dogs used therein. To her right, Viscount Darnell apparently had designs on seducing her into his bed no matter that she ignored his blatant whispers or repeatedly moved her foot from his.

Why I ever wanted to come back to London is beyond me.

Curse be damned, nothing was as interminable as this. When the soup bowls were whisked away by the butler and a maid, two footmen distributed various platters around the table as well as served each of the twelve diners a roasted partridge that rested next to a dollop of potatoes in mash. Emmaline welcomed the chance to look down the table and attempt to catch Miles' attention. In that, fate thwarted her as well, for he remained focused on Georgiana, at his right and at the head of the table, as she regaled the diners around her with a tale from her travels through the Orient.

You've bacon for brains, Miles, if you fall for anything she represents.

"The pheasant is a much greater challenge to shoot than a partridge," the lord on her left said with a jar to her elbow. "I'm anxious to return to the field," he continued around a mouthful of bird.

"Perhaps you should, as soon as possible," Emmaline responded before thinking. "No sense in hanging about here, wouldn't you say?"

The man's scraggly brown eyebrows rose. "Are you mad? Parliament is nearly in session."

"Pity. Imagine how many poor defenseless pheasants will escape your rifle's site." She rather enjoyed his slack jaw probably more than she should. Then, distaste crawled over her skin as the viscount put a hand on her thigh beneath the table and slid his hand upward. Careful to make certain no one saw her, she spirited her fork under the tablecloth and jabbed at the wandering hand. "Pardon, my lord, but I think you've misplaced your appendage, for its somehow come over to my chair."

God, just another reason she abhorred London and its upper-class residents. A title and full coffers did not grant anyone leave to do as they wished.

The viscount leaned close and whispered, "Don't play coy, Lady Emmaline. Everyone knows what sort of widow you are." He never once acted as if her defense caused offense.

Her stomach clenched. "What sort is that?" She jabbed him with the fork again, this time in his ribs. He winced and a thrill of victory climbed her spine.

The pain apparently didn't dissuade him from his purpose. "The sort who is willing to lift her skirts for the right incentive." He put his hand on her leg again and even went as far as to slide it along the apex of her thighs. "I've heard your family coffers are to let, and I wouldn't mind settling an income on you for a few nights a week in my bed."

The little dinner she'd eaten threatened a return trip. Emmaline swallowed hard to keep the urge at bay. "You've been misinformed, my lord," she answered through clenched teeth. "I'm not now, nor have I aspired to be, a kept woman." Her voice rose on the last few words and the low drone of conversation around the table slacked. One by one the diners turned their curious gazes on her.

Bloody hell.

"Oh, I'd tread carefully with her, Charles," Georgiana said into the heavy silence. Amusement threaded through her voice. "Why, not long ago she was under Lord Leventhorpe's protection, God rest his soul." A pout touched her lips. "And we all have heard about what happened to him. Perhaps it's the widow who is bad luck."

Hot anger filled Emmaline's chest at the slight. With quick, efficient movements, she shoved Lord Darnell's hand from her person then glared down the table. "I do apologize in correcting you at your own dinner, Lady Wellesley, but you must have listened to the wrong rumors." She ignored the few gasps that went up from some of the ladies present. What did it matter if she found herself in the gossip columns yet again? "I have had no dealings, scandalous or otherwise, with Lord Leventhorpe, but perhaps you have. Are you not also a widow who has been known to be a close contemporary to him?"

At Georgiana's side, Miles' eyes widened. Almost imperceptibly, he shook his head.

The marchioness lifted her wine glass, while red color blazed on her cheeks. "I am a widow, of course, though my tastes in men hardly run to the likes of Leventhorpe. He and I shared a business relationship only."

"What sort of business?" Miles inquired, and Emmaline threw him a grateful glance for pulling the attention from her.

"You jealous thing," Georgiana purred and smiled when a few of her friends tittered. "Put your mind to rest. Leventhorpe and I shared a love of art, and especially the work from a genius with canvas, a Monsieur Paul." She waved a hand at the wall to her back. "He did these two watercolors, and Leventhorpe owned some gorgeous oils of landscapes. I wonder what will become of them now. Perhaps I should have them relocated to my properties if his heirs don't want them."

Emmaline didn't care what her interests were. She ignored the low drone of conversation centering around art, and when Lord Darnell's wandering hand landed on her thigh once more, she uttered what sounded like a growl. She rounded on him, brandishing the fork still clutched in her hand. "If you touch me one more time, my lord, I swear I will stab you in the eye. At least then you'd only have one eye for roving and if you continue, I'll go after your hands." When he gaped and his mouth opened and closed like a caught fish, she smiled as if she were indulging in tea time banter instead of this disgusting display. "I trust my point has been made?"

"Only time will tell." His grin was decidedly lascivious as he raked his gaze over her bodice. "Spirited women like you need a man in their lives and beds. I'll wait. There will be an opportunity for you to change your mind." He turned to the diner on his other side.

You'll wait an eternity, then. Emmaline relaxed a fraction, even more when the lord on her left murmured, "Good show, girl." She forced a swallow then dropped her fork to the tabletop. Perhaps now would be a good time to feign megrim and take solace in wandering the halls for an empty room. Just as she opened her mouth to manufacture the excuse, Georgiana cut into her musings.

"How is your father, Emmaline?" she asked in an overly sweet voice. "The last I heard, he remained in Egypt, stubbornly clinging to his outrageous theories. Tell me, do you believe he's at death's door due to a curse, or is it another of his insane ramblings?" She glanced around the assembled company with a chuckle. "Perhaps he remains out of the country to avoid attending to his debts and obligations here in England."

"Now that is a bald lie, my lady." Her heartbeat accelerated. Slowly, she rose into a standing position. "My father may be many things, but he is far from mad. There is nothing wrong with his faculties."

"Be that as it may, he certainly has made a muck of his life, hasn't he?" A demure smile curved her lips. "And it seems as if you're following in his footsteps, if your unladylike behavior this evening is any indication."

A few chuckles went around the table.

"Regardless of current popular opinion, a lady can be many things and oftentimes a true lady doesn't fit into an acceptable mold." Emmaline curled her hands into fists. "And as a matter of fact, I'm proud to take after my father, for there is not another man braver or with more of a heart for the Egyptian people or their history." She glared at anyone who made eye contact with her. "All of us should strive to have as much compassion as him."

"A pity." The marchioness clicked her tongue and shook her head. "He spent the bulk of his life caring for other people yet not his own daughter. How many times did he leave you to your own devices in childhood because an Egyptian antiquity required his attention or one of his workers had an issue?"

"That's enough, Georgiana," Miles said, a warning in his low voice. "Leave her be. Emmaline's life is not up for your inspection or critique."

Warmth spread through her chest from his defense. Perhaps he was just as noble as her father. Hadn't he shown that already in the short time she'd become reacquainted?

The blonde turned a wide smile on him. "You're right, Lord Archewyne. No doubt Lady Emmaline already knows how lonely it is, being abandoned and left by everyone in her life. She's quite unlucky, it would seem, or else she's not as she portrays and people cannot abide to be with her. Perhaps she harbors a tainted soul." She patted Miles' hand where he'd laid it on the table between them, while Emmaline continued to quietly seethe. "Keep that in mind next time you pity her enough to invite her to dinner, hmm? I'd hate for disaster to befall you too; your absence from Society would surely be noted." The marchioness glanced at Emmaline. Pity and something else she couldn't identify gleamed in the other woman's eyes. "I don't think anyone would fault you for making your excuses this evening, dear."

"Enough, Lady Wellesley." Annoyance rang in Miles' voice. "She can stay for as long as she likes. She is my invited guest and therefore my responsibility this evening."

"I'd remind you whose home you're currently visiting, Archewyne." The marchioness frowned. "One would think there's something going on between you from the way you talk."

His eyes flashed. "We share nothing but friendship."

"Pish posh, Georgiana." The dark-haired woman on Miles' other side added, "What can you expect for a woman who hasn't been in Society for years? She was almost raised wild, from all I've heard. It's not like she's truly one of us."

Thank God for that.

Lord Gastonberry harrumphed so hard his double chin quivered. "Don't let those vipers scare you, my lady. Flaying the skin off others is all their tiny brains can handle. They hate others with intelligence, for it makes them look and feel stupid."

"I appreciate that, sir." But indignation still burned in her cheeks.

As she beheld the faces of the men and women who openly gawked and ogled with varying degrees of disgust and boredom in their expressions, Emmaline swallowed a few times to stave off the silly, stupid tears building in her throat. She had no reason to feel badly about her life or upbringing, yet when pitted against these dragons, her self-worth wavered. "No, I'm not like any of you. Think of how boring life would be if everyone were alike." The urge to give into the hysterical laughter building in her chest grew strong, for the members of the *ton* strove to be just the same as each other. "And yes, I may not have been within Society for years, but that doesn't mean I haven't contributed or been successful in my own way."

"Well, that is subjective." Georgiana sliced effortlessly into her partridge. "You've failed at marriage twice, haven't you?" She stabbed a bit of bird with her fork. "Or rather, your husbands have died. That's not exactly a success."

"I'm certain you're quite successful in other areas of life." Lord Darnell leaned close once more. "You know where to find me, Lady Emmaline. I have no fear of the curse."

"Bloody hell." Something inside her snapped. Before she could think the better of it, she shot out a hand and slapped the lord's face. At least that knocked the smirk from his lips, but the interest in his dark eyes didn't waver. "Thank you for the blatant offer, my lord, but I would rather die than let you touch any part of my body." Without another word, Emmaline turned and fled the room, never looking back.

Twenty minutes later, she took refuge in a library that was tucked away on the lower level toward the rear of the townhouse. The anemic light from one oil lamp didn't fill the shadowy corners of the room, and neither did she want it to. She welcomed the darkness, embraced the gloom that both hid and enveloped her. At times, her fellow man disappointed her and she wanted no part of their association.

"I'm a horrible person." If her mother could see her now, no doubt she'd express disappointment. Even her father, for all that he'd taught her to assert herself and strive for her dreams, would have gently rebuked her for the rudeness she'd shown tonight.

After moving farther into the medium-sized room, she briefly inspected a few shelves, but finding nothing more interesting than agriculture, politics through the ages or anything else an English lord might peruse to pass the time, she frowned then wandered over to the sideboard where a good collection of spirits resided.

If she were a man, she could take refuge in drinking away her troubles, but since she was not, being discovered imbibing would be the height of scandal and give the gossips even more fodder than she already had this night. No doubt the papers would be full of her antics at the table tonight, for at least one of those dragons would feed the information to the writers. She muttered under her breath then moved away in favor of approaching a grouping of leather sofas, settees and winged back chairs. More watercolor paintings decorated the walls, each sitting in thick gilt frames.

Men were afforded so many freedoms in the world. It was the height of annoyance that ladies were bound by separate and more stringent—and largely unfair—rules.

Good thing I've never put much stock into that sort of thing. Which is why she'd adored living in Egypt. She'd had her own life there, and no one told her she wasn't wanted or wasn't enough.

Throughout the room, many trinket boxes decorated the shadowy shelves. Did antiquities also rest among the books? The question recalled Emmaline to her task—searching for the missing mummy. Where the devil should she start, especially since the bedrooms would be on the second floor, and what if someone caught her as she passed the dining room?

No sooner had she crossed to the opposite side of the room than the door opened and softly clicked closed behind the intruder. She sucked in a breath and darted a glance to the frame. "Miles?" What was he doing here?

"Are you expecting someone else?" Caution infused his voice. Who did he identify with more—her or Georgiana's set—or did he think she'd actually encourage a clandestine meeting with the likes of Viscount Darnell?

"Of course not. After that whole disastrous scene, I'd rather not be with my fellow man in any capacity." She hated the waspish note in her tone but did nothing to soften the words.

"I don't blame you." Relief rang in his words. He advanced into the room toward her position. "I searched the whole of this floor before I finally found you. Why did you hide away here?"

"The mission, remember?" She rolled her eyes. "And I'm not hiding. I'm looking." Ha! What a lie. To change the subject, she rushed on. "How did you manage to escape the marchioness' claws? I thought she'd attempt to keep you close all evening." That sharp stab through her chest wasn't jealousy.

It wasn't.

"Georgiana is currently occupied with the other men she invited. She's never happier than when she's holding court and all eyes are on her."

"Yes, so I surmised. I'll wager she wants you in her court."

He frowned but didn't deny an interest. "I'd pledged my assistance to you, and I refuse to back down from that, regardless of another woman's wants."

"Ah." Was he truly oblivious to Georgiana's none-too-subtle hints? She eyed him as he closed the distance with slow, unhurried steps. "It was a mistake for me to come here."

"To the library of our hostess while we skulk about her home without permission?" He quirked a dark eyebrow and even in the gloom the wicked twinkle in his eye was unmistakable.

Her lips twitched. She refused to give into his attempt to cajole her. Perhaps she didn't wish to be cheered. Even by him. "No, I meant for me to accompany you this evening. I'm only in the way and a detriment." She brushed her fingers over the polished top of a slim table that ran the length of a sofa. A porcelain shepherdess statuette reposed at one end. A silver carriage-style clock marked the time at the opposite end.

"How so?"

Gah, he would want a deeper explanation. "Apparently, the marchioness didn't plan on dancing for her night's entertainment, which means she'll either continue to converse or resort to parlor games. I detest games and the subjects I'd talk about would surely bore her guests. You, on the other hand, could expertly take up any of those things and show nothing except polite attention." He truly belonged in that world. She did not.

"Ah, then you enjoy dancing?" He paused not two feet from her, his expression inscrutable. And he nicely avoided her observations. Bloody man.

"I…" Drat. She'd given him an opening into her life. When it became apparent he wouldn't move past the subject, she sighed. "Ever since I was sixteen, I wished a man would dance with me." Her cheeks burned with the confession. "I was still in Egypt at that age, and the one event I attended where there was dancing, none of the English young men paid me notice. It was vastly disappointing and that disappointment carried itself into England."

Not for worlds would she tell him he'd attended that same party and he'd been one of the boys who'd ignored her in favor of dangling after prettier girls. She'd been too much the outsider, and her skin, instead of the pale, creamy countenances of proper English girls, had been rather too sun-kissed. Add to that her penchant for plain speak and streak of adventure instead of insipid conversation and she'd been an instant pariah.

Emotion flared in his eyes, but she couldn't read it. "Your husbands never danced with you?"

"Not really." She laughed and the sound was forced. The events of the evening still sat heavily on her consciousness. "My husbands were both sweet and kind, but neither could master dancing. They simply hadn't had enough practice at it, and since they weren't *ton*, it wasn't a part of their upbringing. And honestly, there weren't many opportunities to bully them into it."

"Unfortunate, for every lady should indulge, whether or not there is an opportunity." He held out a hand. "Dance with me. Right here, right now."

She frowned. "Don't be a nodcock. We have no music."

He wriggled his fingers. "I'm quite efficient at dancing as well as humming, so none of your excuses are valid."

"You can dance?" She assessed him in the gloom, and in the shadows his shoulders appeared wider, his chest broader and his grin more tempting.

"I can." He pointedly looked at his hand then back to her. "Constance made certain I practiced with some regularity, for like you, she also enjoyed that form of exercise. She often scolded me for not throwing more parties or attending more *ton* functions, merely so she could dance. She used to say what was the point of having a title if one couldn't dance whenever they pleased."

Emmaline forced a swallow into her tight throat. "She wasn't wrong," she said in a low voice. How lucky his Constance must have been.

"Indeed." His soft laugh sent ripples of awareness over her skin. "There are times when I dance Jane around the room for the sheer enjoyment of it and to accustom her to it, for it will be part of her young womanhood."

"How lovely." An image of Miles and his golden-haired daughter flitted across her mind's eye, she standing on his boots and he twirling her about until her giggles filled the room. Her heart squeezed. Tears prickled the backs of her eyelids. Did he realize how fortunate he was? She focused her blurry gaze on him and he dropped his hand to his side. For him and his daughter, she would break the curse. They both deserved to find fulfilment.

It was too late for her own happiness.

"If you won't agree to a dance, perhaps you'll let me hold you? It's the one way I know that brings a woman comfort when her soul is weary and she's valiantly holding back tears." He came a few steps closer. "As you are now."

How could he know exactly how she felt? She nodded. "If you must." Again, a smile tugged at her lips.

"I must. I might be too starched in your opinion, but my mother was of the sort that suggested a comforting touch was infinitely better than awkward, empty words. Much to my father's chagrin." Then he was before her, and he slipped his arms around her waist. With little effort, he held her close and gently encouraged her head onto his shoulder. "Remember, while in Egypt, when we were told to avoid the asps beyond every other danger?"

"Yes." His jacket muffled her word, but she didn't care. She gave herself up to the sensations of being ensconced in his embrace, of the safety he imparted with nothing more than a hug. Heat from his body seeped into hers, both comforting and capable of setting fire to the tinder of awareness she had of him as a man. "What of it?"

"Certain members of the *ton* are the asps of Society. You'd do well to take care and avoid them too. I'm told their bites sting." His voice rumbled beneath her ear. "Their poison runs deeper than a snake and will linger for years in the blood."

Despite herself, Emmaline giggled. "You're right." After all, her mother's own demise was from one of the actual snakes and not of a member of the *ton*. "I have a dual-sided reason to be wary of any representation of such."

"You had no issue holding your own back there. I silently cheered you on even as the conversation rapidly spiraled out of control."

"Thank you." Pulling slightly back and tipping her head to peer into his face, she slipped her arms up his chest and locked her hands behind his neck. "Your analogy does put things into perspective." His praise made the viscount's wandering hand more than worth the aggravation.

"It does indeed," he whispered seconds before his gaze dropped to her mouth. "And I couldn't agree more." He lowered his head and claimed her lips in a tender kiss that both turned her knees to jelly and released a horde of butterflies within her belly.

When the embrace broke and he straightened, Emmaline blinked. She stared at him as confusion clouded her brain and shivers of need played her spine. A man bent only on friendship wouldn't have offered that sort of kiss, even as comfort. "Oh my." She didn't release her hold on him. Neither did he set her away as he should have. "I'll no doubt hate you tomorrow," she whispered.

Tuck your response away, my girl. He is not for you. Leave him alone so he may live out his days.

"Why?" Perplexity lined his face. The shadows couldn't manage to hide the way his eyes had darkened to the color of strong coffee. "Because of the kiss?" Ever so slightly, he drew abstract circles at the base of her spine, which played havoc with her ability to think clearly. What would his fingers feel like on her naked skin without clothing in the way?

"I confessed a secret to you I've never told anyone. Don't we all hate appearing vulnerable due to a simple truth?" But it was more than that. The longer she looked at him, the deeper she fell into the dark depths of his eyes and the more she wanted to lose herself as easily. Could she hide away in his embrace and let him keep her from the barbs the peerage slung her way? Those were her battles and she would fight those dragons herself. In her heart of hearts, she couldn't do it, couldn't let herself feel anything for him in order to keep him safe.

What a horrible thought.

Tears sprang into her eyes once more and this time she let them fall to her cheeks. The faster they came, the more undone she grew. She nestled into his chest and sighed when he tightened his arms around her. He'd held her thus in the sarcophagus. "I want to matter to someone, you know?" She burrowed her face into the wool of his jacket. The citrus and sage scent of him surrounded her, both familiar and arousing. "It's not possible with the curse. At times, I'd do anything to have it out of my life, to look forward to something that doesn't have to do with death." Her voice broke on the last word, and she hated that tell as much as the tears.

"Oh, Emmy. I've promised my help in breaking that curse. You are not alone in this." Miles held her away and put a hand beneath her chin, lifting her face until their gazes connected. He brushed at her tears with the pad of his thumb. "Regardless if the curse truly exists or not, you matter to me. Never think you do not." And he dipped his head, this time claiming a kiss that was neither gentle or in friendship. It set fire to her blood and sent hot moisture between her thighs.

God forgive me. I want him even though I cannot – should not – have him.

Chapter Thirteen

Miles smiled as he pulled slightly away. "I knew properly kissing you would be worth every ounce of retribution you might heap upon my head," he murmured and framed her face with his hands. Thank goodness he'd removed his gloves before gaining the library. Defying convention was worth the ability to touch her bare skin. He wiped away the remaining streaks of tears on her cheeks. Her lips were every bit as soft and plush as he'd thought, and though the tears discomfited him, he wished to banish them and cajole her into a better mood.

"The only vengeance I'll give is taking another," she answered in a voice as breathless as his while standing on tiptoe to indeed claim his lips as she'd warned. Just as she'd done in the British Museum, she kissed him with abandon, but this time was different. This time wasn't fleeting and neither was it in parting. When she ended the embrace, her breathing had elevated, but her smile was as bright and cheeky as ever. "You, Miles, are highly kissable. No wonder the marchioness is angling for your attention." That throaty, velvety voice reached out and grabbed him.

"Georgiana can go hang for all I care." His pulse pounded loud in his ears and his cock sprang to life with a renewed sense of purpose. How was it in less than a handful of days he'd managed to let her captivate him so perfectly? "I much prefer the adventure you represent." He crushed his lips to hers and spent the next few minutes acquainting himself with every inch of her mouth. When he probed the seam of her lips, she opened for him and he took full advantage, slipping his tongue inside and fencing with hers. A hint of the wine she'd had with dinner urged him onward.

Emmaline moaned. She pressed herself closer to him, never breaking their connection. He slid his hands to her back and moved them down until he cupped the rounded curve of her buttocks. She faltered. "Please don't stop." Her voice sounded so small and vulnerable, his chest squeezed.

"As if I could," he murmured and lifted her into his arms. *I've gone mad.* There was no other way to explain what had happened to him; he didn't give a jot to the fact their privacy here could be interrupted at any moment either. Three steps took him to a table that ran flush against the back of a sofa. He deposited her on it, regardless of the few trinkets that crashed to the floor, then drank from her lips again and again. She met each kiss, mimicked every thrust and parry of his tongue, mirrored each nip and nibble until his heartbeat raced and his breathing shallowed.

And it wasn't enough. This woman who'd beguiled him and tempted him since the night he found her in his library continued to tease him, and now his day of reckoning had come. He wanted her, plain and simple, and here she was, more than willing.

Miles couldn't think past the haze of desire. He left her lips in favor of nibbling a path along the inviting column of her throat. Her floral scent intoxicated him and she clutched at his lapels in an effort to keep him near. The underside of her jaw beckoned, so he planted a line of feather-light kisses there. The dip of her collarbone fascinated him, which prompted him to tarry there and lick the darling area. The creamy swell of her breasts called, and he couldn't live with himself if he didn't pay that satiny skin proper homage. When he followed the scooped neckline of her gown with kisses, a shuddery moan left her throat.

There would be no consequences if they were to indulge, for she was a widow.

As she tugged on his cravat, he cupped her breasts. "Look at me, Emmy." Her eyes fluttered open and she held his gaze with a soft smile on her kiss swollen, rosy lips. "I won't go any further without your permission." Regardless of the needs of his body, he was a gentleman and she a lady. Under no circumstances would he treat her as a wanton widow or do anything to give the *ton* reason to think her lacking morals.

"Then by all means ravish me. You have my enthusiastic support." He didn't move. Neither did she, and she heaved a sigh. "Touch me, my lord." One of her eyebrows arched as if in challenge and she pressed her hands atop his.

The saucy "my lord" spurred him into action, just as she'd no doubt planned. *Wench.* He grinned even as anxiety careened down his spine. He hadn't pleasured a woman in two years, really longer than that since he hadn't lain with his wife since she'd became with child. What if his skill had dulled?

Then the hardened buds of her nipples rubbed against his thumbs and he was lost. With a sound akin to a growl, he hooked his fingers into the soft material of her bodice as well as the petticoat beneath and tugged the neckline down until her breasts popped free, exposed and offered for his inspection. "Damnation, you're gorgeous," he whispered seconds before he dipped his head and took one of the pink tips into his mouth.

She whimpered and leaned back to give him greater access. "Mmm," Emmaline whispered while moving a hand to his nape and holding him to her.

Miles tumbled into the heady world opening around him. As he suckled one pebbled nipple, he rolled the other, and when her moans grew in volume, he claimed her lips with his once more, taking the sound into himself. It wouldn't do to alert someone to their presence. Desperation guided his actions as did the pressure throbbing through his aroused member. He fondled her breasts, delighted in the warm mounds of flesh, teased the hardened peaks with his thumbs while he continued his conquest of her mouth.

How was it possible this woman had brought him to such a pass so quickly? He had no idea, but he drank from her mouth as if she held the secrets to the universe and the only way to get at them was to caress them from her tongue.

"Miles…" Her throaty utterance drove him wild and further tightened his cock. She pulled him closer, and he settled between her splayed knees. Her skirts bunched between them as she locked her heels at his arse, effectively trapping him. "Let's move to a more comfortable place."

Ah, God. So close and he could bury himself in her wet heat. "I think I'll take you right here," he murmured and slid a hand up her thigh beneath the rumpled fabric. The silky glide of her thigh against his fingers urged him onward until the soft lace edging her drawers tickled the back of his hand. He sucked in a breath then dared scandal by slipping his hand between her thighs. Heat from her body seeped through the fine lawn of her undergarments and was stimulating enough, but his wandering fingers found the slit in the drawers and with it, her slick arousal.

Bloody hell, she's ready. "It would be fitting and adventurous for us, wouldn't you say?" Unable to stop touching her, he planted a line of baby kisses along the slender column of her throat as he glanced a finger along the still-buttoned opening of the garment.

"There might be hope for you yet." She gave into a shudder.

He nipped the spot where her shoulder joined her neck. It took a mere two flicks of his finger to undo the few buttons. "Meaning?" Why were they still talking when they could be employed in much more pleasurable pursuits?

"The longer you associate with me, the greater likelihood I'll break you of the habit of being a proper, rule-following lord." She caressed a hand down his back and when she came to his rear, squeezed a cheek. "Responsibility is fine in its place, but there is something to be said for following your passion."

Heated desire shot through his member, but her words gave him pause. Despite their every meeting being less than orthodox, did that mean he was essentially leaving who he was behind? He stilled with his lips hovering above one of her nipples. His pulse rushed hard and loud through his ears.

Miles stared down at her. With her flushed skin, her well-kissed lips, the ardent need in her emerald eyes, her skirts rucked up to her waist, and her white stockings and blue ribbons garters on display, she was every bit a woman in the throes of lust. What else could it be? They certainly didn't hold deep feelings for each other.

Which meant they shouldn't indulge in a quick, cheap coupling that had no merit. After everything, he'd never been a rogue, even if he'd been the second son.

"Botheration." He pulled away, then took another two steps from her as he raked a hand through his hair. "We cannot do this. I refuse to do this." Blasted conscience. "I apologize, but after all I'm not able to forget that I *am* a proper gentleman and I *will* respect your honor."

Cursing himself, he pivoted and walked away from her, or rather, he moved with what little dignity a man could have with a painfully aroused cock pressed tight against the front of his dress trousers. Once he gained the sideboard, Miles yanked a glass snifter from the polished mahogany then poured out a healthy portion of fine French brandy.

"Apparently, more work is needed in order to coax you to accept that you're different than most of the *ton*," Emmaline said in a soft voice.

He faced her but didn't move from the sideboard. She'd left her perch on the table and had put the bodice of her gown to rights. Pity, that. Such perfect breasts should never be covered. *Damn it, man, stop thinking about her in that way!* To distract himself, he took a few swallows of the brandy then, realizing the glass had been drained, he poured another two fingers. "Perhaps I'm not all that different."

"What makes you think so?" Her eyes glittered in the dim light as she advanced as far as a leather winged back chair. She rested a hand on its top.

"I still want you." Something about her managed to pull the deepest, darkest confessions from him.

"Yet you stopped the session before it went anywhere." She moistened her lips and he drowned a groan with another sip. "If you were like most men of the peerage, you wouldn't have given consideration to my reputation, or what remains of it."

"Bravo to me." Bitterness rang in his voice. He left the sideboard. "You should go. If someone finds us here together, despite my best efforts, word will get out and your reputation will be sliced to ribbons anyway. They'll think you a wicked widow." He dropped heavily into the wingback chair beside hers. "You'd be fair game to unsavory advances."

"Honestly, those gossips will think and believe whatever they want. Did the dinner conversation not prove that already? The trick is to ignore them and live your life the way you see fit." She came around the side of his chair and trailed her fingers over his shoulder. "Don't worry about philandering lords. I can handle myself." She gazed at him, the emotions in her eyes inscrutable. "What sort of man are you? Which man would you be if no one was looking? What man do you dream of becoming?"

The questions, spoken in her low, throaty voice, speared through him like darts. "I don't know." At least it was honest. He took a sip of the brandy and reveled in the burn as it slid down his throat. Beyond his desire for her, if their association was found out, she'd be a weakness, a way for unsavory people to get to him, leverage that could compromise future missions.

"What sort of man do you wish to be tonight?" In a flurry of skirts and the rasp of satin, Emmaline joined him on the chair. She bunched her dress then straddled his lap before he could protest or even prevent it.

"Bloody hell, woman." His arousal pulsed. The slight weight of her felt right and heated him as nothing else. "I cannot think like this." What the deuce was she trying to do to him?

"Then don't." It only took gentle pressure for her to tug the glass from his fingers. "I don't want proper." As she held his gaze, she lifted the tumbler to her lips then drained the liquid. The tendons in her throat moved with her swallows. She set the tumbler onto a low table at his elbow. "I don't want a commitment or forever."

He couldn't breathe. He could barely exist. With her body pressed intimately to his, she'd have to be daft not to feel the evidence of his desire for her. "What do you want from me, Emmy?" The question rasped from a dry throat. "Please enlighten me, because I don't know, and the longer I sit here with you, the longer we're in such a position, the less strong I am." Not knowing what else to do with his hands, he rested them on the delicate flare of her hips. Which proved to be a bad decision when he enjoyed the feel of her beneath his fingers, so he gripped her with tighter force.

"Then stop being strong. I'd adore seeing you a touch wicked and slightly undone." Her grin held a roguish edge. "Ever since you kissed me in that tomb all those years ago, I've known you weren't like all the other peers or children of those peers. I admired you then, and still do." While she talked, she worked the buttons of his jacket from their holes.

God, such a memory at a time like this. He'd been so nervous then, had thought about stealing a kiss from her before she departed for England for the last time. When he finally got her alone in that tomb, he took advantage and botched it. In his defense, it had been his first attempt, and he'd carried the sweet taste of her lips with him for years. Funny how she tasted as sweet now. "What does any of that have to do with us here now?" If she moved the wrong way, he'd spend and embarrass both of them.

She leaned forward until their lips barely touched. "For this one moment, I want to feel needed by someone. For this one night, I want to forget that I'm alone and probably will be for the rest of my life, however long that will be. I want to forget that everyone I care for leaves me for death's embrace." She held his gaze and hers sparkled with emotion he still couldn't read. "For the next few minutes, I don't want to think at all. I only want to feel, to remember I'm alive." Ever so slowly, she layered her lips to his. Once the kiss ended, she lightly bit his bottom lip then released him. "I need you."

The whispered plea battered at his resistance. She hadn't said want; she'd said need. That was a stronger pull than a mere craving. "This isn't right." He'd try, once more, to skirt scandal.

"Who can say what is right or wrong, Miles? We are both complicated beings in a disordered and oftentimes unfair world. Why shouldn't we find solace in each other?" She slipped a gloved hand between their bodies and ran her fingers along the bulge at the front of his trousers. "Please."

If it hadn't been for the slight wobble of her chin or the wink of the dimple in her right cheek, he would have clung to gallantry and urged her from his lap. He would have gently but firmly escorted her from the house, bundled her into his carriage and made certain she arrived home unmolested. Yet, that tell had always gone straight to his soul; it was the one thing she did when upset, and she probably wasn't aware of that. It was no less effective now.

And it made him lose his mind.

"Emmaline Darling, you'll be the death of me." He kissed her with all the desire raging through him. And after this it would make it all the more difficult to hold her at arm's length for her own safety. "Where?" he asked against her lips.

"Here." Quickly, she manipulated the buttons of his frontfalls and when his engorged member sprang free, she wrapped her fingers around his length. "Naughty boy, hiding such impressive equipage away."

Miles gave into a full-body shudder. The touch of her hand, regardless of the glove she wore, coupled with her teasing words, became his undoing. "So says the woman who has her fingers around said equipage. Now that *is* the height of scandal." And it impressed the hell out of him. Never had he seen a more emboldened woman.

She rose up on her knees and released her grip. "No more talking. We've already been away too long. The marchioness will wonder what has become of her play thing." Once she gathered her skirting out of her way, she took him in hand again, guiding his tip to the slit in her drawers.

Georgiana could go to the devil for all he cared, and he certainly didn't want to think of her right now. "Do you wish to tease or do you want to get to it straightaway?" God that sounded crass and a touch desperate. He adjusted his position, which glanced his cockhead against her slick folds.

With the devil's own gleam in her eyes, Emmaline in her typical adventurous fashion took him more firmly in hand then impaled herself on his length. She bore down without stopping until he was fully embedded. "Oh my," she breathed with wonder in her whispered tone. Pleasure lined her expression. Her eyes dilated with desire. "So marvelous."

"Indeed." He groaned, for by God, this was one of the best things he'd ever experienced. Constance had been a gentle, timid lover who had never once initiated a coupling. They'd shared an idyllic sort of intimacy, but it had not been blood-pumping excitement. There was nothing of his wife in Emmaline, and that both terrified and invigorated him.

Emmaline wriggled, presumably to seat him more comfortably. She rested her hands on the back of the chair at either side of his head and smiled into his face. "I suspected you'd be quite satisfying when we were together in the sarcophagus." Then she moved, stealing away his ability to comment.

Slowly, almost experimentally, she slid along his shaft, her slick arousal easing the passage. Each time she came down, his stones tingled and need raced through his cock. Despite her façade of confidence and plain speaking, in this matter, Emmaline held back. Her muscles tensed but she didn't throw her whole self into the act.

Why?

Intrigued but almost gone from the shuddering sensations crashing over him, Miles renewed his grip on her hips. "Let me help." His ragged request seemed to echo in the empty room. "Move against me, not with me." To help her understand, he urged her downward while at the same time thrusting up. "It's much like making love in a bed except we're vertical."

Yet, this scenario wasn't exactly that. There was no love exchanged and neither did they share this most special of acts out of deeper feelings. This was giving in to a mutual need, slaking lust with heated comfort.

Nothing more.

Sudden understanding lit her eyes and she nodded. "Quite," she said seconds before she uttered a low moan.

They moved in a dance as old as time, and with frantic intensity and friction until their painting breath broke the calm and mutual moans provided background music.

"Miles, hurry." Her whisper warmed his ear as she pressed herself closer.

If he pushed any faster, his damn prick would fall off. But for her, he obliged. He dug his fingers into her hips as she bounced on his lap, her head lolling onto her shoulder, her eyes half closed, her cheeks flushed. "I'm done for." The point of no return had been achieved, for he'd been primed past endurance this night. Intense sensations raced through his shaft. It pulsed and twitched, but he gritted his teeth. He would not finish before her, even if his honor had already been misplaced.

Desperate to spend, he delved a hand between them and around the superfluous fabric. When he found the damp slit in her drawers, it took next to no time to rub a fingertip over the swollen bundle of nerves at her center. At her rapid inhalation, he kissed her and took her cry into his mouth. She shattered in his arms. The walls of her channel quivered and fluttered around his cock, intent on pulling him deeper.

Miles' own release exploded into being, and as his member emptied, he ground his hips into hers while chasing the last bit of exquisite feeling. When she collapsed fully against his chest, he wrapped his arms around her and held her close. Emmaline's heartbeat raced as quickly as his; her frayed breathing steamed his ear. The heat of her skin seeped through her gown and warmed his fingers.

Hellfire and damnation. What kind of bacon-brained idiot was he that he couldn't summon enough self-control to refuse an indulgence into such madness? Though… A satisfied grin curved his lips. What a delicious moment of insanity it had been.

Her earlier utterance filtered into his euphoria-soaked brain. *… I don't want proper and I don't want a commitment…* Still, servants' eyes were everywhere. There was every chance word of this interlude would leak out, and then what? He refused to leave her to the wolves of the *ton* and would die before he'd see villains like Viscount Darnell touch her or treat her as a fast widow. Too bad he hadn't been more mindful of prying eyes before.

I'll ask for her hand tomorrow. And come up with a good explanation for Lord Liverpool the next time he was summoned before the powerful lord to defend his country.

She stirred and pulled slightly back in order to peer into his eyes. "Thank you."

His chest tightened then subsequently burned with guilt. He didn't want gratitude for something he shouldn't have done in the first place. "Emmy, we should discuss what we'll do now." God, how would Jane take the news? Briefly, his mind dwelled on the possibility of the curse being real. If he and Emmaline were to wed, despite the reasons for the union, would the curse transfer to him, or if it already was working in his life, would it intensify?

"I agree." With a smile, she edged off his lap and he regretted the loss of her warmth, the weight of her. "For the time being, you'll return to the dinner party while I root around Georgiana's home and search for the mummy. It'll be easier if I go alone since two of us would be missed and make too much noise." She shook out her skirts so they fell in modest lines as if nothing untoward had occurred.

"That's not what I meant." Miles tucked his now flaccid member into his trousers then did up the buttons. He vaulted to his feet, but she'd already scuttled across the floor toward the door. Hadn't he closed it when he came in? He frowned and planted his hands on his hips. Perhaps it had come open by itself, for it only yawned six inches or so.

"Oh, I know what your proper heart and belated honor meant, and quite frankly, I reject anything that comes from you based in guilt." She patted her hair, absently tucking escaped tendrils into the upswept style.

"Yet, what we've done here tonight..." He gestured between him and her. His jaw worked.

"Was nothing more than you giving comfort to me when I needed it." She gazed at him from over her shoulder. Her eyes glittered, but he couldn't read the emotions in the gloom. "Please don't feel you have to do what you feel is right by me. I'm content being a widow, and until the matter of the curse is cleared, I'm not in the market for a husband."

"But—"

"No." Emmaline faced him and held up a hand. "Miles, tonight was not an effort to trap you or force your hand. I..." She bit her bottom lip and he stifled a groan, for he well remembered what those plush lips felt like beneath his. "I enjoyed every minute spent in your company and I'm glad you were there when I needed you the most."

If another man had followed her into the library, would she have needed him just as much? He refused to think upon that. "Fine. I'll grant this isn't the time or place to discuss our future—"

"Of which we won't have if the curse isn't lifted," she interrupted with an arch of an eyebrow.

"—but know this," he continued as if she hadn't spoken. "I intend to call on you tomorrow."

"Stubborn man."

"Honorable man," he corrected. By God he'd do what was right. But when the needs of the Crown trumped hers? Would she understand if he suddenly had to quit England at a moment's notice for God knew how long?

"Bugger." Her huff sounded overly loud in the room. "Do manage to call after eleven. My mornings are quite busy." Distant footsteps in the hall tugged her attention from him. "I'll meet you at the carriage in an hour. Hopefully, we'll have an answer." Then she exited the room without a backward glance, leaving him alone as if he'd done nothing more with her than executed a dance.

The answer to what? How the deuce had his life gone so off kilter in the span of four days? *The woman will be the death of me. Literally.* He hoped to the devil it wouldn't be true.

And he still didn't bloody know who killed Lord Leventhorpe. What the hell sort of agent was he?

Chapter Fourteen

"Aha!" Emmaline would have danced in triumph if she hadn't been wedged between a broken longcase clock, a giant brass urn filled with what looked like glass stones and a mummy case made of cartonnage—a linen papyrus blend that allowed the case to mold more evenly to the deceased. It was the second of two cases crammed into an upstairs bedroom.

She'd managed to pry open the case, thrust a hand into the small space afforded her in the tight quarters and feel around until she found a femur. Once she'd followed the bone down to the wrist and then encountered nothing, there was no more doubt this was the priest's wife.

Leave the house, Emmy, before it's too late.

So easily could she explore the rooms and make a mental catalogue of the antiquities piled inside, but she'd lingered long enough already. Slowly, she slipped from her hiding place then tiptoed over the plush carpeting toward the door. If she didn't hurry, Miles would depart without her. What would she do then?

As she pulled the door open a crack in order to listen, Emmaline allowed her thoughts to dwell on the man. A warm flush stole over her body. What they'd done in the library had been nothing short of scandalous and wanton, but oh how wonderful it had been, and it had been completely what she'd needed at the time. Everything she'd told him was true, and now? Well, if she knew anything about men and Miles especially, he'd be sitting in that carriage battling his conscience and debating on how he'd demand she marry him.

Despite the circumstances, a tiny smile tugged at the corners of her mouth. He was too proper and starchy for his own good, but sooner or later he'd see they would never suit, not for a lifetime. His life lay in England and in doing things the traditional way for the good of his title and the people he looked after while her path would send her around the world to investigate history and its unsolved cases for the good of those peoples.

That's how life was. Sometimes paths didn't converge forever.

Her stomach clenched, but she ignored the discomfort. Anything between her and Miles needed to remain a diversion, a momentary descent into madness, for to think it might grow into anything else would be a cruel tease. Her luck with the opposite sex, whether curse driven or fortune given, wasn't good. With silent movements, she slipped from the room and stole down the hall only to pause at the banister.

Female voices drifted up to her. Departing guests, no doubt.

"... Georgiana has her sights set on the earl. Make no mistake. She'll have him by the holidays..."

"... She could have at least given some of us a chance with him. Georgiana's already been married once..."

Emmaline frowned. *I had no idea Miles is so sought after.* Of course he was. He wasn't some doddering old lord, and he was certainly still attractive. Any woman worth her salt would try to attach herself to him. Her chest tightened. It was one thing to think Georgiana had gone on pursuit. If his words of earlier were any indication, he didn't return her regard. But to have confirmation other women would welcome a suit from him? *I cannot think of that now. It's not my business besides.*

Yet she'd encouraged him, teased him into intercourse on a whim because she'd let her emotions get the better of her, and in their hostess' library no less. Would that ruin his chances with one of those hopeful ladies who he had every right to want to align himself with? *It cannot happen again.* No matter that she found him appealing and different than other men and interesting in his own right, she must keep their interactions cool and professional.

His life depended on it as well as her sanity. She couldn't bury another man she'd become close to.

"… Lord Leventhorpe should thank his stars he's dead and not dealing with one such as the marchioness…" The woman's voice redirected Emmaline's thoughts.

How *did* Georgiana know Leventhorpe and was it more intimately than socially? She sucked in a breath. How often had she visited or seen the lord? Would anyone accuse the powerful marchioness of having a hand in his death if she was more than a contemporary?

Fat chance, that, Emmaline. She rolled her eyes at herself. In matters concerning the *ton*, there needed to be implicit proof. And the bald fact was, Leventhorpe wasn't a good person. More people than she knew probably hated the man.

Most likely, the peerage would never know who put an end to his life or why. It was a matter those austere members would want closed and forgotten with alacrity.

Then the two women moved out of Emmaline's range of hearing. She scuttled down the stairs and again, looking for lingering dinner guests or worse, Georgiana, she shot to the lower level and darted through the door, past the frowning butler and into the blessedly cool night air. By the time she gained Miles' familiar carriage with the Archewyne crest painted on the dark door in gold and navy paint, the night had swallowed the outlines of the few departing conveyances.

"It took you long enough," he hissed as he swung open the door and helped her up with a hearty tug on her arm. "I was about to let Giles return home, but my honor demanded I wait for you even if you were gone a deuced long time."

That honor would land him in the drink if he wasn't careful. "And a good evening to you too," she quipped, sitting down harder than expected when the carriage lurched into forward motion. She took a moment to rearrange her skirts over her legs. "I apologize for the time it took, but it was put to good use. I found the priestess." As quickly as she could, she related her discovery. "Obviously, I couldn't smuggle it out while she's in residence."

"Goddamn it. Georgiana had it all along." Miles curled the hand resting on his knee into a fist. "How the hell did she get her hands on Leventhorpe's mummy?"

Emmaline shrugged. As much as she wanted to lean across the aisle and squeeze his hand in comfort or reassurance, she remained in place. "There's every possibility she indeed forgot she had it. That room was crammed full of things." She arched an eyebrow. "Which we should either coax her to donate or demand she return to their countries of origin."

"Listen to yourself, Emmaline." Miles shook his head and in his apparent agitation, he shoved a hand through his hair, leaving furrows in his wake. "You sound deranged." He rubbed that hand along his jaw. "We both do. She's a blasted marchioness. Neither of us can barge into her house and demand she do anything. Already we're flirting with disaster from that quarter."

With a huff, Emmaline crossed her arms over her chest and flounced back into the squabs. "Be that as it may, the marchioness has a room, maybe more, of antiquities that do not rightly belong to her. Now you know of their existence, so if you ignore those facts, it's on you if you choose to do nothing about it."

"Do shut up, my lady," he said with a hearty grumble in his voice.

She caught her breath at his slip back into formality when not an hour before they'd been extremely intimate. Why did quick tears sting her eyes? She rapidly blinked away the telling moisture. "I beg your pardon?"

"I simply cannot take on that problem among the others that have cropped up since meeting you." He turned his attention to the window where the velvet drapes had been parted. "For this drive home, allow me peace. I must think."

Home. The place where a person felt welcome and loved. A spot where laughter rang and humor abounded. Much different from her cold, empty townhouse that was a drafty and threadbare as a beggar's pockets. Suddenly she didn't wish for him to see the interior of her home, not after witnessing the dripping opulence of the marchioness' residence.

"I apologize for ruining your evening, *my lord*." She emphasized that last bit merely to annoy him further, but for the first time she truly looked upon him, studied him as she would a scrap of papyrus to understand the hieroglyphics. That's exactly what he searched for in life—peace. He wanted to live and let live, except the curse kept him in a constant state of worry and wondering even if he wouldn't admit it. That and something else she caught lurking at the backs of his eyes occasionally spurred her curiosity.

What other secrets did he keep and why did she want to know?

Her heart tripped and she hated she felt even that sympathy, for the longer she remained in his life, the more likely he'd never find that quiet. Instead, she sought to poke at his ire and thus keep him from thinking he felt anything else for her. "One would think that after having intimate relations with the ever-present threat of scandal lurking and the pure intensity such a thing caused that your mental attitude would have vastly improved." Except, in her case, the releasing of emotions found in spending had dimmed and a blasted ache in her chest kept her company.

How annoyingly inconvenient.

In the dim illumination from a gaslight they passed, the corner of his mouth turned upward slightly. However, all he said as a rejoinder was, "I intend to call upon you at eleven o'clock sharp tomorrow morning. Do be certain you calm the turmoil that surrounds you enough to receive me."

And just like that, he shook off his adventurer's persona and cloaked himself with the glamour of the stuffy, responsible lord.

She stifled a sigh. Annoying indeed.

At eleven o'clock exactly the next morning, Emmaline glanced up and her belly tightened with anxiety. The sound of shuffling footsteps at the doorway of her morning room preceded the ancient Thompson's arrival.

He had arrived.

And she didn't particularly care to hear what he'd say to her, especially not if his grumpy mood from the night before lingered.

Her butler cleared his throat at the door. "Lady Emmaline, Lord Archewyne is here to see you. I've shown him into the gold parlor. Or would you rather I usher him here?"

Oh, good heavens. She shot a glance about her sanctuary on the midlevel of the townhouse. Shabby pale pink curtains at the windows matched the worn and equally shabby Oriental carpet done in pastels. The furniture, though dear to her heart and put her in mind of her mother, showed is age and was unmatched. A few of the legs on the settees had gnaw marks from where Sanura had teethed on them. A rush of doubt raced down her spine as she slowly gained her feet. "That won't be necessary. I'll see him in the parlor. Thank you, Thompson."

"Very well, my lady." The servant turned then made his ponderous way along the corridor then finally down the stairs.

Without the butler present to calm her nerves, Emmaline's pulse beat out a frantic rhythm. She smoothed her palms over her skirts. Was the garnet color too bright, too bold? Did it brand her a fast woman? As she reached the doorway, she tucked a few escaped tendrils of hair into the loose chignon. Would he see the threadbare state of her townhouse and judge her for it? She took two steps into the corridor and paused again. Compared to the brilliant and bejeweled marchioness, would she be found lacking and dowdy?

Stop those thoughts at once, Emmaline. You won't accept his suit anyway, so none of that matters.

After a deep inhale, she slowly released the air from her lungs and nodded. He might be here on guilty honor, but she operated on determined resolve. First and foremost, she needed to break the curse and if possible, save her father. Until that had been accomplished, anything personal she wished to pursue would have to wait.

Even if that meant losing the earl's newly found friendship or seeing him wed to someone else in the meantime.

With a tight chest, Emmaline continued on and when she gained the staircase, she pinched her cheeks for a little color and bit her lips for the same effect. It wouldn't do to appear wan and worried. On the ground level, she took a step toward the parlor when a feline growl halted her progress. "Sanura? What are you doing down here?"

The lion cub growled again and pawed at floor near the front door.

"What is it?" She changed direction and headed for her cat instead of the parlor. At times, the lion tracked a mouse to earth or found a particularly interesting bug to bedevil. "What do you have?" The wink of beadwork on a tiny scrap of fabric caught the morning light. Emmaline frowned, for she didn't recognize it from one of her gowns. The beautiful dove-gray silk held a fine sheen in the sunlight. The crystal beads alone were worth a small fortune. "Let me have it, silly cat." She dislodged the scrap from the lion's claws. Had someone of consequence called while she'd been out and run into the cat? As she crossed the entry hall an odd creaking noise sounded overhead followed by the tinkling of crystals in the chandelier.

A quick glance upward was the only warning she had. With a cry, Emmaline took a few stumbling steps out of the way as the light fixture came crashing to the hardwood.

In the aftermath, bits of crystal littered the floor like tiny broken windows in the sun. The metal structure of the chandelier lay amidst the glass, a sad, dark skeleton of its former framework. The silence left behind was deafening. Sanura, startled from the noise, had run for parts unknown. Emmaline stared at the mess, vaguely aware of Thompson approaching her location.

"Are you all right, my lady?" the elderly butler inquired in a voice that shook. His eyes were as wide as hers felt.

"I think so." Though her knees were decidedly wobbly. She crushed the fabric square in her hand. Had she not moved because of Sanura, the thing would have fallen directly onto her head, rendering her wounded, surely, and perhaps even fatally thanks to the arrow-shaped shaft that pierced through the whole contraption. Shards of crystal lay at the toes of her slippers. So close yet no harm done, yet her heart still beat wildly.

"Damn and blast, what's happened here?" Horror punctuated the exclamation.

She looked down the hall as Miles jogged toward her, his gaze taking in the scene before alighting on her face. "Apparently, the chandelier decided to give up the ghost." It wasn't out of the realm of possibility that the fastenings holding into place on the ceiling were as old and worn out as the rest of the house. "An accident, nothing more."

The earl offered an outstretched hand. Concern shone in his dark eyes. "Come away from the mess."

She glanced at him then at her butler. "Ask Sarah to help with the clean-up," she instructed in a quiet voice. "You know how marvelous she is with a broom." If she let him think that, then her request wouldn't hurt his feelings.

"Very well, my lady."

Only then did she grasp Miles' hand, her own shaking, and let him escort her into the parlor. Once ensconced in that room, she collapsed into the first chair she came to. "I'll admit, that discomfited me more than I'd like."

"Have you previously seen evidence the light fixture was unstable or would need replacing imminently?" Miles didn't sit. Instead, he clasped his hands behind his back and paced the space between her chair and the parlor door.

"Not that I've been aware of." She cringed as she followed his path with her gaze. Did he see the shabby state of the Aubusson carpet beneath his feet, note the threadbare spots on the gold-upholstered furniture that once was shiny and bright years ago? "Why?"

"I'm not sure, but it seems odd, given the circumstances that threw us together a handful of days ago, that your chandelier has suddenly malfunctioned." When he pivoted to return toward her, their gazes locked and one of his eyebrows arched.

"What are you saying?" With more resolve, she rose slowly. When he hesitated, she sucked in a breath. "Surely not the curse?"

He snorted. "I'm not convinced there is such a thing. However," he held up a hand, "I'm willing to admit it might be more than a coincidence."

"It could be merely that. I mean, I employ only two servants and both of them I trust with my life. I highly doubt either of them want to injure or kill me." A sick feeling rolled through her stomach. "And if not them, then who? I haven't seen anyone in the house…" In fact, no one ever visited her here. Miles was the first in many years.

"That you're aware of." If his frown grew any fiercer, he'd be mistaken for a thundercloud. He flicked his gaze to the scrap of fabric in her hand. "What's that?"

Weakly, she held it out to him, being careful not to brush his fingers when he took it from her. "Sanura had it, and if I hadn't gone after her to investigate, the chandelier would have…" She waved her hand and let him come to his own conclusion.

"Interesting." He rubbed the fabric between his thumb and forefingers. "This isn't from one of your gowns?"

"No." She shook her head. "I own nothing in gray. Once I set mourning aside, I never wanted to go back."

"I agree with you on that, at least." He tucked the scrap into an interior jacket pocket. "Rich colors are best suited for you." For long moments, he rested a speculative gaze on her, clouded with emotion she couldn't read. "In the future, I recommend being more vigilant."

"Good advice." Silence reigned between them, boiling into uncomfortable territory. Why wouldn't he say something else, anything else, either in censure or comfort? Finally, unable to stand his intense gaze without the buffer of conversation, she blurted, "The urgency to bring those mummies back to Egypt cannot be ignored any longer." She twisted her hands together. "Now that I know where the priestess is, I can easily—"

"Emmaline, enough." He chopped at the air with a hand. "I am not here to discuss whether or not the curse exists."

"Ah. I'd hoped you'd changed your mind." She brushed two cat hairs from her bodice and shivered.

Perhaps she should have brought a shawl down with her. A chill had pervaded the house and the tension between them didn't help.

"I have not." He laid a hand on the back of her chair. "Please, sit." He gestured to the chair. "There is much to talk about."

Her knees wobbled again, but not out of fear or relief. Without a word of protest, she sank into the chair and fervently wished the cushion wasn't quite so worn out. At least she could have comfort for her rear end while receiving unpleasant news. To add insult to injury, Miles didn't sit. Instead, he lurked at her side so she was forced to crane her neck and look up at him. She cleared her throat. "Perhaps you should make yourself comfortable if you intend to do this."

"I do intend and I don't need to be comfortable." His frown remained in place though he did once more clasp his hands behind his back. "Especially after the whole affair of the chandelier."

"What of it?"

"You need a protector."

Emmaline uttered a most unladylike snort. "And you want that position?" When he merely stared at her, she shook her head. "It was a freak accident. Nothing more. If had you been here, you couldn't have prevented it. How could you have known?" Yet the seeds of doubt were planted. If it wasn't an accident and it wasn't part of the curse…

"Marry me."

"No."

"I mean it, Emmaline. I strongly suggest we marry." A hint of the earl he was rang in the statement.

Could an offer be given any more stiffly and without soft or positive emotion? She sighed. "What of Jane? I've barely met her and haven't spent time with her. Shouldn't we see how that would work? It's ill-advised to install a new mother into a household without introducing your child to her."

He focused his gaze on her shoulder. "I'm hopeful that over the course of a short engagement she will become accustomed to you. That being said, you and she will spend time together in due course." A muscle in his cheek twitched.

"Ah, how flattering. Hoping that your daughter will acclimate to me. Why, I can almost feel the affection." She shook her head. "Don't do this, Miles. It's not what you want."

A tick under his left eye flared. "At this point in time, it doesn't matter what I want—in many things. We must marry."

What else did the man grapple with, and why did he keep such things to himself? Done with feeling ridiculous staring up at him, she clambered from the chair and faced him over said piece of furniture. "We're not in love."

Emotion flared in the depths of his eyes, gone so quickly she couldn't identify it. "Most *ton* marriages don't have love involved and go on to become successful."

"Successful, not embedded in romance." Emmaline gawked at him. Is that what he truly believed? How very sad to go through life with that mindset. "That's not a selling point for me. I'm not like most of the *ton,* and I disdain the practice of marrying for money, power or position. Or convenience. Don't ask that of me because we both know you'd regret it as soon as the vows were recited."

He rested both hands on the back of the chair with a grip so hard the fabric dented beneath his fingertips. "Love doesn't matter now, does it? It didn't matter last night either. After what we've done..." His jaw worked. He softly cleared his throat. "We should marry, *especially* after what we did."

"No, we shouldn't." Her chest tightened. "We did what we wanted in a moment of mutual need." A catch entered her voice. Had she pushed her advantage knowing he'd crumble once desire flared? Perhaps, but her emotion in the library had been all too real and she'd been weak as well. "What we shared is not wrong, and it's not something that warrants immediate matrimony."

"It should." His gruff statement rasped across her ears.

"No." Her smile wavered. "If anything, a couple should marry only after discovering if they'll suit in a lovemaking capacity instead of the other way around." She held his gaze, hoping she conveyed earnestness. "Pity, that. It's seen as scandalous in the eyes of Society." All she wanted to do was pat his hand and assure him that love did indeed exist in the world and one should actively try to pursue it. "You loved your wife, Miles. Why should anything between us be any different?"

"Because, her and I never..." He sputtered. "Because, you and I did..." His jaw. "This is a different circumstance."

She shrugged. "Regardless, I won't marry for obligation or guilt, either." The truth of the matter was she didn't harbor any guilt. "In fact, I refuse to feel shame for last night. I thoroughly enjoyed every moment of it, and if the opportunity presented itself for a repeat..." Belatedly, she cut herself off. "Well, that doesn't matter, does it?" *Stop rambling, Emmaline!* In those precious, abandoned moments when she and Miles had given freely of themselves to each other, she'd glimpsed the true man he could be, the man with a healthy sense of adventure and wicked freedom, the man stifled by tradition and obligation—the man who wanted so much more from life than he'd been given.

Several minutes of pregnant silence reigned before he spoke again. "Then you do plan to marry again?"

Whatever she'd thought he'd say, that wasn't it. "Perhaps." She dropped her gaze to study to faded Aubusson carpet. The beginnings of a hole had started near the edge. "I suppose if I had to put things into words, I'd say I don't want a grand, whirlwind passion. I had that twice and it fled quickly like a spark in a strong wind. I don't need a man to bring me the moon or the stars either." Why was she telling him any of this? It had no bearing on the current conversation.

"What do you want then?" His soft question took her by surprise.

When she focused her attention on him again, his somber expression confused her. Not one of the men in her life had ever asked her that. Not her father, not her husbands, not the men in charge of various museums around the world, not the peers she'd been forced to interact with. The fact that he did sent a tremor down her spine. "I want a man to lay down in the grass and watch those stars with me no matter where in the world I am, because, honestly, I do not feel at home in England. Society and the peerage stand too much on facades and are steeped in lies."

Was that … guilt … in his eyes, gone with his next blink?

Emotion she couldn't—or wouldn't—name clogged her throat and she swallowed around it. "Right now, I don't believe you are that man, Miles. Your life, your home, your purpose, your *heart*, lies in England, beats for the Empire."

"More than you can know." He nodded and pulled away from the chair. "Tell me the truth. Is there a chance I might be in your future?" The hopeful expression on his face tugged at her heart.

"Oh, Miles." She came around the chair and took one of his hands in hers. "How can I know that when I have no idea what the future will hold for me? For the time being, I cannot see past the curse. I don't relish a lifetime already planned out in a world where I'll be forced to act a certain way, say certain things, be a certain way." She bit her bottom lip. "It would be a gilded prison. Also..."

"Yes?" A sparkle of light winked at the backs of his eyes.

"I refuse to let you bind yourself to one such as me because..." As much as she wanted to look at something, anything else in the room, she couldn't tear her gaze away from his. The words would wound him, but they'd make certain he left her alone. "...because you still require the heir and the spare. If the curse is broken, you must continue your line." She dropped her voice to a whisper. "I cannot give you that, and what I can give you would never be enough."

A heavier quiet fell between them, charged with everything they couldn't—or wouldn't—say.

Finally, he nodded, but his eyes were no less intense. "I understand. I won't accept that last bit as an excuse, but I understand." The muscle in his jaw twitched again. "Please know that just because you've declined my proposal, it doesn't mean I withdraw my offer of assistance regarding your mummy logistics. If breaking the curse is what will make you happy, then I shall endeavor to be happy making it so."

Relief swept through her, but now it was tinged with a bittersweet disappointment. "I'm glad. I'd hoped we could continue our friendship." Though she knew as sure as she looked at him that it had changed. How exactly she didn't know. What brewed between them remained perhaps stronger than before, though was it merely friendship?

He briefly dipped his head in acknowledgement. "If you are accosted by unsavory members of the *ton* due to … things between us if they should be leaked for public consumption, I shall defend your honor with everything that I am."

Her chin wobbled as she fought back the need to cry. How did he not realize how different he was from the bulk of the peers around him, that if he would let himself, he could be so much more? "There is no need, but your gallantry is appreciated, especially in today's society." She swallowed around the lump in her throat. "If you should find yourself drawn to a worthy lady in the *ton*, I suggest you give her a chance to win your heart. I refuse to be a weight around your neck in that regard."

"I'll take that under advisement, yet for the moment, it is a comfortable weight to bear." He squeezed her fingers then released her hand. "Now, if you'll excuse me, I have matters of business to attend to."

"Of course." Emmaline escorted him to the door. It was on the tip of her tongue to ask when she'd see him again, but then she thought the better of it. She had no right to make demands on his time. Especially now. "I suppose we'll talk soon."

"Undoubtedly." He quit the room, his back ramrod straight as he traversed the corridor with strong, steady steps. Thompson, still involved in cleaning the wreck of the chandelier, didn't retrieve hat or gloves, but apparently Miles didn't care in his haste to exit her home.

Emmaline stood looking at the front door long after he'd gone, carefully trying not to think of anything related to him and the sudden hole he'd left in her life after a mere handful of days.

How did a lady continue on when something as marvelous as a once-in-a-lifetime gentleman walked away by one's own urging and design?

Chapter Fifteen

Miles sat in a comfortable leather chair at White's club. He was ensconced a front room, a snifter of brandy in his hand—his third, actually, since leaving Emmaline's house—while staring out the window at the afternoon sun slanting over the London streets, but his mind didn't dwell on the carriage traffic or the wealth of pedestrians at this time of night.

Instead, thoughts of her filled his mind. She'd refused his suit. Of course she had. He'd known it all along. So why, then, was he wracked with disappointment? It wasn't as if he was in love with her. Hell, he didn't even fancy her. Not really. Beyond the instant and urgent attraction between them, they shared a friendship.

The woman shouldn't haunt him the way she did.

He took a long sip of brandy, letting the liquid slide slowly down his throat and savoring the burn. The bloody alcohol wasn't dulling the memories of her either; it only made his brain slightly fuzzy on the edges. It was maddening this constant thinking of a female he hadn't considered since his boyhood in Egypt. When she'd left that country for the last time at sixteen, he'd consigned her to the deepest reaches of his mind then went about his life, taking his pleasures where he could, for his father had cared nothing of grooming him for a career and the title. He'd had no idea what had become of the girl he'd known and laughed with in the winters abroad; it had never occurred to him to track her in London or to inquire as to her return to Cairo.

Now, in a scant sprinkling of days, Emmaline had reentered his life in spectacular fashion and he refused to forget her this time. Perhaps his interest went beyond enchantment for the novel idea of her to something else, something that would lead down a road he wasn't certain he wished to travel again, but for the adventure he was willing to try.

Perhaps it was time to retire from espionage and concentrate fully on his own life.

"My lord?" The timid question brought his attention to a young footman bearing a silver salver. "A note had arrived from special courier for you. I'm to make certain you accept it and read it forthwith."

A tingle wound up his spine as he snatched up the envelope of heavy vellum. A thick glob of red wax bore the prime minister's personal seal and his stomach clenched. "Thank you." Quickly, he broke it then pulled a scrap of paper from the envelope, shielding it from the servant as he scanned it.

Your directive has changed with Leventhorpe's death. Our timeline has accelerated. Players are shifting and scattering in the wake of the murder. Do what you must to alienate yourself at all costs. Eliminate distractions. Your removal to the Continent is imminent. Rathesborne will brief you on your next move soon.

Cold dread sat like a stone in the pit of his belly. Devil take it. Anything he'd like to build with Emmaline would need to wait. He stuffed the note and the envelope into the pocket of his waistcoat. "Acknowledged. Thank you." When the servant loped off, he slumped into his chair.

What now? He poured another measure of brandy into his snifter and brought the glass to his lips. His quarry, an elusive French art forger and known Napoleon sympathizer, was on the move, or at the very least running scared, and all because of Leventhorpe's death. Interesting. How was the deceased marquess involved, and why did his compatriots panic? He sipped his drink. Even as the thrill of the chase fired in his blood, this time protest kept pace with it.

Living for king and country was the highest honor, but what of living for the state of his heart? When would he be given the opportunity to find out if the love of a lifetime that Emmaline held out for was indeed something true and worth pursuing?

"If you remain too long in that chair, Archewyne, you will become a statue. I don't believe you've moved in the last two hours." The droll voice of the one person of the peerage he called friend yanked him from his musings.

Miles flicked a glance at the man of average height whose lean muscle would go to fat in a year if he continued to drink to excess and laze about Town. "Trewellain. I'm surprised to see you here. Isn't this a rather too proper establishment for a man of your tastes?" Jonathan Banshire, Viscount Trewellain, the third son of the Duke of Werthsbury, had no expectations placed upon him, and he himself held no aspirations. He spent his days wagering and his nights carousing.

Mostly. He was also a decent spy who could charm the secrets from an ice queen. It was one of the reasons Lord Liverpool let them work together. They played off each other too well.

A trace of a grin touched the man's lips. "It might be too proper, but it is rather too early to inhabit my usual haunts, don't you think?" His blond hair, done in the latest style, caught the sunlight, which rendered him a Greek god as he sat in the chair next to Miles.

"I wouldn't know." What Jonathan did on his own time wasn't his business. Spending time in scandalous clubs where half-clothed women thought nothing of offering services right there at a man's table didn't appeal. If that made him stiff and stodgy, so be it. Men like them had different ways in which to relieve tension and stress, especially when one never knew if a day in the field would be one's last. He took another sip of his brandy and regarded his friend. "What do you want?"

"And it's rather too early in the day to be so disgruntled." The other man cocked a blond eyebrow. "It's been a long time since I've witnessed you stewing." Ever the consummate agent, the other man's gaze roved about the interior of the club.

"I'm not. I've merely come here to think." He frowned but set his snifter on the small round table at his elbow. Though why he couldn't do the same at his townhouse he had no idea. There was more than enough quiet there as well as brandy.

White's didn't hold memories of *her*. Given the shift in his assignment, he didn't wish to remember, to indulge in thoughts of Emmaline. It would invite regret, and that made a man compromised.

"Ah. To think." Jonathan continued to stare at him as he rested an ankle on a knee. "Would you be dwelling on a certain attractive widow, the same woman you brought to the Marchioness of Wellesley's dinner party without an invite?"

Miles' chest tightened. Obviously, the gossip tongues were wagging. *I hope that's all they know.* He glared at his friend. "If I am, what of it?" He wouldn't divulge any information if he could help it, and he and Jonathan obviously couldn't discuss the mission while in public.

Again, he was cornered by the elusive Emmaline.

"For starters, I glimpsed you leaving your birthday ball with that same woman. Plus, I've heard she's garnered attention from Bow Street regarding the death of Lord Leventhorpe." Again, a golden eyebrow rose. "In some circles, that could be seen as damning evidence, Archewyne. What have you gotten yourself involved in?" A double entendre weighed heavily on the question.

"Nothing as far as I'm concerned, where she's concerned as well." Instinct flared and sent cold apprehension through his gut. "How did you know about Bow Street's involvement?"

Jonathan snorted. "It's in the books, my good man. Men are wagering she'll be apprehended as early as this afternoon. It's also wagered on whether or not those two Runners who were at your home on the night of your ball will find themselves sacked for delaying their investigation of said widow."

"Buggar it." He detested that bored peers set money on her misfortune.

Jonathan lowered his voice. "I have it on good authority those two Runners are on their way to her residence as we speak. Apparently, events of that night are not adding up and Lady Emmaline was witnessed at the scene. That's strong enough though I've never heard gossip linking her name with Leventhorpe's." He shrugged. "Could be a piece of the puzzle we're missing."

I refuse to believe she's involved. Even though from her own admission she was in that study. "The Runners are going there now?" Miles shot to his feet too fast and the room spun slightly. "They have no proof of her guilt." Yes, Emmaline had sworn to him that she'd had nothing to do with the lord's death, and he believed her knowing the sort of person she was, but Bow Street didn't. All they knew was circumstantial evidence.

"Most likely they have no proof of her innocence either, and that's what the Runners deal in. We both know that," he added in a low voice.

"I do." Christ, what would happen to her in Newgate? He downed the remainder of his drink and attempted to will away the fuzziness hovering over his mind.

"Not well done of you to let Bow Street make the kill before you." Jonathan frowned. "Where are you going?"

"To the lady's townhouse." She might have rejected his offer of marriage, but he had pledged his assistance to her, and he was a man of his word.

"For what end?" His friend stood. "Is she under your protection? I can't blame you if that's true. She does possess a magnificent figure. Ripe for the plucking, that one."

His friend assumed she was his mistress. The heat of a flush crept up the back of his neck. He curled a hand into a fist, so great was his wont to land the other man a facer for daring to note her figure. "No. She is a friend and that relationship goes back to childhood. I'm merely going to offer assistance and support should she need it." For even though she was not part of his current mission, he couldn't abandon her.

"Then, the widow is available?" A groan left his friend's throat. "I wouldn't mind tarrying between those legs for a while."

Miles whirled around so fast the room spun again. Damnation, but he should have stopped drinking earlier. He narrowed his eyes and concentrated until his friend's visage wasn't blurry. "Lady Emmaline is not for you, Trewellain." Belatedly, he remembered to keep his voice down. Already, the men around him had probably overheard and this scene would add fuel to the rumors. He didn't care. "If I catch you sniffing around her skirts, I'll call you out. See if I don't." He couldn't bear the thought of her being bedded by his philandering friend, covert partners or not. She didn't deserve to become an object merely to slake a man's lust.

Though isn't that what he'd done last night in Georgiana's library?

I'm working to rectify that mistake, damn it! If she wasn't so bloody stubborn…

"Message received." Jonathan held up his hands in surrender. "On second thought, your widow's not as fast as I like them."

My widow. Ha! "You'll do well to remember that." Without another word, Miles made his way from the club and into the bright afternoon sunlight. Pulling down the brim of his top hat to better shade his eyes, he searched the immediate area for his carriage, but his eyesight wouldn't focus into clarity, and he couldn't discern his from the others waiting nearby. "Damn and blast." Why'd they all have to be black?

He shook his head. Perhaps that third snifter of brandy—filled with several fingers—hadn't been quite the best idea. Squinting didn't help overly much. "Bah." He waved off the assistance of one of the drivers. "I'll walk." St. James Street wasn't far from where Emmaline resided anyway and a bracing jaunt would hopefully clear his head.

Or he could go home. It was an equal distance from the club, but in the opposite direction. He could fall into his bed and sleep until things had evened themselves out again. Miles lurched off to the left before he came to a stumbling halt three strides later.

Wait. Shouldn't he be somewhere else now?

This is what I've been reduced to, what she's done to me. He narrowed his eyes as he stared at the dirt beneath his boots. Something about a damsel in distress? A dress? He snickered despite his fuzzy brain. That dress Emmy had on last night had been fine. *I adore when she wears sapphire.* He swore he could still feel the slippery silk of the garment as it brushed his hand when he'd pleasured…

Emmaline!

Jerking upright, he pivoted and headed off to the right. He had to gain Emmaline's house before the Runners arrived. Dear God, what if they didn't believe her protests and hauled her to Newgate? The bottom dropped out of his stomach and for several queasy seconds he feared he'd toss up his accounts. A few hard swallows staved off the urge. No matter what, he couldn't let her rot in prison for something she hadn't done.

Why are you so certain the lady didn't kill Leventhorpe?

He frowned at the voice inside his head. Because … because a woman who could kiss him, seduce him like Emmaline couldn't possibly have poisoned an unsavory lord.

Not that such an explanation would sway a Runner's opinion or anyone with half a brain, really. Damnation, he should know better than to let a distraction like her well … distract him.

With determination, he shoved the missive's directive from his mind for the moment. Miles increased his pace, but it was a difficult endeavor as the London streets were clogged with pedestrian and carriage traffic. The cacophony produced by so many people, animals and vehicles rang in his head and further contributed to his balance issues. Finally, after what seemed an eternity of walking, he spied her house in the row just beyond a slight curve of the street. As he focused, a black carriage—this one a hired hack—came to a stop in front of her townhouse.

"Botheration." He quickened his steps, and when he'd advanced halfway across the teeming street, a carriage waiting opposite her townhouse broke away from the curb and jolted in his direction.

The thunder of the horse's hooves increased as they bore down on him. He had mere seconds to take action and though his responses were slightly dulled by that one too many brandies, he vaulted as much as he could away from the danger. His foot connected with a smallish stone on the road, and when his ankle rolled, he stumbled and couldn't maintain his balance.

The sharp stab of pain was forgotten as he fell to the dirt the same moment the team came upon him. As his pulse thudded in time to the hooves, Miles had enough presence of mind to curl himself into a ball and pray that the worst of the hooves and wheels would miss him. In mere seconds his world narrowed to pawing legs, rapidly turning wheel spokes and the undercarriage of the equipage as the mass passed inches to his left. He didn't pull his left hand in as tightly to his body as he thought and a wheel scraped the back of it. Pain screamed through his hand up into his nerve endings. As he flinched, the wheel caught the shoulder of his jacket and the seam tore open.

Once the dust settled, Miles maneuvered into a standing position with a few more aches and pains than he'd had when he started his journey. Blood smeared on the back of his left hand from the scrape. Damnation, it throbbed, but the incident had cleared his head of the fog, and in that clarity, ire burned. London was full of reckless drivers. They shouldn't be allowed in Mayfair. A handful of people approached but he waved away their offers of assistance. The only thing truly injured was his pride, but that didn't stop him from staring down the road after the departing carriage. No identifying markers set it apart from other growlers in the city. Neither could the driver be immediately picked from a crowd. His nondescript cloak and low-brimmed hat obscured his features.

How utterly annoying and worrying.

He brushed the worst of the dust and dirt from his jacket by the time he gained the Darling's front door. As he'd rapped the tarnished brass knocker against the wood, his ankle had developed a slight throb in time to the wound on his hand. A lifetime passed. Would the ancient Thompson never admit him? He lifted his hand to knock once more when the door swung open and Emmaline herself stood in the frame, her eyes wide, the color washed from her face, her chest heaving with the great gulps of air she took in.

"Oh, thank heavens you're all right!" She grabbed onto his arm and tugged him into the entry hall. "I witnessed the debacle from my bedroom window and ran downstairs as fast as I could, hoping against hope that you weren't horribly mangled."

"Ah, so then reasonably mangled would have been acceptable?" he murmured in a fit of misplaced humor. "I am that, actually."

She quirked an eyebrow. His words, designed to lighten her fears, didn't coax a smile. "How can you not believe it's the curse at work now?"

He shifted his weight from his injured ankle. Not for worlds would he tell her blood from his scrape was now smeared along the shoulder of her dress. "For the last time, there is no such thing as the curse."

"Then an accident?" Doubt sat heavy in her voice.

"Most likely." His gut flared once more. If the carriage incident had occurred before her own accident from earlier in the day, perhaps he could have laughed it off. However, because it happened the same day, he'd be a nodcock not to think it was more than a coincidence, and he had seen less in his profession. "Perhaps someone very much alive had a hand in it."

"You don't think someone wishes you dead or out of the way?" She flicked a glance to his hand and frowned.

He shrugged. "Me or perhaps us both." Which went at cross purposes to his directive from the prime minister. How could he leave her behind if her life was in danger from an outside force that had nothing to do with an ancient curse?

Hellfire and damnation.

"How? Why would…" Her words trailed away, mostly because she'd paused to take another deep breath, but when she gazed up at him with concern clouding her flawless eyes and her lush lips slightly parted, Miles rushed to reassure her before he did something stupid like kiss her for the pure enjoyment such an act would bring.

"Rest assured, I'm not ready to perish yet, and I'm uninjured. More or less." Even as he said the words, his ankle and hand throbbed and he winced.

"You're a terrible liar, my lord," she murmured seconds before she threw her arms around him in her typical way and hugged him close.

He froze, but then that sort of spontaneity was Emmaline. Almost reluctantly, he enclosed her in an embrace and her light violet scent surrounded him. Before he could accustom to the touch of her, she pulled away and he regretted the loss of her warmth. "Perhaps I am," he said in a low voice. On more subjects than an injury. The more time he spent in her company, the more he wished to know about her and that tore at the pledge he'd given to protect England's interests. He shoved the thoughts away. For the moment, it didn't matter. England could wait. "I turned my ankle seconds before the accident and that's what pains me at present." He held up his left hand. "As does this, though a simple cleaning will take care of it."

"Come to the parlor. I'll ring for tea, maybe a take a look at the ankle and—"

The pounding of the door knocker interrupted her offer. Miles turned and groaned. Standing in the still open doorway were the two Bow Street Runners he'd talked with before—Mr. Ratterly and Mr. Flummert. "Oh, bother."

The tall, thin agent smirked and with a lifted eyebrow said, "Fancy finding you here, Lord Archewyne, especially after you told us days ago that you weren't acquainted with Lady Emmaline past childhood friends." He coughed discreetly into a gloved hand. "Yet here you are embracing that same woman."

"It wasn't an embrace," he shot back, vexed beyond measure that the possibility of enjoying the touch of her hand on any part of his person was thwarted by the arrival of these two.

Mr. Flummert, the portly one in the duo, sent a speaking glance to his partner. "I'll wager that begs us to open a new line of questioning, eh?"

"Regarding me?"

"Yes." The round agent nodded.

Emmaline stepped forward with a frown. "What is this about? Are you gentlemen," her tone of voice suggested they were anything but, "here to see me or the earl?"

"Both, actually," Mr. Ratterly answered with a decided gleam in his eye. "Regarding your guilt in a peer's murder."

She sucked in a breath. "Leventhorpe."

"Quite," Mr. Flummert said with a hard glance.

"We have some questions, my lady." Mr. Ratterly looked pointedly at her before resting his dark gaze on Miles. "Will we be invited in or shall we conduct this unsavory business on the stoop for all to see?"

If he wasn't such a damn gentleman he'd land the man a facer merely for the satisfaction. Instead, he deferred to Emmaline. "This is her residence, so I'm afraid you will need to do it up brown to her, not me." He tamped a chuckle when the agents exchanged anxious glances.

Mr. Ratterly shoved a hand through his dark hair, leaving it sticking up in disorganized furrows. "Lady Emmaline, if you please, we should discuss this inside."

"Yes," Mr. Flummert added, "we promise not to take much of your time, unless…" He cleared his throat. "Unless our proof is enough to warrant arresting you," he finished in a soft, lame voice while casting his piggish brown eyes away from her. He scratched at his greasy blond hair. "We've heard rumors—"

"It's bad form to strong-arm a woman into doing anything," she answered in aggrieved tones. "As is assuming rumors are facts. Plus, why you've chosen now to begin an interview, I have no idea. Why did you not visit the day of the incident or even the day following?"

Both men shuffled their feet and wore twin expressions of embarrassment. Neither answered.

"Typical." She shook her head. "However, because I do have a full agenda and don't wish to draw out this bit of unpleasantness," she sniffed in Ratterly's direction, "do follow me to the parlor. I suppose I can convince my butler that tea would be a lovely addition to this poor party."

A smile curved Miles' lips as he let the two agents move into the corridor ahead of him. Though the glass from the crashing chandelier had been cleaned, the managed frame lay off to one side. Why had they not commented on that? Apparently, Runners needed better training regarding observation skills. He closed the door behind them. Whatever else Emmaline was, she could box a man's ears with words alone when she wanted to. If that wasn't an inherent skill for any member of the peerage, he didn't know what was. His approach that she needed protection had been rendered moot.

Emmaline Darling could hold her own in any situation.

Pondering again, he clasped his hands behind his back and sauntered, or as much as a man could saunter with a slightly injured ankle, into the parlor that had seen better days. The ivory and gold draperies and carpeting was threadbare and shabby while the delicate French furniture showed signs of wear and … were those teeth marks on the leg of the settee? Surreptitiously, he looked about for the lion cub, but the feline wasn't immediately in sight. He hoped the lion would make an appearance, merely to witness the fear on the men's faces since the feline had been one reason they'd declined to visit. Of course, knowing their mindset, they'd no doubt declare Sanura a menace to Society or even a dangerous weapon of sorts and they'd take her away.

Not if I can help it.

Once they'd taken seats—Emmaline on a settee by herself, Ratterly in a chair and Flummert on the other settee—Miles skirted the seating area to stand behind Emmaline. The vantage point allowed him to watch both agents' faces.

"Are you sure you wouldn't rather sit?" she asked of him as she tipped her head backward and met his eyes. "There's room next to me." She patted the faded ivory-and-gold striped cushion beside her where the skirt of her garnet gown appeared like spilled wine. The color was exquisite on her, setting off her pale skin to perfection.

Heat shot through him, but he kept his expression schooled into near boredom. "I'm quite all right here."

"But your ankle must pain you." She affected a pout and even upside down, it was endearing and chipped away at his resolve not to touch her. "And I'd rather not have you trail blood on the furniture, even if the fabric is shabby enough."

What would it feel like to kiss her while she was tipped like that? *Stop thinking about her in that way, man!* "If the ankle pain grows unbearable, I promise to make use of your offer." He withdrew his handkerchief and wrapped his hand. "There."

"Very well." She turned her attention to the agents. "You may proceed." Emmaline moved her gaze over Ratterly's form then did the same to the other man. He well knew how powerful her emerald eyes would be, and he hoped the Runners felt unsettled. "It's not every day I'm afforded the notice of Bow Street."

Ratterly cleared his throat, which recalled Miles to the first time he'd been in the man's presence. Damnation. Would he make that noise throughout the entirety of the interview? "Yes, well, be that as it may, Lady Emmaline,

I'm afraid our presence this afternoon isn't a social call, as we've already alluded to."

Miles frowned. As if the man would ever have a shot at moving in the same social circles as Emmy. "Get on with it, Ratterly."

The agent flicked a glare in Miles' direction. "Very well, though we may as well begin with you, my lord."

"Me? Why?"

Ratterly's grin was maddeningly obnoxious. "Following our meeting with you on the night Leventhorpe died, we were apprised of the fact that the British Museum had been vandalized."

"Interesting, but what does that have to do with me?" He willed Emmaline to remain silent on the subject. They didn't need their names linked to that crime at the moment.

"I found it odd such a thing occurred the same night as a murder and your apparent need to take in the air of your garden, in which you returned home dirty and disheveled." He cocked an eyebrow. "What have you to say to that?"

"Nothing." Miles shrugged. "Coincidence. Nothing more."

"Mmm. Perhaps." Ratterly glanced at Emmaline. "What of you, my lady? Where you there that night?"

Her expression went blank. "Gentlemen, have a care. If you're trying to pin Leventhorpe's murder on me, how could I also have been at the museum?"

Miles wanted to hoot with laughter. Was there ever a woman as fantastic as her?

"Point taken." Ratterly reached into an interior coat pocket and withdrew a bauble of some sort, too shielded by his hand for him to see clearly. "Upon further investigating Lord Leventhorpe's home, we came across a rather intriguing piece of evidence." He held up the object—an oval earbob in a delicate silver setting.

An earbob that perfectly matched the emerald necklace and bracelet Emmaline had worn the night he'd first met her.

She gasped and put a hand to her ear. Of course she wasn't wearing any sort of jewelry on those lobes now. An instinctive reaction no doubt. He prayed she wouldn't blurt out ownership just yet. "Where did you find that?"

"Why don't you tell me, Lady Emmaline?" Ratterly's tone was every bit as chilly as hers had been earlier.

Emmaline didn't answer though she did open and close her mouth a few times.

The agent continued. "After the body was removed, we conducted a sweep of the house with particular attention to his study, of course." He let the earbob dangle from his thumb and forefinger. "We almost missed it, wedged as it was behind a leg of the sideboard where Leventhorpe's liquors were stored."

The round Flummert leaned forward and rested his arms on his knees. "Isn't that earbob part of the heirloom St. Ives jewelry, part of the missing pieces your father couldn't find and sell in order to fund his theories?"

The tendons in her delicate throat worked with a hard swallow. "I misplaced those earbobs a week before I was in Leventhorpe's house."

Miles stifled a curse. Not only did she claim the jewelry, she voluntarily placed herself in the peer's home on the night of his murder. Couple that with what she'd told him about the off-handed brandy remark and being in the study where she'd taken Leventhorpe's notebook, and she was well and truly in the drink. In the hope he could misdirect the agents' attention, he said, "Misplaced or stolen, my lady?"

"Pardon?" She turned her head to look at him and the sight of her wide, worried eyes gutted him.

"Isn't it possible those earrings could have been stolen by unknown persons? You said you hadn't seen them for a week before Leventhorpe died." He glanced at the agents. Time for misdirection. "If we're dealing with a murder, why couldn't the jewelry have been stolen ahead of time? For, let's be honest, if Lady Emmaline did kill the lord, why the deuce would she take the time to drop a very distinctive earbob? A killer wouldn't leave a calling card."

"Unless she wanted to make a statement," Ratterly said as he tucked the bauble into his pocket.

"Or be caught," Flummert added with a smug smile.

"No one is that great of a nodcock," Miles shot off.

Emmaline waved a hand in dismissal. "You say Leventhorpe was poisoned?" When the Runners nodded, she continued. "Why would I use poison—if I did indeed kill him—when I carry a dagger on my person at all times?"

Miles groaned under his breath. Dear God, why would she say something like that?

"A dagger, you say?" Ratterly's dark gaze raked over her person. "May we examine it?"

"Of course. I have nothing to hide." She gathered a handful of her skirting, no doubt with full intent of drawing up her gown and showing them the sheath strapped to her thigh.

These men aren't worthy to look upon her limbs let alone the tip of her slipper. "That is not necessary." He dropped a hand on her shoulder and gently squeezed. "You may take the lady's word as truth."

"In our line of work, my lord, we've found the truth is always distorted," Ratterly replied.

Miles rolled his eyes. They had no idea. He came around the settee then sat next to her, needing to protect her but knowing she'd hate a barbaric show of power. "Had your home been broken into that you know of? Perhaps your servants aren't trusted?"

She shook her head, her eyes still large in her face. "I trust them with my life." She licked her lips. "A day after I returned to England I'd accepted an invitation to tea with one of my father's old friends, Vicountess Babbington. She's the one who held the remainder of my family's jewels, the one who advised me not to let my father know of their whereabouts lest he sell them off too."

Flummert cleared his throat yet again. "You took possession of the jewelry after that meeting?"

"Yes." Emmaline nodded.

"Were the earbobs in the collection?" This from Ratterly.

"I have no idea, for I didn't open that particular casket until a week before I decided to…" Her words trailed off when Miles gave his head a hard shake. "I assumed Sanura carried off the earbobs." Light sprang into her gaze. "Though, there might have been a break in. There is every possibility the chandelier was tampered with as well, as you could see from the remaining mess where you came in."

Good girl. She was quick on her feet. A great quality to have in a covert agent. Not that she was.

Flummert colored. "I assumed you were redecorating."

Miles rolled his eyes. "With a smashed light fixture?"

Emmaline covered a laugh with a cough.

This interview had grown tiresome. "So you see, gentlemen, trying to tie the lady to the crime scene with such flimsy information as that won't work. You'll have to do better than that." With the dignity ingrained into him through the title, he rose and looked down his nose at Ratterly. "Wouldn't you agree?"

The Runner's expression darkened. He wouldn't be as cowed as he'd been the last time. "I do not." He gained his feet as well, his gaze not dropping. "However, I would like to question Lady Emmaline privately."

I'm sure you would, but I'd have to be dead first. Miles hurried to answer before she could. "Instead of badgering the lady, perhaps you should investigate the fact I was nearly run down by a carriage not thirty minutes ago by a madman."

Flummert shook his head. "Not exactly worthy of our time, my lord. Reckless drivers abound in this city."

She briefly touched Miles' injured hand and he hissed as pain stung him. "I'm afraid that won't be possible, for my personal schedule won't allow it in the next week. My time is very much spoken for and I simply cannot change the appointments." Emmaline stood in a rustle of skirts. She bestowed a smile upon each of the agents. "I'm sure you understand, and I must adhere to that schedule, especially with the lion in residence."

The agents exchanged fearful glances. "Of course, Lady Emmaline," Flummert said in solicitous tones. "I do hope you'll find a free spot in your calendar to sit down with us again, perhaps here, perhaps while Lord Archewyne is in attendance if you wish." Perhaps he would crumble after all. "We wish to ask a few questions." He cleared his throat, and this time Miles made a strangled sound in his.

"Be assured, if I have free time, I shall send word to Bow Street straightaway." Her eyes twinkled, which signaled mischief for someone, but her carriage and way of speaking screamed *ton* as if she'd been born a duchess.

Hot pride spread through him. "I'm certain my London business will be well and truly ended by next week's end." She extended a hand to Ratterly. "Now, if you will excuse me? I have a pressing appointment that simply cannot be delayed any longer. Plus, my lion cub will be eager for her next feeding."

It took all of Miles' willpower not to dissolve into hearty laughter. How she sensed the Runners' fear of the feline, he'd never know.

Ratterly nearly tripped over his own feet in an effort to take her hand and bring it to his lips. "That would be perfect, my lady."

"We'll await your summons," Flummert agreed as he too rushed to grasp her fingers once his partner had finished. After, he touched the brim of his hat. "A pleasure."

She inclined her head. "Enjoy the remainder of your day, gentlemen."

Miles followed the Runners as far as the parlor door, where Thompson finally intersected them. "Do help these men with their escape, eh old boy?" When the butler nodded and led the way down the corridor with his shuffling steps, Miles returned to Emmaline. "If I didn't know better, I'd say you've performed on Drury Lane, my lady."

A wide grin curved her lips, and he dropped his gaze to her wonderful mouth. "Thank you for the compliment, but I wasn't lying when I said my business would be concluded."

"Oh?" How many surprises would she have this afternoon?

"Yes." She rested her brilliant gaze on him. "After next week, my plans are to return the mummies to Egypt. I simply won't be in London any longer and out of their reach."

Mine as well. Her words pierced his chest with the accuracy of the sharpest daggers. "Is that so?" Now his ankle wasn't the only thing that ached. By sheer force of will he kept his uninjured hand at his side instead of rubbing the skin above his heart. Why should it matter to him if she left? He'd only become reacquainted with her in the last week. He had no right to suggest what she did with her time. Didn't he wish to have her out of his life so he could complete his mission without potential harm to her? This would save him the trouble. "When do you leave?"

"A week from tomorrow." Her grin wilted. "That is if I can obtain the priestess' mummy from the marchioness' home." She batted her eyelashes as she closed the distance and laid a hand on his arm. "Which brings me to the favor I need to ask of you."

"A favor?" Charged impulses raced up his arm to his shoulder. The pain in his ankle and left hand was all but forgotten. Had she always used feminine charms to manipulate men to do her bidding? Quickly he thought back over his interactions with her. She'd used them on him, certainly, but he'd hoped her flirtations had been due to a fondness for him.

Had he mistaken her intent?

"Mmm." She nodded. Gold flecks appeared in her eyes. "You take tea with Georgiana every Tuesday, do you not?"

"I do, but how do you know that?" Annoyance warmed him and beat back some of the enchantment that blanketed his brain when she came near. For a thief, she had honed other skills worthy of the Home Office.

Rosy color infused her cheeks. She squeezed her fingers upon his arm. "I might have taken a peek at her schedule when I perused her study on the hunt for the mummy." She looked away from him then, but it merely gave him a better chance to admire the curve of her cheek and the graceful column of her neck.

"Ah." He shifted his stance as his damn cock tightened. Why couldn't he control his reaction? It wasn't as if his arousal awakened due to kissing. He was only standing close to her, and talking with her for Christ's sake! Realizing she awaited a reply, he said, "Yes, I will go to her home for tea. Tomorrow. Usually, she discusses the women she wants to introduce me to. In her mind, I desperately need a new wife."

Hurt crossed her face so slight he might have missed it if he hadn't been watching so intently. Was it possible Emmaline wasn't as impervious to his attentions as she wished him to believe? "Well done. On both counts." Her throat moved. "I think a wife would be wonderful for you." When she raised her gaze once more to his, hope lurked in the depths. Did she wish to be in that position or was that emotion for something else? And why the devil did he want to know so badly? "But regarding the more urgent issue, I'll need you to provide a decent distraction, for I mean to sneak into her townhouse once more, only this time I'll carry out the mummy."

Well, that answered his question. "A distraction." His jaw slacked and his eyebrows soared. This on the heels of the missive from Lord Liverpool brought his temper into a foul place. He grew deuced tired of everyone tugging on his time without asking his permission or thoughts.

"Yes, so I can kidnap the mummy. Do what you must, even kiss her if that's what it takes, but I need that mummy and soon." She frowned. "After the incidents today, I'm not sure how secure my home will be, and I do not wish to have the original mummy stolen."

Why the hell did everyone in England assume they could order him about on their whim? "Kiss her." He'd turned into the village idiot as he focused on what she'd said. Did she not understand he didn't care for Georgiana that way?

"We all must do things we don't enjoy, Miles," Emmaline told him in a sing-song voice, "but you did pledge to assist me. In order for me to do that, I must appropriate the mummy by any means possible."

"Even if that means using me as bait." That brought him back to his senses though anger still seethed in his chest. She treated him no better than the prime minister. Had his instinct regarding her been so wrong? "There is no curse," he ground out from between clenched teeth. "There is something else afoot here, and it has nothing to do with long dead priests or their wives." That much was true.

She dropped her hand. Some of the light died from her eyes. "Be that as it may, I owe it to myself, my father and," she moistened her lips, leaving them glossy, "and you to attempt this. Only then can we really know which one of us is correct." Her chin quivered. "Please?"

Damnation.

When did he become a slave to a woman's chin or her compassion? "Of course I'd do anything for you, Emmy. Didn't I give you that promise the night you left Egypt?"

Emotion flickered over her face, too quickly for him to read. "Yes."

He nodded. "I'll do this one thing for you, but I'm not happy to know you'll leave England soon." *And without us coming to an understanding or agreement about the future.* Such as it could be now that his orders had changed. "I'd hoped to further our acquaintance, even more so now that Bow Street is sniffing about." He paused as he searched for words. "You don't necessarily need protection, but you do need a powerful advocate."

Those compelling emerald eyes searched his. A trace of moisture pooled in them, blinked away before the tears could fall. "Thank you, Miles. You'll never know how much this means to me."

He'd have to work harder at convincing her leaving the country wasn't the answer, and neither was ignoring what she felt for him. Women like Emmaline wouldn't be intimate with anyone without some sort of feelings driving the coupling. Now was not the time to broach either subject. Damn the prime minister to hell. His hands were tied unless he could procure a new plan. He dropped into the chair, his mind in a spin. "For starters, you could ring for tea, or at the very least, lend me a pillow so that I may prop my poor battered ankle, since you've roundly ignored me in favor of entertaining the Runners." He grinned as she whisked across the room and pulled the bell strap. It wasn't well done of him to lay on the guilt, yet she wasn't the only one who knew how to play for favors. "Plus, my hand does need tending to before infection can set in."

Perhaps his ego would be soothed after all if she'd consent to examine and massage his injuries. In the meantime, he'd need to formulate a plan on many levels, and for that, he'd have to consult his valet and man about town, Peterson.

They hadn't been through military service together for nothing.

Chapter Sixteen

The next morning Miles put the finishing flourish to the knot of his cravat then drifted to the window and gazed down into the bustling London streets below. He glanced back over his shoulder. "I wish to wear a color today. Green perhaps."

"Very well." Peterson pulled a superfine jacket of bottle green from an armoire. "You're troubled today, sir. More than usual."

"Perhaps." He returned his attention to the outside world. "I have much on my mind."

"Beyond Lady Emmaline? Have you heard from the prime minister?"

"I have and I'll brief you soon." The corner of his mouth lifted in a grin. "However, you're right." Peterson understood him like no one else, and so he should. When Miles had come home from Egypt with his brother in order to attend school and gain what his parents considered the best education in the world, he met Casper Peterson amidst the hallowed halls of Oxford. The man was being bullied on account of his penchant for being a loner. Peterson, being a fourth son of a baron, had the world at his feet and the freedom Miles emphasized with. Miles had come to his rescue with threats of roughing up the few fellows if they persisted in their behavior.

The two had been steadfast friends ever since.

Midway through 1806, the year they both graduated, Peterson pledged to fight for the British in The Peninsular

War. Miles, having come away with less than pleasing marks, wasn't any less thrilled when his father bought him a commission onto the same Navy vessel as Peterson. At least it had been a familiar face and their friendship and mutual admiration had deepened as they'd both honed their combat skills.

He might not have been an attentive student, but he'd excelled in a military career. Once Portugal had been secured, and Miles had earned promotion after promotion for valor and leadership, they'd both gone on to fight Boney's forces in Spain, ending only when Peterson had been sliced near fatally in the side by a bayonet. Miles had refused to leave him for dead as instructed by his commanding officer and instead had taken it upon himself to care for his friend around the clock, even went so far as to have him moved to his personal quarters to better oversee his progress.

Softly, Peterson cleared his throat, bringing Miles back to the moment. "Do you think of her now?"

Miles snorted as he faced the other man. "Actually, no. My mind was on my history together with you, and how we'd come to this pass."

Once his commission in the Navy expired, he declined to continue on against the advice of high-ranking officials. That had been 1812, and though France had been beaten into submission, the Empire had other problems with the newly independent American colonies. He'd had no interest in more fighting and instead had come home where Nigel flexed his soon-to-be-earl attitude. Miles had thought to become a rake, but once Constance entered his life, he'd been content to mellow. Except, the Home Office had come calling with offers of the adventure he craved and missed since leaving the military, and he'd answered with his wife's blessing. He'd risen up the ranks and was now one of the Empire's most sought after covert agents.

Through it all, Peterson had been by his side, happily employed and doing the tasks of a valet or whatever Miles could concoct, which was usually being his right-hand-man on various missions Lord Liverpool formulated.

A genuine smile split his friend's lips. "We have had quite the time of it, haven't we?" He came forward with the jacket held up then slightly shook it to encourage him to don the garment.

"That we have." He slid his arms into the sleeves while Peterson tugged the highly tailored piece of clothing into place. "Excellent choice today, sir. The green complements the gold threads in your waistcoat." He brushed a stray piece of lint from one shoulder.

Miles nodded as he did up the buttons. "For whatever reason, I'm favoring green lately."

Peterson chuckled. He brushed back a lock of curly reddish-blond hair from his forehead as he regarded Miles with a knowing light in his blue gaze. "No doubt it helps you to remember the lady's eyes."

"Exceptional insight, my good man." He didn't care that most of what he discussed with his valet could have crossed many lines in other *ton* households. Peterson wasn't merely a servant, and he had enviable talent in procuring necessary paperwork to anything Miles' missions might require. "She does have unforgettable eyes." Now that he thought on it, Peterson and Emmaline would probably get on together well.

God help the Empire if that ever occurred.

The valet snorted. "If you're ready to wax poetic over a woman's eyes, you're already far gone over her."

"I wouldn't say I'm quite there yet." Heat crept up the back of Miles' neck. He ignored the knowing smirk on his friend's face. "Though, if I'm being honest with myself and you, I'd have to admit to a certain interest." He hadn't shared with Peterson what had occurred in Georgiana's library the other night. That was a gentleman's secret.

"Do you want my opinion?" The other man folded Miles' dressing gown then consigned it to a drawer in the armoire.

"Of course." In lieu of having assistance, he rooted out his newly shined Hessians, sat upon a low stool then crammed a foot into the first one.

"I know you've refused, time on end, to let yourself be matched. I also know you believe you've the devil's own luck where it comes to friends, family and loved ones." He held out the second boot.

"What of it?" A note of annoyance had slipped into his voice as he grabbed the boot. Would he, too, extol the virtues of matrimony?

Peterson sighed. "I merely wished to say I understand your position on all. "However." He pinned Miles with a stern look. "I think you're lonely and have been since your wife left this world. It wouldn't be remiss if you found yourself falling for a spirited, adventurous woman who would keep you on your toes and save you from being lost to the demands of your title."

"Thank you." The annoyance vanished under the onslaught on concern. He tugged on the second boot, being careful to avoid overly jarring the still-tender ankle. "I follow and approve of your logic, but convincing said lady that we should be together is another endeavor entirely." Briefly, he told Peterson that he'd asked for Emmaline's hand after a bout of heated kissing in the marchioness' library. If the other man read between the lines, that was his prerogative. He also conveyed the reason she turned him down. "In addition, a match with her is a distraction, a weakness perhaps I cannot entertain at this time."

"Ah, so the lady is as stubborn as you." Both of them grinned. "All the more reason to continue, regardless of what the mission demands."

"Easier said than done, for she intends to return to Egypt within the week, bearing mummies with her. I'm told her father is ailing as well. And Liverpool has hinted I'm for the Continent soon." The ache in his heart from yesterday flared. Did a man truly move past the bruising of his ego when a proposal was rejected? "Perhaps her father needs her more."

"Go with her."

"I cannot," he answered a little too readily. "You know that." Was the man not listening?

"Why? You have a competent estate foreman. Your accounts are flawless. Parliament hasn't yet come into session. If you manage to tie up your mission with your usual finesse, you'll be afforded free time. Return to England from the Continent then accompany the lady. Surely she can postpone her trip by a month." He finished his enumeration with a cheeky grin. "Do consider it."

Ah, God. Peterson made it sound too easy and entirely too feasible. "All of this is true, but—"

Jane pelted into the room at precisely that moment in only her underthings. Laughter caroled around her. "Papa!" She flew at him and he scooped her into his arms. "Good morning."

"Good morning to you, pet." He kissed her cheek. "Where are the rest of your clothes?"

"Nurse has them." She rubbed a small hand along his cheek.

"Why don't you go find her and finish dressing?"

She shook her head and her clouds of blonde hair flowed about her shoulders. "I don't want to."

"You have to."

"Why?"

Miles stifled a sigh. "Young ladies cannot go about their days without being properly dressed." Over her shoulder, he looked at Peterson. "*This* is why. I have responsibilities here that can be threatened with one wrong step in a mission," he said in a soft voice. "Jane has no one else except me. I couldn't live with myself if something happened to me and left her alone."

For long moments his valet studied him before nodding. "Take her with you once the mission has concluded, though I have no answer for what to do with her while you are on said mission. No need for the two of you to be parted after that."

"Take me where, Papa?" Jane bounced with excitement on his hip. "The park?"

Really, she was too precocious for her own good. "Not right now, my girl. Papa has obligations." It seemed that's what his life had boiled down to. "I must tend to business then take tea with the marchioness this afternoon. Perhaps Nurse will take you out."

She pouted, but the bad temper melted away as fast as it came. Her eyes sparkled. "To see the kitty and Wady Emmy?"

He resisted the temptation to tug on his neckcloth even as his throat constricted. "Not today." Yet… A glimmer of an idea took root in his brain. "We shall see about a visit soon."

"Wady Emmy has pretty dresses. I want dresses wike her." She squirmed and he let her down on the floor. "I'm hungry."

Children were always hungry, but in this moment he welcomed the reprieve from having to converse about Emmaline. "If you let Nurse dress you, I'm sure she'll procure you a treat."

Without a by your leave, Jane dashed from the room as fast as she'd entered. Miles stared at the empty doorway then finally turned his attention to Peterson. "The devil's in the details, my good man." His mind spun in turmoil. "In your spare time, run a bit of surveillance on Lady Emmaline's townhouse. The two incidents from yesterday aren't sitting well with me, and I have my doubts that a mere curse is the cause."

Peterson nodded. "Very well, sir. Will there be anything else?"

"Not at the moment." When the valet reached the door, Miles spoke again, almost to himself. "Though, if I were to decide I might like to accompany the lady should my schedule suddenly become free and the mission end sooner than later, would you be up for an adventure?"

A wide smile wreathed his friend's face as he looked back over his shoulder. "There's no place I'd rather be, my lord."

That's what I'm worried about. There was every reason to believe his friend of a lifetime was an enabler.

"You're looking lovely this afternoon, my lady," Miles said, doing the pretty as she led him into the parlor.

"Thank you." Her voice was guarded. "I had hoped to see you before our weekly tea."

"Business kept me away." He owed her no further explanation.

Before she could reply, a scratching on the door interrupted them. Georgiana glared at a slip of a woman he assumed was a maid. "What now?"

"Begging your pardon, my lady." The young woman advanced a few steps into the room. "The, uh, gown I took to the seamstress has returned. Mrs. Lasley said due to the nature of the fabric and beadwork, she is unable to repair the skirt."

Dark anger crossed Georgiana's expression. "Not acceptable. You take the gown back to Mrs. Lasley instantly and tell her I won't hear excuses. I need that gown repaired." She waved a dismissive hand as the young woman pelted from the room. "Training new servants is an exhausting endeavor."

"So it would seem." But his minded turned the information over. Torn gown. Beadwork. He narrowed his eyes. Emmaline had handed him a scrap of fabric after the incident with the chandelier. A coincidence? Damnation. Why couldn't anyone be as they appeared?

"In any event, I feared you wouldn't keep our appointment today," Georgiana purred as she handed him a cup of tea, complete with cream and one lump of sugar.

"Why would you think that?" He blew on the surface of the amber liquid before taking a sip. Though the marchioness sat on the settee perpendicular to his, she perched close enough that when she reached over, she touched his knee. "Obviously, I haven't missed a meeting yet even if my business demands more of my time."

Which, before he'd met Emmaline, it wouldn't have seemed odd. He appreciated Georgiana's penchant for sticking with a schedule, for setting a habit. However, since the advent of Emmaline and everything that had occurred between them, he longed for the freedom her lifestyle represented. What would it be like to knock about the world unfettered or mired down with responsibilities or at the whim of a government?

Her words after she'd turned down his suit rang in his mind ... *you still require the heir and the spare. If the curse is broken, you must continue your line ... I cannot give you that.*

His chest tightened. Damn and blast what a coil he'd landed in. Yes, securing the line would be a good thing; however, securing that captivating woman's hand and promise felt more important than seeing a moldy old title continued.

"This is true. You were mentioned in the *Times* this morning as having some sort of accident with a carriage, though they did wish you well." She arched a perfect blonde eyebrow. "It's good to see you unharmed. I thought you might cry off due to that."

"Ah." He took another sip of tea. How did the vermin who wrote the *on-dits* for the paper even know of the debacle? Obviously, spies were everywhere. Now that she'd mentioned it, the aches and pains made themselves known. He flexed his left hand, the skin tight with scabs. "I'm quite fine even if I do favor my ankle. I'm sure I'll return to full health in no time." What game was she playing, and had she anything to do with that very same incident?

"Thank goodness." She laid her teacup into its saucer then put both pieces on the low table in front of her and focused her full smile on him.

"Why's that?" Her blue eyes twinkled and that alone made him suspicious—of many things.

"I have another prospective match for you."

Bugger it. "Who?" He had no intention of allowing such a thing to move forward, but his curiosity demanded she tell him.

"Lady Anna Fairfield. She's the daughter of Duke Rathesborne and—"

"—and she's as dumb as a sack of rocks," he finished for her. Not to mention her upper teeth stuck slightly out giving her the appearance of a horse. As much as he admired Rathesborne, he simply had no amorous feelings for his daughter. "Honestly, Georgiana, can you not find a suitable woman? I'd rather not sit across a breakfast table for the rest of my life with a female whose conversational prowess consists of the weather, the latest fashions from Paris or the pedigrees of her various dogs." Plus, Rathesborne trotted his daughter out as bait if needed. No way would he allow her to be married off yet. She may be ugly as sin, but she had a knack of making men talk when they didn't wish it.

And he didn't want to know her methods.

"Imagine her dowry or the holdings that would come your way upon your nuptials," the marchioness purred. She appropriated the tea cup from his hand then set it down next to hers. "The duke has deep coffers and expansive properties, and Anna is his only daughter. He's given her every desire of her heart, and right now, he desperately wishes her married."

He barely managed to stifle his snort. His Grace had done well putting forth that rumor through the *ton*. "No doubt he's going mad from her topics of conversation." He eyed her askance. What motivated Georgiana? Best to go along with her and find out. "Either that or he's hoping a suitor won't look past the piles of money to see the vast emptiness that resides between her ears." Remorse assailed him and he held up a hand. "That was unkind of me. Perhaps the right man will find her wildly fascinating." When her father and the Home Office had no more need of her.

Georgiana's tinkling laughter filled the opulently decorated parlor. "Honestly, Miles, you are too picky. The fact is you need a wife. You should be happy with whomever is available."

"Ah, so then mutual regard and respect or even love shouldn't have any bearing on a relationship." He leaned back against the crushed velvet of the settee as his gaze wandered toward the open doorway. "Let alone attraction," he said to himself. His thoughts jogged to Emmaline and warmth spread through his chest. Certainly there was desire between them and he heartily respected her as a person, a woman and an archeologist.

Was that enough? According to her it was not. Yet she refused to allow anything else to bloom between them. Why? It had to be more than the curse or her inability to bear children.

"You've developed quite the sense of humor lately," she answered and stood, smoothing a hand along the front of her gold-colored silken dress. "It's refreshing." She relocated on the settee next to him, so close her skirting fell over his leg.

"I've found a different way of looking at life, I suppose." It would be bad manners to scoop up that fabric and hand it back to her, so he sat still, leaning as far away from her as the arm of the furniture would allow. Her honeysuckle scent was heavy and overpowering.

She touched a hand to his forearm. "I assume you're refusing Lady Anna?"

"Yes, absolutely." Let her think what she would.

"Well, that's for the best, really." Nothing in her tone suggested she took the news badly.

Not even for king and country would he align himself with Rathesborne's seed. "Why?"

"That frees up your attention for another." She drew an abstract figure on his sleeve as he eyes widened. Was she attempting to appear innocent? Foreboding snaked through his gut. That was her motivation—him. Emmaline had been right and he'd refused to see it.

"Who?" Where had his intelligence gone that he now resorted to one-word answers?

"Me, of course." She moved even closer, which pressed her leg and hip against his. "I mean, it's a logical step, wouldn't you say? We've known of each other since we were children. We're well matched and we both still have our looks." The marchioness patted a tendril of hair into her elaborately dressed coiffure. It was nice, of course, and the look sleek enough, but it wasn't the adorable mess that was Emmaline's loose chignon.

"Thank heavens for that," he mumbled. "However, I'm not certain we would rub well together."

"Whyever not?" Her lips, with the bottom one slightly more full than the top, turned down in a decided pout. She didn't have Emmaline's lush mouth, and he didn't find himself wondering what it would feel like to kiss her.

"For one thing, you love to entertain. Not a week goes by that you haven't thrown some sort of rout, soiree or ball. I value my privacy and being left alone." The better to disappear at a moment's notice.

She snorted. "You're wasting away behind the walls of your townhouse, and when you do have business, it consumes you. You need to mingle more; take time for you." She fiddled with the low neckline of her gown, naturally drawing his attention to the creamy curve of her bosom. There was such a thing as being seen as too overblown like tulips two days before their petals dropped.

Miles stopped himself from rolling his eyes. "For another, there's my daughter, Jane. I'm extremely protective of her, and she's young yet. Far too young to send to school or leave to the exclusive care of a nursemaid and a governess later." Would Jane consider Georgiana as pretty as she did Emmy? He took a deeper notice of his companion. Her eyes didn't glitter nearly as much as Emmaline's, nor did she have laugh lines around her mouth or gathered at the corners of her eyes. He put a hand atop hers merely to halt her finger's meanderings. "Plus, you have a son, my lady. You should spend time with him while you can before he assumes the title. Once children are grown, they rarely wish to spend time with their elders." He hadn't when he'd been that age. Granted, he'd been in Egypt and had adventures with his contemporaries and Emmaline to fill his free time…

Have I truly become stodgy and starchy since I assumed the title? How disappointing, though he'd worked hard to cultivate that assumption. It helped hide his covert activities.

She waved a hand in dismissal. "Roderick is but a child yet. Fifteen is a difficult age and he's quite surly when he's home on school holidays." A delicate shiver wracked her shoulders. "I'd rather leave him to his schoolteachers and when he matures, I'll take the credit when I match make for him."

He mentally wished the boy luck. "Regardless, the two of us are too good of friends. A romance wouldn't suit."

Her pout deepened. "Is that what you're holding yourself for then? Romance? Love? That's not how the *ton* works. For us, it's about connections and power. You know that."

Was he? From his handling of the offer for Emmaline's hand, one wouldn't think so. Hell, he'd told her much of the same thing Georgiana just uttered. It was jaded and crass and wrong. Like Emmy had said, he'd loved his wife. Such things did happen in the *ton*. No wonder Emmaline had declined his proposal, and now on the heels of the new missive? Annoyance rose in his chest. Too many demands. The least of which was that damn scrap of torn fabric that may or may not belong to Georgiana. Had she tried to kill Emmaline or warn her for some reason? And if so, why? "What do you wish to gain from me if we were to wed, Georgiana? Power or an addition to your coffers? For we don't share the heat of passion between us like some of those peers who have wed for the things you mention."

"Why, I'd gain you, of course, and how do you know we don't if you've never so much as kissed me?" She covered his hand with hers and squeezed his fingers. Her eyes were soft as she held his gaze. "We should rectify that soon." Her breath skated across his cheek and warmed his skin.

He didn't answer with words. In fact, he didn't answer at all. Instead, he stood abruptly, disentangled his fingers from hers then meandered over the plush Aubusson rug to the window that overlooked the street. As he stared, a nondescript door in the basement level opened and a woman with a black shawl covering her head and lower half of her face emerged. She hunched over as if her back pained her, and in her hand she held a black velvet sack, full but not bulging.

Miles stifled a groan. *Emmaline*. He'd recognize her anywhere, even with the poor disguise and obvious bag of stolen mummy. Continuing to observe, he clasped his hands behind his back. His heartbeat accelerated when a footman followed her out and apparently hailed her. Oh God. Would she be stopped and drug back into the house, perhaps brought to task before Georgiana?

"Miles?" The marchioness' soft inquiry didn't bring him around as his attention remained riveted on the tableau below.

"Hmm?" Emmaline brought forth something from beneath her shawl. It winked in the sunlight and he could only assume it was a piece of jewelry of some sort, for she held it up and she talked to him. The groom's gaze followed whatever it was in her hand, but he crossed his arms over his chest and shook his head. Miles' pulse soared. Would she still be caught? She continued and finally the liveried servant held out a hand. She dropped the bauble into his palm. He vanished back into the bowels of the house and she continued on her way toward the front of the property. Miles released a quick sigh of relief.

"Do you not wish to see if there'd be passion between us?" Georgiana's voice sounded nearby. "I always thought we'd suit, ever since those days in Cairo."

He whirled around, his nerves strung tight since Emmaline was still visible from the window. If he didn't provide that much needed distraction, Emmy would be caught. Miles closed the distance between them and none too gently took the marchioness into a loose embrace, turning them so that the marchioness' back faced the window. "I suppose it wouldn't hurt," he murmured before he'd really thought about what he'd said. His only intent was to protect Emmaline.

"Splendid."

That largely depended on the perspective. To postpone the inevitable, he tossed out, "If you and I were to wed, you must know I require an heir. Would you even wish to be a mother again?" Somehow, he couldn't imagine her as the nurturing type. It didn't matter that he had no wish to align himself with her, nor did he absolutely want more children. He said it to fill the void and keep her talking.

"I think I could be pursued to bear you a child, for the bedding would be spectacular. Though, one, perhaps two babes, for I don't wish to wreck my figure." She cupped his cheek and brought her gaze to his. "I had hope this would occur soon." Her attention dropped to his mouth. "I've always dreamed of it since we were stuck in that nasty desert every winter."

Botheration. That explained why she'd trailed after them everywhere they'd gone. "Is that so?" There was nothing for it now except to do the deed. He swallowed hard past the lump of distaste in his throat. This was worse than anything Liverpool had asked of him in the field. "I shouldn't keep you waiting any longer." Once he'd settled her into his arms more comfortably and she tilted her face as her eyes fluttered closed in expectation, he silently wished Emmaline good luck then lowered his lips to Georgiana's in a perfunctory kiss.

A shuddering sigh escaped her. She slipped her hands up his chest to lock them behind his neck, and when he tried to pull away, she murmured a decided, "No," and renewed the embrace. She curled her fingers into the hair at his nape and it was she who pushed to deepen the kiss by shoving her tongue into his mouth.

Miles reared back and broke the connection. *This is wrong.* To give credit where it was due, the marchioness certainly had skill, but her lips didn't cradle his like Emmaline's and neither did her curves fit to his body quite like Emmy's did.

In short, Georgiana wasn't Emmaline and she never would be.

What the hell do I do about that?

"Well, now that that's finished, you should know we would never suit." Truly what he wanted was a hearty snifter of brandy with which to wash away any trace of this woman. Even her kiss tasted like honeysuckle. Why the need for that much perfume?

Her eyes flashed. A flush of color blazed in her pale cheeks. "That's not well done of you, Miles. It was barely a kiss and not enough for either of us to know anything about the other." She narrowed her eyes. "You have no intention of being anything to me except a friend."

Heat shot up the back of his neck. How horrible it was to be called out in such a fashion, but he couldn't prolong this interview. "I do not, Georgiana, though I do value our acquaintance and would hate to lose that even if we do not suit in a romantic way." Gah, what a lie! But then, wasn't the bulk of his life based on the same?

"You won't give us a chance, and that I take exception with. Is there another you favor?"

"I…" What to tell her when he wasn't fully certain himself?

Georgiana propped her hands on her hips. "Are you involved with that widow, that Lady Emmaline?"

"Involved?" He forced a laugh and hoped it was believable. "I am not." At least that was the truth. Not for his lack of trying.

"Yet you think she's fascinating." The marchioness sniffed as if he'd drug in rubbish from the street. "I cannot imagine why."

Miles remained silent. There were countless reasons, but none of them needed to be brought before Georgiana's condensation, especially if she already harbored ill-will toward the other woman.

"You went after her after she fled my dinner. What happened between the time when you found her and when you returned to my table?" Her tone had turned sharp and direct, her eyes overly bright.

How much did she actually know? The slightly open library door flashed into his mind and anxiety rode his spine. Best to stick with minimal truth. "I found her in your library. She was upset so naturally I spent some time there talking to her and comforting her."

The ticking of the ormolu clock on the fireplace mantle sounded overly loud in the pregnant silence that followed his statement. The marchioness crossed her arms beneath her breasts, pushing those mounds against the neckline of her bodice. "What did that *comforting* entail?" She cocked a perfectly arched eyebrow. "Servants talk, and who knows who could have come upon the two of you when you were … otherwise engaged."

What deuced bad luck. Had she opened that door and spied on them while he and Emmy had shared… Miles shook his head. No sense in denying it, and if she didn't know, he wouldn't tell. The act had been too precious to sully with treating it as gossip. "We are done with this conversation, Georgiana, unless you'd like to confess to tampering with a certain chandelier?" He made sure to infuse every bit of his earl persona into that statement. Yes, she sat in higher rank than he, but he wasn't above throwing his power around anyway. He resisted the urge to stride to the window and check on Emmaline's progress. Surely she'd made good on her escape by now. *Please, Emmy, for once in your life, stick to a plan.* But then, that was her. She was spontaneous and unpredictable. To make her follow a rule or dictate would be to essentially change her.

The marchioness' expression went bland. "I don't know what you're talking about."

Somehow, he doubted that. "It matters not." He couldn't keep a trace of disappointment from his voice. Georgiana and her displeasure could go hang. "Things between Lady Emmaline and I are not to be." If Georgiana did have harm in her heart toward Emmy, it was best to remove that temptation.

"Oh?" Her expression changed to that of a hunting dog who has detected the scent of a fox. "I suppose I can take comfort that you won't dangle after her like an untried youth. After all, why would you want her when you could have someone with more experience in pleasuring a man?"

"That's enough." He clasped his hands behind his back, surprised that they shook, whether in fury or annoyance he didn't know. "She plans to leave England within the week." Not trusting the sharpness in her gaze, he tamped on the plan to tell the whole story. "Her father is very ill and she wants to visit with him one last time before the inevitable." Letting Emmaline go would keep her safe—from everyone. And he could go on to the Continent without guilt. His chest squeezed.

"Ah, then her departure has nothing to do with an attempt to break a curse?" The shock must have flitted over his face, for she chuckled. "That's the scuttlebutt I've heard. Some people are slaves to that sort of stupidity."

And some people thrive off it like he suspected the marchioness did. "She cannot help what she believes, Georgiana. Her life has been a string of hardships." *As has mine.* Perhaps peace of mind was the greatest prize, and if Emmaline could return the mummies to their eternal resting place, so be it. She could finally give herself permission to live again instead of holding everything at arm's length.

She could be happy, and if she could only achieve that by leaving him behind, perhaps he should let her go. Disappointment stabbed through his chest at the thought. At least she couldn't be used against him. She deserved to be safe and happy.

Perhaps in another time or place, he and she could have had a chance.

"Yes, well, sometimes people are merely unfortunate and should let fate play itself out." Her lips curved in a smile, but it didn't light her expression. "In the meanwhile, I shall wait until your temptation is well away before I continue *my* pursuit of *you*." In a rustle of skirting, she headed toward the door. "I trust you can show yourself out, Miles dear. I do hope to see you at Rathesborne's ball later this week. It's time we appear together in public as a united front, don't you think?"

Chapter Seventeen

"Is there nothing you won't do, my lady?" Awe wove through Sarah's voice as she eyed the velvet sack Emmaline handed her that contained the remains of the priestess' mummy.

Emmaline grinned then set about washing her hands in the basin beneath her bedroom window. "If one is motivated enough, one can accomplish anything, even something seemingly impossible." As she scrubbed at the dirt and dust she'd accumulated in the daring apprehension of the mummy, she briefly related the adventure to her maid. "I honestly thought when the footman waylaid me, I was done for."

"How did you manage to get away?" Sarah slid the sack beneath the bed. How amusing and a tad unsettling to have two ancient Egyptian mummies stowed there.

"As luck would have it, I remembered the citrine broach I'd put on my dress this morning. It's at least ten carats and will fetch a prime price if he chooses to sell it on the streets." She shrugged while she dried her hands on a length of scrap linen. "No doubt he will, for I suspect the marchioness doesn't pay a fair wage. There's talk she cannot keep servants in her employ for longer than two months."

"You're a bold one, my lady. I would have fainted from fright."

"You're made of much sterner stuff, Sarah, and you'll need that courage if you still mean to accompany me to

Egypt." Emmaline paused with a frown. She'd only assumed her maid would go with her.

The younger girl nodded. "I do. I'm quite fond of traveling, and were it not for you, I'd not have the chance."

"Good." She exhaled in relief, then a box upon her bed caught her attention. Sanura sat atop the box, idly licking a paw. "What's in the package?"

"The gentleman's jacket you sent to the modiste to have altered." The maid grinned. She rushed over to the bed, and after pushing the cat from the box, handed the package to Emmaline. "I never thought you'd truly attempt to wear something that belonged to the earl, but where you're concerned, you'll dare anything."

"Perhaps." Except give in to that same earl's request that they wed. After the death of her second husband, she'd vowed that unless the curse was broken, she'd never again pledge her troth to anyone. Beyond that, if she did marry again, it would be for an all-consuming, white-hot passion, one that would easily flare into the perfect sort of love she'd spend a lifetime enjoying without the constant fear of either her or them expiring early. "Well, let's see it."

With Sarah watching, Emmaline untied the string that bound the box. Sanura promptly pounced on it then carried it off to a corner. Flutters of anticipation filled her as she removed the top, peeled back the paper and finally held up the altered garment. Instead of a jacket of navy superfine, in its place was a tailored vest complete with feminine silver buttons and silver embroidery around the edges.

"It's lovely," her maid breathed.

"It is," she agreed. A faint sage and citrus scent wafted from the piece and she unsuccessfully stifled a smile. At least it hadn't lost that essential part of him.

Sarah darted away to the other side of the room where she scooped up a few envelopes. "I found the post, meager though it is. Thompson had squirreled it away in the silverware drawer, so I'm afraid it's at least a week old." After she placed the correspondence aside, she made a clicking sound with her tongue. "Come, Sanura. Time for your daily exercise."

Emmaline tucked the vest into her armoire, she glanced at the maid. "You're taking her in the pram?"

"No. The cat jumped out last evening. Tore off down the street where I had to retrieve her at the earl's doorstep. Perhaps she remembered the house from her other visit. Today I thought we'd race up and down the stairs." Trepidation shone from her blue eyes. "If that meets with your approval, my lady."

"It does." And it sounded rather fun besides. "Just stay out of Thompson's way. He's fragile and I don't wish to have him knocked down by your antics."

Sarah left with the lion cub galloping in her wake.

Left alone, Emmaline turned her attention to the small stack of envelopes. As she shuffled them, familiar scrawl caught her eye.

Father!

Dropping the others, she ripped his open and settled upon her bed to read. Dated five weeks ago and written two days after she'd left Egypt for England, the page was filled with her father's thin penmanship, crossed once.

My dearest Emmaline,

You've only just left me and you should be well on your way home. Yes, my girl, England is your home, and it would make me beyond happy if you would take up residence in the Mayfair townhouse and come to grips with the world I have always kept you from. Your mother's fondest wish was for you to marry well and become a valuable member of the ton, *but I know better.*

That world is not for people like you and me – the ones with intelligence and compassion for things beyond ourselves.

Regardless, I know I'm dying. My dear, you can deny it all you wish, but I know the evidence of my own eyes and I've overheard the prognosis from the doctors here. It's only a matter of time, and I probably won't see you again in this life.

I implore you now to find the mummies you seek. It's too late to have an effect on my short time here, but for you it will mean everything. I regret putting myself and my family into something that would mean our eventual destruction. Had I known…

And as I write to you with insight of one who sits and waits for death, I can tell you this. Live your life to its fullest. Find a man who will celebrate you, who will support you without being a fetter, a man who won't demand your talents be shuttered or keep you in a gilded cage. At this point, I'm not sure there ever was a curse. Perhaps we just entered a run of bad luck. Time, my dear daughter, is the most valuable thing we have and it goes by too quickly.

Use it well. Sometimes that means throwing logic and caution aside and chasing your dreams with your heart because life is truly amazing when you allow yourself the freedom to live it.

Above all, I've never been more proud to call you my daughter. You've grown into a fine woman, and no matter what else you do in your life, you have my approval and my love.

Don't rush back to Egypt after reading this, dearest daughter. I'll leave this world when I'm called whether or not you're with me. I'd rather move on to the next life knowing you've found someone worth lingering on England's shores for, someone who makes you feel like you do when stumbling upon a treasure in the sand.

Yours faithfully,

Father

Emmaline stared at the letter for long moments. After she read it again, tears welled in her eyes. When she blinked, they fell to her cheeks and kept falling. "I won't be able to tell him goodbye." She shook her head. "I don't accept this. If I break the curse, I can save him."

Then her shoulders slumped. No she couldn't. Deep down she'd known that.

With shaking hands, she folded the letter and slipped it back into the envelope. Was he even now dead? Taken from her too early? Just like her mother had been. Just like everyone she loved had been.

Which was why, no matter what he'd said in the letter, she would return the mummies to Egypt. If she didn't, she'd always wonder, and she didn't wish to live out her life, keeping herself aloof from others, keeping her heart safe from love out of fear they'd leave her too.

She moved on to the second envelope in the stack. The thick vellum crackled as she broke the seal—the Duke of Rathesborne no less. Her eyebrows rose as she read the invitation to a ball in two days' time. *I'd rather die than attend a* ton *event.* Ready to toss the card away, she paused. Yet her father's words jumped into her mind … *allow yourself the freedom to live your life…*

Perhaps it wouldn't be the worst idea to go, especially if Miles would be there as well. The thought made her smile. And it wasn't as if she'd have the opportunity to attend a ball while in Cairo. Her smile widened. Plus, there was every possibility she could beguile the earl into writing his name upon her dance card.

Besides, the duke had always been rumored to have one of the world's largest diamonds in his possession—the Star of India—which it was also rumored he'd stolen from a visiting Indian rajah—or prince.

Her fingers itched. It wouldn't hurt to take a look around.

Two days later and under cover of the inky night, Emmaline stole up the steps to the duke's expansive townhouse. She'd deliberately waited until the duties of the receiving line would be over. One because she detested being required to do the pretty with people she had little to no interest in and two because most guests would already be inside and not lingering to see that she'd arrived by foot instead of a carriage.

Because she didn't own a vehicle. Long ago her father had sold the equipage in order to fund one of his digs. And one just didn't arrive at a duke's affair in a rented hack.

Once the butler of indeterminate years admitted her and she handed over her invitation, he led the way down a long hallway lined with paintings of landscapes, hunts and horses. Two were portraits of whom she assumed were the duke and his wife. All too soon, he waved her into a large ballroom then bowed his exit.

Anxiety played her spine as she hovered in the doorway. These events always showed her in an awkward light and even her choice of gown didn't impart enough confidence to drive the nerves away. She smoothed a gloved hand over her stomach. The silk skirts of deep royal purple suited her well, and though the top of the gown was ivory silk dotted with tiny clear crystals that caught the light when she moved, she smiled with the knowledge that she was a bit too wicked for the proper *ton*. The back of the gown plunged low where it met a multi-colored silk sash that Sarah had worked into a pretty bow at the small of her spine. Would she be tossed from the ball for her too-scandalous wardrobe?

No doubt I'll end up in the gossip pages tomorrow.

She didn't care and never did she read such trash anyway. It wouldn't be the first time her name had graced those pages. At the very least, perhaps Miles would see her before she was escorted out, for she'd worn the gown partially for his benefit. How lovely it would be to see admiration in his eyes or perhaps heat when he spied the back. Yet … she'd be a fool if she didn't admit to herself that she held certain feelings for the earl. She wished for more than what he could give her physically, and that left her in confusion. Is that where she wished her future to go? Her heeled slippers of matching purple silk, also encrusted with crystals, made little sound as she stepped forward.

The only piece missing from her wardrobe was her jeweled dagger. She'd decided not to wear it tonight due to the fact that, since she hadn't worn undergarments of any sort, the lack of layering material wouldn't conceal the weapon. Besides, what could possibly happen at a staid duke's ball?

The many conversations and laughter swallowed her up and whirled around her. Hundreds of candles gave the room soft, golden illumination, but they also put off heat that blended with the many bodies crowded on the highly polished marble floor. And no amount of searching revealed the tall form possessing the midnight hair she strained to see.

When she reached a Doric column, she rested a palm against it and continued to scan the couples on the dance floor. After recognizing none of them, she moved her gaze over the people gathering along the sides of the room. Some held glasses of punch while others watched the dancers like she did. At the back of the room, young ladies sat with expressions of boredom—wallflowers. She smiled. How well did she remember those early days when she'd first returned to England under the watchful eye of Viscountess Babbington.

I need to visit her, and soon.

It was on the tip of her tongue to tell those girls that this wasn't the pinnacle of their existence, but Viscount Darnell walked into her line of vision—tall, blond and definitely on the prowl. Even from this distance, the gleam in his dark eyes was unmistakable. "Bloody hell." She scampered behind the column and hoped he hadn't yet seen her. As her pulse beat hard, she caressed the pearl choker about her neck and the round amethyst stone that sat at the hollow of her throat.

Please find some other woman to annoy.

She peeked around the column on the other side and breathed a sigh of relief when the viscount had indeed waylaid an unfortunate young woman and was even now attempting to cajole her onto the dance floor as couples set up for what appeared to be a waltz. When she returned to hide behind the shield again, she gasped, for Miles was not three feet from her, a wicked grin curving his lips and an answering light in his deep brown eyes.

"I hope the gentleman you're trying to avoid this evening isn't me," he said in a low voice that sent thrills of anticipation down her spine.

"Put your fears to rest, my lord. I'm very glad to see you." It didn't matter that she'd seen him many times before in the last week, nor that they'd been intimate, she gawked like an untried schoolgirl as he came forward another few steps.

Clad in black evening clothes, he'd once again bucked tradition by donning a jacket of lightweight wool done in a military style. Black braided frogging and silver buttons provided decoration and set off his starched white shirt and cravat to perfection. A sapphire stickpin winked from the snowy folds of his neck cloth. She followed the buttons down the front of his jacket and she gave a mock-pout since the jacket was longer than the current style and hid the front of his trousers from view. Gleaming Hessians completed his ensemble.

"Shall I turn so you can inspect my backside?" His smile widened and as he stood here, a slightly curved lock of his raven hair fell over his forehead.

Heat slapped her cheeks and she snapped her gaze to his face. "That won't be necessary." It was vastly unfair that he looked so dashing, for now she'd have a difficult time concentrating.

"Perhaps another time." He touched a fingertip to her mother of pearl inlaid fan. "Never say you plan to do a bit of exploring while you're here."

She fought off a blush. "I might. How lovely would it be to find the missing Star of India?" Where she expected censure, her mind reeled when he didn't offer a rebuke.

"God, I adore your sense of adventure. We could use a woman with your skills."

"We?" What did that mean?

Guilt and shock cycled through his expression, before they were quelled by mischief once more. He held out a white-gloved hand, deftly ignoring the question. "Would you care to dance, my lady? If I'm not mistaken, you've mentioned how you adore dancing and I'm certain you won't find waltzing much in Cairo."

Butterflies brushed through her stomach at his remembrance. The orchestra completed its warm up. As she looked on, the dance floor had almost filled. After all, she'd come to the ball specifically to partner him once. "I'd like that above all things," she managed in a whispered voice as she placed her fingers in his. When he held her hand in a firm grip, tremors of need raced up her arm from the point of contact.

Seconds after they took a position on the floor and she laid a hand on his shoulder, the five-piece orchestra struck up the first notes of a slow French waltz. Miles set them into motion. His hand at the small of her back tensed then he pulled her inches closer to his body.

"Are you trying to appear indecent?" she whispered but couldn't banish her grin. "I never thought you'd have it in you."

His answering smile held so much heat her knees wobbled and she stumbled on her next step. "Of course not. I'm merely throwing all that I am into this dance." With ease he settled her as they accomplished the first turn of the room. "If others perceive I'm scandalous, so be it."

"Impressive." She glanced at the onlookers and when her gaze landed on the marchioness, who wore a fierce frown, she sighed. "Georgiana is not best pleased to see us together."

He never moved his gaze from her face. "Ignore her. Ignore everyone and give me your full attention if only for the duration of this waltz, Emmy." The earnestness in his voice, the way he tightened his grip, which reeled her in closer still, the intensity in his brown eyes all worked as a web she didn't know if she wished to escape from. "You're beautiful tonight. Each time you wear a brilliant color, it's as if you've tumbled out of a jewel box." He glanced at the cluster of downy feathers pinned into her hair and accented with an amethyst comb. "One of these days I will see your hair down."

That would assume they'd spend more time together than there was allotted, but in her mind's eye she saw herself waking up beside him or perhaps straddling his waist with her hair hiding her naked chest from his view. Her stomach muscles clenched. "I chose this gown specifically for your eyes alone." Would he think she too high-handed or bold?

His gaze flicked briefly to her décolletage before catching hers once more. "I would have seen you in the crowd had you been wearing sackcloth and ashes." The hand at her spine moved slightly upward. Ripples of need followed. Her heart skipped a beat. "Though, I want nothing more at this moment than to explore the back of this gown without gloves." He quirked an eyebrow. Admiration and desire fought for dominance in his eyes. "I appreciate how innovative you are."

"How skilled in flattery *you* are." Her reticule and fan hanging from her wrist swung as they continued.

"Perhaps, but then, where you are concerned, I've only spoken truth." His smile promised much more, and she was lost to the wonder of it. "Your unorthodox approach to life caught my attention in our Cairo days, but you as a woman are quite thoroughly captivating. I..." He cleared his throat. "I'm under your spell."

Warmth swept through her, only building as they turned the next corner of the room. With each step, each movement, their bodies brushed. What would it be like to give in and accept his proposal? "Be careful, my lord. It seems you're growing feelings for me." True, neither of them had professed love for each other, but would such an emotion grow in time? If he were genuine, he was certainly headed in that direction.

Am I?

All too soon, the ending of the musical piece drifted to her ears. A tiny frown marred the perfection of Miles' face as he heard it too. "Emmaline." He tugged her even closer so that barely an inch of space separated them. "Please reconsider your plans to leave England. I promise we'll fight whatever ill wind blows our way." He put his lips to her ear and whispered, "Let me help you. I want to protect you, but I cannot do that if you're halfway around the world from me."

Her breath caught. She almost wavered. It would be so easy to say yes and surrender to all that he offered, yet he was a peer of some high standing. Would he expect her to conform to the *ton's* standards? And what of an heir? Though he'd argued that it didn't matter, they both knew it did. Titles and the obligations therein trumped love.

"Oh, Miles, I..." Her father's words in his letter came back to her and once more her resolve strengthened. "Please understand. I must go. I have to, if there's a chance..."

"I know." As the last notes of the song echoed through the room, Miles led her off the floor and through a doorway into an empty corridor. He gripped her hand while he tugged her along the hall. At a door midway down, he tried the handle and when the portal swung open, he pulled her inside, softly closing the door behind him.

"What are you doing?" Her heartbeat raced. A single lamp glowed on low table near a gray settee in crushed velvet. They'd taken refuge in a small retiring room where ladies could come to regroup or retire from the noise and crowds. As yet, she and Miles were the only occupants.

"I must be insane, because this cannot happen," he said more to himself than to her. "But I'm going to do it anyway. I'm trying to convince you to take a chance on me—on us." He whisked her into his arms and pressed his lips to hers.

If the kisses they'd shared in the marchioness' library were heated, this embrace had all the power of molten lava—destructive and so hot bones had no chance.

Emmaline sighed and twined her arms around his neck, pressing herself shamelessly into the hard wall of his chest. Her nipples tightened, and the friction gained by her movements didn't bring enough relief. So she tugged him even closer and parted her lips to invite him in.

The earl was quick on the uptake. He thrust his tongue into her mouth and fenced with hers. Over and over he chased and she retreated, and then she went on the offensive and did the same. Her pulse ricocheted through her veins, propelled on the wings of the heat licking along her body and the desire throbbing in her core. Miles broke the kiss only to nip a path on the underside of her jaw. "You have to know how much I want you."

He said wanted. Not loved. "I do. It's quite obvious." Now that they were pressed together, she had no doubt since his hardening length made its presence known at her belly. On the heels of a throaty sounding laugh, she slipped a hand down then between them and rubbed her palm against the impressive bulge and he groaned. "How well I remember what you feel like." Need fluttered through her lower belly. Oh, she wished they'd repeat that performance.

"Too much more of that talk and who knows what will happen." He kissed the skin of her throat just above her choker.

"Then, by all means, let us continue the conversation." What would it hurt to encourage deeper intimacy? She'd meant what she'd told him days ago. She wouldn't marry for anything less than love. Was she there yet with him? No, but she was fond of him and the desire was certainly present. That wouldn't prevent her from enjoying a moment of passion. Gently, she squeezed and his cock twitched beneath the layers of clothing.

His groan sounded overly loud in the silence. Miles set her away and she pouted. "You don't play fair and try my gentleman's soul." His gaze smoldered with need as he yanked off first one of his gloves then the other and stuffed them into an inside pocket of his jacket.

"I never said I wanted a gentleman," she reminded him in a hoarse whisper. "However, I do want you." No use trying to hide that. He knew it and she knew that he did. Emmaline didn't have time to remove her own gloves before he'd once again taken her into his arms. "What are you about now?"

"Falling to temptation to caress your delectable backside." He claimed her lips in another searing kiss while he deftly undid Sarah's hard work untying the bow. Once the ends dangled at her sides like vanquished snakes, he made quick work of sliding the few buttons from their holes. He skimmed his fingers up and down her bared back. Heat trailed in his wake.

"Temptation goes both ways," she murmured then lightly bit his bottom lip. When she plucked at the buttons on his jacket, he tugged her loosened bodice off her shoulders and down her arms enough that her breasts popped free. "Unfair, Miles." Yet, she smiled as he devoured her with his gaze.

"No, what's unfair is you not wearing underthings." He cupped her breasts and rubbed the pads of his thumbs over the sensitive tips.

Emmaline shuddered as pleasure flooded her. "How can I when this gown is cut so scandalously?" When would he stop talking and employ his mouth on other things?

"It's quite convenient." Miles dipped his head and took one hard, pebbled nipple between his teeth. Sharp pain from the bite pulled on a current that ran between her breasts and her core.

When he sucked on the bud, she cried out and arched her back while scrambling to clutch his lapels for balance. "More," she urged as her eyes shuttered closed.

"Gladly." He switched his attention to the other nipple and she dug her fingers into the wool of his jacket. Back and forth he flicked his tongue over the tip, and with every pass the fire in her blood raged.

She wanted to tug him to the floor and divest him of clothes until he was as partially naked as she. There was something about this man that slipped past every barrier and defense she had. As he caressed her back and slid a hand beneath her gown to cup a buttock, she moaned her encouragement.

The earl urged her legs slightly apart with a knee. "I want you, Emmy," he whispered as he moved his hand down the slope of her cheek and farther until his fingers brushed the curls shrouding her center. Another scant centimeter would have him dipping into her core.

She almost cried with frustration when he merely hovered there, not moving. Outside, laughter and footsteps intruded on the passionate fog that had descended on her brain. "I wish we could indulge." She buried her face into his jacket and inhaled his citrus and sage scent. "This isn't the place or time."

When next they came together for intercourse, she didn't want a rushed joining. She wanted unhurried lovemaking where they were both naked and in a proper bed.

Sadly, if that occurred, it would be more of a goodbye than anything else.

"I understand." His gaze bore into hers with such intensity she had to drop hers to the sapphire pin in his cravat. "When?" He withdrew his hand but wrapped her in his arms and held her close to his chest.

She tried to regulate her breathing, though the longer she was with him, in his arms, so close the steady beat of his heart thumped in her ear, the more her resistance eroded. Would it be such a horrible thing to allow him into her heart even though the curse would take him from her early? What was the lesser of two evils—sentencing him to death or never seeing him again? "Tomorrow at my home. Around tea time."

"That will have to do." He pressed a kiss into the crown of her head. "Come. Let me put you to rights."

In a daze, Emmaline turned, presenting him her back while she tugged the bodice of her dress into place. The hard points of her nipples clearly showed through the thin silk. Nothing said scandalous widow more than literally wearing her arousal. As he did up the buttons, his knuckles grazed her skin. Tremors of need raced through her veins to seemingly every nerve ending, spiking her awareness of him. Wordlessly, he fussed and worked at making a decent bow with the sash. All too soon, he was finished. "Thank you." *For seeing beyond my father's reputation. For not making light of my beliefs. For pulling me out of the briars I put around me.*

For everything.

"You're always welcome." He dropped his hands onto her shoulders and placed a feather-weighted kiss on the side of her neck. "I'll leave first if you'd like. I refuse to damage your reputation further by quitting the room with you."

She bit her lip to stave off stupid, silly tears. "Will I see you again this evening?"

For the first time since she'd known him as an adult, he dropped his gaze and wouldn't look her in the eye. "I shall do everything in my power to claim another dance."

"Two dances? You'd commit societal suicide. Public opinion would demand we marry else both be disgraced."

A slight shrug lifted his shoulders, and finally he met her gaze once more. His expression was serious as he looked at her. "Let them talk." And then he was gone. Several seconds later, the soft closing of the door rang in the quiet.

Emmaline pressed her gloved hands to her burning cheeks. How could a man she'd re-met a week ago send her into such confusion? With no answers and even less guidance, she quickly crossed the floor. Once she gained the corridor beyond, the sound of angry, raised voices at the end of the hall caught her attention.

With a frown, she walked toward the cluster of men, one of whom was Miles, whose expression resembled a storm in progress. "What is going on here?"

One of the older men glanced at her. His bushy salt and pepper eyebrows were shoved together like one long caterpillar with his scowl. "None of your concern."

She ignored him and caught Miles' gaze. "Why are you arguing with these men?"

He raked a hand through his hair, leaving it disheveled. "I've been accused of something I've not done."

Before Emmaline could form a response, a younger man pinned her with a flashing hazel gaze. Good heavens, the Duke of Rathesborne himself was involved. That couldn't be good. Dukes were a driving force in the *ton*; their every word or whim close to law.

The duke cleared his throat. From his impeccable evening attire to his brown hair styled in the latest fashion, he was every inch a lord of consequence. "I'm afraid certain evidence has come to light that points a finger to Archewyne being the murderer of Lord Leventhorpe. We are now attempting to convince him he needs to turn himself in to the Runners."

She gasped as she looked to Miles again. His eyes had darkened to almost black and his body was tensed as if for flight. Never had she seen his jaw more rigid, his expression so angry, yet… there was *something* in his expression that didn't ring true. What was it? Her mouth dropped slightly open. She might believe in many far-fetched things in her life, but thinking the man before her a killer?

I refuse to entertain that thought.

Chapter Eighteen

Miles' pulse pounded in his temples while he alternately curled his hands into fists then relaxed them. Bloody hell, someone would pay for this insult. It would add an unforeseen complication to the plan he and Rathesborne had already set into motion. He'd barely met with the duke to receive further orders before the rest of the lords were upon them. Truly, it couldn't have been better orchestrated if tricky.

Knowing that didn't make what he had to do any easier, especially not after he'd lost whatever had remained of his mind and threw every bit of romance and charm into pursuing Emmaline, even when it was hopeless.

"How dare you." He infused heavy authority into his voice. That these peers would dare put forth such preposterous claims was ridiculous. He had to be certain not to let the claims sidetrack him. "What the deuce is going on here?" He couldn't look at Emmaline at the moment. Not yet for fear he'd give too much away, not when it was vital she continue on the course she'd already made for herself.

The Duke of Rathesborne crossed his arms over his chest. The tall lord's attire and brown hair remained as impeccable as if he'd just stepped out of his valet's care. There wasn't a flicker of recognition in his hazel gaze. The man was one of the best when it came to subterfuge. "I'm afraid it doesn't look good for you, Archewyne," he said in frosty, ducal tones he'd no doubt perfected at his father's knee. "We've come upon some damning evidence."

"What evidence? I haven't seen or talked with Leventhorpe in months." He scowled at his three accusers. Besides the duke, there was the gray-haired Viscount Dursly and the painfully thin Lord Vitteras, who'd recently come into the title after his father had died from a bout of horrible food poisoning. Gossip held that his mistress had tampered with his meals when he wouldn't buy her the fripperies she wanted.

The duke's frown deepened. "A note was delivered to me earlier today, written in your hand addressed to Leventhorpe. In this note you made a threat against Leventhorpe, saying in short that if he didn't remove your brother's name from his ledgers, if he didn't stop demanding that you pay the notes he held for your brother's gambling debts, the consequences would be dire."

A tiny gasp escaped Emmaline and when he finally glanced at her, she'd pressed her gloved fingers to her lips. His chest tightened. As much as he'd wished to spare her from this ugliness, there was no help for it. Yes, he'd said something along those lines to the now-dead lord, but he'd not issued a threat and he'd certainly not committed any of it in writing. He wasn't a fool. Aside from the fact this bit of alleged foolishness would work well to help his mission, anger toward whomever had planted such "evidence" flared. Who wanted him removed from London and why?

"Miles, is that true?" Her voice conveyed her horror.

The older viscount tapped his cane against the hardwood, removing the need to immediately answer her. "Clear it up now, Archewyne. Did you or did you not have dealings with Leventhorpe?"

"I did; however, I never wrote that note, and I never threatened him." Again, he curled a hand into a fist. Needing something more to play up his alleged outrage, he pounded that fist into his free hand. "Of course I wanted anything having to do with my title above board. When Leventhorpe came to me shortly after I became earl, he presented me with a contract initiated between my brother and him. It outlined the staggering debt Nigel had accumulated that Leventhorpe had paid." He shook his head as the old rage bubbled to the surface. That wasn't manufactured. He'd always warned his brother away from the pitfalls of gaming, but Nigel thought he knew everything. It had been an unfortunate circumstance that reality collided with the need to cause this scene.

"I had no idea my brother had acted so carelessly, but I sure as hell wasn't going to crumble beneath Leventhorpe's thumb and blackmail attempts or succumb to his repayment plan with steep interest. The debt was rendered null and void with my brother's passing." He made a mental note to be sure and rip that damning page from the notebook he'd hidden away in a secret trinket box. At the present time, he didn't plan to destroy the book in the event it was needed as evidence if Leventhorpe's killer came to light.

And it would, especially if someone was as desperate as to try and implicate him with the murder.

Lord Vitteras snorted. "You'd like to think that, but whatever debt is incurred becomes the responsibility of the title." So said the man who had just attained his twenty-fifth birthday as well as *his* title. "Leventhorpe capitalized in shaming everyone."

Miles glared at the lord until he looked away. What did that green young man know about anything in life? "Be that as it may, all of my dealings with Leventhorpe were in person and at his home, and conducted in a civil manner in his study. Inquire through any of his servants. They've witnessed my appointments at one time or another." He waved a hand. "If that will be all? This is a waste of time." It was, but his departure had to appear authentic in front of everyone but Rathesborne. This was the easiest way to cut himself from the *ton*.

His intention to quit the area was staved when the duke raised a hand, just as they'd discussed earlier. "There's the rub, Archewyne. After I received the note, I had my man question Leventhorpe's butler and a maid. Both were adamant that on your last visit the two of you argued, quite strenuously, loud enough that the butler stood outside the room in alarm." His eyes narrowed. "The maid, once she was able to calm down enough, told my representative you visited Leventhorpe's home the day of his demise bearing a goodwill gift—a bottle of brandy. What are the odds that very gift contained the fatal poison?" The sharp words echoed in the sudden silence.

Damnation, but when the duke threw himself into a role, even Miles was hard pressed to discern what was real and what was invented.

"No." Emmaline's softly uttered denial fell on deaf ears.

"Lies. All lies." For the first time, cold panic wound up his spine as he gaped at his accusers. What if the plan failed and he truly fell victim to this complication? "Never have I raised my voice at Leventhorpe, nor did I bring him a gift or anything else."

"It's your word against witnesses, my lord," the viscount said. "It would be in your best interest to turn yourself in to the Runners before this scandal can catch fire."

"Otherwise, you'll be bad *ton* and ostracized," the younger lord added with a smug expression.

That's what I'm hoping for. At the last second, he tamped the urge to smile. "I refuse to admit to something I didn't do!" When did his actions move from believable into a Drury Lane tale? Just minutes ago he was near lost in the wonder that was Emmaline's soft lips and silky skin. Now, his mission from the prime minister had caught up with him and collided with these very real facts. Truly, he was on stage, if only he could play his part convincingly. How much more was needed? He pinned the duke with what he hoped was an angry look. No doubt the man would chastise him for it later. "I demand to see this alleged note, to compare handwriting."

Rathesborne shook his head. "I cannot let you do that given the slant of the investigation."

"Gentlemen, enough." Emmaline stepped forward and stood in their midst. Her eyes flashed. Frosty authority rang in her voice, and once again, Miles couldn't help but admire her confidence and poise. "This is hardly the place to discuss such a delicate matter." She stared down each and every lord, including the duke. "I would like to think all of you have enough integrity that this can be talked through, perhaps in the duke's study at his earliest convenience and most definitely not in a public forum for the lowest gossips to overhear." Her attention jumped to Miles. "You've conducted your life since becoming earl with nothing except honor. Surely your reputation will carry you through now."

Always the peacekeeper. Miles relaxed, but only slightly. Like a fish to a hook, she'd latched onto the story he and the duke hastily concocted. What would those ramifications be when—if—the lady found them out? "Thank you, Lady Emmaline. I agree. This isn't the proper venue for such a sensitive subject." His stomach twisted though he'd been sent on other missions of similar import. The only difference? He was lying to a woman he cared about and he'd have to leave Jane behind.

Never had he done either, for his wife had always been privy to his covert operations, but could he trust Emmaline with the same?

The answer remained cloaked. Emmaline possessed too spontaneous a nature. She'd be liable to do anything, even insist she go with him to defend him and her own interests. While that stroked his ego and would be convenient, it wasn't practical and it wasn't feasible. Lord Liverpool would have an apoplexy.

Before anyone could answer, Georgiana sailed up to them in a rustle of satin skirts with Viscount Darnell at her side. Miles fought to keep his expression neutral. He couldn't have planned a better way for the news to circulate than the gossipy, vindictive marchioness.

"I have to wonder why some of the most sought after men are congregating in this hall instead of making statements on the dance floor," she interjected with a hard glance at the gathering.

Miles glared. God, the last thing this farce needed was her interference. "This is business-related and doesn't concern you." His voice sounded graveled to his own ears, and that was all to the good.

"Is this about Leventhorpe's murder?" the viscount asked in curious tones. His dark eyes glittered in the dim light and the satisfied smirk on his face was unmistakable. "It would only reason it is since the whole of the ballroom is buzzing about it."

"The *ton* is vile like that." Emmaline, with a look of distaste, scuttled to Miles' side, and it took all his willpower not to wrap a protective arm around her. "It's a private matter."

God love her. His heart squeezed. "It's all right." He smiled at her then he focused his attention on the detestable viscount. "As a matter of fact, Darnell, yes. We are discussing Leventhorpe's untimely death—"

"—and the wealth of information that indicates Archewyne had a hand in it," the young Lord Vitteras interrupted with a wide grin. No doubt he thought to elevate himself in the eyes of higher ranking peers.

"Oh?" Lord Darnell's eyes lit and he cast a quick glance to the marchioness. "Now that is an interesting *on-dit* and development."

"Yes," Rathesborne drawled as his eyes gleamed with frustration. "We were just moving to return to the ballroom in favor of taking up this discussion later."

"Is this information credible?" Georgiana asked.

"In my opinion, yes," Rathesborne bit off sharply. "Though we'll need to authenticate the handwriting."

"Then why put off what you can tackle now? If Archewyne can clear his name, let him do it at this moment. No need to have an upstanding member of the *ton* arrested and cause further scandal." Georgiana threw a questioning glance around the assembled company. When Miles remained silent as did the duke, she continued. "Hmm, if he doesn't wish to defend himself, does that assume his guilt?"

"I say yes," Lord Vitteras declared with expectation in his expression.

The marchioness nodded. "Obviously, we cannot have an alleged murderer circulating in our midst," she continued with a sage expression that rang as false as his make believe murder charges. "Think of the talk." She glanced at the duke, whose thunderous frown said more than words ever could. "Would you truly want someone like Archewyne around your innocent daughter, my lord?"

Ha! What an asp she showed herself as. Perhaps she suffered from hurt feelings and was now being spiteful in her attempt to have him hauled away. He tamped on the urge to scoff. The situation would have been laughable had parts of it not been contrived by him and the duke. That a tiny grain of truth made the whole folly believable became a sticky wicket they'd have to play around. Miles concentrated on maintaining an attitude of annoyance. "That's an unfair assessment, Georgiana. I haven't seen the evidence and still maintain my innocence, as should my peers, until they too have a look at such allegedly damning information."

Rathesborne ignored him. No doubt if their gazes met, they'd give themselves away in what was rapidly growing out of hand. "Perhaps you're right, Lady Wellesley." He included everyone present with his dark gaze. "Shall we adjoin to my study?"

"To what purpose?" Emmaline briefly touched her fingertips to his forearm. "So they can continue to accuse you of wrongdoing? To sully your reputation?" With each question, her voice rose in alarm. "Miles, you cannot let this happen. They'll string you up alive and investigate later." She gripped his sleeve. "Look at them! They're fairly salivating for a fight."

"It must be done though, Lady Emmaline, for I shall alert the Runners momentarily of this information. After all, they're as perplexed as to who Leventhorpe's killer is as the rest of us are. It's only right they know." The marchioness took a step toward her with a hand extended. "Come away. This is not a matter for our female minds to worry over, my lady. Perhaps we should let the gentlemen talk it over."

Good God in heaven, the woman was vile and much too cunning to trust in any capacity. Miles' gut clenched. What was she about now? He didn't want Emmaline anywhere in the marchioness' company alone. The beaded scrap of fabric was still suspect and uppermost in his mind. Did it belong to Georgiana, and if so, why did she mean harm to Emmy? "I don't think—"

Darnell cleared his throat as the company looked on. "If I may be of service?" When six pairs of eyes rested on him, he grinned. "As a peer, I agree this matter should be discussed behind closed doors, and as a concerned citizen I think the Runners should be notified, but as a gentleman, I attest this is no place for the ladies. They should be enjoying themselves instead of witnessing such a foul situation." His low voice had a calming effect on the assembled members of the *ton*. He slid his gaze around the company before finally resting it on Emmy. "Lady Emmaline, perhaps you would be more comfortable in allowing me to return you to the ballroom and partaking in a dance?"

"If it's all the same to you, I'd rather remain with the gentlemen. It's an idiotic idea at best that women are not equal to men in brain capacity." She propped one gloved hand on her hip. "In some circumstances, the female insight can vastly differ and solve the problem. Especially when the men involved refuse to think clearly."

Snorts of derision emanated from the group. Lord Vitteras called for Miles' immediate detainment, no doubt in an effort to impress the others. The duke was rapidly losing control of what should have been an easy bit of fancy and misdirection.

Georgiana flashed a smile that bordered on the predatory. Was that the light of victory in her eyes? Miles' belly tightened. "Obviously, Lady Emmaline is overwrought. A nice cup of punch should settle her nerves while the men move to settle what sounds like rather heavy charges against Archewyne." She rested her blue gaze on Emmy. "My lady, it would behoove you to come away with the viscount and me. You wouldn't want additional scandal attached to your already cloudy reputation, would you?"

"I put little to no stock in the current gossip," Emmaline replied and her tones were as icy as a February wind.

Miles arched an eyebrow. This standoff between the women was vastly more interesting than trying to disentangle himself from the current knot. Why did Georgiana try so hard? Cold panic trickled down his spine. Surely the marchioness wouldn't attempt harm in such a public venue? Perhaps he should attempt to let her remain with him and lend whatever protection he could. "Her remaining will entirely depend upon the will of the duke." At least in this, the decision could be taken from him and her rage could fall on someone else. Plus, Rathesborne did drive the current drama.

Poor bastard.

"Capital idea," Rathesborne agreed. His expression eased into relief. "If you four would be so good as to take a few steps backward and give us a modicum of privacy? We'll confer as to the feasibility of that."

The women and Darnell retreated halfway down the corridor while Miles only gave the duke the asked for few steps. He stood by himself between the group of men and the others. Though he longed to take Emmaline aside and reassure her, his hands were figuratively tied. Everyone he knew had to look upon him with suspicion and rumors had to fly. Too bad those rumors and accusations were now much more serious than he had intended.

"Lady Emmaline," Georgiana said in a whisper that he could still hear. "If you think Archewyne will pursue you if he manages to clear his name, you are mistaken."

Miles narrowed his eyes and blatantly stared at them. If she didn't want to be overheard, she would have talked directly into Emmy's ear. The woman had an agenda and he didn't like it by half.

The marchioness practically purred into the relative quiet while Emmaline regarded her with slight interest. "Oh, I have no doubt this whole thing is a misunderstanding of the greatest magnitude. Archewyne could indeed be innocent." She waved a hand with a tinkling laugh. "It's no secret Leventhorpe was disliked by all who knew him. Anyone could have killed him, but if the earl is guilty, it's best the issue is settled now."

Emmaline quirked an eyebrow. Clearly she didn't believe the marchioness. "Even you, my lady?" she murmured with a sweet smile.

A trace of high color infused Georgiana's pale cheeks. "A reasonable assumption, for he did thwart me in my quest to acquire certain … things. Highly valuable pieces of art mostly. He was a self bastard." She sighed and it was a rather dramatic affair. "However, my innocence is not in question at the moment." She pinned Emmaline with a cold stare. "Archewyne isn't for you, pet. Why, the other day he and I took tea together, and we discussed the likelihood of a union between us."

"Georgiana, enough," Miles ordered, and though that part of her speech was correct, taken out of context, it would show him in a damning light.

"Pish posh, Miles. She has a right to know." Another trilling laugh followed. She grabbed Emmaline's hand and patted it as if they were the closest of friends. "He also wished to make certain that, if we were to wed, I'd be in accord with him and birth at least two children, for the dear man desperately wants that heir and a spare. After all, isn't that what all men want from the women they align themselves with?"

"What?" Emmaline's rapid intake of breath pierced Miles' heart. She shot a glance to him. "Is that true?" In one fluid movement, she extricated herself from Georgiana's clutches.

Did every woman of the *ton* manipulate men, or was it just his misfortune to come into contact with those who did? He sputtered at the same time the duke and the others turned to observe his latest *on-dit*. "It's true only insofar as the fact that the marchioness and I did speak of a mutual agreement between us in a theoretical way. I, for one, wasn't remotely serious." He shook his head, and with an outstretched hand, came toward her.

"Archewyne, we need to away." Authority rang in Rathesborne's voice.

"One moment, Your Grace." He didn't look at anyone else except Emmy and didn't care if the others heard what he had to say now. "Emmaline, listen to me, and me alone. Without you being a part of the circumstances of that day, of course the story sounds outrageous."

Her eyes widened, and in the low light, annoyance and disappointment fought for dominance in her emerald eyes. "You're no different after all."

"I am." Obviously, he couldn't remind her that she was the one who begged him to distract the marchioness so she could carry out her theft. Why was what he'd done—at her insistence—any different a crime than hers? He shook off the duke's heavy hand on his shoulder. This night had rapidly grow out of control and now he was caught in the middle. On one side rested the needs of the Crown and his services while on the other side waited his needs for a personal life and happiness. Why couldn't he have both? Why couldn't he keep both safe at the same time? He knew the reason; he cared too much about Emmaline. "You need only remember what I told you regarding offspring. That's the truth."

"Is it?" The sheen of tears filled her eyes, gone with the next blink. Determination settled in past the tiny crack of vulnerability. "It seems like I must reassess what the truth is and how much of it I believe, and what was foolish hope on my part."

"Please hear me out." Again he escaped the duke's hold and closed the distance between them. His pulse rushed loud in his ears, and though alienating her was a direct order, he suddenly hated the restrictions placed upon him. He dropped a staying hand on her shoulder, and when she flinched, he removed it. "Emmy." He lowered his voice, this time not wishing for anyone else to hear. "I've never lied to you." His chest pained him as though someone had punched him in his center. Well, he hadn't, until it had become necessary.

Goddamn the prime minister and the duke!

Behind him, Rathesborne cleared his throat. "Archewyne, we must adjourn." There was no mistaking the authority in that ducal command. "Now."

He forced down a hard swallow as he held Emmaline's gaze that glimmered with confusion. "Remember what I said about the Egyptian asp." He flicked a glance to Georgiana then back at her. "They are as dangerous as they are evil. Avoid them at all costs, for they are always underfoot, biding their time to bite and attack."

"You talk in riddles. There are no snakes here."

"I have to for the moment." Would that he could explain. Instead, he implored her to understand with his gaze. *Please remember.*

Emmaline narrowed her eyes. She whispered, "Why me?"

"I beg your pardon?" He didn't follow her line of thought not when a thousand others crowded his mind.

"Why did you attempt to toy with my affections if you intended to wed another all along?" Then her damned chin wobbled and his resolve did the same.

The use of the word "attempt" nearly gutted him. Had he been winning the upper hand before this? Reality intruded once more and cold disappointment invaded his being. This was for the best, honestly. Without the connection to him, she'd be safe. "I'm sorry." *For many, many things. Please forgive me.*

"So am I." She stood staring at him as the light died in her eyes, and all too soon the duke tugged at his shoulder while Lord Darnell appeared at hers. Georgiana watched with a slight smile curving her lips. It was that grin that chilled Miles to his very bones.

"Emmaline, don't go." And what in hell was she supposed to do while he had the remainder of his part to play?

"My lady, would you care to dance?" the viscount asked, ignoring Miles' entreaty. "There are better men in London than the earl, as we've all borne witness to this night."

He couldn't give her up, not like this. Leaning into her, he pressed his lips to her ear as if he were bestowing a farewell kiss, and said for her alone, "I *will* call tomorrow."

He pulled back quickly and assumed an expression of hurt he desperately hoped was convincing.

At the same time, Rathesborne growled, "We've decided. Lady Emmaline will not be part of our negotiations as she's been implicated herself to a point, and furthermore, we've agreed to reconvene later in the week. I will send out notice. My lady, please remove with the marchioness and viscount."

Miles nodded though his chest squeezed so hard he could barely breathe. "Very well." He wasn't capable of movement as Emmaline, with one last, lingering glance over her shoulder at him, laid her fingers upon Darnell's sleeve then allowed him to lead her down the corridor toward the ballroom.

The marchioness followed, but not before she imparted a statement that chilled his blood. "Our paths will cross again, Miles, once you convince the duke and the others of your innocence, for we both know you had nothing to do with Leventhorpe's death."

He sucked in a quick breath. "You wrote the note damning my name?"

"How rude of you to say something like that." She paused and his jaw worked though no words came forth. "I'm certain you'll smooth over this ugly little distraction. Afterward, you'll come to see that an alliance between us is advantageous to you, for I command influence throughout the *ton* you can make use of. Peers such as us have been born to this. Everything we do is about power and wealth. We are untouchable in all matters—including the criminal."

He gawked. Was that a veiled confession?

The other two lords trailed in her wake, their backs ramrod straight, their hands clasped behind their backs. In short order, Miles stood alone with the duke, his world shattering about his feet, piece by jagged piece.

"That was brutal, Archewyne. I couldn't have asked for it to play out better though I would have wished there truly wasn't a link between you and Leventhorpe." He shook his head. "The business of the note can be cleared in short order."

"Thank you. No doubt you'll soon find it's a forgery." Miles glanced at him, the man to whom he reported if the prime minister was out of pocket and heaved a sigh. "I only hope our plan did what we'd hoped." And not damaged more important things.

"It will if you cut all ties to her." The duke's expression softened. "You know what needs to be done, how vital our plan is. This country cannot return to war."

"I do. The security of the king is my first priority. You know that." He rubbed a hand over his face. "Tell me this. How can you do the same as well as have a wife and a family when you tell me I cannot?"

"One must be sacrificed for the other." A trace of regret lingered in his low-pitched voice. It mirrored what flashed in his eyes. "There was a time when I was first married that I could have been quite blissfully happy."

"What happened?"

"The Crown needed me more, and when I answered Britain's call, my marriage suffered. Couldn't compete." A graceful shrug pulled at his shoulders. "The sting was there surely, but I learned to live with it. Unfortunately, or perhaps fortunately for her, my wife found other interests, and I silently wish her well in the affair she's kept for nigh onto fifteen years. I..." His jaw worked. "I pray she's happy even as she remains tethered to me. At least in this regard, my title and reach can see she's cared for. I love her still."

"But you're not with her." Miles schooled his expression into a blank mask so the other man wouldn't see his shock. What a horrible outcome for one's life, yet the duke was teaching his daughter those same values as she played the part as a spy for him. His throat worked. He peered down the now-empty corridor. "Forgive me if I'm having difficulty in accepting the same fate just yet. It's a lonely endeavor. Especially now."

"I understand." Rathesborne tugged out his timepiece from a waistcoat pocket, consulted it then stuffed it back in. "Things are coming to a head. It would behoove you to have your affairs in order soon, old man. I'll do what I can to smooth your way out of England, but these younger lords are out for blood and accolades. I expect at least one will tip someone's hand, if Lady Wellesley hasn't already done so. It'll prove more of a mess, but rest assured, I will take care of it. Many men owe me favors."

The reach of a duke was a fearsome and fantastic power. Miles didn't answer in words. Instead, he nodded. "If you'll excuse me? I should probably spend as much time with Jane as I can." How could he leave her, when she was the only family he had left?

"Indeed." The duke brushed at his shoulder. "What do you mean to do with her? She cannot come with you."

"I am aware." He shook his head. "At the moment, I do not know." With that, Miles continued along the corridor in the opposite direction of the ballroom where gay laughter and conversation echoed. No way could he bear to witness Emmaline dancing with Darnell or another man, to see the accusation or disappointment in her beautiful eyes.

I'm simply not strong enough.

Chapter Nineteen

Emmaline detested every second she spent in Lord Darnell's arms as they circled the dance floor in a quadrille. She hated that Miles had been accused of Leventhorpe's murder and not given the opportunity to defend his honor.

Above all, she loathed the knowledge that he'd discussed marriage and children with the marchioness, and all but made the blonde an offer, while paying her—Emmaline—pretty compliments and pressing his suit. Why the devil would he do such a thing if not to mock her or try to wound her? Out of all the men of the *ton*, she never thought Miles would be so cruel.

Except… She forced a hard swallow. It had been on her direction he'd been in that situation to begin with. She'd even indicated he should kiss the marchioness for more of a distraction. Apparently, he had indeed.

I'm as guilty as he. And her heart ached all the more because of it. *I need to apologize.*

On one pass of the ballroom, she spied Georgiana standing near a Doric column. Her expression proclaimed her the cat who had caught the canary. *Damn her eyes.* She already considered herself the winner of the earl's hand, providing he found a way out of this current mess.

Silly tears prickled the backs of her eyelids. She blinked. Now was not the time for such maudlin displays, not when all she wanted was to remove herself from this horrible ball and lick her wounds in private while coaxing

Sanura near. Nothing set the world to rights quite like the warm body of a cat in one's lap.

"Come now, Lady Emmaline. Never say you've let that scandalous earl affect you," the viscount said, his voice teasing as he led her to the sidelines once the dance concluded.

"I don't owe you an explanation," she managed to choke out and removed her fingers from his the moment she reached safety.

"No, you do not, but you do owe me your manners." He arched an eyebrow. "Some of us have managed not to kill a peer and some of us look past your father's reputation in order to squire you about the dance floor."

Heat jumped into her cheeks. "I apologize." No matter how much she disliked the viscount, there was no cause of a bad attitude. "The last few days have been fraught with drama." And she'd had a hand in some of that.

"Understandable." He roved his gaze along her person then grinned. That gesture held a predatory edge that sent cold chills down her spine. "Would you care for a glass of punch or perhaps some champagne? At the least it should calm your nerves."

"Punch would be lovely," she replied in some distraction.

"I'll return in a twinkling."

She stood in a daze as the viscount, the same man she'd slapped days before, rushed back to her side with a glass cup three-quarters full of a pink-hued beverage. "Thank you," she murmured and took the offering from him. Emmaline choked down a few swallows of the punch and wrinkled her forehead.

"Enjoy the beverage," he said, his tone intense. "It'll quench your thirst and perhaps give you a second wind.

The ball is likely to go on for hours, and dinner is ninety minutes out. Perhaps we can enjoy the garden beforehand."

Oh God. Dinner. The thought of sitting at a table trying to eat and make insipid conversation turned her stomach as did spending more time in this man's company. "This is vile and bitter. I'm surprised the duke would serve such a brew." Not that she wouldn't mind something to eat since her last meal had been breakfast that morning.

He nudged her elbow. "Perhaps it improves on a second taste?"

Emmaline gulped another mouthful then handed him the cup that was now nearly empty. "It did not." As much as asking for a flute of the sparkling wine would help calm her nerves and help wash the horrid punch from her tongue, she shook her head. "Honestly, my lord, I'd very much like to go home. Please reach deep inside yourself in the event you have some glimmer of redemption and escort me to the door." Gone was the desire to search the duke's home for the India diamond. The enjoyment for thievery had dimmed in the face of worry for Miles. *I must apologize to him.* "Forget that. I need to talk with Archewyne." She took a step away.

"I wouldn't involve myself with him any further, my lady." Lord Darnell caught her arm. His eyes took on an enterprising gleam. He took her hand and patted it. "Your home is the best place for you at the moment. Allow me to escort you there myself."

She frowned. Slight warning bells went off in her mind. "Why would you do that for me?" Leopards didn't change spots overnight.

Or at all.

"Let's just say I have my reasons, and it does appear as if your knight in shining armor has already departed." He offered his arm. "Shall we?"

A look through the crowds didn't show the tall, commanding figure she sought. Did the duke detain him or had Bow Streets come to claim him? Or worse, did he visit a shadowy alcove with the marchioness? Her spirits sank. "Thank you." She laid her fingers on his sleeve and they quit the ballroom. Once or twice her steps faltered, but Darnell wrapped an arm about her waist and kept her upright.

It took mere moments to exit the townhouse, and by the time they reached the street, the viscount's closed, black carriage waited.

The viscount himself swung open the door. "After you, my lady." He handed her into the vehicle and when she'd seated herself climbed up beside her.

Once the door closed and the carriage sprang into motion did Emmaline realize there was another person in the carriage. The heavy scent of honeysuckle reached her nose. "Georgiana? What are you doing here? I don't understand." She shook her head. The interior of the carriage spun. A fuzzy fog invaded her mind and her vision blurred at the edges. She fought against the weird sensations and squinted at the other woman. Had the viscount offered the marchioness a ride as well? That didn't make sense. Of course the marchioness would have arrived in her own carriage.

Her laughter trilled through the darkened interior. "Did you think I'd let you escape this night with only hurt feelings?"

"Meaning?" Her eyelids drooped so heavily she could barely keep her eyes open. What the deuce was wrong with her? She'd barely exerted herself in two dances. Of course, there was the whole heated session with Miles… Miles, the man who'd stomped on her heart and she'd given him the means in which to do it. "Where are you taking me?" Her stomach clenched. Perhaps being so hasty and leaving with an unsavory man such as Lord Darnell hadn't been wise. She swallowed as her mouth went dry. That horrible bitter taste lingered on her tongue. Her pulse increased. Bitter punch. *Oh God, and I was so distracted with worry and self-pity that I didn't notice something was added…*

"Why, to your home, of course. That's where you intended to go, is it not?" The marchioness waved a hand as if Emmaline's questions were a bother. "To answer your first inquiry, Lord Darnell did a special favor for me, now I'm rewarding him with a gift. He's a dear friend and I know he'll enjoy it."

"Of what?" The carriage wasn't moving fast. If she jumped out now, she wouldn't incur many injuries and if fate was with her, she might just manage to stumble home before the inevitable happened. She groped for the door handle. It took three attempts for her fuzzy and lagging brain to tell her hand to grasp it. Once she did and tugged, the mechanism didn't budge.

Locked!

"Rather, of whom," Georgiana purred.

"Whom?" She struggled to focus on the pale face in front of her. Blinking didn't alleviate the sudden onset of lethargy. Panic edged up her spine and she cursed her own stupidity.

The marchioness leaned forward and her grin in the passing gaslights was anything but warming. "You, my dear. The viscount has lusted after you ever since my dinner party; his interest rather borders on obsession. I thought you'd be just the thing for him."

"I refuse." Emmaline vaulted to her feet, but the carriage spun around her and she faltered. Her balance wavered. With growing horror, she stared at the viscount. "What was in that punch?" *Beware the asps. They're underfoot ... ready to bite.* She should have listened to Miles instead of giving in to stupid feelings of petty hurt and jealousy. *I should have believed him, remained true to myself.* The earl she knew would never voluntarily wed the marchioness, nor would he kill a peer. Lord Darnell tugged her down so hard she sprawled inelegantly in his lap. "Let me go."

"Not now, when the game is only starting," he murmured. He pressed her closer to his chest and still she fought her drooping eyelids. "As to your inquiry regarding the punch, I included a hefty dose of laudanum in your cup. It's extremely fine and very pure; the stuff the king uses, I'm told. It should work quickly enough, especially if your stomach is empty."

Bloody hell. She tried to focus on his hated face, attempted to lift a hand to slap him, but her arm was too heavy and her vision darkened. "No." No matter that she wished to say more, she couldn't make her now tingling lips do anything else but form an *O*.

"Yes." Darnell's chuckle held a triumphant edge. "Enjoy the nap. Everything will be well-prepared by the time you wake." He licked the side of her neck. "You won't soon forget this night."

"No." Her whisper faded as the darkness claimed her.

Emmaline came back to consciousness slowly.

Her limbs were heavy and she couldn't move them, but at least her mind was beginning to clear. As near as she could figure, she lay on something cold and hard and unforgiving. Her legs dangled off it, but her feet rested on something solid. The warm scent of candlewax wafted to her nose as did the cloying aroma of Georgiana's honeysuckle perfume. Sounds drifted to her position. She kept her eyes closed in the event someone monitored her while she attempted to identify the noise.

As she concentrated, the low buzz changed into soft conversation, but her parched throat demanded attention. On her quest to swallow, mild panic swept through her system. A rag of some sort had been tied around her head and between her jaws, effectively stifling any sort of moisture or talking. Ignoring that for the moment, she turned her attention to making out the words said.

"Just how do you intend to make certain Archewyne will no longer want her?" Georgiana asked in a petulant tone. "You told me you had methods, and I want assurance that after tonight, she'll be objectionable to him."

"Oh, ye of little faith," the viscount murmured off to one side. "I have my ways, but you need to ask yourself if your ability to turn his head is enough."

A *tap-tap* sounded near Emmaline's opposite ear. Was the marchioness drumming her fingernails on a piece of furniture? "Before the little twit entered his life again, I was more than certain. I had almost won his regard." Annoyance wove through the other woman's voice. "However, I'm not sure now. I've seen the way he looks at her. This might not be enough to keep him away. He harbors a damned noble streak I hadn't anticipated."

Emmaline strained her ears. *How does he look at me?*

Lord Darnell snorted. The tick of metal against metal met her ears. "The man's near gone on her. He'll play a hero to the point of being a fool."

"Yes, I know." The annoyance grew as she ground out the words. "I've seen the love in his eyes. I doubt he's even aware of his feelings, which is all to the good. If he doesn't know, it will be easy enough for me to make him forget."

Gooseflesh popped on Emmaline's arms. He's in love? *With me?* He never said anything nor made a declaration. There was no time to ponder the implications, for the other two continued their conversation.

"*If* you can coerce him into your bed. It would appear he has a strong resistance to you."

"Thanks to his preoccupation from Lady Emmaline." She pinched the skin of Emmaline's inner arm, prompting a soft cry. "It's of no consequence. You break her, and I'll be there to console the earl in good time."

"No one marks her except me," the viscount ordered in a voice that sent cold dread into her stomach. So close, his brandy-scented breath skated across her cheek, he pressed two fingers to her wrist. "Her pulse is faster. She'll wake soon and we'll start the festivities."

"Then you'd best set your stage. I already did my part with the forged note that landed him in the drink rather more nicely than I'd thought." A rustle of satin rasped into the quiet. "What will you do with her after tonight?"

"What can I do?" His hands were at her arm. Something rough and thick slid around her wrist then was wrenched tight, pulling an involuntary moan from her. Did he mean to bind her? Alarm fluttered through her veins. "Ah, she's coming around." Pleasure rode the statement. "I might not be able to keep her as a play thing, but I'll guarantee she won't forget and once word leaks of our time together, of what she begged me to do to her, no respectable man in the *ton* will touch her."

"There are times when you've done a magnificent job at hiding how deranged you truly are," the marchioness murmured. Then she sighed. "Short of keeping her drugged, I suppose you'll have to leave her here. I'm told she's leaving for Egypt in mere days. Poor Lady Emmaline will be so mortified by news of her liaison with you in the scandal sheets that she'll never return to England. Everyone will abandon her, even Archewyne. The man is much too proper to overcome this."

"Perhaps there's no need to turn her loose. My country estate is far removed from London. No one would know if they assumed she had indeed gone on to Cairo…"

"That's your business, and one I won't be privy to. I already have enough complications to manage."

The viscount had moved to her other wrist and gave it the same treatment. The rope's fibers cut into her skin. "You're as devious as I, my lady. If I didn't know better, I'd say you killed Leventhorpe for spite."

"Well, he did grow annoying when he figured out my little scheme with the artwork, but I didn't end him and you know it." A soft chuckle left her. "The little rabbit's eyes are fluttering." The waft of honeysuckle grew stronger, and then soft hands tapped her cheeks none too gently. "Wake up, my lady. It's time to play."

"And before you make any sort of movement, dear Emmaline, do have a care. You mustn't jerk your wrists else death will come immediately."

Not able to feign unconsciousness any longer, Emmaline opened her eyes, and gasped. She was in her father's study at her own townhouse. Even though the sheets covering the furniture remained intact like so many waiting ghosts, she'd been laid out on his massive cherry wood desk with her wrists bound. Heartbeat pounding, she checked the bonds then frowned. What exactly did he mean by this?

"Welcome back to the world, my lady," Lord Darnell greeted as he moved to stand by her legs, which dangled down the side of the desk at the knee. Her feet rested on a stool. "You're probably wondering at my intentions."

When she would have given a short answer, she remembered the gag, and the only sound she emitted was a series of grunts punctuated with growls.

"Poor dear," the viscount said with a mirthless laugh. "No words? Let me explain." He came closer and caressed a hand along her neck. "The rope binding your right hand is attached to that toy cannon on the shelf over there. Inside that cannon is a dart dipped in a fast-acting poison. Move that hand and you'll set off the cannon. I'm afraid you won't live past a few minutes once struck. Don't believe me? You need only to remember Lord Leventhorpe."

Dear God, was that an admission of guilt or did he merely assume? Her eyes widened as she followed his line of sight with her gaze. That cannon had been in her father's possession for years. When she anchored her attention back to him, she recoiled at the dangerous glint in those dark depths.

"Ah, suitably impressed, I see." He slid his fingers down her chest, where he traced the edge of her bodice. "Your left hand is tied to that candle resting on a small table. Beneath the candle as well as around the floor nearby are alcohol-soaked rags and papers. Move that hand and you'll tip the candle, thereby starting a fire. I wonder how long it will be before those flames begin to lick their way to your prone and immobile form?"

Now that he'd mentioned it, the sharp scent of brandy, wine and whiskey flooded her nostrils. She glanced at the table and the single candle that rested in a brass holder. It wouldn't take much movement on her part to send it over. Cold terror washed over her and she focused on him once again. She lifted her head and glared. If only she could work the gag from her mouth. "Bastard," she choked out from around the fabric.

The viscount smiled at Georgiana. "I adore when they have spirit. It makes it more enjoyable for me, for then I must employ methods to subdue them." He lifted an eyebrow. "The knife, if you please, my lady."

While Emmaline watched in horrified fascination, the marchioness procured a knife from one of the desk drawers. She handed it to him. "Enough dramatics, Graham. Move along."

Dear Lord. Did the marchioness mean to stay and witness whatever he would do or did she intend to partake in it as well? Emmaline squirmed, being sure not to jar either hand. She kicked a foot in the viscount's direction.

"None of that." Candlelight winked on the wicked blade as he rested the cold metal against her throat. "Or I shall remove the stool and you'll have to fight for balance?" With the same smile she'd seen at Georgiana's dinner party, he fisted her bodice then deftly sliced the silk, ripping and tearing. Once his handiwork was done, he tossed the knife away then tore her gown asunder, laying her bare to his hot and evil gaze.

"I never thought you'd be such a scandalous baggage," Georgiana commented. "No undergarments tonight." She raked her cold blue gaze over Emmaline's naked body. "No wonder you've manage to captivate the earl. You're no better than a harlot."

Emmaline turned her head away from the marchioness' leer and the blatant lust in the viscount's face. Clad only in her stockings and slippers, she was literally on display and could do nothing to shield herself. The cool air in the room tightened her nipples. His ego probably thought her aroused. When she'd left home *sans* undergarments, she'd only thought to tease Miles. Now, that thought of a romantic interlude mocked her with the raw and somewhat desperate image she had become. Hot, bitter bile hit the back of her throat and she gagged. The rag keeping her from cursing at them only enhanced the need to retch.

"This is what you're waiting for, Lady Georgiana." He twisted a signet ring off his pinky finger and held it up. "It's one of the things I pride myself in. The women whom I wish to remember our time together, I brand them as mine." The man wandered over to the candle on the table she was tethered to. He then proceeded to hold the metal ring over the flame. "I look forward to leaving my mark on this one. She's always held herself aloof from me, fascinated me ever since I saw her that night … well, no need to reveal too much."

Emmaline shook her head. She couldn't tear her gaze away from the flame as it heated the ring. "No." Even with the gag, the horror in that utterance rang in the room.

"Yes." Darnell's smile made him appear deranged in the crazy tilting shadows. "Even if the earl somehow manages to overlook your sins gained this night, he will always have to see this mark and he'll know I had you first, that I left such an impression on you, you'll remember each time he beds you. There is every possibility you'll never crave bed sport again with anyone except me."

A shiver shook Georgiana's frame. "You're insane, Graham." Anticipation lit her eyes as he brought the ring over to Emmaline.

"Perhaps, but then it's also a sign of high intelligence." He flicked a hard gaze to the marchioness. "Do manage to hold her legs steady." He pinned Emmaline with that same look. "Remember, any movement of your arms and death or destruction will claim you before I ever can." He loomed over her; the ring winked in the dim light. "I'm afraid this will hurt, but then, that really does inspire me."

Her pulse raced, pounded in her ears as he came closer still. She attempted to shy away, Lord how she tried, but between the bonds on her wrists and Georgiana's hand on one knee, she couldn't move far. With a grin that bordered on the unhinged, Lord Darnell pressed the white-hot signet ring onto the slope of her right breast, just above the nipple.

Searing pain shot through her, down to every nerve ending and into every pore. She bucked her hips off the desk. A sharp cry tore from her dry throat. And still he held the heated piece of metal against her skin. Tears sprang to her eyes. The moisture welled and overflowed onto her cheeks. "Please. Stop." The rag muffled her plea.

"Enough, Graham. Enough." Georgiana's tone sounded horror-stricken. "I'm satisfied she'll remain damaged for long after you're finished with her."

The viscount removed the ring from her person and Emmaline sobbed with relief. The pain lingered, but at least the horrible heat ceased. His gaze bored into hers. "Your performance this night, my lady, will determine whether or not I put a matching mark on your lower lips." He tossed the signet ring to the desk near her head. "To show you I'm not quite the monster you think, I'll soothe your latest beauty mark."

Georgiana handed him a folded piece of cloth. "I'm leaving. I suggest you finish with her quickly then lose yourself in the city for a few days. Or take yourself off to the country with your little play thing. Make certain there is no evidence to clean up. Archewyne will be incensed, but if we ride out his rage, all will be well and his temptation will be gone. He'll forget her soon enough and will have no cause to search if he believes she's left for Egypt."

"Indeed." He laid the cloth over the skin he'd branded. Emmaline nearly fainted at the coolness that clung to her breast, for the cloth had been soaked in iced water. He waved the marchioness off. "I'll be in touch." Once Georgiana had fully departed, Lord Darnell lifted the cloth. He blew on the newly formed wound, and as much as Emmaline hated anything from him, she closed her eyes against the blessed cool wind his breath provided to her angry skin. "Shall we begin?"

Chapter Twenty

"My lord." Peterson's utterance was as urgent as his knock. "For the love of God, man, open up. This is urgent."

"Enter," Miles finally said as he roused himself from his thoughts as well as the chair in his rooms—the same chair Emmaline had suggested he relocate. After he'd returned home, he'd made good on his word and spent the evening with his daughter, read her a few stories and tucked her into bed himself. Then, he'd retired to his own rooms to contemplate what his life had become. As his valet-turned-companion came into the room, Miles stopped short at the alarm in the man's expression. "What happened?"

"I've been monitoring Lady Emmaline's townhouse for a few days, ever since you asked me to, and tonight there has been suspicious activity." His tone portrayed dire images.

"What?" The question thundered louder than he'd intended.

Peterson rubbed a hand along his rather scruffy jaw. "Viscount Darnell escorted her home from the duke's ball, but he wasn't alone." When Miles glared, his valet rushed onward. "The marchioness accompanied them."

His heartbeat jumped into double time. "How long ago?" He glanced at the ormolu clock on his mantel. Five to midnight. He'd quit Rathesborne's home around eleven o'clock and stupidly gave her into the viscount's care even though his instinct had screamed otherwise.

"Perhaps a quarter hour after you left, sir." Peterson cleared his throat. "The viscount took her out in one dance, pressed a punch cup upon her then they departed straightaway."

"Did she leave the ball under her own power?" Frissons of alarm played his spine.

"More or less, though she was listing a bit. I couldn't determine her state once he handed her into the carriage, but I did glimpse the marchioness in the carriage as well." The red-haired man stood quiet for several seconds. "As we speak, all three remain inside the house. I came here when he carried an unconscious Lady Emmaline into the house. I have no idea how much time we have while she's out. What are your orders?"

"The damn man drugged her punch." Rage sizzled through his veins. Miles raked both hands through his hair. "What the hell do you think my orders are, Peterson?" He met his friend's unreadable gaze. "I have to go to her. I have to break my direct bloody orders and go to her because I care for her no matter what the Crown wants of me."

His breath grew labored the longer he stared at the man who'd been by his side for years. It was true. He *cared* for Emmaline, probably more than he should and especially in the face of her continuing refusals. If he were honest with himself, it was more than that. Could he have been more jingle-brained? In the beginning, it had been a matter of honor and curiosity, but from the first she'd captivated him and now, he couldn't imagine existing in a world without her.

Britain could go hang in this moment. He'd reconcile to his mission once Emmy was safe.

Peterson clapped his hands. A wide grin split his face. "It's about bloody time you got your head out of your arse, sir, if you don't mind me saying so."

"Yes, well, we all make mistakes." He reached to tweak his cravat then realized he'd removed it shortly after returning home along with his dress jacket. "I don't believe there's a dress code regarding rescuing a woman in trouble, is there Peterson?"

"Not that I'm aware of." His lips twitched.

"Shirt sleeves it is." For the first time since the evening's odyssey began, Miles smiled, though it was as tight as his chest. Emmaline's very life might be in critical danger. "Let's be off. I'm concerned that the marchioness has dire plans for Lady Emmaline." As they left his townhouse, he told Peterson of his suspicions regarding Georgiana and detailed the scrap of fabric left at Emmaline's townhouse.

"Then we should hasten our steps," was his valet's only reply.

Never had Miles moved with less decorum through the streets of Mayfair. If anyone spotted them, they'd assume he and Peterson were running a foot race at neck or nothing speed. Or they'd think the two of them were insane.

Perhaps they were.

By the time they arrived at their destination, Miles' nerves were fairly humming with anxiety and alarm. How could he live with himself if harm had come to her when he'd vowed, once again, to protect her and, once more, he didn't follow through on that promise. Only this was worse than the episode in Cairo. Viscount Darnell wasn't a gang of street ruffians and from all accounts, his particular pleasures tended to dwell on the dark side.

I should never have let her go with him. I should have defied Rathesborne. I should have ... well, none of it matters now.

They reached the residence the same time a black carriage pulled away from the curb. As it passed by a gaslight, he recognized the Wellesley crest on the door. *Botheration.* "Come on," he urged his friend as they raced up the front steps. A knock would alert his quarry, so Miles tried the door knob. The handle offered no resistance and the door swung silently inward, opening into a shadow-filled entry hall. "Bugger it. This doesn't bode well." He kept his voice to a whisper.

"Where is her butler?" Peterson threw a glance about their immediate area.

"Not sure. Where is the lion?" He frowned as he surveyed the unpolished floor. "There is a maid as well, but she seems to be missing."

"You take the upper levels. I'll investigate this one and the staff quarters," Peterson offered before melting into the shadows without a sound.

Seconds later, a muffled cry filtered to his ears from above. "Emmaline." He'd recognize that voice for it haunted his dreams.

Miles crept up the staircase. He cringed when one of the treads creaked beneath his weight. When no one dashed out to investigate, he continued until he reached the first floor. Weak illumination escaped from a room at the end of the hall, so he moved toward that, all the while hoping against hope the scene he'd come upon wouldn't be as bad as he feared.

Except, as he gained the room—a study that had been left to dust, time and memories—his stomach bottomed out. It was worse than he could have imagined. Emmaline lay tied to a sheet-covered desk, but he couldn't understand why the ropes were attached to seemingly random objects. Not from this distance at least. But what concerned him was her naked state. He refused to look upon her with lust, for this wasn't the time, yet he did bitterly mourn the fact that his first glimpse of her beautifully bare form was in this way. Darnell had stolen that gift from him, and for that the man would pay.

As quietly as he could, he entered the room, his steps silent on the worn carpeting. With Darnell's back to him, he'd have the advantage.

The viscount kicked a stool out from beneath Emmaline's feet. She scrambled for purchase but her toes barely touched the floor. A chuckle left the other man's throat and the sound sent gooseflesh over Miles' skin. "Do remember, my lady. Any jarring movement from either wrist will be your demise."

What did that mean? Miles sent his gaze roving along the rope that bound her again. One ended with a single, guttering candle surrounded by combustible materials. The man was sick. He slid his attention to the other rope and frowned. What the devil was that? He squinted. A cannon? Another two steps brought the object into better focus. The rope was tied to a trigger mechanism while the sharp tip of a dart winked in the dim light. Miles fought down the bile in his throat. What sort of madness drove this man?

"Hmmm, shall I feast or just skewer you?" Darnell leaned over her, went so far as to put his vile hands on her body, touching her, caressing her, sliding those hated hands over her pale skin then finally grasped her thighs and wrenched them apart.

"Please don't do this." Emmaline's frantic, muffled cry pierced Miles' heart and only then did he see the rag that garbled her voice.

"Ah, begging. How it cheapens the experience for you but thrills me." Darnell manipulated the buttons at the front of his trousers, shoving the fabric out of the way. As he moved slightly, his erect length became visible to Miles. "I wonder how you'll try to save yourself, for I won't be gentle when I claim you. Will you succumb to the poison as you spend at my hand? How fitting, wouldn't you say, dying for pleasure from the last man who'll ever touch you? Perhaps I'll leave you here, laid out in artistic fashion, for your precious earl to find. For him to remember—and to regret." His laugh scraped along Miles' nerves. "Wouldn't the marchioness love that? She's been in a right proper rage since you returned to England."

Miles couldn't stand there another minute. "Not unless you kill me first, you demented bastard." He flew across the room, and as Darnell turned, he landed the man a facer that knocked him backward. Unfortunately, he landed against Emmaline's legs.

She jerked from the impact and both arms moved. The candle tipped and the flame set fire to the detritus around it with a slight *whoosh!* Her cry was his only warning.

Ignoring Darnell's rage-filled shout, Miles grabbed a slim book that rested near her head. He used it to shield the side of Emmaline's face at the exact second the sharp, silver dart imbedded its tip into the linen cover. His heartbeat raced, but he said, "At last I've found a decent use for Keats."

"Damn you, Archewyne, you've ruined everything!" The viscount shoved Miles from his body then got off a kick that connected with Miles' abdomen.

He grunted. "That largely depends on your perspective, and from mine, I've saved everything." He sprang at the viscount, grappling with him and they both hit the floor in a tangle of limbs. The acrid scent of smoke filled the room and lent urgency to his mission, but he couldn't spare a look to gauge the fire. "Give up, Darnell." He attempted to pin the other man to the carpet, but the viscount flipped them both over with surprising strength then knocked Miles' head backward with a powerful uppercut to the jaw.

Darnell sprang to his feet. "I've still won, my lord." As he stuffed his deflating prick back into his trousers, he headed toward the door then skidded to a halt as Peterson blocked his path, the lion cub at his feet.

"Don't let him get away!" Miles shouted to Peterson as he clambered into a standing position. Darnell eluded Peterson then pelted down the hall. The valet's footfalls rang behind him. He looked at the cat, who remained poised, body taut. What the devil was its name? He wracked his brain. "Sanura!" He pointed toward the door. "Chase!"

The cat's ears perked. Seconds later she vanished down the hall after the men. A high-pitched masculine cry followed not too long after.

"One moment, Emmy." Keeping an eye on the spreading fire that now occupied half the room and crept toward the desk, he whisked a dust street from a winged back chair then set about smothering the flames. The deuced fire wouldn't die, and the more he attempted to cover a patch, new danger spots sprang to life.

"I am an earl, not the bloody fire brigade!" His roar of frustration had no effect on the fire, of course, but he felt better for the utterance. With determination and much cursing, he moved from flame to flame until every lick of orange had been killed. Smoke still curled through the room and wafted in strange patterns at the ceiling. "It is done," he proclaimed as if he'd just finished creating the

Universe instead of keeping the townhouse from burning. Panting from exertion, he threw the charred and ruined sheet down.

Satisfied the danger from that quarter had passed, he bounded to Emmaline's side, being sure to keep eye contact instead of looking over her body. "My poor girl." As much as he wanted to ask if she was hurt, it would have been an idiotic question. If she wasn't physically, she would be mentally. Anyone would. It took little time to untie and remove the ropes from her wrists. "Did he, ah, violate you intimately?" God, if the viscount touched her, the man couldn't hide anywhere that Miles wouldn't find him, mission for the prime minister be damned.

She shook her head and only then did he spy the tracks of dried tears on her cheeks. His attention snagged on what appeared to be a burn of some kind on her breast, but he said nothing about it, not wishing to perpetuate her trauma. Her eyes, wide and as large as moons, held relief and was that shame? Humiliation? She glanced over his shoulder when he rid her of the nasty gag. "Will Peterson kill him?" No emotion colored her graveled voice.

"He will not, but I suspect he will rough him up a bit. We have no cause to detain him and Bow Street certainly will turn a blind eye." In the world of the *ton*, the authorities or lawmakers didn't care where or how a man took his pleasures against women. Miles helped her from the desk and when she stood, the remnants of the beautiful gown she'd worn earlier fell from her shoulders. "Your lion cub, however, might have other ideas." When she shivered, he yanked the sheet cover from the desk and wrapped it around her.

"Will you?" It was asked in the same deadened tone.

"Not at this moment. You are of greater importance."

Finally, she met is gaze while rearranging the white fabric about her person so that her arms were free. "Thank you." Her soft voice rasped in the quiet. She looked at the abandoned book of poetry with the dart stuck it its cover. "He wanted me to die even as he intended to do … well, you know."

He did know and he didn't wish to think upon it, though it wouldn't be as easy for her to forget. "Let me help you to your rooms. You should rest. Peterson and I will take care of the viscount and leave you in peace."

"No." She clutched his arm. "Please stay." The muscles in her delicate throat worked with a swallow. "I don't want to be alone." Her chin trembled. "I need you, if only for a little while."

How could he deny her the request after what she'd gone through? Before he could answer, commotion at the door interrupted them. He darted his gaze to the opening where Peterson came in. A smear of blood marred his cheek and his bottom lip was slightly puffy. "Well?" Was it too much to hope that he'd beat the man bloody or dropped him into the Serpentine?

"The viscount is out cold for the moment." He wiped his palms on his tweed jacket. "The lion cub is having a go of chewing on his hand. I didn't see the harm, since she did help bring him down. She wasn't best pleased when I found her locked in a broom closet in the servant's quarters." Peterson's chuckle dispelled some of the horrible tension in the room. "Frankly, the blasted viscount passed out once she pounced. Some men have no backbone."

Miles' lips twitched, but he tamped on the urge to grin. "Well done."

Emmaline took a few steps forward. She swayed and he closed the distance, providing stability if she wanted it.

He wished her to maintain her independence until she said otherwise. "What of Thompson and Sarah?"

"I found your butler locked in his quarters. From what I could ascertain he's unharmed and resting. Never woke with the commotion." Peterson's chuckle held an uncertain edge. "As for your maid." A flush turned his face and neck beet red. "Sleeping off some sort of drug in her bed. She was also tied." He trained his attention on Miles. "I discovered a nearly empty water decanter on her bedside table. Powder residue on both the decanter and glass."

He nodded. "Probably the same drug they gave to Emmaline." He looked at her. "Sarah will be fine tomorrow, if groggy."

"We were lucky," she murmured as her knees buckled. "It could have been so much worse." The color leeched from her face. "I should have known better." Her voice broke.

Miles caught her and scooped her into his arms. Her head lolled onto his shoulder. "Dump the viscount in the Park, preferably on a path footpads favor. Or in the Serpentine. I don't much care." He glanced at the bundle in his arms then back at his friend with a rueful grin. "I'll keep vigil here tonight. I, uh, rather think the lady and I have a few things to discuss."

"I'll see he's left in a real choice spot." Peterson frowned. "What about the marchioness?"

"What about her?" He carried Emmaline out of the room and toward the stairs.

"Shouldn't she find comeuppance for her part in all of this? The lady could have died after…" He cleared his throat.

"It would be our word against hers, and I'm sure the viscount won't corroborate our story. No doubt he's guilty up to his neck in other schemes." A muscle in his jaw twitched. "Georgiana is too high in rank for Bow Street to touch much less molest with an inquiry." That was the sad fact of their world. If one enjoyed a high rank, they were given freedoms not afforded to many. "Perhaps in time, we'll find a way to catch her or enact revenge."

"Very well." He peered at Emmaline who'd closed her eyes. A tear had escaped beneath one lid and now slid slowly down her cheek. "Good luck with your conversation." With a grin that was decidedly more cheeky than respectful, he turned and headed down the corridor in the opposite direction.

As Miles mounted the stairs that would carry him to the second floor, he pressed a kiss to the top of Emmaline's head. "You're safe now."

And, God help him, she'd continue to be so.

Chapter Twenty-one

Emmaline lay awake for a long time after Miles put her to bed. Though she wished for a soaking bath, there was no one to bring up heated water and she didn't wish to disturb him. He'd curled up behind her and she'd made no sound to acknowledge him. When he wrapped a strong arm about her waist and rested his chin on her head, she hadn't moved. She simply couldn't do anything except remain thankful fate had seen fit to spare her from what the viscount had planned.

The ticking of the carriage clock on her mantle marked the time as did the contented purring from Sanura, who'd slumped on her pallet in the corner. Now more than ever she needed to break the curse. What if next time, a man like the viscount wasn't interrupted?

"Why are you not sleeping?" Miles' warm breath steamed the shell of her ear.

"How do you know I wasn't?" She stared at the wall. The drapes hadn't been drawn and the light rain that had moved in sent water droplets down the windowpane that made shadows that danced and slid along the wall and closed door.

"For one, your breathing is too fast and for another, I've watched your face off and on since lying down with you." He stroked a hand along her hip. "Do you want to talk about it?"

Did she? Over the course of her life, she'd seen many dangerous and horrible things. Some of them had happened to her. Knowing that most men only valued women for the space between their thighs had never troubled her, for she'd always managed to deflect or defend their advances, and had full-confidence in her own worth. However, what the viscount had done to her, the things he'd said, what he would have accomplished had Miles not burst upon the scene made her blood run cold and left her sick with worry.

"It's nothing but the curse at work in my life," she finally settled for.

"Oh, my girl, it's not the curse at all. This was the work of a madman and a jealous woman bent on destroying your life."

She snuggled tighter into the curve of his body. A certain hardness against her bottom betrayed what their closeness did to him. It both thrilled and terrified her. She swallowed past the building wall of unshed tears in her throat. Why couldn't she tell him she wanted his arms around her; she wanted him to hold her, protect her from the world, tell her she'd be all right—that she'd survived where others hadn't. It would hurt too much when she left him tomorrow, but she wished for that reassurance anyway. "Perhaps that's why I cannot understand it. Their motivation or why the need to harm me to begin with."

"Because they could." He slipped his hand to her belly and the warmth of his palm seeped through the furniture sheet she still wrapped around her body. "I'd ask you not to give them another thought, but that wouldn't be fair or practical. You've been through hell tonight, and for that, I'm truly sorry." He stroked his fingers up and down her torso, leaving goose flesh behind. "I should never have left you alone at that ball."

"You had enough trouble of your own. I don't fault you, and some of the blame falls on me." She gave into the shivers his touch invoked despite the horror the night had brought.

"The guilt is still there." He moved slightly and caressed his fingers up and down her arm. "I should go."

"Why?" She wriggled her backside against his arousal.

He didn't quite stifle his groan. "I think you know why."

"I do, but that isn't a good enough reason to quit my bed." With slow movements, she encouraged the sheet to fall open on her side that pressed into the mattress.

"Be that as it may, I refuse to take advantage of you following what you've already endured." A touch of the proper lord rang in his statement.

"Not even if I wish it?" She caught his hand and guided it to her belly then encouraged him to lay his palm flat on her naked skin. The heat of him brought her comfort. "Don't assume you know what's best for me." Her jaw worked. She bit her bottom lip to stave off the tears she'd wanted to indulge in since the viscount had marked her. "Miles, I need to know you still desire me even after…" The throb from the wound on her breast reminded her of the worst of humanity.

Mayhap it always would.

If he did still desire her, perhaps he'd acknowledge his feelings for her, if what the marchioness had said was indeed correct. But then, she'd have to break his heart when she removed to Egypt and—

"I do." Slowly, oh so slowly, he brushed his fingers along her belly and paused at the curls shrouding her femininity. "Probably more than I should, more than is good for either of us, more than I want to admit."

She took his hand and guided him to her breast. Thankfully, it was her left so he wouldn't stumble upon the hated brand. "Give me something to think about from this night that will blot out the horror." Her request came out on a whisper. "Continue what we started after that waltz."

"I adore this bold side of you," he uttered against the curve of her ear while he brushed his fingers over her nipple.

Shivers of need fanned out from the point of contact. "There's something about you, Miles, Earl of Archewyne, that took me by surprise." She closed her eyes as he continued to play at her hardening bud. Tingles pinwheeled through her system. This is what a woman should feel when a man put his hands on her. Not the urge to retch or shrink, not the feelings of shame that the viscount's assault gave her.

"I hope you never lose that feeling." Could the dratted man read her thoughts now? He pressed a feather weighted kiss to her temple. "If you grow uncomfortable, tell me to stop and I will."

"I don't want you to stop." *Ever.*

"Truly, I won't rush my fences in the event this may further traumatize you."

"Your solicitation is misplaced, but appreciated." She hated that her voice was sharper than she intended. "Right now, I need you, your touch, to listen to the sound of your voice, to borrow from your strength. I want to feel safe. Just for tonight, let me lean on you." Did that make her seem too vulnerable?

"I'm yours to command. Always." He cupped her breast. "I'd like to hope that whatever is between us will," he stumbled over his words then covered it with a soft cough, "manage to survive anything we might go through after this."

It wasn't the admission she'd hoped for, but it was close. "Make me forget *him*." Her voice broke and she bit back a sob.

"Gladly." Thick emotion rode in his voice. He rolled her nipple and when she gasped, he slipped his hand down her body. "I knew you'd be beautiful." He brushed his fingers over her skin and with each pass ribbons of need unfurled in her lower belly.

"I hate that you had to see me laid out and vulnerable. I was so embarrassed, so ashamed." She stiffened in his arms, and she swore she felt the bite of those ropes on her wrists again, endured the humiliation of having Georgiana look upon her naked body, died a thousand deaths to know Darnell had put his hands on her before Miles had the opportunity. "I felt small, used, unwanted."

"No." Miles nibbled on the sensitive skin beneath her ear lobe. "It wasn't your fault. None of it was, and you fought, survived like you've done everything else." He parted her thighs with a knee then gently encouraged her left leg onto his, opening her. "You're certain about this?"

"Yes." Just like the night in the marchioness' library, the only thing that would calm the storm within her was him. Why was that? She firmly shoved that thought away. There'd be time enough to think of it on her trip to Egypt when missing him ate her alive. "Very much so. I want to remember only you."

He didn't answer with words. Instead, he continued to caress her skin and draw abstract shapes over her belly until gooseflesh popped. Her breasts grew heavy and ached for his touch, but he didn't return to tease them. He circled her belly button with a finger, over and over and over again, and when she wanted to cry with frustration, he guided those naughty fingers along her abdomen, glanced them through her curls and finally slid them down her slick folds.

If she didn't know better, she'd swear her nerves hummed in anticipation. Her breathing labored. "Mmm," she whispered, and the quiet of the night swallowed the sound. She pressed a hand to his urging him onward, and he obliged by thrusting one long finger into her core. "Oooh." She prompted him again, moving his hand. He withdrew the finger only to slide two into her passage. "Yes." She applied more pressure, holding him against her swollen nubbin.

"My lady, did you wish me to leave off, for I'd gladly let you pleasure yourself while I watch." Amusement threaded through his statement.

Heat infused her cheeks. "No, please don't. I merely enjoy your touch." Did he think her too forward? Especially after the events of the night?

"That's good, for I enjoy bringing you to bliss." Again, he went silent, but he continued to work magic. After withdrawing from her core, he circled her swollen button with a slippery finger. "Here's what you want, Emmy."

A keening cry left her throat as he manipulated that small bundle of nerves. Need flooded her body. Bands of intense desire tightened and built low in her belly. She pressed her hand on his, hoping to keep him where she wanted him the most. The dear man did exactly that. He rubbed his finger back and forth over the nubbin, increasing the friction then slowing it down. A flick of the bud had her gasping for breath and writhing against him.

"Miles, hurry." She shook from the effort of prolonging the exquisite sensations swamping her, and still he tormented her throbbing flesh. "I ... I..." He worried that bundle of nerves once more and she shattered. Waves of hot pleasure swept her up in their onslaught and she gave into them. Her eyes shuttered closed and she sighed. In her mind's eye, she saw those waves washing her clean, removing the viscount's touch.

But then, how could anything erase what Lord Darnell done? Perhaps it was impossible.

A rush of tears overtook her as the residual bands of bliss pulsed around her. Every feeling she'd denied herself since she'd entered Miles' library a handful of days ago came hurtling to the surface. The curse continued to follow and plague her. Her father lay dying. Tomorrow, late afternoon, she would leave England and Miles behind without clear knowledge of whether she'd return. So easy could she give her heart into his keeping if it weren't for the obligations that kept her from putting down roots, and even if she did, she couldn't bear him the required children. She mourned for those children, the babes she'd never have, and the force of her sobs rocked her in his arms.

Lastly, the horror of the night she'd endured and the mark she'd forever carry sank into her consciousness and she cried harder.

"What can I do?" Miles whispered, concern in his voice. "What do you need from me?" He held her closer. "How can I make this better?"

From the floor, Sanura uttered a curious mew. The cat would jump on the bed soon to investigate.

"Nothing." She sucked in a hiccupping breath then eased it out, trying to gain control of her emotions. "There's nothing you can do. Not now. Not ever." Another few tears leaked out from beneath her closed lids. "He told me he'd make it so I was damaged so that you'd never want me again."

"Oh, Emmy, that's not true. Nothing would kill my feelings for you."

"No!" She shook her head and fought her way out of his hold enough that she turned to face him. She rose up on her knees. "Look at me, Miles. Look! He *marked* me." She gestured at her breast, made certain that he had to peer at the wound that burned even now. "I'll forever carry his initials. How can you ever ignore that?" Tears continued to fall as she challenged him. "How can I forget?"

"I *am* looking at you and do you know what I see?" He held her gaze in the darkness, never wavering. "I see a beautiful woman with a strong soul, a woman who fights for what she believes in, a woman who has a heart for compassion and a talent for breaking and entering." He rolled off the bed.

Her heart wrenched. Of course he would leave, and why shouldn't he? Fear beat a frantic tattoo through her veins. Defeated, she slumped to the mattress. How had her life come to this pass? "We should never have met that night. How can you not see the curse is destroying me?"

The thump of a boot hitting the floor rang in the silence. Seconds later, the second boot followed. "What happened tonight was not the fault of the curse. People with black souls were at work, and in time they will be punished. That I will promise you." A rustle of clothing rasped in her ears. "Yet you accuse me of not wanting you any longer. Don't assume you know my thoughts."

She turned her head when the mattress depressed and he joined her. A gasp escaped. He was naked, and gloriously so. The one time she could see his form in the way God intended and it was too dark to properly appreciate it. "Perhaps you haven't clearly seen what he did. Wait until the cold light of day and—"

"Emmaline!" Exasperation rang in the utterance. He took her hand and pressed it against the hard, warm length of his cock. "Is this not enough proof that I still want you?"

"You could be that way for any woman."

"There has only been you in recent memory." His tone invited no further argument. "Nothing that man did or said to you can or will change how I feel." When she didn't answer, he sighed and encouraged her onto her back. He followed her down and settled between her splayed thighs. The head of his member slid along her folds. "What I feel for you is … confusing and powerful and maddening. It will take time to sort out, but it's there and it's growing, and it has me at sixes and sevens like you've done from the first."

That was exactly it. She couldn't name what she felt for him either, but it was there and wouldn't be denied. Not willing to analyze such a thing, she buried it in deflection. "So is something else growing," she murmured and blatantly wriggled her hips into his. The base of his manhood rubbed her sensitive nubbin and she gasped as flutters of renewed need filled her belly.

He rested his forehead against hers while leaning the bulk of his weight on forearms which he'd placed on either side of her head. When he grinned, his lips brushed hers. "If you're able to joke then all isn't lost."

"It never was." But then, that was life, wasn't it? A heady, confusing mix of joy and sorrow. "Perhaps misplaced or I'd forgotten all I currently enjoy instead of all I was truly never fated to have." Now that her tears had ceased, traces of her old spirit returned. She looped her arms about his shoulders and twisted her legs around his regardless that she still wore her stockings and heeled slippers. "What do you intend to do about it?"

"Hmm, it would take too much time to tell you." He kissed her, and there was so much emotion in that one meeting of mouths that she drowned in it. At the same time, he thrust his hips and joined with her as deep as he could go. His groan blended with hers. "Would you be amenable to this overture instead?"

"Absolutely," she said and the word was suspiciously breathless.

"So it would seem." Amusement threaded through his words.

Nothing else was spoken, for they communed in a language all their own but as old as time. Emmaline canted her hips. She met his every push until they worked in frantic rhythm. Where their first foray into intercourse had been rushed and fraught with the thrill of discovery, this joining took a decidedly slower path. It was gentle; she even dared to say loving and she lost a piece of her heart to him in that moment.

When the coiling bands of pleasure built once more and she teetered on the jagged edge of madness, Emmaline locked her legs around his waist and clung to his shoulders in an effort to press closer. Her panting breath echoed in the silence in time to her fluttering heartbeat. "Finish me."

"There's nothing I'd rather do," he murmured, and his rhythm changed, becoming more wild and urgent.

On a particularly vigorous thrust, she broke. Light and sound fractured around her as multi-colored bliss rushed through every nerve so powerful her toes curled. Gasping cries blended with the insane urge to laugh and the result was a comical string of hiccupping screeches. Sanura meowed intently nearby, obviously thinking her mistress faced a murderer.

"Damnation, you're potent," Miles muttered as he fell into his own release. Hot seed jetted into her core while his cock pulsed and finally he slumped against her, his breath warming her ear, his stubble grazing her cheek and setting off new frissons of awareness. "Amazing." He sounded exactly so.

She grinned but didn't release her hold. For the night, he was hers and she intended to enjoy every second. When he grunted then sucked in a sharp, surprised breath, she asked, "What's wrong?"

A furry tan paw appeared over his shoulder and she understood. The lion cub had pounced and now she lay sprawled on his back while she chewed on his hair.

"Well, that's deuced uncomfortable. Those claws will leave a mark." But he made no move to withdraw from her body or dislodge the animal, and with that, Emmaline fell a tiny bit deeper for him.

"It's not pleasant, I'll agree." She giggled as she squirmed into a more comfortable position beneath him. "I'll also admit that intercourse in a proper bed is infinitely better than seducing you on a chair."

"Ha!" He nuzzled the side of her neck. "You might think you seduced me, but I wanted that joining as much as you did."

"Perhaps." An ache set up in her heart. Tomorrow, she'd sail out of his life. By the time she returned to England, would he belong to another woman, or worse would he have succumbed to Georgiana's overtures? She had no right to ask him for a promise, especially not when she couldn't make him the same. Instead, she said, "Thank you for this night."

"I am forever your servant, Emmy. I hope you know that."

She nodded. Despite everything, he'd been a faithful friend. Only, did she want more from him than that, and in what capacity? "What happens now?"

"I'm not certain. With the false accusations against my name and your imminent departure..."

"I know." She swallowed down the ball of tears forming in her throat. "Perhaps timing isn't right." Perhaps it never would be.

"I believe in that as much as I believe in a curse." Miles pressed a kiss to her forehead. "Will you take tea with me tomorrow before you go? I shall lend you the use of my carriage to make your transport to the docks easier."

"Thank you. Then I shall accept the invitation." In the light of day, she could commit every part of him to memory. "The carriage should be packed with last minute items, for I've already sent all my trunks and the mummies to be pre-loaded. Sarah will also be with me."

"Good."

The lion cub hopped to the floor and returned to her pallet.

Miles took the sudden freedom to collapse to his side and breaking their connection. He tucked her against his body with a strong grip as if he never meant to let her go. "Forgive me for the liberty of staying the night. I promise to remove myself before your maid rouses in the morning."

"There is nothing to forgive." It was on the tip of her tongue to mention her burgeoning feelings, to ask if he'd go with her, but she tamped the urge. Of course he wouldn't, for his life was here, and his time needed to be spent fighting the accusations of the night. "There never will be."

Long after his breathing deepened and he slept, Emmaline regarded the shadows on the wall once more.

At least this parting would be her choice and not because someone she loved had been ripped from her life due to death.

It didn't make it less painful.

Chapter Twenty-two

Miles paced the floor of his library—the room where his life had been turned inside out by the chance meeting of the girl from his childhood.

She would exit his life today with his heart firmly in her hand. Sad, that. When a man realized he'd been more than captivated by an adventurous lady he should have the freedom to do something about it. Even sadder, he didn't have that freedom since his own flight from England was imminent. As chance would have it, his departure would happen on the morrow. Would he ever see Emmaline again?

A tight smile gripped his lips. Yes, he would because he had no choice except to manipulate fate and make it so. She wouldn't like it by half and neither would he, yet it was insurance of sorts that at some time in the future, their paths would cross once more. Hell, even Peterson would protest, but he couldn't help that. Above all, he had to assure himself she'd be safe, and who better to entrust her life to than his valet-turned-confidant?

Faint scratching on the door frame yanked him from his thoughts. Peterson cleared his throat before he came into the room. "Lady Emmaline has arrived, sir. Currently, she's in the Blue Parlor. Would you like for her to be brought here?"

Wouldn't that be fitting? Miles glanced about the space where antiquities mixed with carefully crafted copies, the potted fern, and the statue she'd inadvertently knocked over. He sighed. "No, too much temptation. I'll join her presently. However, fetch Jane and see that she's installed in the parlor well ahead of me."

"I will." Peterson nodded and his red curls bobbed. "There is one more thing, and it's not quite as welcome as seeing your lady love."

He rolled his eyes. "Yes?" This new penchant of his valet's at hesitation grated.

"I have it on the highest authority that a warrant has been issued for your arrest, put forth by Lord Vitteras."

"Dear God, what an idiot that young man is." Of course, the wet-behind-the-ears lord hadn't been privy to the events he and Rathesborne had set into motion the night of the duke's ball, and he no doubt thought to gain respect and admiration through the *ton* for doing something of this magnitude, for the applause he'd gain by bringing a scandalous earl to justice would be high. He waved a hand. "It's of no consequence, for I quit the country on the morrow."

"It would behoove you to pack your things and hide until your trip across the Channel. If need be, I know of a private house. The owner is a trusted friend and he rents out a room for just this sort of thing."

"Capital. Make the necessary arrangements. Pack my things as well." He crossed his arms over his chest then brought a hand up and stroked his chin. "Peterson, there is one other favor, and I wouldn't ask it of you if I didn't trust you with everything in my life."

"I'm honored, sir." The valet executed a half-bow from the waist. "I'm at your service."

"Your trip to France with me will be re-routed by a couple thousand miles. I have a different mission in mind for you."

A red eyebrow arched. "Oh?"

Miles nodded. "I'd like you to accompany Lady Emmaline to Cairo. Of course, covertly. She'll have her maid with her as companion, but I need to know she'll have protection as well." He pinned his friend with a hard look. "Consider her an extension of me. Lay down your life for her if you must. Defend her from any and all threats. Keep her safe but under no circumstances allow her to see you. We'll both be in the drink if she does."

Though it was an exceedingly wonderful thing to cajole her out of her ire and into a more agreeable mood, he didn't know when he'd be afforded the time.

"I understand, sir. I'll do everything I can until I can hand over that responsibility to you."

"What, no protest? I had assumed you'd argue and tell me the mission for the Crown was of greater importance than guarding a mere woman."

A trace of a flush colored the other man's face. "Let's just say that as you have found yourself at sixes and sevens by the lady, so have I been enamored of her maid."

"Is that so?" Miles snorted then gave into a laugh he sorely needed. "Does the woman know where your affections lie?"

"Of course not." Peterson scoffed. "I worship her from afar, and for the moment it is enough."

"Protect them, all of them. I'll send word of where and when I'll meet you. Hopefully this mission won't drag out." He waved a hand. "Now go. Remember to encourage my daughter into the parlor. I'll be there shortly."

After Peterson had departed, Miles waited a full ten minutes before making his way to the Blue Parlor. Already, tea had been delayed once. The window was closing upon his last moments with Emmy. Playing upon a woman's heartstrings—especially where Emmaline's were concerned—was a dirty, nasty business, but the stakes were too high to consider feelings. This simply must work. He was out of options.

Female voices drifted out to the hall as he approached and he paused, leaning a shoulder against the wall to listen.

"That's a pretty dress, Lady Jane. Pink is such a happy color, don't you think?" Emmaline's soft voice wrapped itself around him and he dared to peek around the doorframe.

Jane stood near to Emmy's position on the settee, her blue eyes sparkling but trepidation shadowed her face. "I have wots of pink dresses." She clutched her favorite linen rabbit beneath an arm. Cook's daughter had sewed the animal for her. As much as his staff doted on the girl, he couldn't, in good conscience, leave his only child in the care of servants.

"I like dresses in every color, for I cannot ever choose a favorite. Today, my favorite is blue."

Miles risked another peek into the room. Emmaline had donned a gown of deep turquoise that reminded him of the color of the seas. Paired with a somber cloak of light gray wool, she fairly invoked the spirit of the oceans. A magnificent pearl and aquamarine necklace hung around her neck, the pendant nestled at the slope of her gorgeous breasts. His cock awoke. How deuced wrong it was the jewelry had leave to caress that silky skin while he waited in the hall.

Jane studied Emmaline's face for long moments before speaking again. "Is Papa coming for tea?"

"I certainly hope so." Emmaline smiled. "Do you and your papa play games? I used to play such things with my father when I was small."

"Sometimes. Papa is busy." She stuck a finger into her mouth and when she pulled it out, a slight *pop!* cut through the silence. "Papa said I could pway with you and the kitty." She glanced around with large eyes. "Where is the wion?"

"Sanura is waiting for me at my house with my maid, Sarah. We're taking a trip soon to see my Papa."

Miles' heart squeezed. Please God, let her father hang on until she arrived to tell him goodbye. He prayed all the harder that the two precious ladies in the parlor would form a bond.

"Papa said I could go on an adventure soon." Excitement hung on the statement.

"That's an excellent idea." The same excitement wove through Emmaline's reply. "Every girl should have as many adventures as life will grant her, to play in the sunshine, to tumble through the grass and laugh, to find out who she really is."

His daughter nodded as if she understood perfectly. Her blonde ringlets rioted about her cherub's head. "Papa cried wast night after he read me stories."

"He did?" Surprise reflected on Emmaline's face. "Why?"

"I think Papa is afraid." Such a bold truth from a child.

Emmaline frowned. "Whyever would you think that? Your Papa is a very brave man. He's a hero." She leaned forward on the settee. "He rescued me from a bad man last night."

"Papa is a hero?" Jane's eyes rounded. "Are you a princess?"

In the hall, Miles was hard put to stifle unexpected laughter. Of course his daughter would assume any maiden rescued would be a princess, thanks to her fairy story books, but he strained to hear Emmy's answer nonetheless.

"No, I'm not a princess, and neither do I wish to be. Princesses don't have many adventures." She held out a hand and after a few seconds, Jane put her free hand into Emmaline's gloved one. "Yes, your Papa is the best sort of hero, but why do you think he's afraid?"

A shrug lifted Jane's tiny shoulders. "He's afraid of monsters he has to fight when he goes away."

"Your father is taking a trip?" Suspicion rang in the question.

Bloody hell. This covert agent business was tricky. How could he have explained his imminent absence to his daughter without saying he'd be gone?

"Yes." Jane nodded, but she didn't say more about it. "He kept hugging me and saying he would miss me, but I was sweepy and he kept tawking." She shrugged again. "Papa is so siwwy."

Delighted laughter spilled from Emmaline and the sound alleviated the tightness in his chest. "Jane, your father is a wonderful man and he's doing good work. Never doubt that, especially if someone tells you nasty things about him."

The girl nodded. "Do you wike my papa?"

Miles held his breath and expelled it when she answered, "I do like him, very much. At times I wish … never mind. That's a story for another time." He couldn't remain in the hall any longer. Too much of this talk would be … well, it would be too much talk and none of them needed maudlin ties that would be difficult to sever. He forced a cheerful expression on his face he didn't feel. How was a man supposed to survive watching the two most precious people in his life go away? "This is what a man's parlor should have all the time—two beautiful ladies."

Both Emmaline and Jane's eye lit upon seeing him. If that didn't bolster his ego and reinforce that his decision was the right one, nothing would.

"There you are!" Jane's exclamation made it seem as if he'd been gone ages instead of mere minutes. She ran across the room and into his waiting arms.

He scooped her up and placed a kiss upon her baby soft cheek. "Have you been conversing nicely with Lady Emmaline?"

"Yes." The little girl nodded. "She wikes adventures too."

"That's marvelous!" Miles set her down then gave her bottom a light pat. "Go find your nurse, poppet. Papa needs to talk with Lady Emmaline for a bit. I'll call you for tea."

That ordinary afternoon respite would be the last time he saw his precious child for far too many weeks. He cleared his throat to stave off showing weakening emotion while Jane ran from the room. When he rested his attention on Emmaline and a knowing light flashed in her beautiful emerald eyes, he sighed.

"Are you always suspicious, or is it just me who makes you think that way?" Every instinct screamed, urged him to take a seat next to her and chance touching her, but he fought it. He might be a hero in her eyes, yet even heroes had their limits, and Emmaline was too great a temptation.

"You've given me a few reasons to act so," she replied with an arched eyebrow. "Here we are, the morning after another wonderful session of intimacy, yet you do not act as if your stress had been relieved."

Heat crept up the back of his neck. How could he pass a day, let alone many, without her brand of humor? "One single coming together is not enough to make me forget all the cares and concerns that ride my shoulders," he said with more frankness than he'd thought possible. "Though, I must admit our time together has been beyond compare."

"I understand." A pleased smile curved her lips. "Pray, tell me what haunts you. Jane alluded to monsters, though I'm not certain that is an accurate assessment."

That depended on one's perspective, and only monsters would attempt to start another war or restore a Bonaparte to France's throne. He clasped his hands behind his back and held her gaze. "I'm afraid I must ask a rather personal favor of you." There was no sense putting off the inevitable.

"Ah. I see." She brushed at her skirts. "Out with it then, Miles. I've never known you to procrastinate."

Would Jane learn to be forthright and bold while in Emmaline's company? He both hoped she might and feared it. "A warrant for my arrest has been issued today."

"What?" Emmaline scrambled to her feet as apprehension clouded her eyes. "What will you do?"

"Fight to clear my name, obviously." The lie slid from his tongue like rancid oil. "However, in order to do that, I must essentially vanish from the *ton* for a time." When she said nothing that would make his task easier, he pressed on. "Due to that, I need you to please take Jane with you to Cairo."

The ensuing silence roared as loud in his ears as a den full of hungry lions.

Her jaw fell slightly open. Her eyes rounded in shock. She clasped and unclasped her hands in front of her. "How can you ever think I could do such a thing? The child belongs with her father."

"I agree, but consider my circumstances. I cannot flee with her and neither can I entrust her to the care of servants." He forced a hard swallow. No one should be put into this position, and to her ears, of course his insistence sounded insane. Would that he could share the real reason he couldn't take Jane with him. "She's the only family I have, Emmy. Please do this."

She shook her head. "Telling me to care for your only child… You must be mad to ask it of me. I'm not her family either."

"There are times when I think I *am* mad." He closed the distance between them and clutched her upper arms. "And you could be if you would marry me." Perhaps old habits died hard. The insanity continued, for if she accepted, what the devil would he do then?

"Oh, Miles, not this again." A trace of aggravation lingered in her voice.

But then, a man halfway in love with an enchanting woman would do many a mad thing. "Marry me, Emmy."

"I refuse. I won't marry you out of desperation." Yet longing appeared in her glorious eyes, and that gave him hope.

"Then come away with me instead." God, what would the prime minister say to that if Miles showed up for his next set of orders with a child and mistress in tow?

She dropped her gaze to his cravat. "I cannot, and you know why. I must attempt to break the curse or at least return the mummies to their graves or else I'll always wonder. Don't ask me to throw away my freedom for your convenience."

The woman was both vexing and intoxicating. He couldn't help a grin even as his worry flared. "I'd never deny you freedom." Pursuing her once his mission ended would be the greatest pleasure. "Emmy, please. Say you'll take Jane. I cannot bear to throw her to fate and hope for the best. She's my daughter. She deserves a chance in life." Did his voice really crack? God, he wasn't cut out for this sort of Drury Lane theatric.

"But, I don't think—"

Damnation, did she have nerves made of iron? He went for her heartstrings and lowered his voice. "What will become of the child if I'm tossed into Newgate? One never knows for how long one will languish there. Just imagine bright, blonde, curious little Jane wasting away in a dim, dirty orphanage somewhere. Or worse. I cannot bear to have her told lies about her father. It would break me."

Tears sprang into Emmaline's eyes. "How long do you anticipate I shall have her?"

While the urge to shout in victory climbed his throat, he tamped it. Instead, he bundled her into his arms. "I'm not certain, but I will send word. Either I'll ask that you return to England or I shall come find you and claim you both." He pressed a kiss into her hair.

"Oh, Miles. This situation is untenable."

"I know." He inhaled her violet scent for the last time. "Then you'll take her, care for her, love her as if she were your own?" His heart squeezed. This was, by far, the most difficult thing he'd ever done. "I have set aside a fair amount of blunt for you to take with you to offset her care and to keep you in style while you travel." It was a gambit and could, in *ton* circles, be considered gifts to a mistress, but he had to risk it. He refused to see her off without being properly cared for.

"Yes." She pulled out of his arms enough to peer up at him. "I'll endeavor to do my best by her. For you." The tendons in her throat worked with a swallow. "Please keep yourself safe. I rather enjoy *our* adventures together."

"As do I." He had to do something, he had to leave an indelible impression on her. So he kissed her. Claimed her lush, soft mouth beneath his and drank from her again and again, never pushing to deepen it into passion, but hoping to convey without words that he'd continue to fight for them and for a life where they would be together. When they parted breathless, he sighed. "You have no idea what this means to me."

"And you have no idea what you've asked of me. I've wanted a child for such a long time. Never did I dream I'd be given yours." She stood on tiptoe and briefly kissed him. "Thank you for this most precious of gifts, Miles. I hope things here allow you to return quickly."

The terrible pressure in his chest flared and for one horrible moment, he feared he'd lose his grasp on the typical stiff upper lip and come undone in front of her. However, he mastered his emotions only to engulf her into a tight hug, much like he'd given Jane the night before. "God, Emmy, how can I go on now?" Fear took hold and whispered into his ear, told him he was a nodcock to do this, that she could take his child and vanish anywhere in the world.

Apparently he hadn't mastered those emotions enough. He shoved them away. He trusted Emmaline implicitly.

"You can and you will, my lord," she said in her typical managing way, though her words shook with unshed tears. "We all do what we must in order to live the life we've dreamed of. Someday. Keep the faith, always. That's what I will do."

When Alfred cleared his throat at the doorway, Miles released her and looked at his butler. "Tea, my lord," the older man said in the way of explanation as he carried in a silver tray with the accompaniments and placed the service on the low table. "Also, Lady Emmaline's carriage is here."

"Thank you, Alfred. We'll go out presently. If you could have Jane's nurse dress her for travel? Have a footman bring down her trunk as well." For he'd had the liberty of having his daughter's belongings already packed, knowing Emmaline would agree. The bottom fell out of his stomach as the butler exited. This was it. No more time remained. His life and his focus belonged to England now. He cleared his throat, but that didn't remove the urge to rail at the heavens. "Well."

"Well." Emmaline's chin quivered and he nearly fell to his knees in supplication. "Shall I write to you?"

"No." He shook his head. "The post will likely be monitored." Whether it was or not, he couldn't say, for he wouldn't be in the country to see. "Your father's estate in Cairo is well known. I'll send word there once matters are settled."

She nodded and said nothing else, only rested her emerald gaze on him with emotions clouding the depths he couldn't read. "These last two weeks have been wonderful. Mostly."

"They have. I'm grateful to have discovered that the treasure I liked best in all of Egypt had come back to me." Would she think his words mere flattery instead of the honest truth he'd intended?

A sob tore from her throat and her smile wavered. "Don't make this more difficult than it needs to be," she whispered, then in her usual spontaneous fashion, she threw herself into his arms and held him close. "You stubborn earl. Keep yourself safe, for if something happens to you, no force on earth will keep me from tracking your sorry arse down."

"Now that's what I call a right proper motivation." He kissed her again, savoring her lips. "How can I win your heart, Emmy?" If he could win it, he'd keep that in the back of his mind as a prize for concluding his mission early. "How can I have you in my life forever and always?"

"Do something that no one has done for me before. Don't be like the rest of them, Miles. No lady wishes for exactly the same courtship as every other lady."

"Right." That told him absolutely nothing. Reluctantly, he yanked his gaze away from her. "I hear Jane coming down the stairs."

Emmaline nodded. She rooted in her reticule and pulled out a starched white handkerchief bordered with lace. "Here." She thrust it into his hand. "Every lady should give her knight a favor to remember her by."

Clutching the fabric, he delved a hand into his waistcoat pocket. "This is for you. It's Napoleon's map of the Valley of the Kings. You might perhaps need it."

She nodded and then shoved the paper into her bag.

The opportunity for further conversation expired as Jane appeared in the doorway. A smart ivory spencer, cap and gloves completed her traveling ensemble. Miles tucked the handkerchief into his waistcoat pocket. Alfred led a footman along the hall.

"Where are we going, Papa?"

He crossed the room and lifted her into his arms as he walked. "You are going on a long trip with Lady Emmaline to a place so different that you've only seen its likes in story books."

Down the front steps he went, Emmaline following behind. His black carriage waited at the curb, the gold-painted crest glimmering in the sun, and through the open door he spied Sarah as well as Thompson along with Sanura on her lead. The sapphires in her collar winked in the light.

"Is the wion coming too?"

"Yes, poppet." When she squirmed, he set her on her feet and she immediately ran to the carriage, hopping up the steps as soon as Alfred put them down. "Kitty!" She briefly glanced out the window and waved. "'Bye, Papa!"

His heart shredded, for she didn't fully comprehend that not only would he not be going with them, he wouldn't see her again for quite some time. But the young were resilient. She'd survive, and she had Emmy for guidance.

Emmaline held out a hand and he took it, carrying her fingers to his lips. "Goodbye, my lord, and good luck," she said out loud for the benefit of the few pedestrians on the street, but she lowered her voice for his ears only. "And Miles, should you ask me again, the answer next time will be yes." With that, she turned, hurried to the carriage then let Alfred assist her inside.

The ache in his heart eased slightly. At least there was hope, and now he had her promise. For all intents and purposes, Emmaline had accepted his proposal. That was reason enough to remain alive and unscathed during his upcoming mission.

Still, he stood at the curb for long moments until the carriage turned and went out of sight. Cursed, indeed. He considered himself the most fortunate man in all of England.

And for the love of an incomparable woman, he'd make certain he stayed that way because, in the end, he would finally claim her hand as well as a place by her side.

The End?

Continue the adventure with Miles and Emmaline in *Engaged to a Scandalous Earl,* releasing in January 2017.

If you enjoyed this book, please leave a review on the retailer's site where you purchased the story. I'd love to hear what you thought of it!

Blurb for *Engaged to a Scandalous Earl* (Thieves of the Ton series, book two)

Three months have passed since Lady Emmaline Darling left her lover and fellow adventurer, Miles. Not certain she's in love with him, they're bonded in a miraculous way—she's enceinte. Yet, despite his promises to write and make plans, there's been nothing but silence. When she discovers he's lied and has been out of pocket on a secret mission for the Crown, she's convinced she can go it alone despite the scandal—and he can't be trusted enough to know her secret hope.

Watching Emmaline slip from his life with his daughter broke his heart, but as fifth Earl of Archewyne, Miles Lawrence Hawkins' responsibility to England called louder than his heartstrings, as does the lingering hope to bring Lord Leventhorpe's killer to light. While chasing a faction of Bonaparte sympathizers intent on starting war anew using an obscure relic of great power, his fate crosses Emmaline's—and she's as volatile as the earthquake that puts them both in peril.

They strike a tentative peace, for the opportunity to adventure—and to survive—together is stronger than their hurt feelings. Mutual need collides in the course of duty, but before the state of their hearts can be realized, fate, with danger as a companion, intervenes. With betrayal, insidious peril and a killer lurking, finding their happy ending will be a harrowing prospect indeed, but adventure—and love—doesn't come without risk.

Author Bio

Sandra Sookoo is a bestselling author who firmly believes every person deserves acceptance and a happy ending. Most days you can find her creating scandal and mischief in the Regency-era, serendipity and happenstance in Victorian America or snarky humor in the contemporary world. Reading romance is a lot like eating fine chocolates—you can't just have one. Good thing books don't have calories!

When she's not wearing out computer keyboards, Sandra spends time with her real life Prince Charming in central Indiana where she's been known to goof off and make moments count because the key to life is laughter. A Disney fan since the age of ten, when her soul gets bogged down and her imagination flags, a trip to Walt Disney World is in order. Nothing fuels her dreams more than the land of eternal happy endings, hope and love stories.

Sandra's newsletter

Sign up for Sandra's bi-monthly newsletter and you'll be given exclusive excerpts, cover reveals before the general public as well as opportunities to enter contests you won't find anywhere else.

Just send an email to sandrasookoo@yahoo.com with SUBSCRIBE in the subject line.